P9-DXI-287

STRANGER IN THE MOONLIGHT

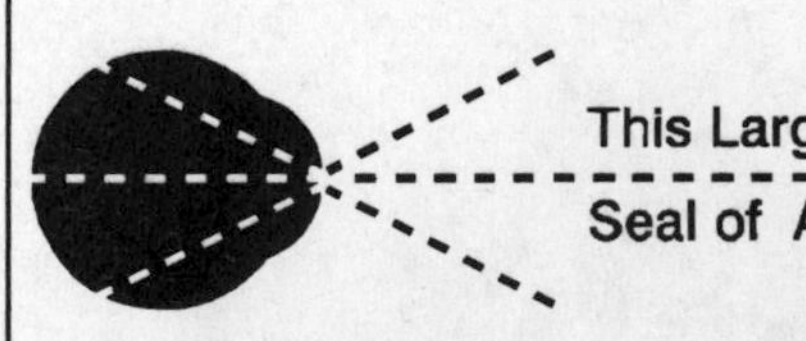

Stranger in the Moonlight

Jude Deveraux

THORNDIKE PRESS
A part of Gale, Cengage Learning

GALE
CENGAGE Learning®

Detroit • New York • San Francisco • New Haven, Conn • Waterville, Maine • London

Thorndike Press, a part of Gale, Cengage Learning.

Thorndike Press® Large Print Core.
The text of this Large Print edition is unabridged.
Other aspects of the book may vary from the original edition.
Set in 16 pt. Plantin.

LIBRARY OF CONGRESS CATALOGING-IN-PUBLICATION DATA

Deveraux, Jude.
Stranger in the moonlight / by Jude Deveraux. — Large print ed.
p. cm. — (Thorndike Press large print core) (Edilean trilogy)
ISBN 978-1-4104-5115-6 (hardcover)— ISBN 1-4104-5115-1 (hardcover) 1. Reunions—Virginia—Fiction. 2. Female friendship—Virginia—Fiction. 3. Domestic fiction. 4. Large type books. I. Title.
PS3554.E9273S77 2012
813'.54—dc23 2012028336

Published in 2012 by arrangement with Pocket Books, a division of Simon & Schuster, Inc.

Printed in the United States of America
1 2 3 4 5 6 7 16 15 14 13 12

Stranger in the Moonlight

Prologue

Edilean, Virginia
1993

In all of her eight years, Kim had never been so bored. She didn't even know such boredom could exist. Her mother told her to go outside into the big garden around the old house, Edilean Manor, and play, but what was she to do by herself?

Two weeks ago her father had taken her brother off to some faraway state to go fishing. "Male bonding," her mother called it, then said she was *not* going to stay in their house alone for four whole weeks. That night Kim had been awakened by the sound of her parents arguing. They didn't usually fight — not that she knew about — and the word *divorce* came to her mind. She was terrified of being without her parents.

But the next morning they were kissing and everything seemed to be fine. Her father kept talking about making up being the best, but her mother shushed him.

It was that afternoon when her mother told her that while her father and brother were away they were going to stay in an apartment at Edilean Manor. Kim didn't like that because she hated the old house. It was too big and it echoed with every footstep. Besides, every time she visited the place there was less furniture, and the emptiness made it seem even creepier.

Her father said that Mr. Bertrand, the old man who lived in the house, had sold the family furniture rather than get a job to support himself. "He'd sell the house if Miss Edi would let him."

Miss Edi was Mr. Bertrand's sister. She was older than he was, and even though she didn't live there, she owned the house. Kim had heard people say that she disliked her brother so much that she refused to live in Edilean.

Kim couldn't imagine hating Edilean, since every person she knew in the world lived there. Her dad was an Aldredge, from one of the seven families that founded the town. Kim knew that was something to be proud of. All she thought was that she was glad she wasn't from the family that had to live in big, scary Edilean Manor.

So now she and her mother had been living in the apartment for two whole weeks and she was horribly bored. She wanted to go back to her own house and her own room. When they were packing to go, her mother had said, "We're just going away for a little while and it's just around the corner, so you don't need to take that." "That" was pretty much anything Kim owned, like books, toys, her dolls, her many art kits. Her mother seemed to consider it all as "not necessary."

But at the end, Kim had grabbed the bicycle she'd received for her birthday and clamped her hands around the grips. She looked at her mother with her jaw set.

Her dad laughed. "Ellen," he said to his wife, "I've seen that look on your face a thousand times and I can assure you that your daughter will *not* back down. I know from experience that you can yell, threaten, sweet talk, plead, beg, cry, but she won't give in."

Her mother's eyes were narrowed as she looked at her laughing husband.

He quit smiling. "Reede, how about you and I go . . . ?"

"Go where, Dad?" Reede asked. At seventeen, he was overwhelmed with importance at being allowed to go away with his dad. No women. Just the two of them.

"Wherever we can find to go," his dad mumbled.

Kim got to take her bike to Edilean Manor, and for three days she rode it nonstop, but now she wanted to do something else. Her cousin Sara came over one day but all she wanted to do was explore the ratty old house. Sara loved old buildings!

Mr. Bertrand had pulled a copy of *Alice's Adventures in Wonderland* out of a pile of books on the floor. Her mom said he'd sold the bookcase to Colonial Williamsburg. "Original eighteenth century and it had been in the family for over two hundred years," she'd muttered. "What a shame. Poor Miss Edi."

Kim spent days reading about Alice and her journey down the rabbit hole. She'd loved the book so much that she told her mother she wanted blonde hair and a blue dress with a white apron. Her mother said that if her father ever again went off for four weeks her next child just might be blonde. Mr. Bertrand said he'd like a hookah and to sit on a mushroom all day and say wise things.

The two adults had started laughing — they seemed to find each other very funny. In disgust Kim went outside to sit in the fork of her favorite old pear tree and read more about Alice. She reread her favorite passages, then her mother called her in for what Mr. Bertrand called "afternoon tea." He was an odd old man, very soft-looking, and her father said that Mr. Bertrand could hatch an egg on the couch. "He never gets up."

Kim had seen that few of the men in town liked Mr. Bertrand, but all the women seemed to adore him. On some days as many as six women would show up with bottles of wine and casseroles and cakes, and they'd all laugh hilariously. When they saw Kim they'd say, "I should have brought —" They'd name their children. But then another woman would say how good it was to have some peace and quiet for a few hours.

The next time the women came they'd again "forget" to bring their children.

As Kim stood outside and heard the women howling with laughter, she didn't think they sounded very peaceful or quiet.

It was after she and her mother had been there for two long weeks that early one morning her mother seemed very excited about something, but Kim wasn't sure what it was. Something had happened during the night, some adult thing. All Kim was concerned with was that she couldn't find the copy of *Alice's Adventures in Wonderland* that Mr. Bertrand had lent her. She had *one* book, and now it was gone. She asked her mother what happened to it, as she knew she'd left it on the coffee table.

"Last night I took it to —" The sentence wasn't finished because the old phone on the wall rang and her mother ran to answer it, then immediately started laughing.

Disgusted, Kim went outside. It seemed that her life was getting worse.

She kicked at rocks, frowned at the empty flower beds, and headed toward her tree. She planned to climb up it, sit on her branch, and figure out what to do for the long, boring weeks until her dad came home and life could start again.

When she got close to her tree, what she saw stopped her dead in her tracks. There was a boy, younger than her brother but older than she was. He was wearing a clean shirt with a collar and dark trousers; he looked like he was about to go to Sunday school. Worse was that he was sitting in *her* tree reading *her* book.

He had dark hair that fell forward and he was so engrossed in her book that he didn't even look up when Kim kicked at a clod of dirt.

Who was he? she thought. And what right did he think he had to be in *her* tree?

She didn't know who or what, but she did know that she wanted this stranger to go away.

She picked up a clod and threw it at him as hard as she could. She was aiming for the top of his head but hit his shoulder. The lump crumbled into dirt and fell down onto *her* book.

He looked up at her, a bit startled at first, but then his face settled down and he stared at her in silence. He was a pretty boy, she thought. Not like her cousin Tristan, but this boy looked like a doll she'd seen in a catalogue, with pink skin and very dark eyes.

"That's *my* book," she yelled at him. "And it's *my* tree. You have no right to them." She grabbed another clod and threw it at him. It would have hit him in the face but he moved sideways and it missed.

Kim had had a lot of experience with older boys and she knew that they got you back. It didn't take much to set them off, then you were in for it. They'd chase you, catch you, and pin your arm behind your back or pull your hair until you begged for mercy.

When she saw the boy make a move as though he meant to get down, Kim took off running as fast as she could. Maybe there'd be enough time that she could reach what she knew was a great hiding place. She wedged her small body in between two piles of old bricks, crouched down, and waited for the boy to come after her.

After what seemed like an hour of waiting, he didn't show up, and her legs began to ache. Cautiously and quietly, she got out from the bricks and looked around. She fully expected him to leap out from behind a tree, yell "I got you!" then bombard her with dirt.

But nothing happened. The big garden was as still and quiet as always and there was no sign of the boy.

She ran behind a tree, waited and listened, but she heard and saw nothing. She ran to another tree and waited. Nothing. It took her a long time before she got back to "her" tree, and what she saw astonished her.

Standing on the ground, just under her branch, was the boy. He was holding the book under his arm and seemed to be waiting.

Was this some new boy trap that she'd never seen before? she wondered. Is this what foreign boys — meaning ones not from Edilean — did to girls who threw dirt at them? If she walked up to him, would he clobber her?

As she watched him, she must have made a sound because he turned and looked at her.

Kim jumped behind a tree, ready to protect herself from whatever came flying, but nothing did. After a few moments she decided to stop being a scaredy-cat and stepped out into the open.

Slowly, the boy started walking toward her, and Kim got ready to run. She knew not to let boys she'd thrown things at get too close. They prided themselves on the quickness of their throwing arms.

She held her breath when he got close enough that she knew she'd not be able to get away.

"I'm sorry I took your book," he said softly. "Mr. Bertrand lent it to me, so I didn't know it belonged to anyone else. And I didn't know about the tree being yours either. I apologize."

She was so astonished she couldn't speak. Her mother said that males didn't know the meaning of the word *sorry*. But this one did. She took the book he was holding out to her and watched as he turned away and started back toward the house.

He was halfway there before she could move. "Wait!" she called out and was shocked when he stopped walking. None of her boy cousins *ever* obeyed her.

She walked up to him, the book firmly clutched against her chest. "Who are you?" she asked. If he'd said he was a visitor from another planet, she wouldn't have been surprised.

"Travis . . . Merritt," he said. "My mother and I arrived late last night. Who are you?"

"Kimberly Aldredge. My mother and I are staying in there" — she pointed — "while my father and brother go fishing in Montana."

He gave a nod, as though what she'd said was very important. "My mother and I are staying there." He pointed to the apartment on the other side of the big house. "My father is in Tokyo."

Kim had never heard of the place. "Do you live near here?"

"Not in this state, no."

She was staring at him and thinking that he was very much like a doll, as he didn't smile or even move very much.

"I like the book," he said. "I've never read anything like it before."

In her experience she didn't know boys read anything they didn't have to. Except her cousin Tris, but then he only read about sick people, so that didn't count. "What do you read?" she asked.

"Textbooks."

She waited for him to add to that list, but he just stood there in silence. "What do you read for fun?"

He gave a slight frown. "I rather like the science textbooks."

"Oh," she said.

He seemed to realize that he needed to say more. "My father says that my education is very important, and my tutor —"

"What's that?"

"The man who teaches me."

"Oh," she said again, but had no idea what he was talking about.

"I am homeschooled," he said. "I go to school inside my father's house."

"That doesn't sound like fun," Kim said.

For the first time, he gave a bit of a smile. "I can attest that it is no fun whatever."

Kim didn't know what *attest* meant, but she could guess. "I'm good at having fun," she said in her most adult voice. "Would you like me to show you how?"

"I'd like that very much," he said. "Where do we begin?"

She thought for a moment. "There's a big pile of dirt in the back. I'll show you how to ride my bike up it then race down. You can stick your hands and feet straight out. Come on!" she yelled and started running.

But a moment later she looked back and he wasn't there. She backtracked and he was standing just where she'd left him. "Are you afraid?" she asked tauntingly.

"I don't think so, but I've never ridden a bicycle before, and I think you're too young to teach me."

She didn't like being told she was "too young" to do anything. Now he *was* sounding like a boy. "Nobody teaches you how to ride a bike," she said, knowing she was lying. Her dad had spent days holding her bike while she learned to balance.

"All right," he said solemnly. "I'll try it."

The bike was too short for him and the first time he got on it, he fell off and landed on his face. He got up, spitting dirt out of his mouth, and Kim watched him. Was he one of those boys who'd go crying to his mother?

Instead, he wiped his mouth on his sleeve, then gave a grin that nearly split his face in half. "Huzzah!" he said and got back on the bike.

By lunchtime he was riding down the hill faster than Kim had ever dared, and he jerked the front wheel upward, as though he were going over a jump.

"How'd I do?" he asked Kim after his fastest slide down the dirt hill. He didn't look like the same boy she'd first seen. His shirt was torn at the shoulder, and he was filthy from head to toe. There was a bruise forming on his cheek where he'd nearly crashed into a tree, but he'd pulled to the left and only grazed it. Even his teeth were dirty.

Before Kim could answer, he looked over her head and stiffened into the boy she'd first seen. "Mother," he said.

Kim turned to see a small woman standing there. She was pretty in a motherly sort of way, but whereas Travis had pink in his cheeks, she had none. She was like a washed-out, older, female version of him.

Without saying a word, she walked to stand between the two children and looked her son up and down.

Kim held her breath. If the woman told Kim's mom that she'd made Travis dirty, Kim would be punished.

"You taught him to ride a bike?" Mrs. Merritt asked her.

Travis stepped in front of Kim, as though to protect her. "Mother, she's just a little girl. I taught myself to ride. I'll go and wash." He took a step toward the house.

"No!" Mrs. Merritt said, and he looked back at her. She went to him and put her arms around him. "I've never seen you look better." She kissed his cheek then smiled as she wiped dirt off her lips. She turned to Kim. "You, young lady . . ." she began, but stopped. Bending, she hugged Kim. "You are a truly marvelous child. Thank you!"

Kim looked up at the woman in wonder.

"You kids go back to playing. How about if I bring a picnic lunch out here for you two? Do you like chocolate cake?"

"Yes," Kim said.

Mrs. Merritt took two steps toward the house before Kim called out, "He needs his own bike."

Mrs. Merritt looked back, and Kim swallowed. She'd never before given an adult an order. "He . . ." Kim said more quietly. "My bike is too small for him. His feet drag."

"What else does he need?" Mrs. Merritt asked.

"A baseball and bat," Travis said.

"And a pogo stick," Kim added. "And a —" She broke off because Mrs. Merritt held up her hand.

"I have limited resources, but I'll see what I can do." She went back to the house and a few minutes later she brought out sandwiches and lemonade. In the afternoon she returned with two big slices of freshly baked chocolate cake. By that time Travis had learned to do wheelies, and she watched him with a mixture of awe and terror. "Who would have thought that you're a natural athlete, Travis?" she said in wonder, then went back in the house.

In the early evening, Kim's uncle Benjamin, her cousin Ramsey's father, yelled, "Ho, ho, ho. Who ordered Christmas in July?"

"We did!" Kim yelled, and Travis followed her as she ran to her uncle's big SUV.

Uncle Ben wheeled a new shiny, blue bicycle out of the back. "I was told to give this to the dirtiest boy in Edilean." He looked at Travis. "I think that means you."

Travis grinned. He still had dirt on his teeth, and his hair was caked with it. "Is that for me?"

"It's from your mother," Uncle Ben said and nodded toward the front door.

Mrs. Merritt was standing on the step, and Kim wasn't sure but she looked like she was crying. But that made no sense. A bicycle made a person laugh, not cry.

Travis ran to his mother and threw his arms around her waist.

Kim stared at him in astonishment. No twelve-year-old boy she knew would ever do something like that. It wasn't cool to hug your mother in front of other people.

"Nice kid," Uncle Ben said, and Kim

turned back to him. “Don’t tell your mom but I went over to your house and did a little cleaning. Any of this look familiar?” He pulled a box toward the back of the car and tipped it down so Kim could see inside. Five of her favorite books were in there, her second-best doll, an unopened kit for making jewelry, and in the bottom was her jump rope.

“Sorry, no pogo stick, but I got one of Rams’s old bats and some balls.”

“Oh thank you, Uncle Ben!” she said, and followed Travis’s example and hugged him.

“If I’d known I was going to get this, I would have bought you a pony.”

Kim’s eyes widened into saucers.

“Don’t tell your mom I said that or she’ll skin me.”

Travis had left his mother and was looking at his new bike in silence.

“Think you can ride it?” Uncle Ben asked. “Or can you only handle a little girl’s bike?”

“Benjamin!” Kim’s mother said as she came out to see what was going on. Mr. Bertrand was still inside. As far as anyone knew he never left the house. “Too lazy to turn a doorknob,” Kim’s father once said.

Travis gave Kim’s uncle a very serious look, then took the bike from him and set off at a breakneck speed around the house.

When they heard the unmistakable sound of a crash, Uncle Ben put his hand on Mrs. Merritt's arm to keep her from running to the boy.

They heard what sounded like another crash on the other side of the house, and at last Travis came back to them. He was dirtier, his shirt was torn more, and there was a streak of blood across his upper lip.

"Any problems?" Uncle Ben asked.

"None whatever," Travis said, looking the man straight in the eyes.

"That's my boy!" he said as he slapped Travis hard on the shoulder. He closed the lid of the SUV. "I've got to get back to work."

"What work do you do?" Travis asked in an adult-sounding voice.

"I'm a lawyer."

"Is it a good trade?"

Uncle Ben's eyes danced with merriment but he didn't laugh. "It pays the bills, and it has some good points and bad. You thinking of trying the legal profession?"

"I rather admire Thomas Jefferson."

"You've come to the right place for him," Uncle Ben said, grinning as he opened the car door. "Tell you what, Travis ol' man, you get out of law school, come see me."

"I will, sir, and thank you," Travis said.

He sounded very adult, but the dirt on him, the twigs, and the bruises, made what he was saying funny.

But Uncle Ben still didn't laugh. He looked at Mrs. Merritt. "Good kid. Congratulations."

Mrs. Merritt put her arm around her son's shoulders, but he twisted away from her. He didn't seem to want Uncle Ben to see him so attached to a woman.

They all watched Uncle Ben leave, then Kim's mom said, "You kids go play. We'll call you in time for dinner and afterward you can catch fireflies."

"Yes," Mrs. Merritt said. "Go play." She looked as though she'd been waiting for years to say that to her son. "Mr. Bertrand is going to teach me how to sew."

"Lucy," Kim's mom said, "I think I should tell you that Bertrand is using you for free labor. He wants his curtains repaired and —"

"I know," Lucy Merritt said, "but it's all right. I want to learn to do something creative, and sewing is as good as anything else. You don't think he'd sell me his machine, do you?"

"I think he'd sell you his feet, since he rarely uses them."

Lucy laughed.

"Come on," Kim's mom said, "and I'll show you how to thread the machine."

For two weeks, Kim lived in her idea of heaven. She and Travis were together from early until late.

He took to having fun as though he'd been born to it — which Kim's mom said he should have been.

While they played outside, inside the two women and Mr. Bertrand talked and sewed. Lucy Merritt used the old Bernina sewing machine to repair every curtain in the house.

"So he can get a better price when he sells them," Kim's mom muttered.

Lucy bought fabric and made new curtains for the bathrooms and the kitchen.

"You're paying him rent," Kim's mother said. "You shouldn't be paying for them too."

"It's all right. It's not as though I can save the money. Randall will take whatever I don't spend."

Mrs. Aldredge knew that Randall was Lucy's husband, but she didn't know any more than that. "I want to know what that means," she said, but Lucy said she'd told too much already.

At night the children reluctantly went inside their separate apartments. Their mothers got them washed and fed and into bed. The next morning they were outside again. No matter how early Kim got up, Travis was always waiting for her at the back of the house.

One night Travis said, "I'll come back."

Kim didn't know what he meant.

"After I leave, I'll return."

She didn't want to reply to that because she didn't want to imagine him being gone. They climbed trees together, dug in the mud, rode their bikes; she tossed the ball, and Travis hit it across the garden. When Kim brought her second-best doll out, she was nervous. Boys didn't like dolls. But Travis said he'd build a house for it and he did. It was made of leaves and sticks and inside was a bed that Kim covered with moss. While Travis made a roof to the house, she used her jewelry kit to make two necklaces with plastic beads. Travis smiled when she slipped one over his head, and he was wearing it the next morning.

When it got too hot to move, they stretched out on the cool ground in the shade and took turns reading *Alice* and the other books aloud to each other. Kim wasn't nearly as good a reader as he was, but he never complained. When she was stumped by a word, he helped her. He'd told her he was a good listener, and he was.

She knew that at twelve he was a lot older than she was, but he didn't seem to be. When it came to schooling, he seemed like an adult. He told her the entire life cycle for a tadpole and all about cocoons. He explained why the moon was different shapes and what caused winter and summer.

But for all his great knowledge, he'd never skimmed a rock across a pond. Never climbed a tree before he came to Edilean. He'd never even skinned his elbow.

So, in the end, they taught each other. Even though he was twelve, and she only eight, there were times when she was his teacher — and she liked that.

Everything ended exactly two weeks after it began. As always, as soon as it was light outside, sleepy-eyed Kim ran out the back door, past the back of the big old house, to the wing where Travis and his mom were staying.

But that morning, when Travis wasn't already outside and waiting for her, she knew something was wrong. She started pounding on the door and yelling his name; she didn't care if she woke the whole house.

Her mother, in robe and slippers, came running out. "Kimberly! What are you shouting about?"

"Where is Travis?" she demanded as she fought back tears.

"Will you calm down? They probably just overslept."

"No! Something is wrong."

Her mother hesitated, then tried the knob. The door opened. There was no one inside, and no sign that anyone had been there.

"Stay here," her mother said. "I'll find out what's going on."

She hurried to the front of the house, but Mrs. Merritt's car wasn't there. It was too early to disturb Bertrand, but she was too concerned about Lucy and her son to let that stop her from going inside.

Bertrand was asleep on the sofa — proving what everyone suspected, that he didn't climb the stairs to go to bed. He came awake instantly, always glad for a good gossip. "Honey," he said, "they tore out of here at two this morning. I was sound asleep and Lucy woke me. She wanted to know if she could buy that old sewing machine."

"I hope you gave it to her."

"Nearly. I charged her only fifty dollars."

Mrs. Aldredge grimaced. "Where did they go? Why did they leave in the middle of the night?"

"All Lucy would tell me is that someone called to say her husband was returning and she needed to leave. She said she *had* to get there before he did."

"But where? I want to call her to see if she's all right."

"She asked us to please not contact her." He lowered his voice. "She said that no one must know that she and Travis were here."

"That sounds very bad." Mrs. Aldredge sat down on the couch, then jumped up. "Heavens! Kim is going to be heartbroken. I dread telling her. She'll be devastated. She adores that boy."

"He was a sweet one," Bertrand agreed. "Skin like porcelain. I do hope he keeps it, and doesn't let the sun ruin it. I think my good complexion comes from a lifelong belief in staying out of the sun."

Mrs. Aldredge was frowning as she went to Kim to tell her that her friend was gone and it was likely that she'd never see him again.

Kim took it better than her mother thought she would. There were no tantrums and no tears — at least not that anyone saw. But it was weeks before Kim was herself again.

Her mother took her into Williamsburg to purchase an expensive frame for the only photo she had of Travis. Kim and he were standing by their bikes, both of them dirty and smiling hugely. Just before Mrs. Aldredge clicked the shutter, Travis put his arm around Kim's shoulders, and she clasped his waist. It was a sweet portrait of childhood and it looked good in the frame Kim chose. She put it on the table by her bed so she could see it just before she fell asleep and when she awoke every morning.

It was a month after Travis and his mother left that Kim brought down the house. The family was just sitting down to dinner when Reede, her older brother, asked what she was going to do with the bike Travis had left behind.

"Nothing," Kim said. "I can't do anything because of Travis's bastard father."

Everyone came to a halt.

"What did you say?" Mrs. Aldredge asked in a whisper of disbelief.

"His bas—"

"I heard you," her mother said. "I will *not* have an eight-year-old using that kind of language in my house. Go to your room this instant!"

"But, Mom," Kim said, bewildered and already close to tears, "that's what you always call him."

Her mother didn't say a word, just pointed, and Kim left the table. She barely had the door to her room closed before she heard her parents burst into laughter.

Kim picked up Travis's picture and looked at it. "If you were here now I'd teach you a dirty word."

Sighing, she stretched out on her bed and waited for her dad to be sent to "talk" to her — and to slip her some food. He was the sweet one while her mother did the discipline. Kim thought it was very unfair that she was being punished for repeating something she'd heard her mother say several times.

"Bastard parents!" Kim muttered and held Travis's picture close to her chest. She would never forget him and she would *never* stop looking for him.

ONE

New York
2011

The big office sprawled across a corner of the sixty-first floor. Full-length windows went along two sides, offering breathtaking views of the skyline of New York. The other two walls had tasteful paintings chosen by a designer, but they gave no hint of the occupant. In the middle was a desk of rosewood, and sitting in a steel and leather chair was Travis Maxwell. Tall, broad shouldered, and darkly handsome, he was bent over papers and frowning.

Another damned merger, Travis thought. Another company his father was buying. Did his desire to own, to control, never end? When Travis heard the door to his office open, he didn't look up. "Yeah? What is it?"

Barbara Pendergast — Penny to him, Mrs. Pendergast to everyone else — looked at him and waited. She didn't put up with bad

moods from anyone.

Travis looked up at the silence and saw her. She was twice his age and half his size, but she intimidated the hell out of everyone but him. "Sorry, Penny, what is it?" She had worked for his father until just a few years ago. Together the two of them had gone from owning nothing until Randall Maxwell was one of the richest men in the world. When Travis joined the business, Penny decided to help him out. It was said that Randall Maxwell's protests could be heard six blocks away.

Penny waited a moment to give the full weight to her announcement. "Your mother called me."

"She what?!" Travis forgot about the merger as he leaned back in his chair and took a couple of deep breaths. "Is she all right?"

"I'd say she's better than all right. She wants to divorce your father because there's a man she wants to marry."

Travis could do nothing but stare. Penny wore her usual boring, but expensive, suit. Her hair was pulled back, and she was looking at him over her reading glasses. "My mother is supposed to be in hiding, keeping a low profile. How can I protect her if she's out in public? And she's been *dating?*"

"I think you should see this," Penny said and handed him a photocopied newspaper article.

It was from a Richmond newspaper and told of a fashion show for kids that had taken place in Edilean, Virginia, where his mother was staying, or more accurately, hiding. He scanned the article. Some rich woman had thrown a lavish birthday party for her daughter and there were some clothes designed by a Jecca Layton and — He looked up at Penny. "Sewn by Ms. Lucy Cooper." He put the paper down. "That's not so bad. Cooper is an assumed name, and there's no photo."

"It's not bad unless your father decides to go looking again," Penny said. "Her love of sewing is a dead giveaway."

"What else did Mom say?"

"Nothing," Penny said. "Just that." She looked at her notepad. "To quote her directly: 'Tell Travis I need a divorce because I want to get married,' then she hung up. You know she thinks you, her precious son, makes the world spin on its axis."

"My one unconditional love," Travis said with a half grin. "Did she say who she wanted to marry?"

Penny gave him a look. Travis knew there had always been great animosity from his mother to Mrs. Pendergast. For many years, Randall left his wife and child home, but he never went anywhere without Penny. "Of course she didn't tell me," Penny said. "But to answer before you ask, I don't think she would have been stu— uh, unwise enough to let this unknown man in on who she is currently married to. So no, I don't think the man is after her money."

"Would that be the money she stole from Dad, or the money she could get in a divorce settlement?"

"Since I don't believe in fairy tales, I'd say the three point two million she stole."

"I watch her accounts pretty carefully, and there have been no unusual charges. In fact," he said proudly, "she's been self-supporting for years now."

"Are you referring to the living she's been earning with the hundred grand in equipment and supplies she bought with the embezzled money?"

Travis gave her a look to let her know he'd heard enough. "I'll take care of it." Even as he said it, he dreaded what he saw as the future. His father would make a war of a divorce. It wouldn't matter if his wife relinquished all claim to his assets and paid back what she ran away with — a pittance to him and legally half hers — he'd still use everything in his power to make his wife's life a living hell. The deal Travis had made with his father four years ago was that he'd work for him if his father would leave Lucy alone. He wasn't to move heaven and earth to find her, and if he did find her, he couldn't torment her. It had been a simple bargain. All Travis had had to do was sell his soul to the devil — i.e., his father — to obtain it.

"Anything else?" he asked Penny.

"Mr. Shepard has asked to have dinner with you tonight."

Travis groaned. He was doing the legal work needed to buy Mr. Shepard's company out of bankruptcy. Since the man had started his business thirty years ago, it wasn't going to be a pleasant meal. "Helping Dad destroy a company will be a picnic after today."

"What do you want me to do?" Penny asked, her voice with a hint of sympathy in it.

"Nothing. No! Wait. Don't I have a date tonight?"

"Leslie. This will be the third one in a row that you've canceled."

"Call —"

"I know. Tiffany's."

For all his complaining, when Travis

glanced at the newspaper article on his desk, he couldn't help smiling. Edilean, Virginia, had been the site of the happiest memories of his life — which is why when his mother ran away, she went there. Kimberly, he thought and couldn't help the feeling of peace that came over him. He was twelve and she was just eight, but she'd taught him everything. He didn't know it then, but he was a boy living in prison. He hadn't been allowed to be with other children, had never watched TV or read a work of fiction. He may as well have been living in a cave — or a past century. Until he met Kim, he thought. Kim with her love of life. On his desk was a little brass plaque, the only personal item in the room. It read: I'M GOOD AT HAVING FUN. WOULD YOU LIKE ME TO SHOW YOU HOW? Kim's words to him. The words that had changed everything.

Penny was watching him. She was the only person he trusted to know the truth about his life. "Shall I make your plane reservations, or do you want to drive?" she asked quietly.

"Drive where?" When she didn't answer, he looked at her. "I . . ." He wasn't sure what to say.

"How about if while you're at dinner

tonight I buy a normal car — something that's legal to drive on the streets — and you pack a bag full of normal clothes? Tomorrow you can drive down to see your mother."

Travis still wasn't sure what to say. "Leslie . . ."

"Don't worry. I'll send her enough diamonds that she won't ask questions." Penny didn't like Leslie, but then she didn't like any of the girls Travis dated. "If you can buy her off, it's not love," she'd said several times. Penny wanted him to do what his dad had done and find a woman who loved her family more than the contents of any store.

"All right," Travis said. "Get Forester to handle this merger."

"But he can't —"

"Do it?" Travis said. "I know it but he doesn't. Maybe it'll fall through and Dad will fire the ambitious little twerp."

"Or maybe he'll succeed and your father will give him your job."

"And you said you didn't believe in fairy tales," Travis said, grinning. "All right, where's this reunion?"

She gave him the time and address.

He stood up, looked at his desk, and all he could think of was seeing his mother again. It had been too long. On impulse, he picked up the brass plaque of Kim's words and slipped it in his pocket. He looked back at Penny. "So what do you call a 'normal' car?"

As she left, she gave him one of her rare smiles. "Wait and see."

That evening a Town Car and driver were waiting downstairs for Travis. It stopped at his apartment building, the doorman opened the door, and the elevator was held for him. He spoke to no one.

His was the penthouse apartment, with views all around. The same decorator who'd done his office had filled his apartment with her idea of good taste. There was a huge antique Buddha in an alcove, and the couches were upholstered in black leather. Since Travis was in the apartment as little as possible, decorating it had never interested him.

There was only one room that held truly personal items, and he went to it now. It had originally been a walk-in closet, but Travis had requested that it be filled with glass shelves. It was in this small room — which he always kept locked — that he put his trophies, awards, certificates, those symbols of what Kim had taught him about having "fun."

It was those two weeks in Edilean, spent

with feisty little Kim, that had given him the courage to stand up to his father. His mother had tried, but her sweet nature was no match for a man like her husband.

But Travis had found that he could hold his own. The first time he saw his father after having met Kim, Travis said he wanted physical instruction as well as academic. Randall Maxwell had looked at his young son in speculation and saw that the boy wasn't going to give in. An instructor was hired.

As Lucy had said about her son, he was a natural athlete. For Travis, the strenuous activity was a release from the grueling academic work he was given to do, and as Travis learned what they had to teach, the instructors left and a new one arrived. By the time Travis was college age, he was trained in several martial arts. His nose had been broken twice, once in boxing, once by an instructor's foot in his face.

His father had wanted Travis to continue being tutored for college, but Travis said that the minute he was of age, he'd leave and never return. At that time his mother was still living at home. Her life was as isolated as Travis's, but then, she'd never been a very social person.

Travis went to Stanford, then Harvard

Law, and it was while he was away from the prison that was the only home he'd ever known that he discovered life. Sports — extreme sports — drew him. Jumping out of planes, being dropped by helicopter onto a snow-covered mountain, cliff diving. He did it all.

He passed the bar exam but had no interest in spending his life in an office. Even though his father demanded that his son work for him, Travis refused. In anger, his father shut down his trust fund, so Travis got a job as a Hollywood stuntman. He was the guy who got set on fire.

When his father saw that his ploy didn't work, that he hadn't made his son knuckle under to him, he turned his attention to his wife and made her miserable. One afternoon Lucy accidently saw a way to intercept a business transaction of her husband's. With only a moment's hesitation, she sent $3.2 million into her own account. She then spent about ten minutes packing a bag, took one of her husband's cars, and fled.

Randall told his son he wouldn't go after Lucy if Travis would stop trying to kill himself and work for him.

Travis would have done anything for his mother, so he left L.A., went back to New York, and worked for his father. Whenever possible, Travis relieved his stress by participating in any violent sport he could find.

Now, he looked about the room at the trophies, the medals, the souvenirs. On the wall behind the shelves were many framed photos. The Monte Carlo races. His face was dirty and the champagne he'd sprayed when he'd won had made streaks, but he'd been happy.

There were pictures of some of his more outrageous Hollywood stunts with fire, explosions, leaping off buildings. Interspersed among the pictures of the sports were the ones with the women. Movie stars, socialites, waitresses. Travis hadn't been discriminate. He liked pretty women no matter where they were born or what they did.

He closed the door, leaned back against it for a moment, and looked around him. He would turn thirty this year and he was tired from all of it. Tired of being under his father's control, tired of making money for a man who had too much of it.

His mother had been right to run away and hide, but he knew how guilty she felt that Travis was protecting her. But the way he saw it was that she'd spent a lifetime protecting him, so he owed her.

Right now Travis's worry was that his

mother was marrying some man just to release her son. His fear was that his mother's guilt was overwhelming her, and she was going to start the divorce proceedings just to give her son freedom.

But Travis knew that his mother had no true idea what she was asking for if she went for a divorce from Randall Maxwell. *Ruthless* was too mild a word for the man.

On the other hand, there was no way Travis could describe how much he'd like to have his own life back. Even though the last four years had worn him down, before he got out, he wanted to make sure that his mother wasn't walking into something just as bad as her marriage had been.

Travis left the trophy room and locked it securely. Only he knew the combination, and none of his many girlfriends had ever seen inside it.

He went to his bedroom, a sterile place with no personality, and into his closet. One side contained his sports clothes, the other his work suits. At the end were what Penny would call "normal" clothes, jeans and T-shirts, a leather jacket. It took only moments to throw them into a duffle bag.

He stripped down to his briefs and glanced at his body in the mirror. He had almost no fat on him and he worked to keep his muscles strong. But his skin was marked with scars from burns, punctures, surgical repairs. He'd broken his ribs more times than he could count, and under his hair was a deep scar from where a misfired piece of steel had come close to killing him.

Minutes later, Travis was dressed and ready to go to dinner with a man who needed some reassurance that the business he'd started from scratch would continue. Travis knew that what the man really needed was a shoulder to cry on. With a sigh, he left the apartment.

It was 8:00 P.M. and Travis had been driving for hours to reach Edilean. The car Penny had bought for him was an old BMW. The engine sounded good, but he could barely get eighty out of it. No doubt that was Penny's idea of how to keep him from exceeding the speed limit. She'd put a packet of hundreds in the glove box, and he'd had to smile. If Travis used a credit card, his father would know where he was. He well knew that his father kept close watch on him. It was one thing to have charges in Paris but another to have little Edilean, Virginia, show up on the statement.

"Just until Mom is safe," he said aloud as he downshifted. At least Penny hadn't insulted him by getting an automatic. She'd let him have some fun!

At the thought of that word, Travis thought of last night. Trying to comfort a man nearing seventy hadn't been easy. But Travis knew that if he didn't attempt it, no one else would. His father often said in disdain that Travis didn't have a shark's heart. It had been meant as a put-down, but Travis took it as a compliment.

He'd managed to get away from dinner by eleven. He wanted to sleep because he planned to leave early for Edilean.

But the next morning, just as he was ready to leave, his cell rang. It was his father. It was 7:00 A.M. on a Saturday morning but his dad was at work.

"Where are you?" Randall Maxwell demanded.

"Leaving town," Travis said in a cold voice that matched his father's.

"Forester can't handle this deal."

"You're the one who hired him."

"He's a good number cruncher and he sucks up to the clients. They like him."

"Then when he tells them their jobs are gone, he can hold their hands," Travis said. "I have to go."

"Where is it this time?" Randall muttered.

"Watch the sports pages."

"If you get yourself killed," Randall said, "I'll —"

"You'll what, Dad? Not attend my funeral?"

"I'll say hello to your mother."

For a moment Travis froze in place. Why had his father spoken of her *now?* Had he heard something? That a Lucy Cooper had been mentioned in a Richmond newspaper hadn't been enough to alert him, had it?

Travis decided to brazen it out. "You're pulling out the big guns this morning. You must want something bad."

"I need you to go over this deal. There's something wrong in this contract, but I can't figure out what it is."

One thing Travis knew about his father was that his instincts were infallible. If he thought there was something wrong, there was. In the last four years there'd been a hundred times when Travis had wanted to say there was nothing wrong, that no one was trying to put one over on him. Travis couldn't help thinking that if he screwed up, his father would let him out of his devil's deal. But he knew that wouldn't happen.

Randall knew when he was pushing his son too far. "Give me this morning and you can take a couple of weeks off."

Travis was silent as he thought that his

father knew him too well. But then, Randall Maxwell was a brilliant judge of character. Many years ago he'd rightly judged that Miss Lucy Jane Travis would be too afraid of him to do anything but comply with whatever he told her to do.

"Take three weeks off," Randall said. "This deal will take that long. Just figure out what they're trying to put over on me in this contract and you're free."

The last thing Travis wanted was to leave his father in anger or suspicion. The rage would come later when Travis helped his mother in the divorce. "Send the contract to me."

"There's a man waiting outside your door now," Randall said.

Travis couldn't see his father's smile of triumph, but he felt it. The only thing in life that really mattered to the man was winning.

It had been two in the afternoon before Travis got away. He'd wanted to call his mother and tell her he was coming, but he didn't have a throwaway phone, and he didn't dare use his cell.

In the end, the second he finished with the contract, he left. He called his father from the car. "That old man is as big a crook as you are," Travis said. "Page 212, last paragraph, says that if you don't agree to his terms you're in default and the company goes back to him."

"Terms?" Randall shouted. "What *terms?!* What's he talking about?"

"I have no idea. You'll have to ask old man Hardranger that."

"You have to —"

"No I don't," Travis said. "Get Forester to find out what the old man wants. Or sic Penny on him. Anybody but me. See you in three weeks," he said, then clicked off the phone. "Or not," he added.

It was difficult for Travis to imagine that possibly — maybe — he was about to get out from under his father's thumb. If his mother had had enough time to get up her courage to actually go through a divorce, Travis would be free.

The thought made him smile for most of the drive down to Edilean.

It was eight o'clock on a Saturday night, and as far as he could tell, the town was dead. Every store was closed, no all-night drugstore, no one sauntering by walking a dog. All in all, he thought the little town with its old buildings was a bit eerie, rather like a sci-fi B movie where all the inhabitants had been abducted by aliens.

It wasn't easy finding Aldredge Road, but

when he saw the sign he smiled more broadly. He knew Kim didn't live on the road but her relatives did, and the ancestral home, Aldredge House, was there.

But Aldredge House wasn't where he was going. His mother had rented an apartment in the home of Mrs. Olivia Wingate, which was just behind where Kim's cousin lived. Travis's original plan was to arrive there in the afternoon and see his mother. Since he didn't want anyone knowing who she was or who he was, he planned to park along the road and call her on the cell phone Penny had sent him that morning. After he'd seen her and made sure she was all right, he'd find a hotel.

He hadn't changed his plan, but it was growing dark and he didn't like her walking out alone. He'd have to meet her close to the house.

Travis was thinking about this as he drove down the tree-lined road when a big teenager wearing a yellow reflective vest and carrying a flashlight stepped out of the bushes in front of him. As Travis slammed on the brakes, he thanked his years of race car driving for his quick reflexes.

There was a tap on his window and another kid was motioning for him to put down the window.

"You wanta slow down, mister?" the boy said. "There are kids around here, and besides, people are leaving. Park over there by the Ford pickup."

"Park?" Travis said. "I wasn't planning on going to —" He didn't finish, as he didn't want to tell anyone his business. He could hear music and see lights through the trees to the left. It looked like there was a party going on. Travis thought of turning around and leaving, but there was a car behind him. A U-turn would draw too much attention to himself.

"You take any longer, mister, and the place will be empty. You already missed the wedding cake," the kid said.

"Yeah, sure," Travis said and pulled in beside the truck. Wedding? he thought and couldn't help grimacing. Was it Kim who was getting married? After all, it was the Aldredge House so it could be.

As he got out, he put his hand up to block the light from the next car, and also to hide his face.

A very large man was standing outside a truck that unless Travis missed his bet, had been revved up to illegal street use. He was looking at Travis as though trying to figure out who he was.

"You with the bride?" he asked as he

opened the door to help his pregnant wife out.

"Colin!" she said. "You're off duty now, so stop interrogating people." She looked at Travis. "Welcome to Edilean," she said, "and please go inside. Let's hope there's some champagne left. Not that I'll be having any."

"Sure, thanks," Travis said.

As the two of them walked toward the house, the big man gave Travis a look up and down.

"Great," he mumbled. It looked like he'd raised the suspicions of an off-duty cop. More people walked past, most of them leaving, and looked at Travis. It was then that he realized that all the people he saw were in their finest. He was wearing a gray shirt and a pair of jeans.

For a moment Travis contemplated what he should do. Leave? See his mother tomorrow?

On the other hand, he thought that it was possible that his mother was at the wedding. He didn't think so, as she had always been a quiet, retiring woman, but maybe so. It was even possible that the man she was thinking of marrying would be there too.

He had a vision of the two of them sitting in a corner holding hands and whispering sweet words to each other. It might be a nice thing to see.

And maybe Kim would be there — if she wasn't the bride, that is. Not that he could introduce himself to her again. Not that he hadn't seen her as an adult, but it had been a while. She'd been a very pretty little girl and she'd grown into an even prettier woman. The vision of her riding down the hill, her auburn hair flying out behind her, would stay with him forever.

Maybe he could change into some more appropriate clothes and maybe he could go and see the wedding. Not stay. Just look, then leave.

He opened the trunk of the car.

Two

"So how are you and the new boyfriend — Dave, is it? — getting along?" Sara Newland asked as she sat down across from Kim. Each table had a different color cloth on it, what the bride called "Easter colors." The band was taking a break, and the big dance floor was empty. Overhead, the tent was strung with tiny silver lights that cast pretty shadows everywhere.

Sara's twin boys were now a year old and were at home with a babysitter. The wedding was a rare night out for her and her husband, Mike.

"We're doing great," Kim said. She had on her bluish purple bridesmaid dress, with its low, square neckline and swishy skirt. Jecca, who was the bride as well as Kim's best friend, had designed it for her, and Lucy Cooper had made it.

"Think it's permanent between you two?" Sara asked.

"It's too early to tell, but I have hope. How are you and Mike doing?"

"Perfectly. But I'm not making much progress in taming him into a domestic life. I wanted him to help with the garden. Know what he did?"

"With Mike, I can't imagine."

"He chased off the guy who runs the backhoe, taught himself how to use the big machine, and he's cleared a strip about two acres long for the new fence. You should have heard him and the owner of the backhoe yelling at each other!"

Kim smiled. "I would have liked to have been there. I spend most of my life with salesmen. Every word they utter leads back to me buying more from them."

Sara learned forward and lowered her voice. "So how was Lucy Cooper with your dress?"

"I never saw her," Kim said. "Jecca did the one and only fitting."

"But you saw her dancing with Jecca's dad a few minutes ago, didn't you?"

Sara and Kim were cousins, the same age, and they'd played together since they were babies. For the last four years they'd talked about how odd it was that Lucy Cooper, an older woman staying at Mrs. Wingate's house, ran away whenever Kim appeared.

Other people saw her at the grocery, the pharmacy, even in Mrs. Wingate's shop downtown, but when Kim showed up, Lucy hid. One of her cousins had snapped a photo of Ms. Cooper and shown it to Kim, but she saw nothing familiar in the face. She couldn't imagine why the woman avoided her.

"I couldn't miss something like that, could I?" Kim said. "Down and dirty. Raunchy. More than a little embarrassing at their age."

"But did you see Lucy's face?"

"Yes and no. She had it buried in Jecca's dad's body parts, so I'd see an eye here, and an ear there. I'd have to get one of those police artists to draw a full face for me."

Sara laughed. "When I saw her, she looked like the happiest woman alive."

"No, that would be Jecca."

"It was a beautiful wedding. And her dress was divine! She and Tris are a stunning couple, aren't they?"

"Yes," Kim said with pride. She and Jecca had been roommates all through college and had remained BFFs, even though Jecca lived in New York City and Kim in Edilean. A few months ago Jecca had come to Edilean to spend the summer painting, had met the local doctor, Kim's cousin Tristan, fallen in love, and had married him today.

"How's Reede doing?" Sara asked, referring to Kim's brother. Reede had volunteered to help Tris while he recovered from a broken arm, but now it looked like he was going to have the responsibility of Tris's medical practice for the next three years.

"Reede is not a happy camper," Kim said. "I didn't know a person could complain as much as he does. He's threatening to jump a freighter and leave town."

"He wouldn't do that, would he? We *need* a doctor on call here in Edilean."

"No," Kim said. "Reede has too much of a sense of duty to do that. But it would be nice if he didn't look at this as a three-year prison sentence."

"Everyone will be glad for Tris to come back and be our doctor again."

"Especially the women," Kim said, and they laughed. Dr. Tristan Aldredge was a truly beautiful man, with a sweet temperament, and he genuinely cared about people.

"Who's that man who keeps staring at you?" Sara asked, looking behind Kim.

She turned but saw no one she didn't recognize.

"He stepped outside just as you turned around," Sara said.

"What's he look like?"

"Your typical tall, dark, and handsome," Sara said, smiling. "It looks like his nose has been broken a few times — or maybe I see that in all men since I met Mike." Her husband was a master of several forms of martial arts.

"My secret admirer, I guess," Kim said as she stood up.

"Is Dave here tonight?"

"No. He had to cater a wedding in Williamsburg."

"That must be difficult for you," Sara said. "He's gone every weekend."

"But home during the week," Kim said. "His home, not mine."

"Speaking of which, how's your new house?" Sara asked as she also stood. It hadn't been easy, but she'd managed to lose the baby weight and now had her slim figure back.

"Wonderful," Kim said, and her eyes lit up. "I turned the big garage into a workroom, and Jecca helped me decorate the inside. Lots of color."

"Does Dave like it?"

"He likes my kitchen," Kim said. "When I get more settled, we'll have you and your three kids over. But tell Mike he can't bring his new toy, the backhoe, with him."

"I'll do that." Smiling, Sara said good-bye

and left. The band was returning, and she wanted to get away where she could talk.

Kim stood there for a moment, looking at the friends and relatives around her. There were also some newcomers in attendance, meaning people who weren't descended from the seven founding families, and they'd come to see Dr. Tris get married. He was beloved by everyone, and she wondered how many people were there uninvited because they wanted to see Tristan again. He had saved many lives in their small town.

It had been Kim's hope that Jecca would marry her brother, Reede, but she'd fallen for Tris almost the day she met him. Because of job changes, Kim's dream of having her best friend live in the small town of Edilean had been postponed for another few years.

Kim couldn't help thinking that by that time she would be almost thirty. I'll be a statistic, she'd often thought but had said to no one. She was successful in business, but her personal life didn't seem to be going anywhere.

The bridal couple had left some time ago — Kim hadn't caught the bouquet — but some of the guests were hanging around to dance as long as the band played.

As she walked toward the side of the tent, she again thought how much she wished she could have had a date tonight. She'd met Dave six months before, when she'd gone into Williamsburg to talk to a nervous bride about the rings she and her fiancé wanted. The girl had been maddeningly indecisive and her groom was even worse. Kim had wanted to start giving them orders, but she could do nothing but make strong suggestions.

After an hour, and still no decisions, the girl's father had come in, instantly sized up the situation, and told his daughter which rings to get. Kim had looked at him in gratitude.

When she went out to her car, her way was blocked by a big white truck with BORMAN CATERING written on the side. A good-looking young man came running toward her.

"Sorry," he said as he pulled out his keys, but then he saw that the bride's father had blocked him in. Since the father was locked inside his study on a conference call, Kim and the man had introduced themselves. The first few minutes they'd exchanged complaints about the bride's inability to make a decision.

"And her mother is just like her," Dave said. He was David Borman and he owned the elegant little catering company.

By the time the father got off the phone and moved his car, she and Dave had a date. Since then, they'd gone out twice a week, and it had been quite pleasant. There were no fireworks, but it had been nice. The sex was good, nothing outrageous, but sweet. Dave was always respectful of her, always courteous.

"So where are the bad boys when you need them?" Kim mumbled as she took a flute of champagne off a tray and went outside.

She knew Tristan's house and grounds as well as her own, so she headed toward the path that led to Mrs. Wingate's house. To her left was the old playhouse. She'd spent a lot of time there when she was a child. Her mother and Tris's were good friends, and when they got together, Kim would go to the playhouse. It was in bad shape now but Jecca had plans to restore it.

Kim sat down on a bench at the head of the path. The moon was bright, the lights from the big tent twinkled, and the air was moist and warm. She closed her eyes and let it all seep into her. Was there a way to make jewelry that looked and felt like moonlight on your skin? she wondered.

"Do you still teach people how to have fun?" asked a man's voice.

Abruptly, she opened her eyes. A tall man was standing in front of her, looming over her. She couldn't see his face, as the moon formed a circle behind his head. His question was so suggestive, so provocative, that she couldn't help feeling uncomfortable. There was no one else around them, just this stranger and his creepy question.

"I think I should go," she said as she got up and headed toward the tent with its light and people.

"How long did the house I built for your doll last?"

Kim halted, then slowly turned back to him.

He was taller now, and from what she could see of his face in the low light, he was no longer choirboy-pretty as he had been when he was twelve. There were lines at his eyes and, as Sara'd said, his nose looked as though it had been hit a few times. But he was very handsome, with dark eyes as intense as the night around them.

"Travis," she whispered.

"I told you I'd come back and I have."

His voice was deep and strong, and she liked the sound of it. As she took a couple of steps toward him, she felt as though she were looking at a ghost.

"I thought maybe you wouldn't remember

me," he said softly. "You were so very young then."

She was reluctant to tell him the truth, of the depth of her despair after he left. She'd cried herself to sleep many nights. The photo of the two of them was still her most prized possession, the thing she'd grab if the building caught on fire.

No, she thought. It was better to keep it light. "Of course I remember you," she said. "You were a great friend to me. I thought I was going to lose my mind from boredom, but you came along and saved me."

"Saved you by being someone who knew nothing. You were a good teacher."

"You on that bike!" she said. "I've never seen anyone learn as fast as you did."

Travis had an image of the things he'd done on a bicycle since then, of leaps and jumps, and turns in the air. He wondered if Kim had any idea how good she looked. The moonlight on her hair, still with a hint of red in it, and the color of that dress in the silvery light — it made a beautiful picture. Had she been any other female in the world, he would be making a pass at her right now. It had never mattered to him if the woman was the wife of a diplomat or a barmaid, if Travis was attracted to her, he let her know.

But Kim had lived all her life in a small

town where everyone knew her. She wasn't the type of woman he could make a move on five minutes after seeing her.

Kim felt the awkward silence between them and thought that he hadn't changed. When he was twelve, he hadn't said much, just watched and listened and learned.

"Would you like to go back to the wedding?" she asked. She was still holding her champagne flute. "Get something to drink?"

"I . . ." Travis began, then seemed to hear himself say, "I need help." He doubted if he'd ever before said those words. His life had made him fiercely independent.

Immediately, Kim went to him. "Are you hurt? Should I call a doctor? My brother, Reede, is here and —"

"No," he said, smiling down at her. She was even prettier up close. "I'm not hurt. I came to Edilean for a reason, to do something. But now that I'm here I don't know how to go about it."

Reaching out, Kim took his hand in hers. It was a large hand, and she could feel calluses on it. It looked like he did something in his life that required physical labor. She led him over to the bench and had him sit down beside her. The light from the wedding celebration was behind her and she could see him better. He had on a dark suit that looked as though it had been tailored for him. His cheekbones reflected the moonlight, and she saw lines between his eyes. He looked worried. She bent toward him in concern.

When she leaned forward she unintentionally gave Travis a view down the top of her dress. Kim had told Jecca the neckline was too low, but she'd laughed. "With a set of knockers like yours you should show them off." With a compliment like that, Kim couldn't insist that the bodice have a modesty panel put in it.

Travis was so distracted by the view that for a moment he couldn't speak.

"You can tell me anything," Kim said. "I know we haven't seen each other in a long time, but friendship lasts forever, and you and I are *friends.* Remember?"

"Yes," he said, swallowing. He had to take his hand out of hers or he'd be pulling her closer to him. Why hadn't he used the drive down to think about what he'd say if he did see Kim again? Instead, he'd spent most of the time on the phone planning the rock climbing trip he was going on in six weeks. Equipment had to be purchased and Travis needed to do some training. Wonder if there was a cliff he could climb in little Edilean? And did this backwoods town have a gym?

He didn't want his body turning to mush while he was here trying to figure out his mother's problems.

He saw that Kim was still waiting for his answer. He hadn't planned to ask for help, hadn't even planned to see her again, but seeing her inside the tent, in that figure-hugging dress, had been too much for him. When she'd slipped out and disappeared into the woods, he'd followed her.

Now, he couldn't keep sitting there in silence. Kim was going to think he was a moron.

"It's my mother," he said. "She's living here in Edilean." He fell silent again, not sure what to tell and what to keep back. He didn't want to scare Kim away.

"What about her?" she coaxed as she tried to remember what she knew about his mother. When it had all happened, Kim had been too young to understand what was going on, but over the years she'd figured out some things. Lucy Merritt had been hiding from her abusive husband.

At the memory of the name, Kim gasped. "Lucy! Your mother's name was Lucy. Is she Lucy Cooper, the woman who runs away every time I get near? She's lived in Edilean for four years, but tonight was the first time I saw her, and even then it was only a partial view."

Travis was genuinely surprised. He'd asked his mother about Kim a couple of times, but she'd always said that they traveled in different circles, then changed the subject. "I didn't know that she hid from you, but I'm sure she would feel that she needed to. She didn't see many people when we were here before, just that old man and your mother. And you."

"Mr. Bertrand died the next year, and my mother would never tell anyone that Lucy was here."

"What about you?" Travis asked. "If you'd recognized her, would you have told?"

"I —" Kim broke off. If she'd seen Travis's mother here in Edilean she would have been on the phone to Jecca two minutes later. And she would have told her cousin Sara and maybe her new relative by marriage, Jocelyn, and she rather liked her cousin Colin's new wife, Gemma, so maybe she would have told her. And she would have *had* to tell Tris, as he was Mrs. Wingate's friend.

"Maybe," Kim said in a way that made Travis smile.

"If this is your cousin's house and Mom lived next door, it must have been difficult for her to hide from you."

"She managed it," Kim said but didn't elaborate on the many times Lucy Cooper had escaped her view. Jecca had lived in Mrs. Wingate's house for a while, and every time Kim visited, Lucy would magically disappear. Now Kim wondered if the poor woman had slipped into a broom closet. Whatever she did, Kim knew one thing for sure: Her mother had told Lucy not to let Kim see her.

Kim wanted to get the focus off her. "Is your mother here because of your father?"

"Yes," Travis said as he leaned back against the bench. He was silent for a moment, then turned to smile at her. "I'm keeping you from your friends — and your relatives. Mom said everyone in Edilean is related to one another."

"It's not that bad, but close," Kim said.

"Is that dress one of those . . . bride things?" He waved his hand.

"I was the maid of honor."

"Oh," he said. "Doesn't 'maid' mean that you're not married?"

"I'm not. What about you?"

"Never married. I work for my father," Travis said. "The deal is that if I work for him he won't pursue Mom." He was telling her things that he never told unless necessary, but the words seemed to pour from him.

"That doesn't sound pleasant," Kim said and again wanted to reach for his hand, but she didn't. She couldn't imagine being in such a situation, but she thought how . . . well, how noble, heroic even, it was of him to sacrifice himself for his mother. Who did that today?

"It seems that now my mother wants to get married, but she's still legally married to my father."

Kim didn't understand the problem. "She can get a divorce, can't she?"

"Yes, but if she files that will let my father know where she is and he'll do what he can to make her life unpleasant."

"There are laws —"

"I know," Travis said. "I'm not worried about the divorce. It's the aftermath that I fear."

"I don't understand," Kim said. The band was playing their last set, and she could hear people laughing. She wondered if Travis had ever learned to dance.

Travis turned to her. "Can I trust you? I mean, *really* trust you? I'm not used to confiding in people." Every word he said was from his heart. This was Kim, the grown-up version of the little girl who'd changed his life.

"Yes," she said and meant it with great sincerity.

"My father is . . ."

"Abusive," Kim said, her jaw set.

"He is to anyone who is weaker than he is, and my mother is a delicate woman."

"Jecca adores her."

"Mom mentioned her. She's the young woman who lived in the apartment next door."

"And she's the bride. I guess you know that Jecca and your mother became great friends. They worked out together, sewed together. There was a point when I was becoming downright jealous."

Travis was looking at Kim in shock. He talked to his mother once a week — even if he was out of the country — but he'd heard nothing of this. He'd seen the article that said she'd made clothes for some woman, but he'd thought that meant his mother stayed in her rooms and sewed.

"Jecca is Joe Layton's daughter," Kim said when Travis was silent.

"Joe Layton?"

"I assume that's the man she wants to marry, isn't it? Tonight the two of them were dancing together as though they were about to tear each other's clothes off. Jecca said

Lucy was very flexible, but I had no idea she could do a back bend like *that.* I hope that when I'm her age I can —" She broke off at Travis's look. "Oh. Right. She's your mother. I feel pretty certain that the man she wants to marry is Joe Layton."

"What's he like? What does he do?"

"He owns a hardware store in New Jersey, one that's been in his family for generations. But he's turning it over to his son and opening a store here in Edilean."

"Can the small population of this town support a hardware store?"

"We are near some large cities," Kim said coolly.

"I didn't mean to insult Edilean. I was thinking in terms of money. My mother stands to make a profit by the divorce."

"I've known Jecca for many years," Kim said tersely, "and I can assure you that her father is *not* after your mother's money." She really and truly did *not* like what he was insinuating. She stood up. "I think I'll go back to the reception now."

Travis didn't say a word. Just as he'd known he would, he'd blown it with Kim. But then, he always messed up when it came to good girls. He didn't call when he was supposed to, forgot birthdays, didn't send a gift that she'd expected. Whatever he did seemed to be wrong — which is why he tended toward women like Leslie. Give her something shiny and she was happy.

Kim got to the end of the path before a strong sense of déjà vu hit her. She was eight years old again, she'd just let her temper override her and thrown a clod of dirt at a boy. She then ran away and hid, waiting for him to come after her. But *that* boy hadn't come. She'd had to go after him. In the weeks that followed she'd found out that the boy didn't know how to do much of anything. Couldn't skip rocks, couldn't ride a bike. He knew lots about science but couldn't put a blade of grass between his thumbs and make a whistle. He didn't know anything about the really important stuff in life.

She turned back to Travis. Just as he'd done so long ago, he was sitting there, not moving. She didn't know what was in his head now — probably something he'd learned in a book — but it was obvious that he was as socially awkward now as he was then.

Slowly, she walked back to the bench and sat down beside him, her eyes straight ahead. "Sorry," she said. "My temper sometimes gets the better of me."

"Then you haven't changed."

"And you just sat there, so neither have you."

"Maybe as children we're the purest forms of ourselves."

"In our case, I think so." She took a breath. "Joe Layton isn't after your mother's money. As far as I know, no one knows she has any or will receive any. I don't mean to reveal a confidence, but Jecca said that her dad knows little about Lucy, whether she has kids or not, anything. Whenever he asks about her personal life, Lucy starts kissing him and — I guess you don't want to hear the rest of that."

"I would prefer your descriptions to be less graphic."

She smiled at the way he spoke. His extensive schooling was in every syllable. "I understand. I think you can rest easy that they are together for love, not money."

When he said nothing, she put her hand on his arm — and Travis put his hand over hers. He had almost forgotten how caring she was. When they were kids she was appalled at the things he didn't know. She seemed to have a checklist of what each and every kid in the world *must* know and she'd set about teaching him.

Right now there were a few things he'd like to teach her. She looked so good in that dress in the moonlight that it was difficult to keep his hands off her. But she was looking at him as though he were a stray dog that she needed to rescue. He had to work to keep desire out of his eyes, but she seemed to want to give him a bandage.

He knew he should let go of her hand, but her long fingers were — He lifted her hand. "Is this a scar?"

She pulled out of his grasp. "Very unfeminine, I know. But it's a hazard of my trade."

"Your trade?" Thanks to the Internet, he knew all about her jewelry shop. He'd followed her all through school, then back to Edilean, where she'd opened her own business. Kim never knew it, but Travis attended every one of her one-man shows while she was at school. One time, he'd barely escaped being seen. She'd come in with two other girls, a tall, slim, dark-haired one, and a short blonde girl with a figure that had every male in the room staring.

But Travis only had eyes for Kim. She'd grown up to be as pretty as she'd been when they were children. And he liked the way she laughed and seemed to be so happy. Travis didn't think he'd ever been that happy in his life — at least not since he'd left Edilean and Kim so many years before.

"I make jewelry," she said.

He turned on the bench to look at her. "The jewelry kit!"

She smiled. "You remember that?"

"You had me open it. You got it . . . ?"

"My aunt and uncle had given it to me for Christmas, but I wasn't interested enough to even open it. I was an ungrateful child! It was in that box Uncle Ben brought to us."

"With my bicycle," Travis said, his voice softening with the memory. "You were very creative with everything in that kit. I was amazed."

"And you were an excellent model," she said. "No boy I knew would have let me put a necklace of beads around him." She didn't tell him that the pleasure of those two weeks and the jewelry kit were all tied together. Travis and jewelry and happiness were synonymous to her.

"I still have that necklace," he said.

"Do you?" she asked.

"Yes. Kim, that was the best two weeks of my childhood."

She started to say it was for her too, but she didn't. "What are your plans about your mother?"

"I don't really have a plan. I just heard of this yesterday. She called . . ." He thought it best not to say "my secretary." "And left a message saying she wanted to get married, so she needed a divorce. That's all she said. It was a total shock to me. I thought she was living in an apartment in a house owned by a respectable older widow and they were sewing children's clothes. Now I find out that Mom is doing back bends in front of the whole town." He looked at Kim. "So, no, I haven't come up with a plan. Mainly, I want —"

"What?"

"I want to know if this man Joe Layton is good for my mother. Forget love — she thought she was in love with my father. I want to know if he's a good person and that he's not going to browbeat my little mother."

Kim drew her breath in sharply. Jecca's mother had died when she was young, and she'd been raised by her father. Joe Layton was a very strong-willed man who liked things done his way. All through college, there had been hundreds of girlfriend sessions where Jecca was tearing her hair out about some maddening thing her father had said or done. While the man could be very sweet, he could also be a serious pain in the neck. And he was *very* possessive! When Jecca fell in love with a man in Edilean, Virginia, Joe Layton had moved there to be with her — and his stunt had almost caused Jecca and Tris to break up.

"What is it?" Travis asked.

"I, uh . . ." She didn't know exactly what to say. She was saved from replying by the sound of voices coming their way.

Kim could tell from Travis's expression that he didn't want to be seen. At least not yet, before he saw his mother. "Follow me," she said as she stood and lifted her long skirt to start running down a narrow path through the woods.

"Gladly," Travis murmured as he followed her. It was dark in the heavily wooded area, but there was enough moonlight to see Kim's pale skin and the silvery blue of her dress. He loved watching her run.

His eyes were so focused on her that he almost collided with what looked to be an old playhouse. The tall turret, shadowed in the moonlight, looked like where the evil witch in a fairy tale would live.

"In here," Kim said as she opened the door, then locked it behind them.

Travis started searching for a light switch, but Kim caught his wrist and put her finger to her lips indicating he should say nothing. She motioned for him to get out from in front of the window.

He leaned back against the door, close

beside Kim.

Outside they heard the voices of what sounded like teenagers.

"Come on. I'm over here," came a loud male whisper.

"We'll get caught." It was a girl's voice.

"By who? Dr. Tris? He's already on his honeymoon." There was the sound of kissing. "I'll bet that right now he's doing what we want to do."

"I'd trade places with her," the girl said in a dreamy voice.

Kim looked at Travis, and they grimaced. The girl had said the wrong thing.

"So now I'm not good enough for you?" the boy asked.

"I just meant . . ." the girl said. "Oh, never mind. Let's get back to the tent. My mom will be looking for me."

There was a loud turn of the door handle on the playhouse. "The damned thing is locked anyway," the boy said.

"Good!" the girl said and footsteps ran down the leafy path.

When it was silent again, Kim let out her breath, looked at Travis, and they laughed. "Tomorrow the entire teenage population of Edilean will be wondering which couple got to the playhouse first."

"But it was just us oldies," Travis said.

"Speak for yourself. You're the one about to turn thirty. I have years and years to go." She moved to the right. "Come through here, but duck. The doorway is low."

He followed her into a very small second room, with a short daybed built into the wall.

Kim motioned to the bed. "You are now looking at the love capital of Edilean. Well, the indoor one."

"If you have two in a town this size that must make Edilean the romance capital of the world."

"You have to have something interesting to do in a town that doesn't have a Walmart."

Travis laughed as Kim sat down at one end of the bed and motioned for him to take the other. He had trouble fitting his long legs into the small space.

"Here, stretch out. See how we fit?" she said. Their legs went to the sides of each other.

"You and I always have fit together rather well," Travis said.

Kim was glad that the lack of light hid her expression. We're friends, she reminded herself.

"So tell me about Joe Layton," Travis said and his voice was serious.

"I don't know him well, but he did boss Jecca around a lot while we were in school. But to be fair, all our parents did. My mother never let up on me. She wanted to know who I was dating, when I got in, and if I'd applied for a job yet."

"Sounds like she cares about you. How is she now?"

"She demands to know who I'm dating, when I got in, and what the weekly gross for my shop is."

Travis laughed. "And your dad?"

"My father is made of sugar. He truly is the sweetest man alive. My parents and my little sister, Anna, are on a long cruise right now. They won't be back until the fall."

"So you're in town alone?"

"My brother, Reede, is here, and I do have a few relatives." She thought he was being polite to ask so many questions about her when what he wanted to hear about was the man his mother wanted to marry. "I think Mr. Layton is a good man, but it depends on your mother, doesn't it? From what you've said, she doesn't seem to stand up for herself very well."

He took his time answering. "When I was growing up, my mother was a very quiet woman. I think she'd learned that to stand up to my father just made him worse. If she stayed in the background, it gave him the illusion that everything was under his control, so he didn't need to reassert his authority."

"And what about you?" she asked. "What was *your* life like?"

Travis tried to move on the little bed, but there wasn't room. "I'm about to fall off this thing. Your feet are . . . Do you mind?" he asked as he picked up her feet and put them on his thigh.

Kim would have died before she protested his movement.

"Ow! Sorry, but the heels on your shoes are rather sharp and . . ."

It took her about a quarter of a second to flick her pretty high-heeled sandals off and put her feet back on his thigh. He made it seem natural when he began to massage them. Kim thanked the Spirits of the Spas that yesterday she'd had a mani-pedi. Her heels were as smooth as glass.

"Where were we?" he asked.

"Uh . . ." Kim couldn't remember. No man had ever given her a foot massage.

"Oh yes, you asked about my life. The truth is that you changed everything."

"Me?"

"I didn't grow up like other kids. We had a big house on a hundred acres in upstate New York. The place was built by a robber baron around the turn of the last century and it was a testament to his greed. Very high ceilings and lots of dark paneling. It suited my father perfectly. My mother and I lived there with a houseful of servants — all of whom became like family to us. We hardly ever saw my father, but his presence was always there."

Travis's thumbs caressed the ball of her left foot, his fingers sliding between her toes. It wasn't easy for her to comprehend what he was saying.

"Until that summer when my father went to Tokyo and my mom drove us to Edilean, I had no idea that my life wasn't like other people's. You taught me how other kids lived, and I'll always be grateful to you for that."

"I think you're making it up to me now. Travis, where in the world did you learn to do that?"

"Thailand, I think," he said. "Or maybe it was in India. Somewhere. You like it?"

"If I pass out from ecstasy, pay me no mind."

"Can't have that, can we?" he said and tucked her feet to the side of him. "Tell me more about Joe Layton."

Kim let out a sigh of disappointment that he'd stopped rubbing her feet, but she sat up straighter. "I don't have any answers. Jecca complained a lot about her father, but she also loves him very much. I know she's the light of his life. When she was younger, he wanted her with him every minute. The first summer she went back home from college, she had to beg and plead to get to visit me for just two weeks. And Mr. Layton scrutinized every man Jecca so much as looked at. She said that Tristan — the man she married — paid a bride price by giving her dad a building."

"For his hardware store?"

"Yes," Kim said.

"Is the store open yet?"

"No. There was a lot of remodeling, rebuilding actually, that had to be done. Mr. Layton had some friends of his come down from New Jersey to do it. He and Jecca had a big fight, as she said there were good contractors in Virginia, but he wouldn't listen to her."

"Sounds like a man who likes to have his own way," Travis said, frowning. "My father is like that. He has to rule over every situation."

"You think your mother said yes to Mr. Layton because he's . . . He's what's familiar to her?"

"That's exactly what I'm afraid of. I wish

there was a way I could see them together — but only if he didn't know who I was."

"You're right," Kim said. "If you're introduced as Lucy's son, Mr. Layton will be on his best behavior with you. You'd never see anything close to the truth." Her head came up. "Would your mother agree to —"

"Not telling him who I am?" Travis asked. "That's what I'm wondering. I don't know. I find women extremely unpredictable. My mother could laugh and agree, or she could get angry and ask how dare I think I know more about people than she does."

Kim had to laugh. "Spoken like Mr. Spock."

"Is he someone in Edilean?"

"No," she said. "He's someone from TV. My parents' generation. Do you often find missing pieces in your education?"

"Whole decades," he said with sincerity. "People make references to things I've never heard of. I have to watch other people to see whether to laugh or not. However, I've learned to *never* ask what the hell they're talking about. That gets me branded as something akin to being an alien."

Kim laughed more because that's just what she had done. "You can ask me anything and I'll do my best to answer it."

"I'll take you up on that." He paused. "So

tell me, are Dr. Spock and Mr. Spock the same person?"

"No. Far from it. My dad has DVDs of *Star Trek* episodes, so I'll lend them to you."

"I'd like that very much," Travis said as he suppressed a yawn. "Sorry, but it's been a very long day. I meant to be here this afternoon so I could talk to my mother right away. But my father had something he wanted me to do, so I got a late start."

Kim turned around and put her bare feet on the floor. "Have you eaten? And where are you staying?"

"Unless Edilean has a hotel and a restaurant open past — what is it now? Nine-thirty? — I'll be going into Williamsburg."

Kim decided not to think too hard before she spoke. "I have a guesthouse and a refrigerator full of food. It's really just a tiny pool house that the previous owners made into a place for their son to stay when he visited. When I bought the house, my brother, Reede, said he would move in there, but it's too small for him. He took over Colin's — he's the sheriff — old apartment, but he hates that too. Reede does, not Colin, although Colin hated the apartment too."

She stopped before she made a complete fool of herself.

"I would be honored to accept," Travis said softly. "As for dinner, I'd take you out, but . . ."

"The old cliché: We roll up our sidewalks at nine."

"When did you get sidewalks?"

"I am wounded!" Kim said. "We've had sidewalks for three years now. Next year we're getting electric streetlamps."

"I bet the lamplighter is crying over the loss of his job," Travis said.

"We married him off to the cobbler's daughter, so they're happy."

They laughed together.

Three

As she drove home, Kim marveled at the fact that Travis had returned. She kept checking the rearview mirror to make sure she hadn't lost him. He was driving an old BMW that didn't even have an automatic transmission. Maybe she could teach him that he didn't need to shift gears.

She was dying to ask him thousands of questions about what he'd done in the last years, but she thought it would be better if he told her at his own pace. She knew he worked for his bastard of a father — the word made her smile in memory — and his father had money. But if his car was any indication, it looked like he didn't share it with his son.

Kim thought about the horror of what Travis's current life must be like — and why he was doing it. To give up his own life to protect his mother! How heroic was that?

As she pulled into her driveway she remembered that he'd asked for her help, and she vowed to give it.

Travis parked beside her and got out. "You don't use your garage?"

"I have it set up as a workroom." She fumbled for her house key on the ring.

"So when it snows or rains or gets really hot, your car is outside?" He took the keys from her and unlocked the door.

"Yes," she said as she went inside. She switched on the lamps by the couch she and Jecca had chosen. The room was done in shades of blue and white. One wall was bookcases and a TV, a fireplace below. The ceiling went up to the roof, with big white exposed rafters.

"Nice," Travis said. "It looks like a home." He was wondering why his expensive decorator couldn't have done something like this. But then, he'd not given the woman any help by telling her what he liked.

"Thanks," Kim said and turned away so he wouldn't see her grin. "Kitchen's this way."

"Kim, you don't need to feed me," he said. "That you're giving me a place to sleep is enough. I can —" He stopped talking at the sight of her kitchen. It opened into the dining area, and all of it was warm and cozy. There was a big pink granite island, with copper pots hung along one wall. The dining table was big and old, with cut marks from hundreds of meals.

"I like this," he said. "Have you had this house long?" He knew the answer to that because he'd followed the sale every inch of the way. He'd even had Penny make a couple of calls to the bank where Kim was applying for a mortgage. He wanted to make sure everything went through smoothly.

"Less than a year," she said.

"And you made it look like this in that time?"

"Jecca and I did it all. We . . ." She shrugged.

"You two are artists, so you knew what you were doing. What can I do to help with dinner?"

"Nothing," Kim said, but she wondered how he knew that Jecca was an artist. Had she told him? "Just sit down and I'll get you something to eat."

He took a seat on a stool on the far side of the counter and watched her.

Kim could feel his eyes on her as she started going through the refrigerator. She felt guilty that everything in there had been made by Dave and his catering crew, but there didn't seem to be any need to tell Travis that. To say that she had a fairly regular boyfriend would be to assume that something could possibly happen between her and Travis. Foot massage aside, he didn't seem to be interested in anything besides friendship. And he was looking at her as though she were still eight years old.

She put a place mat on the counter in front of him, then a plate and the matching knife and fork. Her mother had tried to get Kim to save money by using her grandmother's dishes, but Kim had refused. "You just want to get rid of the old things," Kim had said, and her father had suppressed a laugh. In the end, her mother gave the whole set to Colin and Gemma Frazier for a wedding gift, and they'd loved them.

"What's that look for?" Travis asked, and Kim told him.

"Gemma is a historian and she knew the history of the company that made the dishes. She treated them like they were treasure."

"But not you?" Travis asked.

"I like new. What would you like to eat?"

"Anything," he said. "I'm a pure omnivore."

She put spoons in each of the nearly dozen plastic bowls she'd taken from the fridge and let him help himself. She couldn't help sitting on the stool next to him and watching him. He ate European style, with his fork turned over in his left hand, his knife in his right. His manners were those of a prince.

Without the sharp contrast between shadows and harsh white light on him, she could now see some of the angelic look that he'd had as a boy. In adulthood, his hair was midnight black, his eyes were as dark as obsidian, his cheekbones angular, and his jaw strong. It looked like he hadn't shaved in a day or so, and the whiskers further darkened the look of him. All in all, she thought she'd never seen a better looking man in her life.

Travis saw the way she was leaning on her elbow and looking at him. If he didn't distract her he was going to put his hand on the back of her neck and kiss her. "Aren't you afraid of getting something on that dress?"

"What? Oh yeah, sure." She broke her trance of staring at him. "I guess I should put on something more comfortable."

Travis gave a little cough, as though he nearly choked on his food.

"You okay?"

"Yes," he said. "I'll just finish here while you . . ."

Reluctantly, she got off the stool. "Sure, of course." She hurried down the hall to her bedroom and closed the door. "I am making a fool of myself," she whispered aloud.

It wasn't easy to reach the zipper in the back of her dress, and for a moment she thought of asking Travis to unzip her. That thought made her giggle — which disgusted her. "You *are* eight years old," she said aloud and began to undress.

In the kitchen, Travis breathed a sigh of relief. Kim, so beautiful in her low-cut dress and sitting there watching him, had been too much for him. Had he been in a normal situation, he would have given her looks to let her know how interested he was in her. He knew from experience that girls who looked at him as Kim did were an easy make.

But then what would happen? he thought. Would she start talking of *their* wedding?

The truth was that Travis didn't think he'd mind that. So far, everything around Kim had felt like he was coming home. Her, her house, even what he'd seen of her friends, had been pleasant and welcoming.

But what happened when she found out more about him, about his past, about who his father was? He'd see the stars fall out of her eyes — and he couldn't bear that. No, it was better that he let her keep her ideas that he was noble, someone who had done only good deeds in his life. Better to never let her find out the truth.

He'd finished eating by the time Kim returned wearing jeans and an old T-shirt. Unfortunately, Travis thought she looked even more desirable than before. It hit him that it had been a mistake to accept her invitation to stay at her house. He stood up.

"Ready to go to bed?" she asked.

Travis didn't dare answer that question. He just nodded, but when Kim started toward the back door, he halted. He wasn't going to be in the same room with her and a bed. "Why don't you give me the key and point me in the right direction?"

"But I need to show you where things are."

"I'm sure I can find everything." He smiled at her in a way that said he wouldn't take no for an answer.

Kim handed him her key ring.

There was an awkward moment at the back door when they parted. Kim bent forward, as though she meant to kiss him on the cheek, but he pulled back. For a moment she thought he was going to shake her hand, but then he gave her a brotherly pat on the shoulder and left the house.

As Kim put away the leftovers, she couldn't help grimacing. She was the one who'd said they were friends, so she had no right to complain when Travis stuck to that.

The next morning she awoke to the smell of cooking, and her only thought was *Travis!* She rapidly dressed and put on a bit too much eye makeup, but then her brows and lashes had always been too pale. She cursed herself for not having them dyed before the wedding. But then, she had an idea that Travis liked women who could pull off the no-makeup look. It took three shades of brown to achieve that look.

She had on nice black slacks and a crisp linen shirt when she went into the kitchen. Pausing in the doorway, she saw Travis with his back to her as he cooked something on her new Wolf range. He had on jeans and a denim shirt. She wasn't sure, but he looked to have a truly magnificent body under his clothes.

"Good morning," she said.

Travis turned, skillet in hand, and smiled at her. She so badly wanted to put her arms around him. For a moment he seemed amenable to that idea, but then he broke eye contact.

"It's my turn to feed you," he said and

nodded toward the island that had one place setting.

"You aren't eating?"

"I got up a couple of hours ago and ate then. I hope you don't mind that I did laps in your pool."

Kim was very, very sorry that she'd missed seeing him in swim trunks. "I'm glad someone is using the pool. That was my only hesitation about buying this house. I liked the layout and I loved the three-car garage for my work, but I don't know how to take care of a swimming pool."

He slid an omelet onto her plate. "I thought maybe that was the case, so I did a little cleaning for you and checked the pH. There were some chemicals in a closet, so I used some of them. I hope I wasn't being presumptuous."

"Presume all you want," Kim said as she looked at her plate. There was an omelet with peppers and onions in it and two pieces of whole wheat toast. "I'll put on weight eating like this," she said, then waited for him to say something nice.

But there was no way Travis was going to comment on the state of Kim's body. She looked great! She'd grown taller than he'd expected; she was the perfect height for him. Her white blouse clung to her, and the black pants curved around her bottom half.

His silence at her hint made her tell herself that Travis really didn't know how to act around a woman. "So what are you planning to do today?" she asked.

This morning, Travis's first thought had been to call his mother and tell her he was in Edilean. He should arrange to meet with her somewhere private where they could talk about the divorce, the man she wanted to marry, and what she planned to do with her life. He should then spend the next three weeks getting ready for the divorce case that would, no doubt, make all the newspapers.

But as he looked at Kim, he tried to think of a reason to take as long as he could to postpone all the bad that was coming. "What were you going to do today?"

"Church if I got out of bed early enough." She looked at the clock. She still had time to get ready and go, but that would mean leaving Travis behind. She thought it was entirely possible that when she returned, he'd be gone. He'd probably talk to his mother, be reassured that Joe Layton was a good man, then Travis would go back to . . . to wherever he lived. To whomever he lived with but wasn't married to.

She searched her mind for a reason to

make him stay — and for her to be with him. "I'm sure you want to see your mother, but maybe you should see Mr. Layton's new hardware store before you do."

Travis smiled as though she'd said something brilliant. "I think that's a great idea. You can tell a lot about a man when you see where he works." Which is why Travis's office had no personal items in it, he thought but didn't say. "Would you mind going with me? If you're too busy to go, you could draw a map. I could —"

"I would love to!" she said. "We'll take my car. Could you excuse me for a little bit? I have to make a phone call first, then I'll be ready to go."

The minute Kim closed her bedroom door, she called Carla, her assistant.

"Hello?" Carla asked, obviously half-asleep.

"It's me," Kim whispered as loudly as she could. "I need you to finish the Johnson rings today."

"What? I can't hear you."

Kim went into her closet and shut the door. "Carla, please wake up. I need you to finish a couple of rings for me today."

"Kim, it's Sunday. I was at the wedding until after midnight. I drank too much."

"I did too," Kim said, "but those rings

need to be done today. The wedding is tomorrow."

"But you were going to do those and —"

"I know," Kim said. "I'm a rotten, lazy boss, but something's come up. An emergency. I need for you to come over here to do them. They've been cast. They just need sanding and polishing."

Carla groaned. "That's hours of work, and it's Sunday."

"Time and a half."

Carla was silent.

"Okay," Kim said. "Double time. I just need them done today. All right?"

"Sure. Fine," Carla said. "But I want Friday the eighteenth off *and* double time for today."

Kim glared at the phone. Oh how she used to dream of being the boss, of setting her own hours, and having employees to follow her orders! "All right," Kim said. "You know where the key to the garage is, so come over here and get it done."

"Do you have a hot date?" Carla asked. "Dave planning to pop the question? You design your own ring yet?"

Kim wasn't about to tell Carla about Travis. "I have to go. And remind me to order more rouge tomorrow."

"For your face or the jewelry?"

Kim grimaced. Carla's humor often left people groaning. "See you tomorrow," she said, then hung up. Minutes later, she was in the living room. Travis was in the big navy blue chair with the matching ottoman and reading the Sunday paper. Jecca had chosen that chair. "It's for the man in your life," she'd said.

"Which one?" Kim had asked sarcastically.

"The one that's going to come along and sweep you off your feet."

"Like Tris did to you at Reede's Welcome Home party?"

"Yes," Jecca had said with a dreamy sigh, and Kim knew she had managed to get the conversation away from her.

Kim quietly sat down on the couch and picked up the Sunday magazine.

Minutes later, he asked, "Ready?" without looking up.

"Any time," she answered, but she wasn't in a rush to leave. Usually on Sunday morning she was hurrying to get ready for church, answering the phone to her mother's calls, and thinking about the work that needed to be done that week. Sunday afternoons were quiet for her. Her past boyfriends, the ones with the normal jobs, would sometimes come over to visit, but Dave was always busy on weekends. Since she'd met him, her weekends had been solitary.

"You look like you're miles away," Travis said.

She smiled at him. "I was thinking how I usually work on Sundays."

"That doesn't sound like fun," he said.

He was repeating her words of long ago. "I can attest that it is no fun whatever," she said, quoting his response, and they laughed together.

"Shall we go see what my mother is getting herself into?"

"Since you don't want to be seen, how about if we take a back way? There's an old forest road, but I don't know what shape it's in. I'll try not to lose us in any potholes."

Travis still had her keys from last night. "In that case, how about if I drive? And we'll take my old car so we don't hurt your pretty new one."

"All right," she said, but there was caution in her voice. The area around Edilean was rough. It was a wilderness preserve, maintained by the state of Virginia, but she knew that her cousins often took care of the trails. The question was whether anyone had looked at that particular road in the last few years.

A few minutes later, she and Travis were in his old Bimmer and sitting at the head of a trail that looked like it hadn't seen any traffic in years. There were holes, ridges, fallen rocks, and a dead tree was taking up half the roadway.

"Looks like we should turn around and go by the road," Kim said. "I'll tell Colin about this and he'll get it fixed."

"Colin?"

"The sheriff. You may have seen him at the wedding. He's big, dark hair."

"Pregnant wife?"

"That's him. Did you two meet?"

"Sort of," Travis said, and he thought about the risks of what Kim was saying. The sheriff would ask why she wanted the road cleared, and how she'd discovered it was a mess. And then there was what would happen if they didn't go in this way. A ride through town with Kim seated beside a stranger was bound to cause comment — and he'd be damned if he'd hide in the back!

"We could walk," Kim said. "It's only about two miles to the building."

"Those are awfully pretty sandals you have on," he said.

"Thank you. I just bought them. They're made by Børn and I love the soles. They're —" She broke off. "Oh right. They'd be destroyed walking through that."

"Kim . . ." he said slowly as he looked

into her eyes.

She could almost read his mind. He *wanted* to drive down that old road. If they went slowly and carefully, they might be able to do it. If it got to be too much for him to drive, they could walk — and maybe Travis would give her a piggyback ride. She checked her seat belt to see if it was securely fastened.

"Once I get going, I can't stop," he said in warning. "This car isn't four-wheel drive, so if I slow down we'll get stuck."

"Then you'd have to call a Frazier to get you out."

"A Frazier?"

"The sheriff's family. They know about cars."

"Do they?" From Travis's perspective, the road was easy. It would do some damage to the undercarriage of the car, but he might be able to avoid that. The question was whether or not a girl like Kim could stand it. "The sheriff would drive over that?"

"Colin? Are you kidding? He'd drive up the mountainside. He's nearly always the first person to arrive if someone needs rescuing. I keep telling him what a great team he and Reede would be. My brother goes down on helicopter cables to save people. He —"

Travis was looking at her in such an odd way that she stopped talking.

"This is like the bicycle, isn't it? You need to do it even if you fall on your face."

He smiled at her because she understood so completely. On the other hand, her talk of what other men could do was crushing his ego.

"I'm game if you are," she said.

"If we do this, you have to trust me," he said, his face serious.

"Didn't I ride on your handlebars when you rode up that dirt hill?"

He smiled at her in such a way that Kim wanted to kiss him. There was gratitude as well as pleasure in his eyes.

"All right," he said as he glanced out the windshield, his hand on the gearshift. "Put one hand on the armrest and one here and hold on. And don't scream. Screaming distracts me."

At that last, Kim's eyes widened and part of her wanted to say, Let me out of here! But she didn't. She put her hands where he told her, braced her feet on the floor, then nodded. She was ready.

With a grin, Travis put the car in low and took off. To her shock, he started out going fast and he didn't slow down for anything. With lightning reflexes, he went around potholes, or straddled them precisely. When a fallen tree blocked the way, Travis went up onto the side of the road. The car banked left at what Kim was sure was a forty-five-degree angle, and he was heading straight for a giant oak. Kim wanted to scream. She wanted to warn him that they were about to crash, but she held her breath — and kept her eyes open.

Travis swerved to the left and missed the tree by no more than an inch. It was so close that Kim's intake of breath sounded like a mouse's squeak.

He never let up speed as he put the clutch to the floor and upshifted. When he hit a hillock made by years of overgrown weeds and a rotten tree trunk, all four wheels left the ground.

As they sailed through the air, Kim thought it could be the end of her life. She glanced at Travis, the last person she'd ever see alive.

He turned his head a bit, his dark eyes wildly alight — and he winked at her.

If Kim hadn't been terrified, she would have laughed.

When the car hit the ground, her body jolted hard — but he kept going at what seemed to be warp speed.

Travis took the car to the side again,

riding on the bank, then twisting hard to the left, then to the right and back again.

Finally, before them loomed the back of the huge building that used to be a brick factory. But Travis didn't slow down. He went around, over, and across three more big holes.

The solid wall of the brick building was straight ahead and Travis was flying toward it.

When she saw a pile of dirt in their way, Kim again had to work not to scream.

"Hold on, baby," Travis said, then hit the hill at full speed. They went through the air and landed hard on the other side, but they were still heading toward the building.

He turned the steering wheel so hard to the left that he looked like he was about to wrench his shoulders out of their sockets. The car skidded to a halt so close to the building Kim could have put down the window and touched it. But she didn't move. She was frozen into place. Her body was rigid from what she'd just gone through.

Travis turned off the engine. "Not bad. Not nearly as bad as I thought it was going to be." He looked at her. "Kim, are you all right?"

She stayed where she was, eyes straight ahead, her hands white as they gripped the handholds. She doubted if her legs were ever going to work again.

Travis got out and went around to her side to open the door. The building was so close that the edge of the door nearly scraped. Nearly. There was about a half inch of clearance. His parking had been precisely perfect.

When he opened the door, Kim's hand stayed on it and her arm was so stiff he couldn't get the door open all the way. Slowly, one by one, he pried her fingers up.

When he finally got the door open, he leaned across her and loosened her other hand, then unbuckled her seat belt. But she was still rigid in the seat.

Bending, he slid one arm behind her back, the other under her knees, and lifted her out of the car. He carried her to the shade of a tree, sat down on an empty wooden spool, and held her on his lap.

"I didn't mean to scare you," he said as he put her head on his shoulder. "I thought —" At the moment he didn't know what he'd been thinking. He'd been around too many women who wanted nothing but thrills. Yet again, he'd screwed up.

Kim was beginning to thaw out. But her first thought was that she didn't want Travis to put her down. She wanted to snuggle on his lap for as long as it took to get him to kiss her.

"Should I take you to your brother?" he asked softly.

She had no idea what he meant until she remembered that Reede was a doctor. "I'm fine," she said.

"You don't seem fine." He pulled her head from his shoulder and looked at her. Her skin was pale and her eyes were wide. She looked like a shock victim — but at the same time there was something else deeper in her eyes.

He leaned back and studied her. "You enjoyed yourself, didn't you?"

"I've never done anything like that before," she said. "It was . . ."

She didn't have to say any more. He could see it all in her face. The ride down the old road had made her feel *alive*. It's how he'd felt that first day when he'd ridden her bicycle.

Smiling, Travis stood her on the ground. "So how do we get inside this place?" He started walking away.

Kim was still a bit dazed, her legs felt weak, and her mind was full of images of what had happened in the car. She could see the tree coming at them, then swerving just before they hit. Twice Travis had taken the car through the air, all four wheels off the ground.

"Is there an alarm system?"

She had to blink to focus on him. "What?"

"Do you know if there's an alarm system on the building?"

"I have no idea." As she walked toward him, she nearly fell once when her legs buckled, but she held her balance.

"I'm going to look around," he said. His eyes were twinkling, as though he knew something she didn't. "Stay here and I'll be back in a few minutes."

"Okay," Kim said, "but if you need help, I'm here."

"I'll keep that in mind." Smiling, Travis went around the side of the building. He'd seen how scared she was during the drive. It was the kind of thing he'd done a hundred times in his stunt work. He had to make the star look as though he could actually *do* things. But Kim hadn't screamed, even though he'd seen that at times she'd been terrified. If at any time he'd felt out of control he would have stopped, but he hadn't. He liked that she'd been brave. Most of all, he liked that she'd trusted him.

Kim went back to the big wooden spool and sat down. "He seems to have learned how to do a lot of things since he rode my bike," she said aloud.

She was sitting there, looking at the old BMW, amazed that it wasn't in flames of protest, when a door in the building opened. She expected to see Mr. Layton, but Travis stepped outside.

"No alarm," he said. "Come inside."

"How'd you get in?" she asked as she went to him.

"He left a window open and I climbed in it. He needs better security."

Kim had only been in the old building once and that had been before the rebuilding had begun. Jecca said her dad had worked the men from New Jersey in shifts 24/7. Whatever he'd done, the transformation was stunning.

They were in a big room with tall ceilings and all around them were boxes. From what was printed on the cartons they appeared to be full of equipment and tools.

"Looks like he kept some trucking companies busy." Travis's frown was deep.

"What's that look for?"

He hesitated.

"We're friends, remember? We share secrets."

He smiled at her. "That's not easy for me to remember, but I'll try. My mother . . . Well, when she ran away from my father, she also took some money from him."

"Six or seven figures?"

"Multiple seven."

"Yeow!" Kim suddenly realized why Travis was frowning. "You think maybe Mr. Layton used your mother's money for . . ." She waved her hand. "To buy all this?"

"What hardware store owner do you know who could afford this much?"

"I don't know," she said, but the truth was that Kim did know quite a bit about opening a business. Her little jewelry shop was a quarter the size of this room, and to get it she'd had to take out a mortgage, borrow from her father, and max out her credit cards. She'd only paid it all off a year ago. She'd celebrated by putting herself back into debt by buying a house that was a bit more than she could afford. At first the bank had said no to the mortgage, but then the bank president had personally called her and said they'd be happy to give her financing. No one ever said, but Kim was sure her father had arranged it.

But Kim said none of this. Jecca was her best friend and this was her father they were talking about.

She looked around the big room and noticed that way up in the top, high above the exposed steel rafters, was an open window. Everything else looked sealed shut. "Is that the window you came through?"

Travis didn't glance up. "Yeah." He was reading the labels on the boxes. Saws, hand tools, power equipment, garden implements. Even at wholesale prices this had cost a lot. Had his mother told this man Layton about the money she had hidden away? She knew Travis had access to her account, so maybe she'd used it as collateral to buy the man's tools.

"Travis?" Kim asked, getting his attention. "That window is at least twenty feet up. How did you get up to it from the outside and down from the inside?"

"Climbed," he said distractedly. "I'm going to look around."

She followed him into a smaller room that held two large restrooms. Travis went past them but Kim stopped. She knew that Jecca had sent her dad designs that the New Jersey workmen were to follow.

In keeping with the age of Edilean and the fact that the building used to be a factory to make bricks, Jecca had used a color palette of cream and Williamsburg blue. She'd left the bricks exposed wherever she could, and trimmed them in that soft blue that the Colonials had so loved. Kim wasn't sure, but she'd be willing to bet that Lucy

Cooper had made the curtains.

Smiling, Kim went back out into the big hall to see that Travis was gone. She found him standing in the next room, which had three offices in it, with windows facing into the hall. He tried the doors, but they were locked.

"I'd like to get into his computer and see his source of income for all this." He looked at Kim as though asking her a question.

"I don't know how to hack into a computer."

"Me neither," he said, sounding as though his education were lax.

"Nice to know there's something you can't do," Kim muttered. So far he'd cleaned her pool, cooked breakfast, driven like something out of an action movie, and scaled a brick wall.

She hurried after him. He was standing in a long, narrow room with windows that opened to the front. He had an expression on his face that she couldn't read. There was nothing in the room, no boxes, no desks, just the walls on three sides, the windows on the other.

She waited, but he just kept staring, saying nothing. "Want to see the room Mr. Layton planned for Jecca to use? She likes to paint and she's quite good at it, so he was going to make her a studio. But Jecca said she'd never get any work done if she was so near her father. She said he'd bully her into working for him because, you see, Jecca knows how to take chain saws apart. She can put them back together too."

Travis was looking at the room as though he were in a trance and she didn't think he'd heard a word she'd said.

"But Jecca would rather raise pink unicorns, so she didn't take her dad up on his offer."

"Where did she get a breeding pair?"

"What?"

"Of pink unicorns?" Travis asked.

"I thought you weren't listening."

"Didn't I tell you that I'm a good listener?"

They exchanged smiles. They had been children and it had only been for two weeks, but they both remembered every minute of that time.

"Do you know what Layton plans to do with this room?" he asked.

"I have no idea. Why?"

Travis went to the windows to look out at the big parking lot. "Where do you buy your outdoor equipment around here?"

"You mean like fishing gear?"

Travis smiled. "I was thinking more of

climbing paraphernalia and kayaks. Where do the local guides get their equipment?"

Kim was blinking at him. "Guides?" she said at last.

"Edilean is surrounded by some incredible wilderness. I saw online a place called Stirling Point."

"It's the outdoor make-out point," Kim said, but Travis just looked at her. "The playhouse is the indoor and the —"

"I get it," he said, his face serious. "I saw online that there's hiking, boating, your fishing, and some climbing in the preserve. Where do people buy their gear?"

"I don't know," Kim said yet again in answer to his questions. "Virginia City, Norfolk, maybe Richmond. And Williamsburg must sell that stuff."

"But nothing here in Edilean?"

"No kayak store anywhere."

Travis didn't smile. "Interesting. So where is your friend's unicorn studio?"

Kim opened the connecting door to a big, airy room, this time with the windows along the back, looking out into the woods. Like the other one, the room was empty. It had been restored and the floor rebuilt. All the windows were new, some with the Pella stickers still on them.

"This is great," Travis said softly. "Really great."

Kim went to stand in front of him. "I want to know what's on your mind."

He turned away for a moment. "With every word I hear about Layton, the more concerned I am. You said he's a bully. He —"

"No," Kim said. "I said he bullied Jecca. That's what parents do. They say it's for our own good. My mother bullies me. Doesn't your father use anything he can to make you do what he wants you to?"

"Incessantly," Travis said, "but that's beside the point. I don't know if I'll get my mother to agree to this, but maybe I can rent these two rooms as a sports shop." And get someone to run them, he thought.

Kim's heart instantly jumped into her throat. That would mean he'd *stay* in Edilean. But then she deflated. "Oh," she said. "You'd fake it. You'd get your mother to lend you some money so you could pretend to open a store so you could be around Mr. Layton."

Travis was perplexed by what she'd said, especially about the money, until he thought of the car Penny had bought for him. To tell Kim the truth would mean telling her about his father. He didn't want to do that and see her eyes change.

"More or less," he said.

They heard a car door slam.

"Stay here," Travis said as he went into the narrow room to look out the front windows. He came back to Kim seconds later. "It's a man. He looks like a block of granite with a head on it."

"That's Mr. Layton," Kim said.

"A man that size with my little mother —" Shaking his head, he took a step forward, but he stopped and looked back at her. "Let's go," he said as he grabbed her hand and they ran out the back door.

"He's not real," Kim said aloud to herself as she wiped down the kitchen counter. "He's not real and he won't stay," she added to make sure she heard herself.

A few hours before, she and Travis had run out the back of what was to become Layton Hardware and into the woods. "He'll see your car," Kim said, out of breath as she leaned against a tree and looked at him.

Travis was so big and so *male.* She still couldn't believe that the boy she'd thought about for so many years had grown into this great, virile being. His shirt clung to his chest and she could see the muscles. What did he do to be built like that? she wondered. Spend six hours a day in a gym?

When he looked at her, she turned away. She didn't want to see that look of his that said she was a little girl.

"Only if he goes out the back," Travis said, smiling at her. "Wait!"

They listened and heard the sound of gravel crunching.

"He's leaving," Travis said. "Shall we return?"

Kim looked about the woods. What she wanted to do was walk with him deep, deep into the forest and —

"Kim?"

"I'm coming," she said and followed him the few feet to the back of the big brick building. Travis held the car door open for her, then got into the driver's side.

"We go out the way we came in, right?" he said.

"But this time I get to drive."

Travis laughed. "Maybe we'll try the paved road."

"Coward!" she said and laughed with him.

He'd driven her home, walked her to the door, unlocked it, but didn't follow her inside. "I need to see my mother," he said. "We have some things we have to talk about."

"Of course," she said as she went inside. She had no doubt that as soon as he returned he'd tell her he was leaving town, nice to have seen her again.

Her cell rang as soon as she closed the door.

"Miss me?" Dave asked.

So much had happened in the last day and a half that she hardly recognized his voice. "Of course I did," she answered. "What about you?"

"I missed you a lot when you didn't answer any of my messages."

Kim pulled her phone from her ear and pushed a button. She had four voice mails. "I'm sorry," she said. "I've been so busy that I didn't check."

"I know. The Johnson wedding, right?"

Oh no! Kim thought. The rings. Please, please let Carla have remembered her request to do them. She started toward the garage door. "Yes, the wedding," she said. She flipped on the light. There on the workbench were two gold rings, their intricate surfaces perfectly polished. Thank you, she mouthed as she left her workroom. "What about you? Busy?"

"If you'd listened to my messages — not that I'm complaining, of course — you would know that I'm swamped. But I'm trying hard to get away this weekend."

She turned off the light and shut the door. "Oh?"

"Kim!" Dave said. "You sound like you forgot. The weekend?"

"Oh, right," she said. She had completely forgotten. But then, the trip hadn't been her idea, but one concocted by her friends and relatives.

"You made the reservations, didn't you?"

She took a few steps to her desk in the corner of the kitchen and looked at the printout. One double room at the Sweet River B&B in Janes Creek, Maryland, for Friday, Saturday, and Sunday nights, this coming weekend. Carla had said she thought Dave was planning to propose to her while they were there. It was true that he'd pretty much invited himself to go with her.

"I've only known him for six months," Kim had said, frowning. "He asked to go with me because he wants some time off from his catering business."

"Uh-huh," Carla said. "You're forgetting that I know his last girlfriend. He *never* took off a weekend for her, and they were together for over two years."

Kim had said she needed to . . . She couldn't think of an excuse, but had just left the room.

"Kim?" Dave asked. "Are you still there?"

"Yes. It's just that a childhood friend of mine has shown up and is staying in my pool house."

"That must be nice for you," Dave said, "but, Kim, no playdates this weekend. I want you all to myself. For our own playdate."

"Okay," she said, and after a few more murmurings, Dave said he had to go, as thirty pounds of shrimp had just been delivered.

She'd put her phone in her pocket and set about cleaning the kitchen — and looking at the clock. It didn't make any sense that she'd be nervous about how long Travis was spending with his mother, but she was.

An hour went by, then two. At the start of the third hour she was sure she'd never see him again. When he tapped on the back glass door, she jumped, then gave him her best smile.

He didn't look to be in the best mood, which was confirmed when he sat down on a stool by the bar and said, "You have any whiskey?"

She poured him a shot of McTarvit single malt, a drink she kept on hand for her male cousins.

He downed it in one gulp.

"You want to talk about it?" she asked gently. When he looked at her, she saw pain in his eyes.

"You ever have a feeling that the thing you dread most in life is coming true?"

She wanted to say that she feared being a fifty-year-old businesswoman with no private life, and so far, that's where she was heading. "Yes," she said. "Is that what you think is happening to you?"

"My mother seems to think so."

She waited for him to elaborate, but he didn't say any more. When they were kids he'd always said as little as possible, and it had been her job to pull him out of himself. "So what are you planning to do tomorrow?"

He looked at her for a moment and smiled. "Not what I'd like to do, but I'm open to alternate suggestions."

"What does that mean? That you can't do what you want to?"

"Nothing," he said. "What are you going to do tomorrow?"

Kim felt the tension in her chest release. She'd been afraid that now that he'd seen his mother he'd say he was leaving. "Work," she said. "What I do every day. You're the one with open plans. Did your mother tell you to leave town?"

"Actually, just the opposite. Is there anything to eat? I burned off a little energy after the mom-talk."

Kim had been so concerned that he was going to leave that she hadn't noticed that his shirt was torn and dirty, and there was a leaf in his hair. Just like when we were kids, she thought. "What in the world did you do?" she asked as she opened the fridge.

"A little climbing. That's a nice cliff you have at Stirling Point."

"How'd you get so dirty going up that trail?"

"Didn't use the trail," he said as he went to the cabinet and withdrew a couple of plates.

She halted with a bowl in her hands. "But that's a sheer face."

Travis gave a half shrug.

Kim didn't smile. "You had no ropes, and you were alone. That was dangerous. Don't do it again," she said sternly.

"For fear of dismemberment?" he said, and something about the word made him grimace. He put potato salad on the plates. "So what did you do while I was out?"

"Tried to form wax into moonlight."

He looked at her in curiosity. "What does that mean?"

"Last night at the wedding I thought the moonlight was so beautiful I wondered if I could translate it into jewelry."

"What does that have to do with wax?" he asked as he began eating.

Kim sat down next to him and took the plate he'd filled for her. It ran through her mind that the food had been cooked by Dave and she really ought to tell Travis about him, but she didn't.

"I make jewelry by construction, welding on a small scale, or the lost wax process."

"Lost wax? Didn't I see that on TV? Some mysterious method that had disappeared over the centuries."

Kim gave a derogatory snort. "Those idiots! It's called 'lost wax' not because the process was lost but because the wax melts and it flows out. The wax is lost in the making."

"You'll have to show me. Maybe you could —"

"Travis!" Kim said, "I want to know what's going on. You said you needed my help and I'm sure it's not to give you a course in jewelry making."

He hesitated. "I have three weeks," he said.

"Three weeks until what?"

"Until I have to face my father with the news that his wife wants a divorce."

"Then what happens?"

"Legal battles," he said. "Dad will fight and I'll fight him. It will be a war."

"But once it's done, will you be free?" she asked.

"Yes," he said. "I don't know what I'll be free to do, but I will no longer have an obligation to either of my parents. Except morally and ethically, and through affection, and . . ."

"But what are your plans for now? For these three weeks?" Kim asked.

"Maybe I'll harness some moonlight so you can put it in wax and lose it."

Kim smiled. "That would be nice. I need some new ideas. I've always been inspired by organic forms and I've pretty much run through the ones I know."

"What about those flowers you used to tie together?"

"They grow from clover, and they're considered weeds."

"I liked them," he said softly and for a moment their eyes locked. But then Travis turned away and picked up the empty plates and put them in the dishwasher.

"If you're going to be here for three weeks we need to tell people who you are."

"People?" he asked. "Who would that be?"

"Travis, this is a small town. I'm sure they

are all talking about how I picked up some dark stranger and took him home with me."

"Has your mom called you yet?" he asked, smiling.

"Last I heard she was in New Zealand so the news will take — I hope — another twenty-four hours to reach her. But my brother is here. And so is my cousin Colin."

"The town doctor and the sheriff. You are a well-connected young woman."

"What's our story going to be? Will you tell people Lucy Cooper is your mother?"

"She asked for a week to break the news to Layton that she's married and has a kid."

"If she says it like that he'll be expecting a nine-year-old."

"How old does your mother think *you* are?" Travis asked.

"Five," Kim answered, and they laughed. "What if we tell the truth but leave out that the lady who sews, Lucy Cooper, is the same as Mrs. Merritt? You visited as a child, we met, you grew up, and have now returned to Edilean for a three-week holiday."

Travis's eyes lit up. "If I can get Mom to postpone telling Layton, I could get to know him before she tells who I am."

"I think we have a plan," Kim said and they exchanged smiles.

Four

Joe Layton unlocked his office and grimaced at the sight of the papers on his desk. Yet again he wondered what the hell he was doing starting over at his age. The old feeling of resentment welled up in him. He'd thought he was going to spend his life in New Jersey running the hardware store his grandfather had started. He'd never thought of it as wildly ambitious or something that anyone would covet. But then his son, Joey, got married, had kids, and his wife had seen Layton Hardware as a gold mine, something that she'd kill to have.

If she hadn't wanted it all for Joe's grandkids he would have fought her with all he had. But Joe's heart wasn't in the battle. In fact he rather liked that the woman was ambitious for her children.

When his daughter, Jecca, decided to marry some man in little Edilean, Virginia, Joe saw it as a way out of the whole mess.

At the time, it had seemed simple. He had money in the bank, so he'd use that to open a store in Virginia. His daughter-in-law, Sheila, had screamed that Joe had "no right" to take what he'd earned over the years, that he should "leave" it for them. She spoke as though Joe's death was imminent. Joe had reached his limit of generosity. He knew his daughter-in-law wanted to buy one of those big houses in something called a "gated community."

"Gated?" he'd said with a smirk when he'd first heard the term.

"Yeah!" Sheila had said with her usual belligerence. Unless she was trying to sell someone something, she let people know she was ready to fight. "With a guard out front. For protection."

"From what?" Joe asked in the same tone. "From all the photographers hounding you? They want a picture of Joe Layton's daughter-in-law?"

Whenever Sheila and he got into it, Joey left the room. He refused to be drawn into their arguments. But Joe knew his son wanted to run his own business. Sometimes Joe wondered if his son had married Sheila because he knew she'd stand up to his father. There were even times when Joe thought maybe his son had put his wife up to taking over the store. Heaven knew Sheila didn't have enough brains to figure out how her father-in-law could leave his own business.

One afternoon when Sheila had been on Joe's case about selling some damned curtains in his hardware store, he received a text message from some man he'd never heard of. The man said he was in love with Jecca, wanted to marry her, and how could he win her?

Love was the last thing Joe was thinking of. Between Sheila shouting, Joey skulking off in the next room, and hearing that some guy wanted to marry his daughter, Joe cracked. On impulse — something he never gave in to — he replied to the man by asking if that little town had a hardware store. If Joe's dear, sweet daughter was going to move there, he might as well go too. He was about to push send when he added that he wanted more photos of the pretty woman, Lucy Cooper, who Jecca had sent pictures of and who she'd raved about.

At the time, Joe had only thought how the woman had been the mother Jecca had never had. Joe's wife, the love of his life, had died when Jecca was little more than a baby. After that he'd been too busy with earning a living and raising two kids to try to find another bride. He'd made do with a few dates now and then, and even one sort of serious affair, but all the women came up short. Jecca said he wanted a clone of her mother, not a real person, and Joe knew she was right.

But then, Jecca almost always was right. Not that he would ever tell her that, but that's how he felt.

When he'd heard she was marrying a doctor, he was sure she was making a big mistake. Jecca came from a solidly blue-collar background. How would she deal with a la-di-dah doctor? But Dr. Tris — as people called him — had turned out to be okay. More than okay. He was mad about Jecca and gave up a lot to be with her.

It was through Tristan that Joe was going to be able to open the hardware store in Edilean. Tris pretty much gave him the old building. That it needed a massive renovation was beside the point.

In New Jersey, over the years Joe had helped out a lot of men. When they were out of work, he'd found them jobs. When they needed supplies for a job, he'd let them have credit. When they didn't get paid, Joe held their notes for as long as it took.

They'd repaid him in loyalty, by going to him instead of the big franchises, but even with that, Joe's business was going down. He would have died before he admitted it, but Sheila's idea of opening a design department might have been a good one.

He also would never have admitted that he had less money than he said he did. He didn't lie exactly, just sort of rounded off the numbers.

He and Jecca had had one of their big fights when Joe said he was bringing in construction guys from New Jersey to do the remodeling. He'd said the reason was because he trusted the men. The truth was that Joe collected on a lot of favors. He called men he hadn't talked to in ten years. With few exceptions, they drove down to little Edilean and put in one, two, or three days of work. Some men had been with Joe so long they sent their grandsons — or daughters, an idea Joe had no problem with. His daughter had always worked for him.

For the most part, they worked at their own expense. Joe paid some of the younger guys, but his old friends refused any payment.

"See that Skil saw?" one man asked. "You sold that to me seventeen years ago this June. It's been repaired by your two kids more times than I can count. I figure I owe you the money I saved by not buying new every time the old one broke."

Joe had acted as the contractor on the job and had overseen the men who came in at all hours of the day or night. Some guys needed no direction, but some of them were so green he had to show them which end of a nail gun to hold.

Joe's expenses had been for materials. The I beams for the roof and the crane to put them in place had nearly cleaned him out.

There were a dozen times when he thought he'd give it up and go home to fight Sheila for what was his. But that meant fighting his son and his grandchildren. What was Joe to do, go back to New Jersey and throw out Sheila's curtain display? Would he try to take the hardware store back to what it was when his kids were little?

It was an absurd idea, but he would have done it, except for one thing: Lucy.

Lucy, he thought as he stared at the papers on the desk. His whole life was coming to revolve around her.

Jecca had met her when she'd rented an apartment in Mrs. Wingate's house. The three women had hit it off so well that every e-mail Jecca sent him had been about those two women. Later Joe found out that Jecca was covering the fact that she'd met a man. She knew her father would ask a lot of questions, so she'd left him out of her correspondence.

Jecca didn't realize that her letters — and photos — of Lucy, and Lucy, and, well, Lucy, had intrigued her father. Lucy Cooper had come to remind Joe of what he'd missed in life. Now that he'd lost his son, and was about to lose his daughter *and* his business, thoughts of Lucy filled the void.

When Joe drove down to Edilean to see the building Dr. Tris was offering, he'd reminded himself that Miss Cooper knew nothing about him. He couldn't greet her as though he knew her from the hundred or so photos he'd seen of her and all that he'd conned Jecca into telling him. He had to be reserved, cool. Play James Bond, he told himself, not be the New Jersey guy who was so old-fashioned he refused to use an electric drill to put in screws.

By the time Joe got to Edilean, Jecca and Tris had had a big fight. She'd run off to New York and Dr. Tris was frantic that he was going to lose her.

Right away Joe saw that everyone was giving the young man lots of sympathy when what he needed was a kick in the pants. Joe gave it to him. He was astonished at the curse words that came out of the man's mouth! And Joe changed his mind about a doctor being too prissy for his Jecca. Over the course of one long night, Joe gave the boy a piece of his mind and lots of advice about Jecca.

It took the boy three days to get over his hangover — Joe was up by nine the next morning — then he started doing what he'd been told he needed to do to get Jecca back.

After Joe got Tristan straightened out, he found Mrs. Wingate's shop in Edilean and asked to rent a room in her house. She was a tall, elegant lady — not his type at all — who looked him up and down and said she didn't have any vacancies.

When he told her he was Jecca's father, she softened. She had some customers then, so he asked if he could go see the house. She hesitated. "I hear you need some repairs," he said. "Maybe I could look at them."

That had made her give in and she had quickly drawn a map. "I'll call Lucy and tell her you're coming," Mrs. Wingate said, again looking him up and down.

He knew that look. Ladies like her didn't want to meet men like him in the dark.

He'd taken his time driving down Aldredge Road to Mrs. Wingate's big old house. He was seriously afraid of meeting Lucy. He had a feeling that he could like her. But what if he'd misjudged what he'd heard about her and she was as snooty as that Mrs. Wingate? She'd looked at him as though he were a tradesman using the wrong entrance. If Lucy looked at him like that too . . .

"I'll go to a motel," he told himself.

The house was big, and as Jecca had said, it was set in a beautiful garden. The house needed a bit of work here and there, but it was in good shape.

He got his old suitcase out of the truck, took a deep breath, and went inside. The house was so girly inside he felt like he was entering a harem — and he sure as hell wasn't the sheik.

He stood at the foot of the stairs a moment and listened. Just as Jecca had said, he could hear a sewing machine running. It was a sweet sound to a man like him whose whole life had been about tools.

He slowly climbed the stairs and when he got to the top a pretty woman with her arms full of what looked like dresses for baby angels ran smack into him. Hard. She would have bounced off his chest and landed on the floor if Joe hadn't caught her arm and pulled her up. He was pleased to see that she had strength in her legs, good reflexes, and she was very flexible. She came up so fast her soft front was pressed against Joe's wide, hard chest.

For a moment time stood still. They looked into each other's eyes and they *knew.* Just plain *knew.*

"I assume you're Joe and I need your help," Lucy said as she stepped away from him. "Harry's acting up and a table leg is wonky and I need help cutting. Put your suitcase there and follow me."

She bent over to pick up the little white dresses, and he admired her lithe, firm figure. She stopped in the doorway. "Come on. We haven't got all day." She disappeared into the room.

Joe stood there for a moment and it struck him that he and his son might be more alike than he thought. "I *love* bossy women," he said aloud, then followed Lucy into the sewing room.

FIVE

Kim was in her shop, showing some rings she'd made last summer to a young married couple. They were in town just for the day and couldn't stop talking about how "quaint" Edilean was. The word always made Kim smile. Her cousin's wife, Tess, said they should put up a sign on the road into town saying WE AIN'T QUAINT.

Kim tried to give her attention back to the couple, who she felt sure were going to buy an inexpensive piece.

"Which one do you like best?" the girl asked Kim as she gazed at the tray containing six rings.

She wanted to tell the truth, that she liked them all, since she had designed everything in the shop. "It all depends on what *you* like, but I think —"

There was the whoosh of the door opening, and she heard Carla draw in her breath. That was her "man sound," as Carla was always on the make.

Kim looked up to see Travis standing in the doorway. He had on a forest green shirt and jeans, and with his dark hair and eyes he looked as virile as any man ever had. He seemed to exude masculinity, as though it were an aura around him.

"I am in love," Carla said under her breath as she moved next to Kim. Since Travis had eyes only for Kim, Carla added, "Please tell me he's one of your relatives so he's available to the rest of us."

Kim didn't answer as she gave her attention back to the couple — but the girl was looking at Travis, and her young husband was frowning. Customers lost, Kim thought.

Travis came forward and stopped close to the young woman. When she smiled at him, he smiled back.

"I think we should go," the young man said, but his wife ignored him.

"I see you in aquamarines," Travis said in a voice Kim had never heard him use before. It was soft and sultry, silky.

"Really?" the girl asked, sounding about fourteen.

"With your eyes, what else could you wear?"

The young woman wasn't especially pretty and her eyes were a nondescript brown. On the other hand, the ring Travis was nodding toward was one of the most expensive in the shop.

"I've never thought of wearing aquamarines before." Turning, she batted her eyelashes at her husband. "What do you think, honey?"

Before the young man could answer, Travis leaned across the counter so his upper torso was in front of the girl. "But if you want something less expensive, those little amber rings would be all right. They don't sparkle in the same way, but the price is easier on the credit card."

The young woman was looking at Travis's neck, at the way his hair curled along his golden skin. She looked as though she were in a hypnotic trance. When she lifted her hand as though she was going to touch his hair, her husband leaned in front of her. Travis stepped back.

"We'll take that ring and the earrings too," the man said, pointing to the aquamarines.

"Good choice," Travis said as he turned and smiled at Kim.

Part of her wanted to say thanks, but the larger part was disgusted by what he'd just done.

"You ready for lunch?" he asked Kim.

She nodded to Carla to write up the sale,

then went behind the far counter with Travis following her. "It's ten A.M.," she said, her voice cool. "It isn't time for lunch."

"Are you angry at me?"

"Of course not!" she snapped as she pulled out a tray of bracelets and began to rearrange them.

Travis picked up one and held it up to the light. "Nice."

The bracelet was the smallest but the most intricate, and the stones were the best quality. It was also the most expensive item she carried. She took it from him. "You seem to have learned something about jewelry."

"I've had a lot of experience." He leaned toward her. "I have things to tell you, so let's go walk somewhere and have lunch."

"Travis, I have a business to run. I can't come and go at your whim."

He looked at Carla, who hadn't stopped watching him, and smiled at her. "She looks capable of taking care of the place."

Kim lowered her voice. "Stop flirting with the women in my shop."

"Then come out with me."

"Where were you this morning?"

His face turned serious. "I got up at five, drove into the wilderness, and went for a run. When I got back you'd left for work. It's nice of you to be concerned."

"I'm not," she said as she locked the glass case. He was smiling at her. "All right! So I was worried. With the way you drive you could have run off a mountain and no one would know you were there."

"Sorry," he said, and he did look contrite. "I'm not used to telling anyone where I'm going or when I'll return." He hesitated. "Or anyone caring. Can you go out with me now? Please?"

His dark eyes were pleading, enticing even. She gave in. She went to Carla and asked if she'd look after the store for a while.

Carla bent down behind a counter and motioned for Kim to come down too. "Who is he? Where did you find him? Is *he* the emergency you had Sunday? Does Dave know about him?"

Kim stood up.

"Does *he* know about *Dave?*" Carla asked from her squatting position.

Kim rolled her eyes, got her purse out of the back, and left the store with Travis.

Before them was the entire town of Edilean, which meant there were two squares, one with a giant oak tree in the center of it.

"Shall we go sit over there?" Travis asked as he nodded toward the benches under the tree. He'd dropped his flirtatious demeanor and was again the Travis she knew.

There wasn't much traffic in the little town as they crossed the road. Politely, he let her sit down before he sat beside her.

"Your shop is nice. Maybe someday when there are no customers, you'll show me around it."

"But would you enjoy it without customers?"

"I promise, no more flirting with them. Although they did buy some nice pieces. I like your things better than what I've seen in jewelry stores in New York."

She knew he was flattering her, but he looked so worried that she wouldn't forgive him, that she did. She smiled at him. "So what did you want to talk to me about?" When he didn't answer right away, she said, "Last night, how bad was it with your mother?"

For a moment he looked ahead and didn't answer, and she got the idea that something was bothering him. "Remember that I said she could go either way, happy or angry?"

"I know that you said women are unpredictable."

"And you promised me *Star Wars* disks."

"*Star Trek,* and no they're not the same. Which way did your mom go?"

"Angry."

Kim looked at him in sympathy, and she could tell that there was more to what had been said than just for Travis to stay out of it. "Was it very bad?"

He was quiet for a moment. "My father bawls me out all the time. He has a vile temper and he uses it to scare people."

"Are you afraid of him?"

"Not in the least." Travis gave a little half smile. "In fact, I like to do things to set him off."

"But if he fired you . . . ?"

Travis laughed. "Think I don't want him to? Which he knows. Anyway, Dad says things to me that should be demoralizing and I laugh at him. But my sweet little mother . . ." He waved his hand.

"I understand," Kim said. "My mother screams at me until her face is red, but I pay no attention to her. But one time when I was in the fourth grade my father said, 'Kim, I'm disappointed in you.' I got so upset my mother made him apologize to me."

Looking at her, Travis shook his head. "Your family sounds so normal. I can't imagine my mother 'making' my dad do anything. She crumbles in front of him."

Kim had some ideas about how his mother *should* have stood up to her husband when

Travis was a boy, but she didn't think now was the time to say so. "If your mother thinks this is none of your business, why did she call and tell you she wanted a divorce?"

"That's exactly what I asked her. Unfortunately, it was after I had made some rather unfortunate remarks about the man she wants to marry."

"You didn't!"

"I'm afraid I did. Between seeing all the equipment he'd bought for that new shop, and the sheer size of him, I jumped to some conclusions. And maybe I told her too much of what I thought."

"I told you Joe Layton was a good guy."

Travis picked up her hand and kissed the back of it. "So you did. I wish I'd listened to you."

Kim was looking at him with wide eyes. He was holding her hand, massaging it actually, as he stared ahead. He didn't seem to be aware of what he was doing. "What exactly did she say?"

"She told me to stay out of it. She said she'd get herself a lawyer and that she'd fight Dad on her own." He took a breath. "And she said I was free to stop working for him because she no longer needed my protection."

"Oh," Kim said as she looked at his profile. He was frowning. "Is that what you're going to do?"

"Certainly not!" he said as he put her hand back on her lap.

In front of them was a mother with two young toddlers, a boy and a girl, probably twins. Kim didn't know the family. The children had balloons on long strings that they were looking at in fascination.

When Travis said nothing more, she looked at him. "What's your plan?"

"I haven't made one yet."

A howl made Kim look at the children. The little boy's balloon had escaped his hold and was floating up into the tree.

Seconds later, Travis stood up and looked up into the tree, as though surveying it. To Kim's astonishment, he grabbed a branch and swung up. Standing on a limb, he looked down at her. "I talked to Mom this morning and told her I wanted to meet this guy, so she's given me a week before she —" He walked out on the branch, then swung up on a higher one. "Before she tells him that I'm here," he said down to her.

By now the little boy had stopped yelling as he watched the man in the tree, and a couple of teenagers were also looking up at him.

Kim was pretty much speechless. She stood up.

"You think you could help me arrange a meeting with Mr. . . ." He glanced at the people near her. He didn't want to say the man's name in public. "With him?" He was now quite high up, on his stomach, and easing out onto a branch that didn't look large enough to hold his weight.

Kim held her breath as she nodded yes to his question.

"And I have to decide about the . . ." He was inching his way out on a very fragile-looking branch, his left arm extended toward the yellow balloon.

Kim put her hand up, her knuckles in her mouth.

"Who the hell is that?" came a voice in her ear.

Turning, she looked at the wide, solid chest of her cousin Colin, Edilean's sheriff.

Kim looked back up at Travis in the tree. She couldn't get any words out.

Colin stood by her and watched as Travis moved forward until he reached the balloon string and grabbed it.

"Vacation." Travis looked back down at Kim. "Good morning, sheriff," he said just before the branch broke.

A girl screamed, and everyone drew in

their breaths.

On his way down, Travis grabbed a branch with his right hand while holding onto the balloon with his left. He twisted the string around his fingers, then threw his legs over the branch. He pulled himself up, straddled the limb, stood up, and walked his way back to the core of the tree and went down.

He landed on two feet, walked a few steps to give the balloon back to the little boy, and dusted himself off as he went back to Kim. "What do you think?"

She just stared at him.

Colin said, "He's asking what you think he should do on his vacation in Edilean." He seemed highly amused by what he'd just seen.

"Travis!" Kim said at last.

Colin snorted. "You're in for it." When Kim started to speak again, he interrupted her. "You do that kind of thing often?"

"I used to," Travis said. "I worked in L.A. as a stuntman for a couple of years."

Colin was looking him up and down. "Still keep in shape?"

"I try to. What do you have in mind?"

"Sometimes tourists get stuck in situations in the preserve and we have to get them out. I'm the closest, so I usually get there first. Sometimes I need help."

Travis smiled as he remembered the way Kim had gushed about this man and her brother being superheroes in rescuing people. There was no way Travis was going to turn down the opportunity to help out — and maybe to impress Kim. "Do you have your cell phone with you? I'll put my number in it."

Colin handed him his cell, Travis called himself, then put his name by the number. He returned the phone. "Any time, night or day, I'd be glad to help. I've had some experience with ropes and climbing, but I've never rescued anybody. Not for real anyway."

Colin smiled. "Welcome to Edilean." He looked at Kim. "Glad to see you got a *useful* one this time," he murmured, then started toward his office.

"Say hi to Gemma for me," Kim called after him before looking back at Travis.

"I have three weeks' vacation." He still seemed to be waiting for an answer.

"My son wants to say thank you," the mother said, and Travis knelt to the little boy.

"Thank you," the child said, and hugged Travis. The little girl, not to be left out, hugged him too.

The mother smiled at Travis, her eyes

lingering on him a bit too long. "Maybe we could have you over for dinner some night."

Travis's dark eyes went to that smoldering look again. "That would be —"

"He's busy," Kim said and her look told the woman to go away.

Still smiling, she took her children and left.

"Can you arrange a meeting?" he asked.

"Travis," Kim said, "what you just did was very scary. You could have been seriously hurt. You could have —"

Bending, he kissed her cheek. "I find that having someone worry about me feels good."

"Does that mean you're going to pull more stunts like that one? It doesn't make sense to risk your life for a balloon."

"At no time was my life in jeopardy and I couldn't care less about the balloon. It was the look in the eyes of that little boy that made it all worth it."

Kim had no reply to that, as he was right.

"So what about a meeting with the man my mother wants to marry?"

"This is Edilean. You don't need an appointment. Mr. Layton's probably at his store right now, so we can just go over there and you can talk to him."

"What excuse will we give him for showing up?"

"To say hello," Kim said, frustrated and somewhat annoyed at his formality — and the way he had flirted with the pretty young mother. "I'll ask how Jecca is or something. Uh-oh."

"What is it?" he asked.

"Here comes my brother. I bet Colin called him. The snitch! Now you'll be grilled within an inch of your life. This won't be easy."

Travis couldn't help smiling at her words. In courtrooms all across the U.S. and in a couple of foreign countries he'd been interrogated by some of the most brilliant lawyers in the world. He had no doubt he could hold his own against Kim's physician brother.

But when Travis saw the man walking toward them, he turned pale. He'd seen Reede Aldredge before, and not under the best of circumstances.

Travis and his mechanic had been in a car race in Morocco. As they came around a corner outside a remote village, they saw a man leading a heavily laden donkey right across their path.

Travis had done well in not hitting the man. He'd turned his car so hard that it had spun in a circle. It had been difficult to keep it under control and not turn over, but he'd done it.

Unfortunately, in the near crash, the boxes on the donkey had hit the ground. When Travis got his car heading back in the right direction, he saw that there was liquid seeping out of the boxes and the man was shaking his fist at them. His furious face was embedded in Travis's memory.

As they drove away, he'd told his mechanic to call Penny to find out who the man was and to replace whatever had been lost. Days later she'd mentioned that the man was an American doctor and that she'd sent him replacement supplies. And she'd also made a donation to his clinic. She'd not told Travis the doctor's name and he hadn't asked for one.

That man, the doctor who'd yelled obscenities at him in Morocco, was now walking toward him.

"Can I tell him the truth about you?" Kim whispered.

For a moment he thought she meant about the race, but she was talking about their childhood. "Sure," he said, "just don't say that Lucy Cooper is my mother."

"Wouldn't dream of it," she said under her breath as she smiled at her brother.

"Kimberly," Reede said rather sternly. "I

hear that you've been causing some commotion this morning."

"Travis rescued a kid's balloon," she said as she looked up at him, but he had his hand up by his face. "This is —"

"Not *the* Travis," Reede said. "Not the boy you've fantasized about since you were a kid?"

"Reede!" Kim said as she felt her face turning red. "I never did any such thing!"

"It's good to meet you at last," Reede said, extending his hand to shake.

Travis shook it, but he kept his left hand by his eyes.

"I've seen you somewhere," Reede said. "I've done a lot of traveling. You weren't ever a patient of mine, were you?"

"No," Travis said as he turned his head away.

Kim looked from one man to the other. Reede was staring intently as he tried to remember where he'd last seen Travis. And Travis was acting like some trapped animal that desperately wanted to hide in its burrow. "We have to go," she said. "Travis has to go see Mr. Layton about opening a sporting goods store."

"This area needs one," Reede said. "What do you plan to carry?"

"Things for sports," Kim said quickly,

wanting to get away from her brother as soon as possible. "Is that one of your nurses waving at you?"

"Yeah," Reede said. "I left two exam rooms and the waiting room full. Let's get together for dinner." He started to walk away but turned back to Travis. "I look forward to hearing about what you've been doing since you were first in Edilean."

As soon as she was alone with Travis she said, "What was that all about?"

"I, uh, I do believe I may have seen your brother somewhere."

When it didn't seem as though he was going to say anything else, she turned and started walking toward her shop.

Travis caught up with her. "What are you doing?"

"If you aren't going to be honest with me I might as well go back to work. I have a new necklace I'm designing right now. I'd planned to use Australian opals in it, but maybe I should get more aquamarines since they go so well with brown eyes."

"All right," he said. "How about if we go somewhere and talk? Maybe you can help me figure out what to do about my mother."

An hour later they were sitting at a picnic table in the preserve. They'd stopped at the grocery and bought sandwiches, salads, and drinks, but it was still too early to eat.

"This is beautiful," Travis said as he looked out over the lake. "You live in a nice place."

"I like it," Kim said. It was so peaceful there that she could barely remember what had made her so angry. Something about Reede. But then lately everything about her brother seemed to make her angry. He didn't want to be a doctor in his little hometown and he complained often — and she was tired of hearing about it.

"I've never actually met your brother before but I nearly killed him," Travis said, then briefly told the story, including that he'd replenished Reede's supplies.

"Reede never mentioned the incident in his letters," Kim said. She could imagine how angry her brother would have been. "Reede thinks everyone should forgo frivolities such as car races and dedicate himself to worthy causes."

Travis was watching her. "Doesn't know how to have fun, does he?" he asked softly.

"Hazards of growing up," she said. "What *have* you done since I met you?"

"Lived by what you taught me," he said, smiling.

Kim didn't smile back. She was noticing that he evaded her questions, skirted around them. Today she sensed that something was bothering him. He'd been quite flippant about what had gone on between him and his mother, but she was beginning to think there was a great deal more to it than he'd told her. "Tell me more about your talk with your mother. What exactly did she say?"

Travis turned away but not before Kim saw his dark brows furrow into a deep frown. It looked like whatever had been said between him and his mother was too unpleasant for him to talk about.

When he looked back at her he was smiling. "She assured me that Joe Layton was a good man and that he loves her. He doesn't know my mother has any money and she doesn't know how he financed the remodeling of that old building."

Kim could tell that he was concealing something from her, and she had an idea that he wasn't going to tell her what it was. All right, she thought, if he could keep secrets, so can I. "When do you want to visit Mr. Layton?"

Travis could tell that Kim had closed down on him and he knew why. The truth was that he'd love to tell her about his talk with his mother, but he couldn't because the worst of it had been about Kim.

Last night he'd met his mother in the

garden of Mrs. Wingate's house, and after several minutes of hugging and tears of joy at seeing each other again, Travis had taken on the task of trying to find out about Joe Layton. But from his first word, she had been different from the way he remembered her. She wasn't the quiet, browbeaten little woman he'd grown up with. She thanked Travis for coming to her rescue but she'd made it clear that this was a battle she needed to fight for herself.

Travis had used his best lawyer voice to point out the error of her thinking. He thought he'd made his side clear until she told him he was sounding like his father. That had so completely taken the air out of him that he'd slumped in the chair and stared at her.

In the next second she'd asked him what he was doing with Kim and why hadn't Travis told her the full truth about his father. "Does Kim even know your last name?"

Her words made them settle back into the roles they'd always played, that of mother and son.

"I just . . . I'd like a woman to care about me, not be dazzled by the Maxwell name," Travis said. "And you know what, Mom? I'd like to know if I can handle being normal. My isolated childhood didn't exactly prepare me for an ordinary adult life."

Lucy winced, but Travis kept on. "And since then the women —"

"Please don't elaborate."

"I didn't plan to," he said. "It's just that I've not had the possibility of . . . well, love."

"So what if you do make Kim fall in love with you?" Lucy asked. "What then?"

"What if I fall for her?" He was teasing, trying to lighten the mood.

But Lucy was serious. "Travis, you have been in love with that girl since you were twelve years old. What I want to know is what happens if she falls for you. Will you look into her eyes, say, 'Wait for me,' then go skiing down some mountain? Will you expect her to be like me and spend every day in fear that I'll receive a call saying you've been paralyzed or dismembered or killed? Will you expect her to share your vagabond life and never settle anywhere?"

"I don't know!" Travis said in frustration. "My life —"

"Hasn't been normal," Lucy said. "I know that better than anyone."

"I went to work for my father to protect —"

"You cannot put that burden onto me," Lucy said loudly. "Travis, you have thrived working for Randall. The excitement, the money, the . . . the power. You've blossomed in it."

Travis fell back against the chair hard. "Are you saying that I'm becoming my father?" he asked softly.

"No, of course not. But I'm afraid . . ."

"Of what?"

"That you could be."

He took his time before speaking. "That's my worry too," he said at last. "Sometimes I see things in myself that I don't like. Whenever I please him I displease myself — and I worry that my displeasure is as strong as his pleasure." He looked at her. "But I'm not sure how to get away from the part of him that's inside me."

Lucy took her son's hand in hers. "Spend time with Kim. Forget about Joe and me. We're fine. He's not after my money and wouldn't be if he knew I had any. He loves me."

"You're sure of that?"

"Absolutely and positively."

"But didn't you once love Dad?"

"I was a girl from a very sheltered upbringing and your father went after me just as he does those companies he buys."

"I'd like to go after Kim like that," he said under his breath.

"Well, don't!" Lucy half shouted. "Don't do it to her! Don't use the Maxwell charm and money and all you've learned with those awful women you date on Kim. Don't dazzle her. Don't fly her off to Paris to wine and dine her so she's swooning over you. She doesn't deserve treatment like that."

"Whose side are you on?"

"Yours!" she said, then made herself calm down. "Travis, I love you much more than life. I'd die for you, but I want what's real for you. Don't just take this girl to bed and show her what you learned from some ambitious starlet. Find out about her. See if you really do love her. Or is it just gratitude that she showed you how to ride a bicycle? Get to know her now. And let her know you — the real you. Not the slick, smooth lawyer who can outtalk anyone. Let her see that boy who was awed by a little girl who put a string of beads around his neck."

"I'm not sure I know how to do that."

He looked at Kim. She was staring out at the lake, and he didn't know that he'd ever seen anyone as pretty — or more desirable. If she were any other girl he'd be making a pass at her and using anything he could to get her into bed. But then, as his mother had said, he'd leave her. It seemed that all his life he'd had to rush off to somewhere else. If it wasn't to some business meeting for his father, it was to some race or to a climb, or to do some other thing that could possibly, as his mother said, dismember him.

"I guess we should go," Kim said into the silence, startling Travis back into the present.

He didn't move. "I don't mean to be so secretive."

"Then tell me what's bothering you!" she said. "Are you concealing some horrible thing you've done? You couldn't be a wanted criminal, because by now I'm sure Colin has looked you up. If you have a record he knows about it and he would have warned me."

Since neither the sheriff — nor Kim — knew Travis's real last name, nothing would be found, he thought. "No criminal record," he said, and smiled at her. "The truth is that I'm not proud of some of the things I've done in my life."

"Does that mean being a stuntman or running down doctors in Morocco?"

He laughed. "Morocco for sure. But why the hell was your brother leading a donkey across an area that had been marked off for a car race?"

"My guess is that Reede thought everyone should stop for him. His work is important; yours is not."

"I have to agree with him on that. Kim . . . ?"

"Yes?"

"I have some big decisions to make in my life right now."

"About what?"

"What I'm going to do with the rest of it. In three weeks I'm going to stop working for my father."

"What do you do for him now?"

"Put people out of work," Travis said.

Kim looked at him sharply.

"It's not as bad as I'm making it sound. The businesses were going under and all the employees were going to be fired. My father buys the company and fires a mere two-thirds of them." He looked out at the lake. "I'm tired of it and I need some changes. You have any openings in your jewelry store? I think I could sell things."

"By flirting with the customers? No thanks. What do you want my help with?"

He wanted to say, To run away with me, but his mother's words rang in his head. *Get to know her now. And let her know you — the real you.* "To be my friend," he said. "We were friends as children, so maybe we can be again."

"Right," Kim said as she looked back at the lake. Friends. Story of her life, it seemed. Her last two boyfriends had broken off with her because she was more successful than they were. Whenever Kim got a new contract from a company that wanted to sell her jewelry, there would be a fight. She'd calculated that it took just three major arguments to end a relationship. She was sure that the only reason she and Dave had lasted for six whole months was because she hadn't told him that Neiman Marcus wanted a trial run of a display of her jewelry.

"Now you're the one being silent."

"I need a friend too," she said. "In the last couple of years every friend I have has married and most of them are pregnant."

"Why aren't you?" he asked solemnly.

She knew that if she told him the truth it would sound like self-pity and she couldn't bear that. "Because my doctor brother refuses to tell me how a woman *gets* pregnant. I don't think it's from swallowing a watermelon seed, which is what he told me when I was nine. After he said that I refused to eat anything with big seeds in it for two years. My mother threatened to force-feed me. But then I found out that French kissing — which I thought meant kissing in France — made a person pregnant."

Travis was smiling. "And who told you the truth?"

"I've held on to the French idea, since I've never been there and never been pregnant."

"How about if you and I —" He cut himself off as he'd been about to suggest that they fly to Paris for a few days.

"If we what?"

"Eat our sandwiches?"

She knew that yet again he'd held back from telling her something. She handed him a sandwich and began unwrapping hers. It seemed that Travis's idea of friendship was a lot different from hers.

Six

When Joe Layton saw Kim and the young man get out of the car, he knew two things. One, the man was related to Lucy, and two, he was in love with Kim. The first one made him frown and the second one made him smile.

Since Joe had met Lucy he'd tried to get her to tell him about her past, but she would say nothing. If he were a different kind of man he would have enjoyed her attempts to redirect his inquiries. But he didn't like her discomfort, so he was careful not to ask.

But it was easy to see that this young man was connected to Lucy. Her son? he wondered. They had the same eyes, only his were darker. The way his hair curled around his neck was just like hers, and the way he held his hand as he closed the car door was pure Lucy.

So she had a son, he thought. The real question was, Who was the father?

As for the second observation, Joe had felt bad for Kim as all her friends got married and moved on to a different life. She and Jecca had kept in close touch over the years, and Joe had heard how, one by one, all Kim's friends and cousins got married. Even Jecca had left. She'd gone to Edilean to visit Kim but had ended up spending all her time with Dr. Tris.

Now, it was good to see some man in love with Kim. She deserved all the best life had to offer.

Joe cleared his throat and put his shoulders back. It wouldn't do to let his sentimentality show. He opened the front door. "You here for the job?"

"What job?" Kim asked as she kissed Joe's cheek. She'd known him for many years, had spent several nights at his house in New Jersey. One night when she was in college he'd stayed up listening to Kim cry over what some fraternity guy had done to her.

"To help me get this place set up. I had to fire the first one I hired."

Travis was looking hard at the man. He was short and solidly built, and he seemed to be scowling.

"This is my friend Travis" — she hesitated — "Merritt, and I was telling him about your new store. Is that big room you were going to use for Jecca still empty?"

Joe was looking at Travis. His father must be tall, he thought, as the boy was, but his resemblance to Lucy was uncanny. It was a moment before Joe realized that Travis was holding out his hand to shake. Joe took it and kept looking in the boy's eyes. When Travis pulled his hand away, Joe felt the calluses. "You in construction?"

"No," Travis said. "Just a misspent life."

"He was a Hollywood stuntman," Kim said.

"That right? What tricks can you do?"

"Get shot, mostly," Travis said. "I'm the guy in the police uniform who gets killed by the bad guy. I've been killed four times in the same movie. Low budget."

"You'd think that as pretty as you are that you'd be the star of the picture," Joe said.

Travis laughed. "I agree. I even suggested that to a director, so he gave me a screen test. The verdict was that I have no acting talent at all."

"Why would that stop you from being a star?" Joe asked, his face serious.

"Beats me," Travis said. "But anyway, I never liked sitting around in a trailer doing nothing. What's this job you need done?"

"Manager," Joe said. "I need someone to look after the place so I have time to spend with my girls."

"Girls?" Travis asked and his smile disappeared.

"Maybe we could —" Kim began.

"My daughter and my intended," Joe said. "You think you could handle the job? You need to know a lot about tools."

"Travis knows about . . ." Kim began but hesitated. "Balloons," she said at last.

Both men looked at her.

"You the guy that got that kid's balloon out of the tree?"

"Yes," Travis said, "but I didn't think it would be known all over town so fast."

"The sheriff stopped by." Joe nodded toward the doorway to the other side of the building. "You want to see Jecca's studio?"

"Yes, we would," Kim said, and they followed Joe.

"What do you think?" Kim asked Travis. They were in a booth in a little restaurant off the road into Williamsburg, eating dinner.

"About what?" he asked as he toyed with his fork.

"Opening a sporting goods store?"

Travis took his time answering. "I liked him."

"Mr. Layton? Of course. He's a nice man.

And he was certainly taken with *you.* I couldn't believe he was asking your opinion about his finances."

"Me neither. You don't think he knows . . ."

"That you're Lucy's son? How could he?"

"I've been told that I look like my mother, so maybe he recognized me."

"Since I've never seen your mother, at least not clearly anyway, I wouldn't know." Kim looked at him, at his dark brows like gull wings over his eyes, at his jawline with its dark whiskers just under the skin. She couldn't imagine that anyone as masculine-looking as he was could resemble any female.

What Travis saw in her eyes made him want to reach across the table and drag her to him. She had a pretty mouth that he'd very much like to kiss. When his mother's words rang in his head, he looked away. He didn't know where his life was going and it wasn't fair of him to pull Kim in with him.

Kim had seen the glow in his eyes, had felt the spark between them — but then he'd turned away. For some reason she didn't understand, he wasn't allowing the attraction between them. The normal, sexual pull that men and women felt for each other was being stomped down by him.

So be it, she thought. Friends is what he'd said and friends is what they were going to be. But she couldn't help the anger that rose in her. Was there someone else in his life? Had he decided that a small town girl wasn't good enough for him? Or was it that he just couldn't see her as anything but a child?

Whatever it was, she didn't like it one little bit.

"You mind if I make a phone call?" she asked in the sweetest voice she could muster. It looked like in her case, the old adage about a woman scorned was true.

"No, go ahead. You want some privacy?"

"No, it'll just take a moment. I'm sure he's working."

"He?"

"Dave, my boyfriend."

Travis nearly choked on the bite he'd just taken. "Boyfriend?"

Kim started to speak, but then Dave answered.

"Hey, babe, what's up?" he asked.

Kim held the phone away from her ear so Dave's voice could be heard. "I was wondering if you had any ideas about what to pack for this weekend. Is this B&B formal? Should I take a long dress?"

"I don't know," Dave said. "You found

the place, but I can tell you that I'm not taking my tux. I have to wear it too often at work. Hey! Why don't we solve the dilemma by having dinner in bed every night?"

Kim was smiling as she looked at Travis. His eyes were wide, as though he couldn't believe what he was hearing. "I thought breakfast in bed was more usual." Her voice was low, sexy — the same one she'd heard Travis use with women. Women other than her.

"How about if we compromise and do them both in bed?" Dave's voice was low.

"What in the world would we do for lunch?" she asked innocently.

"You're the creative one, so I'll let you figure that out. I gotta go. We're loading the truck for a dinner party. See you Friday at two. And Kim?"

"Yes?"

"Don't pack *anything* to wear at night."

Laughing, she hung up, put her phone away, then took a long sip of her drink.

Travis was staring at her. He hadn't moved a muscle since she opened her phone. "Boyfriend?" he said at last, his voice close to a whisper.

"Yes. What's wrong? Don't you like your sandwich? We could get something else. You want me to call the waitress?"

"The food is fine. Since when do you have a boyfriend?"

"Dave and I have been together for six months now." She smiled at him. "I think it's serious."

"Serious as in how?"

She gave a one-shouldered shrug. "The usual. Why are you looking at me like that?"

"I'm just surprised is all. I didn't realize there was someone . . . important in your life."

"Please tell me that you didn't assume that since I live in a small town that I was . . . . What? Waiting for some big city man to come and rescue me? Not quite."

"Actually," he said, "I thought maybe the wedding going on when I arrived was yours."

If Kim had had any doubts that their relationship was only friendship, it vanished with that statement. He didn't seem bothered that he'd thought she was about to get married. But why should he? They hardly knew each other, and he'd made it clear that in three weeks he was leaving. "So what about you? Anyone special in your life?"

"I don't know . . ." he said. It hadn't occurred to him that Kim had a boyfriend, certainly not one that she called "serious."

"You don't know if there's a woman in

your life? If there is and you two need wedding rings, I can design and make them for you. Are you ready to go?"

"Sure," Travis said, but he hadn't recovered from the blow. He didn't know what he'd imagined, but Kim talking of meals in bed with another man hadn't been part of it.

He put money on the table and walked out of the diner behind Kim. A pretty young woman smiled at him, but Travis paid no attention to her.

Kim got behind the wheel of her car. "I have work to do at home," she said, her voice cool.

"Have I made you angry?"

"Of course not. What would I be angry about?" She wanted to yell at him. He flirted with other women but looked at her as though she were his sister — or an eight-year-old girl.

She took a deep breath and when she let it out, she released her anger. It wasn't fair of her to be angry because he wasn't attracted to her. How many times had men come on to her but she'd shot them down? At least once a week some man came into her shop and let her know that he was available. Sometimes his wife would be standing three feet away.

You really can't control sexual attraction, she thought. You either felt it or you didn't. She'd thought she felt it coming from Travis, but it looked like she was wrong. He'd been very clear that he wanted and needed friendship, so that's what she was going to give him.

"How serious are you with this man?"

Think of him as a girlfriend, Kim thought. Don't look at him, don't get pulled in by the smoldering good looks of him. He's a buddy, a friend, and nothing else.

"I think it may be permanent," she said. "Carla giggles every time she mentions this weekend, and one of my best rings is missing from the case. A big sapphire. I can't find the receipt and when I asked her about it she said . . . I don't remember her excuse, but the register receipt isn't there."

"You don't seem worried that this Carla could have stolen it. I guess that means you think this guy is going to give you one of your own rings. As an engagement ring?"

"Maybe," Kim said.

"What was it about a B&B?"

"My cousin Luke's wife, Jocelyn, has been doing the genealogy of the seven founding families of Edilean, but there's a gap in the Aldredge family. A female ancestor of mine went to a place called Janes Creek, Maryland, in the 1890s and came back pregnant. Joce wants to try to find who the father was. But she has two little kids, so she asked me to go up there and see what I could find out."

"And this man is going with you?"

"Yes," Kim said. "Dave owns a catering company and weekends are his busiest time. He's had to pay his employees a lot to cover for him this coming weekend."

"That he's taking off and that a ring and its sales receipt are missing is what makes you think he's going to . . . What? Ask you to marry him?"

Kim could again feel anger rising in her, but she stamped it down. She pulled into her driveway, turned off the engine, and looked at him. "There is also the fact that Dave is mad about me. We spend every day he's off work together. We call each other. We talk about our future together."

"Future? What does that mean?"

"Travis, I really don't like this inquisition. I agreed to help you with your mother and I will, but I'd just as soon keep my private life to myself." She got out and went into the house.

Travis stayed in the car, too stunned to move. Kim was about to accept a marriage proposal from some man who ran a catering company! How could he have ever been so wrong about a person? He'd thought that she was, well, interested in *him!*

He flipped open his phone and punched the button to reach Penny. As soon as she answered he said, "I need to know about a man named Dave, don't know his last name. Lives in a city around Edilean, owns a food catering company. He's registered for this weekend at a B&B in Janes Creek, Maryland. I want to know everything about him, and I mean *everything.*"

"Should I cancel the B&B?" Penny asked.

"Yes! No. Book me a connecting room. And fill up all the other rooms. In fact, fill up all the rooms in the entire town."

"Any choice of guests? Leslie has been calling."

For a moment Travis thought of inviting her. He didn't know whether he was angry at Kim or jealous or . . . well, hurt. Whatever he was feeling, he didn't think Leslie's presence would help.

"She'd probably love Miss Aldredge's jewelry store," Penny said into the silence. When Travis didn't reply, she said, "Life isn't so easy without the Maxwell name, is it?"

Her words came too close to home for Travis's comfort. "Just put some people in the rooms. Your relatives." It occurred to him that he knew nothing about Penny's personal life. "Do you . . . ?"

"Have relatives?" she filled in for him. "Yes I do. Rather a lot of them, actually. My son is your age. I'll e-mail you what I have," she added and for the first time ever, she hung up first.

Travis closed his phone and stared at it for a moment. This was a day for surprises! Kim was about to accept a marriage proposal and his faithful right-hand man, Penny, had a son Travis's age.

At the moment he thought of returning to New York and going back to destroying people's lives. It played less havoc with his emotions.

He got out of Kim's car and wasn't sure what to do. Go inside and talk to her? About what? Ask her to give up her boyfriend in case she and Travis felt something for each other and maybe someday he'd sort out his life and they might possibly get together? Not exactly something any female would accept. Certainly not one like Kim who'd known what she wanted since she was a kid. She was making jewelry at eight and at twenty-six she was still doing it.

"And I haven't decided —" he said aloud, but he didn't want to finish that statement.

He saw that Kim had turned the lights on in her garage, which meant that she was working. He didn't like to be disturbed when he was working, so maybe she didn't either. Besides, he didn't know what to say to her.

He walked around the house to get to the guesthouse and went to bed.

Seven

Travis had a sleepless night, and when he awoke the next morning, Kim had already gone to work. His car, the old BMW Penny had bought for him, was in the driveway. He wanted to see Kim. But if he did see her, he didn't know what he'd say. His system was still shocked at the news that she had a boyfriend. A "serious" boyfriend.

Without thinking what he was doing, Travis got into his car and started driving. His first impulse was to do something physical. That's what he did when his father demanded too much of him. Climb, run, drive, ski, surf, skate. It didn't matter what he did as long as it left him too tired to think.

But he didn't drive into the preserve, didn't seek out a lake or a cliff. Instead, he found himself pulling into the parking lot of Joe Layton's hardware store.

He sat in the car, looking at the brick front

and wondering what the hell he was doing there. When someone opened the car door, he wasn't surprised to see Joe.

"You're just in time. I need to check inventory. You open the boxes, pull the stuff out, and I'll mark it off on the papers."

"I need to . . ." Travis couldn't think of anyplace he needed to be. "Sure. But I warn you that I don't know a saw from a hammer."

"I do, so we'll be fine." Joe held the door open while Travis got his long body out. "Yesterday you looked happy. Now you look like the world came crashing down on you. Kim throw you out?"

Travis wasn't used to revealing his thoughts and certainly not his feelings to people, and he had no intention of starting. But maybe unloading boxes of tools would help him release some energy.

"So she dumps it on me that she's got a boyfriend," Travis said. It was four hours later and he was covered in sweat, grime, and those plastic foam packing beans that someone was going to hell for inventing. Travis had told Joe the story of how he and Kim had met as children, and one thing had led to another until he was telling much more than he'd intended to.

While he talked he had single-handedly unloaded what seemed to be hundreds of cartons and crates of tools and supplies. That there were no shelves to put them on didn't seem to bother Joe Layton in the least. But then he just sat in a big leather chair with a clipboard and checked off whatever Travis opened. Joe had let his disgust be known when Travis didn't know a Phillips screwdriver from a flat head.

"My daughter knows —" Joe started again. According to him, his daughter could run the world.

"Yeah, well I know how to hire a mechanic to keep the machines running," Travis had at last snapped. That seemed to release something inside him and in the next minute he was talking about Kim.

"I don't get it," he said as he pulled some electrical tool out of a box. It looked like a plastic wombat.

"Router," Joe said. "Look in there for the bits."

Travis bent over into the box, foam beans sticking in his hair and wiggling their way down into his T-shirt. He couldn't help thinking of the Frankenstein movie. "It's alive! It's alive!"

"What don't you get?" Joe asked.

"I came to this town to see Kim. We were

great together as kids. I mean, she was just a little girl and I was close to puberty, but still . . . I helped her with her jewelry. I wonder if she'd have that shop of hers now if I hadn't —"

"Liar!" Joe said loudly.

Travis pulled his head out of the carton. Packing beans stuck out all over him. "I beg your pardon."

"You came here to see your mother about me."

Travis's mouth opened, but no words came out as he stared at Joe.

"Don't look so surprised. You look like my Lucy, talk like her. Did you two think I was so stupid that I wouldn't see the resemblance?"

"I . . . We . . ."

"You want to check me out," Joe said. "It's what a good son would do. Lucy is a prize worth protecting. But I warn you, boy, if you tell her that I know who you are I'll show you what a chain saw can do."

Travis blinked a few times. His mother had made him swear not to tell Joe about her, and now Joe wanted Travis not to tell her that he knew.

"You find those bits yet?" Joe growled.

"No . . ." Travis said softly, still staring.

"Then get busy!" Joe said. "You expect

me to look for them?"

Travis bent back into the carton, found two more boxes, and pulled them out. When he came up, he looked at Joe in speculation. Where did they go from here? he wondered.

Joe marked off the items Travis held up. "So you came here to see if your mom had gone crazy when she said she wanted to marry some nobody that owned a hardware store."

Since that was pretty much the truth, Travis gave a curt nod.

"And you thought you might as well see Kim, since you were in the same town."

"I saw Kim first," Travis said, feeling defensive as he cut open another carton.

"Only because the wedding was going on and you got sidetracked."

"I told you too much," Travis muttered.

"What was that?" Joe asked.

Travis turned to him. "I told you too much. You know too much. You *see* too much."

Joe chuckled. "That's because I raised two kids on my own. The things I went through with my daughter! Joey was no problem. When he started staying in the bathroom too long I handed him some condoms. I didn't have to tell him anything. But Jecca! She fought me every inch of the way. So who's your dad?"

Travis caught himself before he blurted out the answer. Could he trust this man he barely knew? But there was something about Joe that engendered trust. The expression "salt of the earth" had been created just for him.

"Randall Maxwell," Travis said.

For a second, Joe looked shocked, scared, impressed, horrified. But then he recovered himself. "That explains everything," he said. "So you came here to see if the New Jersey guy was after your mom's money."

"More or less. She's still married to him." Travis looked hard into Joe's eyes. "The divorce is going to be brutal. You think you can handle that?"

"If I get Lucy all to myself in the end, yeah, I can handle that."

Travis didn't try to contain his smile. "I'm a lawyer and —"

"And here I was beginning to actually *like* you."

Travis groaned. "Don't start on me and no lawyer jokes. I've heard them all. How did we go from my problems to yours?"

"It started with you lying to me. You came to see your mother, not Kim. You left that girl alone for all those years, then you came back here for something else, accidently saw the girl you left behind, and now you're whining because she has a boyfriend she might marry. What did you expect? That she would stay a virgin and wait for you? You got any brothers or sisters?"

"No to every question. What is this thing? The egg of some extinct species?"

"Orbital sander. You didn't expect Kim to wait for you?"

"No I didn't, but then I did know —" He bent back into the carton to pull out sandpaper disks.

"Did know what?"

"A bit about her life."

"You've been stalking her?" Joe asked, his voice full of horror.

Travis refused to answer that. It would take too much explaining and he didn't want to have to defend himself. "When are you going to get shelves?"

"They're in those big boxes over there and you're going to put them up."

"No, I'm not," Travis said. "If you need help and can't afford it, I'll hire —"

"With Maxwell's money?"

"I have my own," Travis said, glaring at him. "Where'd you get the money to buy all this?"

"Thirty years of hard work — and a mortgage on my house in New Jersey. Not that it's any of your business. If you're so in love with Kim, why are you here with me now? Why aren't you courting her?"

"Should I be making her do back bends in public?" Travis asked, his eyes narrowed.

Joe grinned. "Heard about that, did you? Lucy can pole dance. I tell you, she can —"

"Don't!" Travis said sternly.

"Understood," Joe said. "The problem seems to be that you don't know how to court a woman."

"You've got to be kidding, old man. I've done things with women you've never even heard of. One time —"

"Not sex, boy! The only sex that matters is if you make the woman you love happy. You can do a threesome with half a dozen gorgeous dames, but if the one you love ain't smiling at you over breakfast, you're a failure in the sex department."

Travis stood still as he thought about that, and it made sense. He bent back to the box but then straightened up again. "Just so you know, a threesome is with three people, not half a dozen." He went back into the carton.

"Make her *need* you," Joe said after a while. "Not want you, but deep down need you. Whether it's to give her a foot rub at the end of the day, or to fix the kitchen sink, find an empty place in her life and fill it."

"Does my mother need you?" Travis asked in curiosity.

"She can hardly thread those sewing machines of hers without me."

Travis smiled at that. Since they'd first visited Edilean his mother had sewn, and she'd never had trouble threading anything.

Joe seemed to understand his smile. "Okay, so Lucy pretends she can't thread the serger or change the needles. But she gave me pointers on filling out the form for the mortgage application. She even told me what to wear and what to say when I went to the bank. She helped me order everything in here, and she and Jecca picked out all the colors of paint and tile. Lucy made the curtains."

"Sounds like you need her more than she needs you."

"That's just it!" Joe said. "She needs me and I need her. We're twisted."

"Intertwined," Travis said.

Joe narrowed his eyes. "You may have been to school more than me, but I got the woman I'm in love with."

"You have a point. What am I supposed to do with these pieces of metal?"

"I'm going to show you how to use a screwdriver."

"My life is at last complete," Travis muttered and picked up a socket wrench.

EIGHT

"Hello," Travis said softly as he opened the door that led to Kim's garage. She was bent over a sturdy workbench, looking through a lighted magnifying glass at something that appeared to be made of gold. "I don't mean to intrude, but I wanted to apologize for yesterday evening."

"It's okay," Kim said without looking up.

"No, it wasn't. I was rude and . . . I guess I just feel protective of you, that's all."

"You and Reede both," Kim said under her breath. Just what she needed, two brothers.

Travis was looking about the large room at all the equipment. There were deep shelves full of boxes, a couple of what looked to be microwaves, a large safe in the corner, a desk with a computer beside a foot-tall stack of fat folders, and three workbenches filled with more tools than Joe had. "This is some workshop," he said. "You need all this to make jewelry?"

"Everything in here. In fact, I need a drafting table, but I don't have the room, and it would get dirty."

Travis thought that what she needed was some natural light. There were three little glass panels in the big garage door and one small window on the far wall. It was night out, but he'd like to see the stars.

Kim glanced up at him and did a double take. "What have you been doing all day?"

"I went to Joe Layton's place and ended up unpacking boxes for him."

"You have . . ." She touched the side of her head.

Reaching up, Travis removed three foam beans from his hair. "Damned things are all over me. Joe made me sweep the floor and flatten boxes before I left." He went to the chair by the desk and dropped down on it. "I wasn't this tired after I climbed Mount Everest."

"What an exciting life you lead." She was using a tiny file on what looked to be a ring held in a padded vise. She had put a black cloth around it to catch the gold shavings.

"So far, the excitement here in Edilean beats everything I've done. Between your brother, who's going to come after me with a shotgun when he remembers where he saw me, your sheriff wanting me to rescue injured tourists, and Joe belittling me because I don't know what an orbital router is, my dad is looking pretty good."

Kim laughed. "Orbital sander. A router is something else."

"*Et tu,* Brute?" Travis said as he put his hand to his heart.

"Just keeping you straight," she said, smiling.

He was looking at the papers and folders on the desk. "Speaking of straight, what is all this?"

Kim groaned. "Money. Accounts. The bane of my life. I used to have a part-time secretary who put it all in the computer for me, but she got married and quit."

"Pregnant yet?" Travis asked. "That seems to be the main occupation of this town. You guys should invest in cable TV."

"You should try not watching TV," Kim retorted. "It's a lot of fun."

"You'll have to show me sometime," he said softly.

Startled, Kim looked at him, but he had pulled the folders onto his lap and was reading the labels.

"Mind if I look inside these? I know some about financial organization."

"If you don't mind seeing how much I

make, and how much I spend on everything from groceries to diamonds, go ahead." Kim tried to sound light, but she was actually holding her breath. Never before had she allowed a man other than her father to see her finances. Her success was what had ended her romantic relationships.

But Travis was different. They were *friends.* She nearly choked on the thought.

"Did you say something?" he asked.

"No, nothing."

"Have these receipts been entered into some system?"

"Not for weeks. My accountant is going to scalp me."

"Do you mind?" Travis asked as he nodded at her computer.

Kim shrugged. He could look if he wanted to. She listened as he settled into the chair and started going through the folders. She heard the click of the keys, and now and then looked up, seeing him bent over the papers. She was sure that if anyone knew what she was doing she'd be told she was a fool for letting a man she hadn't seen since she was a child look at her accounting charts, but whatever else she had to say about Travis, she trusted him.

It was nearly two hours since Travis had

returned and they were in the kitchen together. He'd gone into her accounting software — but had insisted that she type in her password — and looked at the way her secretary had set it up. He asked if he could consolidate the accounts, and she'd said yes. After that he'd asked some questions about companies and about a few receipts, but for the most part they were quiet.

All in all, it had been very pleasant working with him in the room. As they had when they were children, they just seemed to naturally meld together.

"I can't believe you drove all the way into Williamsburg and got barbeque," Kim said as she pulled the package out of the fridge. As often happened, she hadn't thought aloud about dinner. She'd been surprised, and pleased, when Travis said he'd brought food home.

She'd smiled at his use of the word *home.* It sounded almost as though he lived there too.

"Joe told me about a back road, so it didn't take long," he said, and they looked at each other and laughed. "I went the speed limit and used asphalt." He glanced at the clock. It was late.

"You and Mr. Layton seem to have hit it off well."

Travis took his time answering as he put coleslaw on plates and took them to the table. "He knows who my mother is."

"You're kidding!" Kim said.

"No, he saw the resemblance right away. But he made me swear not to let her know that he'd figured it out."

"And I guess she doesn't want you to tell either."

"Precisely. I have been placed in the middle of my mother and him," Travis said as he looked at her across the table. He'd liked being in her workroom — but he'd always enjoyed the outdoors and he wanted to see it day or night. The converted garage was too closed-in for him. "Joe has no use for that big room at the end of his store. It has windows that look out into the forest. He says Jecca will never use it and I understand why. He greatly admires her ability to reassemble electrical tools and he'd put her to work."

Reaching over, Kim removed a foam pellet clinging to the back of his shirt.

"I feel like I have those things crawling all over me. Could you — ?" He held out the back of the neck of his shirt.

Standing, she put her hand on his collar but she didn't touch him. She glanced down his shirt but saw only sun-bronzed skin. And muscles. “Nothing,” she said.

“Sure? I itch in places. I should have taken a shower first, but I saw your light on and I wanted to see you.” He took her hand in his and kissed her fingertips. “Oops, sorry,” he said and released her. “You’re soon to be married so you’re a ‘no touch.’ ”

Frowning, Kim sat back down. “Hardly that. I haven’t been asked, much less said yes.”

“So you really like this guy?”

“He’s nice,” Kim said, but she didn’t want to talk about Dave. “What are your plans for tomorrow?”

“According to Joe, I’m to be his slave. Kim, if you want that shop that’s supposed to be Jecca’s I can get it for you. I’ll get Joe to give it to you as a wedding gift. Free rent for at least three months, and very reasonable the rest of the time.”

“My garage is fine and why would he give me a gift for his wedding?”

“Not *his* wedding. Yours. To Dave. He’s a man and he’ll want a place to put his car. Or one of those catering vans. He is going to move in with you, isn’t he? I can’t imagine that he earns enough to buy a house like this one. But then what you made last year was substantial. Congratulations! You are truly a success.”

What he was saying was wonderful. Truly great. But, somehow, it was upsetting her. She hadn't thought of the fact that Dave came with a lot of equipment. He owned five big vans and he had enormous pieces of cookware. He lived in a small apartment and rented a commercial kitchen. But still, he did some cooking at his house. One Sunday afternoon she'd gone to pick him up and had ended up helping him make four gallons of tuna salad. Her clothes had smelled so bad she'd had to soak them before putting them in the washer.

"Dave and I haven't discussed anything like that," Kim said. "The truth is that it's only Carla who's saying that I'm about to receive a marriage proposal, but then she looks at all men as marriage material. She even suggested that the two of you —"

"Me?!" Travis's eyes were wide. "Me and Carla? She is cute. Think she'd go out with me?"

Kim looked at Travis in speculation and suddenly had the feeling that she was being manipulated, but she wasn't sure how. "Are you up to something?"

"Just trying to be your friend is all. I enjoy your company and I want to help out around here so you don't throw me out. Edilean is scary."

Kim couldn't help laughing. "It will be when my brother remembers where he saw you! I couldn't understand why you were standing there with your hand over your face. Did you really come close to killing him?"

"Yes," he said. "I don't know why my heart didn't stop. There I was in Morocco, trying my best to beat Jake Jones's time, Ernie my mechanic was with me, and he had the map out. I went around a corner and there's this guy crossing the street with a donkey so covered in boxes the poor thing was bowlegged."

"That sounds like Reede," Kim said.

Travis got up and pantomimed being behind the wheel of his car. "Before I hit that curve, there were Moroccans on the sides shouting at us in Arabic. I don't know about you, but my Arabic consists of *la* and *shukran* — *no* and *thanks.* How was I to know they were telling us that a crazy American doctor was meandering across the raceway?"

"You were the only car?"

"Hell no! I was eating Jake's dust every two miles. He'd done something to the fuel injection system but I didn't know what. Every time I got near him, he'd upshift and spew rocks at us. My windshield was a mass of scars."

Travis bent forward, his hands on the wheel. "So there I am, yelling at Ernie — no sound absorption in a race car — about what the hell the Arabs were shouting at us and he's telling me that if I don't slow down the transmission is going to fall out when bam! There's this man."

"With a donkey," Kim said.

"Which froze. The donkey had sense enough to know danger when he saw it."

"But my brother didn't."

"You're right on that! He looked at a car coming at him doing at least a hundred and twenty and —"

"You'd slowed down for the curve," Kim said solemnly.

"Yeah, I did," Travis said and seemed pleased at her understanding. "If your brother had any fear at all, I didn't see it. He just frowned at me like I was an annoyance, then turned back to pull on the donkey's rope."

"When was this?"

"2005."

"Oh heavens!" Kim said. "That wasn't too long after Reede's long-term girlfriend dropped him. He was probably still in that stage of not caring whether he lived or died."

"Like I'd feel if you told me to get out of your life and never come back," Travis said, then quickly went on with his story. "When I yelled, Ernie looked up from his map and screamed like a girl. I turned the wheel as hard as I could, braked until my ankle felt like it was cracking, and we nearly turned over."

Kim was blinking at his statement about how he'd feel if she told him to go away. "I guess . . ." she began.

"Your brother stood there and watched the whole thing. For seconds we looked into each other's eyes; we had a clear view of onc anothcr. It was one of those moments when the world seems to stand still. The donkey collapsed from sheer terror, and that's when the boxes it was carrying hit the ground and broke."

"And Reede —"

"By the time I got the car headed back toward him, he was in a rage and shouting at us." Travis put his hand over his heart. "I swear this is true, but I wanted to stop and see about the donkey. I didn't know the contents of the boxes were important. It was Ernie who said, 'Good God! He's an American. Don't stop or he'll have us arrested. Go! Go! Floor it and *go!*' I did."

"Did you win the race?"

"Of course not. The transmission fell out about fifty miles down the road. We were so far from anywhere we had to be helicoptered out."

Kim looked at him as he sat back down. She couldn't help remembering the boy who'd ridden her bicycle. "I agree," she said.

"About what?"

"When my brother remembers where he saw you, he's going to come after you with a shotgun."

"You're no help at all," Travis said, smiling. "I want you to be on *my* side."

"I am. Reede probably knew about the race and wanted to provoke a fight. At that time, he had so much anger inside him about his girlfriend dumping him, he probably wanted to get it out."

Travis sobered. "He came very close to getting himself killed."

She smiled. "Thanks for taking care of my brother. Thank you for not hitting him and thank you for replacing his supplies. If you weren't so good at handling a car, all three of you — and the donkey — could have been killed."

For a moment they looked at each other and again Kim felt drawn to him. It was as if his body called to hers, as though some electrical charge ran from her to him and back again. She could feel the pull, the tingle, the desire that passed between them.

Of its own will, her body took a step toward him. She wanted him to put his arms around her and kiss her. She saw him look at her lips and his eyes grew darker, warmer, hot even.

But in the next second, he turned away and the moment was gone. "It's late," he murmured, "and Joe . . . I'll see you tomorrow." In an instant he had left the house.

Kim sat down on a chair. She felt like a balloon that had its knot untied. Deflated. Worse, she felt defeated.

When Travis got inside the guesthouse, he was shaking. He knew he'd never wanted a woman as much as he did Kim, but the problem was that he cared about her. He didn't want to hurt her, didn't want —

He sat down on the side of the bed and punched Penny's number. "Did I wake you?" he asked.

She hesitated. Never before had Travis been concerned about his secretary's sleeping habits. "No," she said, lying.

"Did you find out anything about the caterer?"

"Just his name, but I sent my son to Edilean to see what he could find out."

"What's your son look like?"

"What does that matter?" Penny asked.

"There's a girl, Carla, who works for Kim, and she's after any half-decent-looking man who comes in the store. She knows something about a missing sapphire ring. I think it's connected to the caterer and I want to find out about it. Can your son handle that?"

"Easily," Penny said and seemed to be amused. "What else have you found out?"

"Not much, just that Kim is doing quite well in her little shop."

"Enough to make this man want it?"

"Yes," Travis said. They knew a lot about what a person would do to own a lucrative business.

"You don't think it's possible that this caterer is actually in love with pretty Kim?"

"He may well be, but let's just say that if he touches her, I'll be needing a pair of dueling pistols."

"Well, well, well," Penny said.

"How's it coming with your relatives in Janes Creek?"

"Everyone is happy for the free weekend. But I need to warn you that even your dad might not be able to afford my uncle Bernie's room service bill."

"That's all right. I'm getting used to dealing with relatives. Mom's new . . ."

"Her what?" Penny asked. She was marveling that they were having a personal conversation that included *her* life.

"The man she's planning to marry. I've been working for him."

"Good dental?" Penny asked, covering her surprise.

Travis scoffed. "No pay, just advice. Lots of advice."

"Good or bad?"

"Depends on the outcome, which I don't know yet. I have to come up with a reason why I should go with Kim to Maryland."

"You're asking her permission to go?" Her surprise turned to shock.

"Yes," Travis said. "I can't talk anymore. Joe wants me at work at seven A.M. tomorrow. I'm attaching steel shelves to brick walls. I can hardly wait."

"I, uh . . ." Penny didn't know what to say so she murmured good night and hung up. "I think I like this Edilean," she said as she got back into bed.

NINE

"So what's it like living with him?" Carla asked Kim the next morning. "Great sex, huh? He looks like he'd be fabulous in bed. How's his endurance? Does he — ?"

"Carla!" Kim snapped. "Could you please be a bit more professional?"

"Not getting any, are you? Not with an attitude like that. Saving yourself for Dave? But if you change your mind, I know this perfume you could try that might help. It —"

Kim went into her office and shut the door. She hadn't seen Travis this morning, as he'd already gone to work at Joe's new store. He'd left her a funny note on the kitchen counter about how he was looking forward to learning how to drill holes in brick. *They should have turned the bricks on their sides. They already have holes in them,* he'd written, making her smile.

It was nice to start the day with a laugh,

but she would have liked to have seen him.

Her cell rang with a number she didn't know.

"Meet me for lunch?" Travis asked. "Please?"

Instantly, her bad mood lifted. "Where?" She refrained from saying, When? How? Should I bring food? How about a few clarity three diamonds?

"How about Delmonico's circa 1899?"

"Love it. I'll get my corset out of storage."

"Can you put it on all by yourself?"

"I may need help," Kim said and felt her heart beating in her throat. She loved this teasing!

"I would like to volunteer to help you, but at the present I am a conjoined twin. Joe has attached himself to me. Can you bear to have lunch with the two of us?"

"I'd be honored," Kim said. "If it's Joe, he wants to go to Al's Diner."

"I've seen that place and I'm not sure it's right. Joe specifically said that he wants al dente pasta and steamed broccoli for lunch. And a tablecloth and —"

"Limoges and Christofle," Kim finished.

"Exactly! See you at the greaseburger at noon?"

"My arteries are looking forward to it," Kim said and went back into the shop with a big smile.

Carla looked up as she was putting a tray of bracelets away. "Whatever made you smile like that isn't half as good as what just happened to *me.*"

"Oh?" Kim asked as she glanced at the trays. The bracelet Travis had admired was gone and so was the ring with the big pink diamond. "Good sale?"

"Tremendous! A man was buying for his mother. He had an eye and picked out the best in the store with hardly a glance. And . . ."

"And what?"

"He asked me to go out with him tonight."

"Don't half the men who come in here ask you out?"

"The sleazebags do. And the married losers," Carla said. "The classy ones like him want *you.*"

Kim was in such a good mood she was willing to listen to Carla, but the door opened and a very handsome man came in. Not as dark as Travis, and he didn't have that world-weary look that Travis often had, but this man was gorgeous. And the suit he wore must have cost thousands.

He glanced at Kim, gave a quick nod of greeting, then went straight to Carla.

Standing to one side, Kim watched the

two of them. They were an incongruous pair. Although Kim had had numerous talks with her about the way she dressed, Carla's blouse was always opened one button too far, her skirt an inch or two too short, and she wore too much makeup. The man looked like he'd just left an exclusive club, while Carla . . . Well, there was a lot of discrepancy between their looks.

"I think I'll take the pearl earrings as well," he said in a smooth, silky voice as he looked at Carla as though he wanted to devour her.

"Sure, Mr. Pendergast," Carla said.

"I told you to call me Russell," he said.

"Will do," Carla said but continued to stand there staring at him.

Kim went to the far counter and got out her best pearl earrings. Since he'd bought two expensive items, she figured they were the earrings he wanted. A curve like a shell, the pearl embraced by it. She put them on the counter, then nudged them along between the two people, who were staring at each other.

The man turned to her, his almost black eyes looking at her with a remarkable intensity, as though he was studying her. If Travis weren't here now, she thought, she'd look back at this man. But she just smiled at him in a professional way.

"You're the designer? Kimberly Aldredge?"

"Yes I am."

"I'm Russell Pendergast. I'm just passing through town and I had no idea there would be a store of such quality here. Your designs are exquisite."

His voice and pronunciation spoke of a very good education. Like Travis, she thought.

Behind him, Carla was glaring, her eyes threatening that if Kim made a play for the man, blood might be shed.

"Where could I get lunch in the area?" he asked.

"I know some places," Carla said from behind him. "I get off at one."

"And what about you, Miss Aldredge? When do you have lunch?"

Kim took a step away from him. As enticing as he was, she wasn't interested. "I'm meeting friends at the local greasy spoon. I wouldn't recommend it to an outsider. Excuse me." She went back into her office.

Interesting, she thought as she picked up her sketchbook and put her mind back on work. Maybe she should make some more designs based on shells. She had to come up with a theme for Neimans, so maybe she'd do something about the sea.

An hour later she left for lunch. Mr. Layton and Travis were already in a booth with their drinks. As soon as he saw her, Travis's dark eyes lit up in a way that made Kim smile. He stood up, kissed her on the cheek, then let her in first.

"Have any idea what you want for lunch?" Travis asked as he nodded toward Joe. "The old man couldn't wait so we ordered."

"Al knows," she said and waved to the big man they could see in the kitchen. It looked like Travis and Mr. Layton were getting to know each other well.

"No kisses for me?" Mr. Layton asked. "You just pass them out to the young bucks now?"

"Sorry," Kim said as she stretched across the table to kiss his cheek. She didn't see Travis as he admired the view of her body. And she didn't see Mr. Layton give him a look that said Travis owed him one.

"What have you two been doing?" she asked.

"Him nothing; me everything," Travis said.

She looked at him. His shirt was dirty and there was sawdust on his temple. Reaching up, she brushed it away, then was aware of the way Mr. Layton was staring at them.

Kim moved a bit farther down on the seat.

"We had an exciting morning."

"Better than cutting pieces of lumber to make sawponies?" Travis asked in sarcasm.

"Saw*horses,*" Kim corrected. Mr. Layton's eyes were twinkling. "You're being wicked and I'm going to tell Jecca on you." She looked back at Travis. "A young man came in this morning and bought my three most expensive pieces."

"Did he?" Travis asked.

"He told Carla they were for his mother. He had on a suit that looks like the one you were wearing when I first saw you."

"Before I discovered the joys of T-shirts with trucking logos on them?" Travis asked.

Mr. Layton didn't smile. "What's his name?"

"Russell Pendergast and he asked Carla out on a date tonight."

Travis choked on his drink. "Pendergast?"

"Yes, do you know him?"

"Never met the guy," Travis said and could feel Joe Layton's eyes boring into him. "What's he like?"

"Gorgeous," Kim said. "Smooth. He exudes education and wealth."

"Does he?" Travis asked in curiosity. "And he bought your most expensive pieces for his mother? Interesting. Where'd he go to school? Maybe I know him."

"I have no idea. But after his date with Carla I'm sure I'll hear everything. I can't really see the two of them together. He —"

"Did he come on to you?" Travis asked, his dark brows in a scowl.

"I don't think that's any of your —" Kim began and could feel her temper rising.

"Ah, good!" Joe said loudly. "Our food is here. If you two'd rather fight than eat, let me know so I can sell tickets."

"There will be no argument," Kim said. "Russell and I are going out Saturday night."

"On Saturday you're going to be in a B&B with your almost fiancé," Travis said grimly.

"That's right," Kim said, smiling at Mr. Layton. "I can't keep all my men straight."

"You ought to take young Travis here with you."

"With me where?" Kim asked.

"Over the weekend," Joe said.

"Take Travis on my weekend with my boyfriend?" Kim asked. Truthfully, she liked the idea but she wasn't going to say so. If Dave did propose, Travis's presence would give her time to think about an answer. And if Dave got too . . . insistent, too whatever, Travis would be there. But she'd eat one of Al's '57 burgers and have an immediate coronary before she told him so.

"Yeah," Joe said as he bit into a pound of meat that dripped juice — a.k.a. grease — down to his wrists. "Travis here said you were going to do some work. How can you do that if you're fooling around with your boyfriend? Take Travis and he can do all the work."

Travis gave Joe a look that was half thanks, half murder.

"That's not a bad idea," Kim said as she used her fork to move around what was Al's idea of a salad. Lots of fried chicken, not much lettuce. "I'll think about it," she said and didn't dare look at Travis. She had an idea he was smiling much too broadly.

As the morning sunlight came through the windows, Travis was sitting in Kim's living room and trying to concentrate on the newspaper, but he couldn't. She'd left for work an hour ago, and since then he'd been waiting for Penny's son to show up.

Yesterday after lunch at Al's with Kim and Joe, Travis had gone to see his mother. As he entered Mrs. Wingate's house, the hum of his mother's sewing machine reached him, and the familiarity of the sound felt good. When he got upstairs, it was easy for him to fall into place with her and begin cutting out a pattern. Sewing was something they'd done together when he was a child. They never talked about it, but it reminded them of their time in Edilean, a time of peace for both of them. Those two weeks had changed both their lives.

Travis had been a bit concerned about what his mother knew about him and Joe, but she soon made him relax. They'd always been close and nearly always in agreement. At first he'd been afraid she'd again lecture him about Kim, but the anger she'd displayed on their first meeting was no longer there.

Instead they easily fell into talking about Joe. Travis told her everything — except that Joe knew Travis was Lucy's son. But all the rest of it, from unpacking to being told saw-ponies were sawhorses, to having to attach steel shelves to a brick wall, was there.

When Lucy began laughing at Travis's stories, he got her away from the machines — she worked too much — and down to the kitchen. As they'd done when he was growing up, Travis made tea while she made the sandwiches. When they were ready, Lucy led him into the conservatory. For a while he walked around, admiring the orchids that filled the room. When he sat down, Lucy asked him about Kim.

Travis hesitated.

"You can tell me," she said softly. "Are you still in love with her?"

"Yes," he said, then looked at his mother with eyes that showed the depth of his feeling. "More than ever. More than I thought possible."

For a moment tears gathered in Lucy's eyes. She was a mother who hoped her child would find love.

"She's funny and perceptive," Travis said as he picked up a sandwich wedge. When he was little his mother had cut off the crusts and sliced the bread diagonally into four pieces. As he grew up, she'd continued. "And very smart. And you should see the jewelry in her store. It's all beautiful!"

"I have seen it," Lucy said. "Whenever I heard that Kim was out of town, I visited her shop. I like the olive leaves."

"So do I," Travis said. He stood up and fiddled with a long orchid leaf for a moment before turning back. "I feel comfortable with her. I don't feel like I have to impress her. Although I do work at that."

"Joe said you drove down the back road and he couldn't see how you'd done it."

Travis shrugged. "Stunt work. It wasn't difficult."

"And something about a balloon?" Lucy asked.

"I couldn't stand to hear the kid cry, so I climbed up a tree and got it down for him."

"You always have had a soft heart."

"No one in New York would say that," Travis said.

"No, I guess not. You have both your father and me inside you. What are you going to do now?"

Travis sat back down. "Joe fixed it so I'm going to spend the weekend with Kim. I'll be in a connecting room, and she might be with her boyfriend. But still . . . I'll be near her."

"He told me," she said as she smiled at her son. She'd never seen him this way, and it did her heart good.

"Did he? What other of my secrets did that nosy old man blab to you?"

Lucy smiled. Since the two of them had met, all she'd heard from Joe was "Travis." What Travis said, did, his worries, his deep love for Kim, Travis's suggestions about the hardware store. Every word of it, Joe repeated to Lucy.

"You should have seen him with Kim," Joe'd said when he'd called her after their lunch at Al's. "The poor guy can't take his eyes off her."

"What about *her?*" Lucy'd asked. "What does Kim think of my . . . of Travis?" If Joe heard her slip, he didn't seem to register it.

"She acts like she pays no attention to him, that he's just another guy, but if he moves, she sees it. When I suggested that she take young Travis with her to Maryland, her face lit up like a New Year's spotlight."

Lucy looked at her son. "Joe likes you a lot."

"You'd never know it from what he says," Travis said, but he was smiling. "According to Joe Layton, any man who can't use a handsaw properly isn't worth much. I told him I was a lawyer and you know what he said?"

Lucy had heard the story from Joe but she wanted to hear it again from Travis. "I can't imagine."

"He said . . ."

Now, with the newspaper in front of him, Travis couldn't help smiling. Last night had been the way he remembered with his mother, her kindness, her humor, her sweetness. He was glad he hadn't had to endure another session where she bawled him out.

On the other hand, *that* woman might be able to handle Randall Maxwell in a courtroom.

That evening when Travis had returned home — as he'd begun to think of wherever Kim was — she'd been about to throw a couple of frozen dinners into the microwave. When Travis was going through school he'd spent more than one summer crewing on private yachts. One year, to his horror, he was assigned the position of "chef." He didn't know how to boil water.

He put the dinners back in the freezer and looked to see what else was in there as he told Kim the story. "So there I was, not knowing an egg from a watermelon, and I was supposed to spend six weeks cooking three meals a day for the rich old man and his young wife."

Kim crunched on the carrot stick he'd cut for her. "So what did you do?"

"I put on my most helpless look" — he demonstrated — "and asked the wife to help out."

"Did she?"

"Oh yes," Travis said as he put chicken breasts in the microwave to thaw. He was glad his back was to Kim as he thought about that trip. He didn't want her to see his face.

But she'd understood. "What else did she teach you?"

Travis started laughing. "A little bit here and there." Moonlight, stars, the old man snoring below. He'd been nineteen years old and innocent. Not so innocent when they got back to the U.S.

He and Kim had a dinner that he'd never wanted to end. She told him more about her jewelry and what she hoped to do. "I have a big commission coming up and I need some new inspiration."

"This trip to Maryland will be good for you."

"That was my idea when I let Joce talk me into going."

"You didn't originally plan to go with this guy, did you?"

"Dave? No, I didn't."

"He invited himself?" Travis asked.

"More or less," Kim said, "but I do think he has something important to say to me. Between him and Carla I've been given enough hints."

A lot of things came into Travis's mind that he wanted to say, but he thought he'd better keep his opinions to himself. Penny's son, Russell, was on a date with Carla and the plan was for him to meet Travis in the morning and report on what he found out.

But it was now midmorning and Russell still hadn't shown up. At that thought, Travis had to smile. The small town mind-set was getting to him. In New York he often didn't get up until this time. But then he'd usually been out late the night before.

Clients loved to be entertained and shown New York nightlife.

When the doorbell rang, Travis put down the paper and went to the door in a few long strides. He was curious to see this man Kim had described as "gorgeous," and he wanted to meet the son of the woman who his father had described as his "most trusted employee." She'd worked for Randall Maxwell since she was young, and when Travis had been coerced into working for him, Randall had released Penny to Travis to "take care of him."

Travis opened the door to find himself staring into the angriest eyes he'd ever looked into. Considering all the things his father had had him do, that was a lot.

The two men were almost exactly the same height, appeared to be the same age, and they were both handsome. But Travis's face showed a lifetime of struggle, a life of loneliness. Every time he'd faced death in his extreme sports was in his eyes, and the war between his parents showed on him.

Russell's eyes were angry. He'd grown up in the shadow of the powerful Maxwell family, and he'd come to hate the name because whatever that family wanted came first. This week he hadn't been surprised when his mother asked him to help Travis Maxwell.

It was a name he'd known before his own. He hadn't even been shocked to be told that Travis had never heard of Russell, didn't know he existed. The anger he'd felt was on his face, in the way he stood, as though he'd just love for Travis to say something that would allow him to fight.

"You're Penny's son," Travis said as they stood at the door. "I didn't know she . . ." He trailed off at the look in the man's angry eyes. "Please come in," he said formally, then stepped back as Russell entered the house and went into Kim's blue and white living room.

"A bit of a downsize for you, isn't it?"

Behind him, Travis let out his breath. The Maxwell name! Being in Edilean and especially being around Joe, had nearly made him forget the preconceived ideas people had about him. All his life he'd heard, "He's Randall Maxwell's son so he is —" Fill in the blank.

It seemed that Penny's son had already decided that Travis was a clone of his father.

Travis's face went from the friendly one he'd adopted in the last week to the one he wore in New York. No one could get to him, so no one could hurt him.

Russell took the big chair and Travis saw it for what it was: establishing that he was in charge.

Travis sat on the couch. "What did you find out?" he asked, his voice cool.

"David Borman wants control of Kimberly Aldredge's business."

Travis grimaced. "I was afraid of that. Damn! I was hoping —" He looked back at Russell and thought, the hell with it! This was Penny's son, and this was about Kim. It had nothing to do with the Maxwell name. "You want some coffee? Tea? A shot of tequila?"

Russell stared at Travis as though he were trying to figure him out — and whether or not to take him up on his offer. "Coffee would be fine."

Travis started toward the kitchen but Russell didn't follow. "I need to make it. You want to come in here and talk while I do?"

The ordinariness of the invitation seemed to take some of the anger out of Russell's eyes as he got up and went to the kitchen. He sat down on a stool and watched Travis get a bag of beans out of the refrigerator and pour some into an electric grinder.

"I guess I was hoping," Travis said loudly over the noise, "that I was going to have to fight him over Kim. A duel, I guess." He lifted his hand off the top of the machine and the noise stopped. “It’s going to hurt Kim to find this out.”

Russell’s eyes were wide as he watched Travis put the grounds into a filter and drop it into a machine. He didn’t seem to be able to grasp the concept that a Maxwell could do something so mundane as make coffee. Where were the servants? The butler? “He’s the third one.”

“Third one what?”

“He’s the third man who was more concerned with her success than with her.”

“What does that mean?”

“According to Carla . . .” Russell paused as he ran his hand over the back of his neck.

“Was the date bad?” Travis asked.

“She’s an aggressive young woman.”

Travis snorted. “Seemed to be. Keep you out late?”

“Till three,” Russell said. “I barely escaped with . . .”

“Your honor intact?” Travis gave a half smile.

“Exactly,” Russell said.

“Have you had breakfast? I make a mean omelet.”

“No. That is . . .” Russell was still staring at Travis as though he couldn’t believe what he was seeing.

“It’s the best I can do for Penny’s son after

all she's put up with from *me*."

"All right," Russell said slowly.

Travis began getting things out of the fridge. "Tell me everything from the beginning."

"Do you mean Carla's complete sex history that she delighted in telling me in detail, or what I could dredge out of her about Miss Aldredge?"

Travis laughed. "No Carla, but lots of Kim."

"It seems that small town men can't handle a woman who earns more than they do."

Travis would have liked to think that he could deal with that, but he'd always had the opposite problem. "So they dumped her?"

"Yes," Russell said as he watched Travis pour him a cup of freshly brewed coffee and set it on the counter along with containers of milk and sugar. He wasn't surprised that the coffee was excellent. "St. Helena?"

"It is," Travis said. "I get it here in Edilean at the local grocery. Can you believe that?" He was pleasantly surprised that Russell had recognized the taste of the rare and expensive coffee. "I take it that this Dave is different from the others."

"Carla and Borman's ex-girlfriend are

friends, and Carla told the girl all about Kim, even about the men who'd walked away from her. Carla has no understanding of the word *discretion.*"

"Or *loyalty,*" Travis said. "Onions, peppers, and tomatoes all right with you?"

"Yes," Russell said. "As far as I can piece together, the girlfriend told Borman and he made a plan."

"Let me guess. He dropped the girlfriend and went after Kim."

Russell reached into the inside pocket of his coat and pulled out several pieces of paper folded together into a thick stack. "These are the financials of Borman's company for the last two years."

Travis let the vegetables sizzle while he went through the first pages, but then he had to stop to add the eggs to the skillet and put bread in the toaster. "Would you . . . ?" he asked Russell.

He took the papers and started to go through them, but then paused to remove his suit jacket and drape it over a dining chair. He loosened his tie. "The bottom line is that David Borman isn't a good cook, he spends too much, and he's lazy."

Travis slid the omelet onto a plate, put it before Russell, and got a knife and fork out of a drawer. "So he dropped his girlfriend and went after Kim — or rather, her business."

"It gets worse," Russell said as he took a bite. "Not bad."

"Worse isn't bad?"

"No. Borman gets worse; the omelet isn't bad."

"Oh," Travis said as he watched Russell eat. He could see things about him that reminded him of Penny. He'd spent a lot of late nights with her and they'd shared many meals. Now he wondered why he'd never asked her about her personal life. But then, he would have thought that if he had, Penny probably wouldn't have answered.

Russell looked up at him as though expecting something from Travis.

"The ring," Travis said. "What about the ring?"

"Borman took Carla out to dinner, told her a sob story about how he was in love with Kim. He got Carla to 'lend' him a ring to give to her when he proposed this weekend."

"Then Carla told the whole town that's what Borman was going to do." Travis handed Russell the toast and got out the butter. "That's why Borman invited himself to go with her to Maryland."

"Carla didn't seem to see anything wrong

in the fact that you and Miss Aldredge are living together just before she's to get a marriage proposal from Borman. Carla's exact words were, 'I think you should take things when they're offered.' "

"I'm staying in the guesthouse," Travis said absently as he thought about what he'd just heard.

"The whole town thinks you and Kim are . . ."

"It's just gossip," Travis said, then looked back to see Russell staring at him, his eyes disbelieving. Travis felt anger rising in him. "It looks like you believed them."

Russell looked back down at his food. "It's not for me to judge."

"And a Maxwell takes whatever he wants, is that it?" If Travis had been hoping for an argument, he didn't get it.

Calmly, Russell finished his coffee. "In my experience, yes."

The truth of that made Travis's anger calm down. He refilled Russell's cup. "Maybe so," Travis said. "Taking what he wants is a creed of my father's."

"But not yours?" Russell asked.

Travis wasn't fooled by the man's nonchalant tone. He was asking a very serious question. "No, it's not what I believe in at all."

Russell ate his toast and for a moment he didn't reply. "How do you plan to get the ring back?"

"I'm a lawyer, remember? I'll threaten him with grand larceny and prison."

Russell used the napkin Travis had given him to wipe his mouth. "And what will you tell Miss Aldredge? That her boyfriend only wanted her for her successful little shop?"

Travis grimaced. "That will kill her ego."

"And this weekend you'll have a depressed, crying female on your hands."

Travis looked at Russell and they exchanged a male understanding between them. An unhappy woman wasn't a good companion.

Russell stood, picked up his coat and prepared to leave, but then he turned back to look at Travis. There was no humor in his eyes. "If you leave your father's firm, what will happen to my mother? Will she be thrown out with the rubbish?"

Travis was used to being attacked, used to barely suppressed rage from people who'd had encounters with his father. But this man was different. His resentment was for Travis. "It's all happened so quickly that I haven't had time to think about it. I guess I assumed she'd go back to working for my father."

"No," Russell said. His expression said that he wasn't going to elaborate on that statement, but it was final.

"Tell me what she wants and I'll see that she gets it."

"It must feel like being an emperor to have such power," Russell said.

Travis understood the man's hostility toward him. He knew the late hours, weekends, and holidays that Penny had worked for his father. And Travis hadn't been much better. He'd never thought twice of calling her on Sunday afternoons — and Penny had never complained, never even commented. Her son must have spent most of his life without his mother. He must hate the Maxwell name. And it looked like he especially hated Travis, the Maxwell son who was the same age as he was. But then, did he think Travis grew up with loving parents who doted on him?

"What do you do? For a living, I mean?" Travis asked.

The friendliness that had started between them was gone. Russell's face was hard, unforgiving. "I don't need anything from you or your father, so there's no need to pretend interest. I'll get back to you about my mother and I expect you to keep your word."

The hostility in his voice and eyes made Travis's hair stand on end. To lighten the mood, he said, "Within reason, of course. I can't give her the Taj Mahal. It isn't for sale."

Russell didn't smile. "If it were, your father would have bought it and fired the caretakers. Are we finished here?"

"Yes, I think so."

As soon as Russell was out of the house, Travis called Penny. She seemed to be expecting the call because she answered before the first ring finished. The first thing he needed taken care of was business. He wanted to know where David Borman was right now. As Travis expected, Penny said she'd find out and text an answer.

That was Travis's cue to hang up, but he didn't. "I met your son," he said tentatively. "He, uh . . ."

Penny knew what he was trying to say. A few weeks ago, she wouldn't have dared comment, but lately Travis seemed to be jumping off the fast track to becoming a second Randall Maxwell. "Hates everything with the Maxwell name on it," she finished for him.

"Exactly. Is it curable?"

"Probably not."

Travis took a breath. "I promised him that

when I leave the Maxwell firm I'd see that you got whatever you wanted. To make sure I get it right, why don't you tell me what it is you want?"

"Happiness for my son. Grandkids," Penny said quickly.

"You sound like my mother."

"From you, that is high praise indeed," she said. "But let me think about this. From what Russ says about Edilean, I may want to retire there."

"Not a bad idea. You see the jewelry he bought for you?"

Penny chuckled. "I did. Quite, quite beautiful! Your young Kim is very talented."

"She is," Travis said, smiling.

They exchanged good-byes and hung up. She texted him the address of where Borman was working before he got the kitchen cleaned up.

"I'm going to kill him," he muttered and started for the door.

TEN

But Travis didn't make it to the door. His male instinct was to find the man and tear him apart. He could almost feel his fists in his face. But then what? Do as he'd told Russell and threaten the man with prosecution? With prison time? Would Travis use the Maxwell name to intimidate the man?

And what would be the repercussions? A man like Borman who had no morals — or he wouldn't have planned to marry for money — wouldn't skulk away quietly. He'd go to Kim and . . . Travis didn't want to think what damage the man could cause.

For a moment Travis stood there and tried to cool his temper enough that he could think clearly about what needed to be done. He had to become more calm and figure out how to solve this in a way that would guarantee that Kim wouldn't be hurt.

Travis realized that this meeting could be the most important of his life. The last thing he should do was go in there with guns blazing, so to speak. Travis had dealt with men like Borman before, ones who thought that whatever they did to obtain what they wanted was permissible. If it took marrying a woman to get her business, then that was all right with them.

Travis had also learned that men who lost in a big way tended to retaliate in a like manner. If he threatened the man and forced him to get out of Kim's life, Borman could contact Kim, and maybe he could turn it all against Travis.

No, it was better to get rid of the man in a way that made him believe that he had won, even that he'd put one over on someone. That way, he wouldn't feel a need for revenge, wouldn't want to get back at Kim, wouldn't want to hurt her.

Travis called Penny again, and she picked up immediately.

"Rethinking the dueling pistols?" she asked.

"Yes," he said.

"I thought you might," she said and seemed to be proud of him. "The Maxwell in you always keeps a cool head."

Travis wasn't sure he was pleased by her words. "I want you to set up a meeting between Borman and me for today. I need for it to be held somewhere impressive. Maybe a library. Big desk. Rich surroundings. All the grandeur you can find. Talk to him, tell him I want to buy his catering business, that I'm in awe of what he's done with it. Flatter him."

"I'm not sure I'm that good of a liar."

"If you worked for my father, you can lie."

"More than you know," she said, sounding amused.

"I'll need a contract saying he turns everything over to me, equipment, employees, all of it. Leave the price blank. I'm planning to give him a ridiculous amount of money to buy that dying business of his. Then I want you to tell him — in confidence — that you happen to know that I'm afraid of the competition from him so he has to leave the state. Today. Before nightfall. He can't even take time to move out of his apartment."

"What name do you want to use on the contract?"

Travis frowned. "If Maxwell is on there, he'll come back to get more."

"How about if it's signed by Russell Pendergast? I can run the money through his account."

"Perfect," Travis said.

"Want Borman to call Kim to say goodbye?"

"No! But I'll take care of that. Let me know when it's all set up. Think you can do all this in just a few hours?"

Penny didn't bother to answer his question. "How about four P.M.? That'll get you home in time to have dinner with Kim."

"Penny, I love you!" he said.

She took a while to respond and he thought maybe he'd overstepped himself. "I'm going to have a Realtor send me some information about living in Edilean. I think it must be a magic place."

"Dad will be glad to buy you a house."

For some reason, Penny found that statement downright funny. She was laughing as she hung up.

At a quarter to four, Travis drove onto the palatial estate of a man who'd benefitted greatly from his association with Randall Maxwell. It was an hour outside of Williamsburg and Travis had had three calls with Penny on the drive down. The idea was for him to be familiar with everything in the room where he was to meet Borman so it looked like the place belonged to Travis.

"The contract will be on the desk," Penny said, "and both Russell and I have already talked to Borman. He's primed to sell, and he thinks you're so afraid of the competition of his company that you'll pay anything to get him out of your way."

"Which I will," Travis said. "Just not for the reason he thinks. What's it worth?"

"Russ said no more than a hundred grand, if that. He has too much equipment and not enough commissions. Last week he used a cheap fish in place of crab for a job. He told an employee that no one would be able to tell the difference, but the bride's mother did. The father refused to pay him."

"Good to know," Travis said. "Wish me luck on this."

"I do, and you may not believe this, but so does Russ. Whatever you did this morning has softened his edges more than I've been able to do in his lifetime."

Travis smiled. "For all that a couple of times he looked at me as though he wanted to burn me at a stake, I liked him. He reminds me of you."

"Does he?" Penny asked, sounding pleased. "I'll see you tomorrow in Janes Creek."

"I'm looking forward to it," Travis said and hung up. If this came off all right, tomorrow night he'd be in a cozy little B&B in a room with a connecting door that led to Kim.

A few minutes later he pulled into the huge circular drive of the Westwood estate and turned his key over to the young man who was waiting for it. If this place was like his father's, when Travis left, his car would have been vacuumed, washed, and waxed.

A uniformed butler opened the door before Travis got up the stairs. "Mr. Pendergast is waiting for you in the south parlor," he said as he led Travis to a large, pretty room with walnut paneling and a blue and cream rug. The furniture was meant to look as though it had been there for years. Old money. But Travis's discerning eye saw that it was all new.

"This is more your style," Russell said as he walked toward Travis.

"Cut it out or I'll tell your mother on you."

Russell caught himself before he smiled. "I was told to tell you that Borman will take two hundred grand, two fifty tops. But that's way too much. Those vans of his aren't worth much, and he owes some back wages."

Travis nodded. "Where is he?"

"In the library. Got here twenty minutes early."

"Eager to get rid of everything, isn't he? Has he been told the terms?"

"To get out of town fast. To help him

along, I used Mom's AmEx to buy him a plane ticket to Costa Rica. You'll get the bill."

"I bet you enjoyed doing that," Travis said.

"Very much."

Shaking his head, Travis looked at his watch. He had on his best suit and a black tie with a gold stripe. He still had three minutes before four. "Your mom wants to retire to Edilean."

"So she told me."

"What about you? Where do you live?"

Russell didn't answer the question. "I think it's time you went in. Should I carry the papers for you?"

"I believe I can manage." As Travis went to the doors leading into the library he remembered that Penny had told him the contract would be on the desk. But Russell had been here to hand it to him — which meant that he'd shown up without his mother's knowledge. Interesting. "You ever do any climbing? Skiing? Sailing?"

"Yes," Russell said, then nodded toward the door. It looked like he wasn't going to reveal any more about himself. "You might like to know," Russell said, "that I got Borman down to one seventy-five."

Travis blinked a few times. He wasn't used to anyone else doing his negotiating for him, but in this case, he was grateful. "Thank you," he said. "I appreciate —"

Russell cut him off. "It's four."

Travis took a breath and opened the door. David Borman was sitting in a leather chair so big that it made him look small and insignificant — and Travis was sure that Russell had put that chair there on purpose. It was difficult not to smile. In spite of Russell's hostility and his refusal to answer questions, Travis was beginning to like the guy.

As Travis looked at the man sitting in the big chair, his first thought was: Kim could do better. Borman wasn't tall, was slightly built, and was so blond he was almost invisible. It wasn't easy for Travis to reconcile what he knew of this man to what he saw. He certainly didn't look treacherous.

"You're Westwood, the owner of this place?" the man asked. His wide eyes showed how in awe of it he was — which was what Travis had wanted.

Travis didn't answer, just looked at him with what he'd heard people call "the Maxwell glare."

Borman sat back against the chair, his nervousness obvious.

Travis sat down and took his time looking over the contract. It was very simple. He was buying Borman Catering et al. He would get the name, the equipment, and even keep the employees.

The document had been signed by Russell Pendergast. Travis took more time looking at the signature than he did at the contract. It was bold, sure of itself — and it reminded him of something but he couldn't think what.

When he looked up, Borman was chewing on his thumbnail and there was sweat on his upper lip.

"Mr. Borman," Travis said as he folded his hands on top of the contract. "I have just been informed of a situation that may cause insurmountable problems."

Borman drew in his breath and muttered, "What is it?"

"It has come to my attention that there's something about a missing ring. I don't want any problems with law enforcement."

Borman gave a sigh of relief and lifted to one side to remove his wallet from his hip pocket. "That has nothing to do with my business. It's personal." He withdrew a small square of paper from his wallet and leaned forward to put it on the desk. "I must say that you have been doing your homework. So where do I sign?"

"This is a pawn ticket," Travis said and

knew what it meant. The employee that Kim trusted had given this man a ring, and Borman had pawned it. But Travis had long ago learned that he couldn't jump to conclusions, that he shouldn't base his assessments of a situation on hearsay. When it came down to it, he only had Russell's word about what this man had been up to.

As much as Travis wanted to get rid of the man, get him out of his sight, at the same time he wanted evidence directly from the source. He leaned back in his chair and pointedly looked at the ticket on the big desk. "Mr. Borman, I run a legitimate business. I don't sign contracts if pawnshops and the police are involved."

"Police? I don't know what you're talking about. I owe a little money, for supplies and that sort of thing, but I've done nothing illegal."

"From what I heard, this ring is worth several thousand dollars. I don't want to retrieve it from the pawnshop then find out that it's been stolen."

Borman leaned back in the leather chair, glanced at the unsigned contract on the desk, then back at Travis. He looked thoroughly annoyed. "It's nothing," he said. "It's about a woman, that's all. Get the ring out of hock and return it to her. No one will press charges."

Travis's face was stern, the one he wore when he was working for his father. "Perhaps you should tell me exactly what this is about. Or maybe I should cancel this." He picked up the contract and acted as though he was about to tear it in half.

"No!" Borman shouted, then calmed. "It's just women stuff, that's all." When Travis didn't relent, he said, "There was a woman, a cute little redhead. She has a jewelry store near here. It's little, nothing special. The problem was that she's a woman. You know what I mean?"

"I'm not sure I understand." Travis put the contract down and gave Borman his full attention.

"The problem was that she worked on a small scale when she should have been thinking big. I tried to talk to her about it, for her own good. But she wouldn't listen to me. I wanted to take her store national, make it into a chain. I was going to call it The Family Jewels. Get it?"

"I get it," Travis said. Under the desk his hands were in fists.

"But she just laughed at me. Not that I told her I was serious about the name, as she can be a real prude. She's the kind of girl that goes to church every Sunday.

Anyway, she wouldn't even consider going national, so I decided that the best thing would be to marry her, then I'd be able to help her out. I was really thinking of her. Know what I mean?"

"Yes, I do." Travis took a breath. "Did she know why you wanted to marry her?"

"Hell no! She's a clever little thing, so I had to be careful. I was very nice to her, sweetest person imaginable. Treated her with the respect of a choirboy. Even in the sack I was good. Nothing creative, if you know what I mean."

Travis had to work to keep from diving across the desk and going for the man's throat. "What about the ring? Where did it fit into all this?"

Dave shrugged, and his expression said that he was pleased by Travis's interest. "If I was going to ask her to marry me I had to give her a ring, didn't I? But why should I go buy one when she has a store full of them? They were just sitting there in her shop, about fifty of them, and they were free — or would be once we got married." He leaned forward, as though he was about to reveal a confidence to Travis. "She has a safe inside her garage that's full of . . . I can't imagine what's in there. She lives in a world of gold and jewels. An Aladdin's cave of diamonds and pearls. She likes pearls. One time she even tried to lecture me on the different kinds of them. Like I care, right?"

"Did you see inside the safe?"

"Naw," Dave said with a grimace. "I tried to get her to show me but she wouldn't. I even tried to get her to give me the combination, but she refused."

In his entire life, Travis had never felt such anger, such *hatred* for anyone before. "You understand the terms of the contract, don't you?"

"Of course I do." He looked at Travis as though they were men who shared a secret. "You don't want any competition. You're like me. We're both businessmen and we understand each other. Too bad the women don't get that."

Travis didn't dare respond as he didn't trust himself not to say what he was actually feeling. He gave Borman a fake smile, as though he thought the man was a genius, then filled in the outrageous price Russell had negotiated for him. Travis would have paid more. He pretended to sign it in the place where Russell's name already was.

Eagerly, Dave leaped up, signed the bottom without reading it, and Travis handed him his copy.

"Planning to call her to say good-bye?" Travis asked even while his hands were itching to hit the man.

"Don't have time," Dave said as he turned toward the door. "I have important things to do, including getting my old girlfriend back. Now there's a girl who knows what to do to make a man happy in bed. If you get my meaning."

"Yes I do," Travis said, then stood there and watched David Borman leave the room. He felt like he needed a shower with a disinfectant.

Travis didn't know how long he stood there before Russell came in through the side door.

"Did he take it?"

Travis hesitated. "The money? Of course."

"What's this?" When Travis didn't immediately turn around, Russell stood quietly and waited.

Finally, Travis looked at what Russell was holding. "That's a pawn ticket."

"I can see that. What's it for? Oh! The ring." Russell looked at the address on the ticket. "Wonder what his plan was going to be for this weekend when he asked Miss Aldredge to marry him but didn't have a ring to give her?"

"My guess is that he'd say he knew nothing about a missing ring."

"His word against Carla's, and she was the one who stole it from the shop."

"That's what I think," Travis said as he reached out to take the ticket. "I'll go by there and get it."

"Do you have any cash on you?" Russell asked.

"A few hundred, but I have cards."

"A pawnshop that takes credit cards? Besides, you can't use yours." Russell raised an eyebrow.

Travis knew nothing about pawnshops and what kind of payment they took.

"I'll get the ring out of hock and you can go with me. Besides, your car has two flat tires."

"My car — ?" Travis began but stopped. He had a feeling that Russell was lying about Travis's car being incapacitated, but he didn't mind. Right now he felt like he needed some company, needed something to take the stench of Dave Borman from him. "Fine," Travis said, "but I drive."

Russell gave a noise like a snort.

Two hours later they had the ring and were almost back to Edilean. Russell was driving. For the most part it had been a quiet ride, and Travis wasn't feeling that hostility from Russell that he'd first seen.

"What does Miss Aldredge think your last name is?" Russell asked.

"She hasn't asked and I haven't told her."

"Good, solid foundation between you two," Russell mumbled.

"Your life is better?" Travis snapped.

"Certainly not as complicated," Russell said calmly.

Travis looked out the window. "Yes, I think it's time to tell her."

"Are you going to tell her why Borman won't show up in Janes Creek? About the little play you put on in the library? How about that you're now the owner of Borman Catering?"

"What are you? A federal court judge? You want all the facts?"

"Just curious how the great Maxwell son conducts his life."

Travis started to reply to that, but they'd reached Kim's house and there was a strange car in the drive. "You don't think that's Borman's, do you?"

"I wouldn't think so," Russell said, "but I wouldn't put it past him."

"Park around the corner and I'm going to go in through the back door." Minutes later, Travis was heading toward Kim's house, Russell close behind him. "Where are you going?"

"Mom said to help you in any way I can. If it's Borman, you might need backup."

Travis knew that if it came to a confrontation, he wouldn't need help with Borman. On the other hand, Travis didn't know how Kim was going to react to what he had to tell her. And how much should he tell her? If he was going to tell her the truth about himself, maybe he should tell her about Borman and the ring as well. Or maybe he'd postpone the part about setting Borman up and buying his company and —

"I can see the yellow stripe down your back through your clothes," Russell said.

"I wish Penny had spent more time with you and taught you some manners."

"She tried, but she was too busy working for your family to do much for me."

"If you ever want to compare childhoods, I'm ready," Travis said.

"At least you had —" Russell began but they both stopped talking when they heard a man's voice raised in anger.

Travis hurried to the back door. As usual, it was unlocked. He slipped inside, Russell right behind him.

As soon as Travis heard his name, he knew he should leave, but he couldn't make himself move. He could feel Russell beside him, and he was as transfixed, and as immobile, as Travis was.

"Kim! Are you crazy?" Dr. Reede Aldredge was shouting at his sister. "You don't even know who that man is."

"That's a stupid thing to say. I've known him since I was eight years old. He's Travis . . ." She wasn't sure if his last name was Cooper or Merritt or something else.

"He is John Travis Maxwell and his father is Randall Maxwell."

"So? I've heard the name but . . ."

"You ought to read something besides jewelry magazines. Look on the *Forbes* Web site. Randall Maxwell is one of the richest men in the world. And his son Travis is his right-hand man. Maxwell specializes in taking over other people's companies. When some guy is down and out, Maxwell steps in and buys the place for a song, then he sends in his crew to clean it up. He fires people by the thousands, puts them out of work. And you know who makes all this possible? His brilliant son, Travis the lawyer — the guy living in your guesthouse."

Kim set her jaw. "There are extenuating circumstances that you know nothing about."

"So tell me."

"I can't. I promised Travis —"

"Are you insinuating that *I* wouldn't keep

a confidence? Do you have any idea how many lies and secrets and intrigues I know about in this town? I want to know why Travis Maxwell is here in Edilean. If he's planning to buy some business for his father, I think we should tell people."

"It's not like that," Kim said. "Travis only works for his father so he can protect his mother."

"That makes no sense. Is that the crap he's been feeding you?"

Kim's hands made into fists. "His mother is Lucy Cooper, the woman who's been hiding from me for four years. She was afraid I'd recognize her from when I was a kid."

Reede took a breath to calm himself. He could see that he was making his sister angry, and an angry Kim didn't listen to anyone. "Maybe that's so," Reede said. "Maybe this guy Maxwell came here because of his mother. But what does that have to do with *you?*"

"Nothing, I guess," Kim said. "Except that I'm helping him. We're making plans about what to do. We're —"

"You think you're helping him to make plans?" There was contempt in Reede's voice. "Kim, I don't want to burst your bubble, but Travis Maxwell is a notorious playboy. And now he's using you."

"For what?"

"For what all men want!" he said in exasperation. "He's already manipulated you into giving him the guesthouse you promised to *me.*"

Kim looked at her brother in surprise for a moment, then couldn't help laughing. "You're talking about sex, aren't you? You think Travis conned me into lending him the little guesthouse that you don't want just so he can have sex with me."

Reede glared at her in silence.

"You know what, Reede, I have never been so flattered in my life. That a man would go to so much trouble to get me into bed is the best thing I've heard this century. Men today don't make any effort to get a woman. If they ask you on a date, they tell you when and where to meet them. That's so if you don't pass their every test for beauty and for making less money than they do, they can walk out and leave you. They don't even have to drive you home because you have your own car."

"Not all men are like that," Reede said. "And they're not the point. This man you're playing around with isn't like Paul the Caterer. Maxwell is —"

"Dave!" Kim said. "His name is Dave and I've been going out with him for six whole months and I've withstood the most boring sex imaginable. Someone should tell David Borman that there is more than one position."

"I'd prefer not to hear —"

"Not to hear that your baby sister isn't a virgin?"

"I never thought —" Reede began, then threw up his hands. "I knew you wouldn't listen to me. You never do. Kim, you're my sister and I don't want to see you hurt. Whatever reason Maxwell is here for, when he's done, he'll leave you." He looked away for a moment. "Kim, I know what it's like to have your heart ripped out. I don't want to see that happen to you."

Kim saw the pain in his eyes. When Reede was in high school and through most of college, he'd been in love with a hometown girl. He never looked at anyone else. Then suddenly, she dumped him, said she was marrying someone else. It had taken Reede years to get over the pain. "I know," she said softly. "I understand why you're so upset, but Reede, I know what I'm doing. I know that Travis is a long way from being someone from Edilean. He's not here to get married, move into some three/two house, and have kids."

"But that's what *you* want," Reede said. "I

know it is. When Jecca and Tris got married you cried through the whole ceremony."

"Yes," Kim said gently. "It *is* what I want. With all my soul. Do you think I bought this big house because of the damned garage? I . . ." She had to hold back tears as she said what she knew to be true; it was going to hurt to say it out loud. "Sometimes I think I bought it as bait, to lure some nice guy here, to make it easy for him to move in, to —"

Reede put his arms around her, held her head to his chest, and stroked her hair. "Don't say such things. Any man would be honored to have you. You're smart and funny and caring and —"

"So where is he?" Kim said as she hugged her brother. "Where is this man who is going to see my good qualities and overlook my bad ones? I've spent six whole months with Dave the Caterer and I've never complained about how boring he is." She pulled away from him and wiped her eyes. "At least Travis made an effort."

"Yeah, but for what?" Reede asked as he handed Kim a tissue.

She blew her nose loudly. "I hope it's because he wants wild, all-night sex with me."

"Kim!" Reede said, sounding like a Victorian father.

"Look, I know Travis is going to leave. Once he fully believes that Joe Layton is a great guy who is mad about Lucy, Travis will leave as abruptly as he arrived. It'll be like when we were kids and one day he just wasn't there. No note, nothing. And he came back just as abruptly, with no warning. I know that he appears and disappears according to his own whims, without regard to other people."

"I agree," Reede said. "He'll go back to his dad's empire and . . . Someday, Kim, Travis Maxwell will be just like his father. You don't want to be part of that, do you?"

"No," Kim said, then looked at her brother over the tissue. "But right now while he's here, I'll take all the passionate sex I can get. Days of it. Weeks if I can get it. Months would be divine."

"That's —" Reede said sternly, then shook his head. "It's difficult for me to think of my little sister doing —" He couldn't seem to find words to express his feelings. Instead, he looked at his watch. "I have to go. I'm already late. I want you to promise me that you'll do an Internet search on Travis Maxwell and see what you're up against. He's been dating some model named Leslie who is a truly beautiful woman."

"Not like me, huh?"

Reede groaned as he knew he'd said that wrong. "That's not what I meant and you know it. I just don't want you to be hurt. Is that bad of me?"

"Of course not. You better go now. Your patients need you."

"I'll talk to you later," he said, then kissed her on the cheek.

"I'll walk you out," she said and followed him outside.

Even after the door closed, Travis stood where he was, unable to move, just stood there, staring at the doorway into the living room. He hadn't liked what he'd heard about himself.

"We'd better leave," Russell said softly. "It wouldn't be good for her to know that you heard that."

Travis's mind seemed to race forward and to stand still at the same time. He couldn't figure out what to do. Go to her? Run away? Stay and defend himself? Reassure her that he wasn't what she'd been told?

Russell put his hand on Travis's arm and turned him toward the back door.

"Ironic, isn't it?" Travis said. "I want love and *she* wants sex."

Russell gave a bit of a laugh then pushed Travis to take a step toward the door. But they were too late.

"Stop right there," Kim said from behind them.

ELEVEN

Russell dropped his hand from Travis's arm and stepped away.

"When were you going to tell me?" Kim asked, her eyes on Travis. If she thought about what she'd just said to her brother and that Travis had heard every word of it, she knew she'd die of embarrassment.

Travis took his time turning around, and when he did, he wished he'd made it outside without seeing her. He'd never seen any woman with such anger in her eyes. That's the second person who has hated me, he thought. Russell this morning and now Kim looking at him like he was the devil's spawn. "I came in here to tell you about me."

"How convenient," Kim said. "But why didn't you tell me before? You told me about your mother hiding from your father, about her wanting to marry Joe Layton, but you didn't happen to mention that you're a lawyer and your name is Maxwell. Did you think I'd turn greedy and go after your family's wealth?"

"Of course not," Travis said. He didn't know where to begin. "I just thought . . . I mean . . ."

"Excuse me, but I'm a bit peckish," Russell said. "Do you mind if I . . . ?" He gestured toward the refrigerator.

"Help yourself," Kim said, still looking at Travis.

"Kim, honey," Travis said. When Kim's eyes looked like they were about to emit fire, he backtracked. "I didn't mean —"

"He was afraid you'd hate him because of the Maxwell reputation," Russell said from behind the refrigerator door.

"Yes," Travis said. "The Maxwell name brings out the bad in a lot of people."

"Does in me," Russell said. "Is there any mustard? Ah, here it is."

Kim turned to look at him. "You're the man in the shop. The one who was after Carla."

"Russell Pendergast," he said, smiling. "I'd shake your hand but . . ." He had his arms full of deli meat and bread. "Anyone else want a sandwich?"

"No!" Travis and Kim said in unison.

"He's my secretary's son," Travis said. "I only met him this morning. I didn't even know he existed until a couple of days ago when Penny said her son would help me. From the way she said it, she could have been talking about a six-year-old. But then she is his mother. You and I talked about how parents do that. Remember, Kim?"

She was still glaring at him. "What did your secretary's son help you with that involved *my* shop and *my* employee?"

Travis drew in his breath. It looked like his attempt to distract her hadn't worked.

Russell didn't help matters by chuckling.

"You want to leave us alone?" Travis said to him, frowning.

"Actually, no," Russell said. "No Broadway show has ever been this good, but I'll leave if Miss Aldredge wants me to."

"I never want to be alone with this man ever again. And please call me Kim."

"Gladly," he said as he gave her a look of appreciation.

"Russell!" Travis snapped. "So help me if you —"

"If he what?!" Kim said loudly. "Travis, I am waiting for an answer."

Never in his life had Travis ever found himself in a situation that he couldn't talk his way out of. But too much rested on this now for him to think coherently. "I . . ." He hesitated, not sure what to say, then he reached into his trousers pocket and withdrew the big sapphire ring that Borman had stolen.

"I got this back for you," he said, his voice hopeful.

Kim didn't take it, so he set it on the kitchen countertop. "I see. The missing ring." She took a moment to think. "If you have the ring, that means that whatever you two have been up to involves my boyfriend, Dave. You must have met him."

Travis's face grew serious. "Yes we did and, Kim, you don't know him. He's not what you think he is. The truth is that he's after —"

"He wants to take my jewelry business national and name it The Family Jewels. I treated it as the joke it was. Not the national part, but the name."

Both men were so shocked at her words that Russell stopped eating and Travis stared at her.

Kim turned away. There was so much anger in her that she could hardly breathe. Her friend Gemma was a boxer. Right now, if Kim had the know-how, she'd hit Travis so hard his head would roll across the floor.

She looked back at him. "Why did you assume that I didn't know what Dave was after? Did he seem subtle to you? Secretive?"

"No," Travis said. "But if you knew the truth, why would you consider marrying him?"

Kim was almost sure that if Dave had asked her she would have said no. Before Travis had shown up she might have said yes, but she blamed that on her friend Jecca's recent wedding. Of course, when she came to her senses, she wouldn't have gone through with it. But she was damned well not going to tell Travis that! "Is there a man on earth who *doesn't* have his own agenda for marriage? At least Dave was *honest* with me. He let me know that he was very interested in my business, and he had some good ideas."

"But . . ." Travis said.

"But what? I should wait for a man like *you?* Compared to the amount of lying and manipulation *you* have done, Dave is up for sainthood."

She wanted to get this back on track. This was about him, Travis, and what he had done, not David Borman. That was none of Travis's business. "I want to see if I get your story straight. You're a Maxwell, son of one of the richest men in the world." When Travis just stood there, she looked at Russell and he nodded in verification.

"You came to Edilean when you were twelve, spent two weeks with me, then left without so much as a note."

"Kim," Travis said, "come on, I was twelve. I did what my mother told me to."

"You could write," Russell said, his mouth full.

Travis glared at him.

"Do you know that for eighteen years I searched for you? I used to sneak into my brother's room to use his unblocked Internet service to try to find you."

"But you couldn't find him because you didn't know his correct last name," Russell said. "Mind if I get a beer?"

"Please do," Kim said. "Eighteen years and nothing. I was forgotten by you."

"That's not really true. I always knew where —" Travis said, then shut his mouth.

Kim looked at Russell in question.

"Mom said that you were never out of his radar. She said he used to —"

"I saw your shows," Travis said quickly before Russell could say any more.

Kim's eyes widened. "You! It was *you.* Jecca saw you there. She used to call you the TDH Stranger. She even drew your portrait, but I had no idea who you were."

"TDH?" Travis asked.

"Tall, dark, and handsome," Russell said. "This beer is good. I've never had it before." He looked at Travis. "Want one?"

"Only if it doesn't have hemlock in it," Travis muttered as Russell, smiling, got a beer out, opened it, and handed it to him.

Travis drank half of it in one gulp, then dropped down onto a stool. He looked back at Kim as though to say he was ready to receive more of her verbal lashes. "I thought I was watching over you," he said.

"Ah, right, how noble. 'Watching over me.' 'Looking out for me.' Is that right?"

"I thought so," Travis said and drank more beer.

Russell started making a sandwich for Travis. Neither of them had eaten since breakfast.

"So now," Kim said, "you returned to Edilean not for me — oh no, not for *me* — but because your mother called you."

"Actually," Russell said as he cut the bread, "she called my mother and told her."

"Even better," Kim said. "Lucy Merritt or Cooper or Maxwell called . . . What *is* her name?" she asked Russell.

"Cooper and Merritt are made up. Her name is Lucy Jane Travis Maxwell of the Boston Travises. She got the name and education but none of the family's old money. My mother is Barbara Pendergast of no money and no name. Just hard work."

"Thank you," Kim said. She looked back at Travis as he bit into the sandwich Russell had made for him. He looked like a man walking up the gallows steps. "Whatever the name, the point is that you didn't come back for me, but for your mother."

Travis got up to get two more beers.

"Because of Jecca's wedding you happened to see me and . . . one thing led to another."

Russell looked at Travis in question.

"She means inviting me to stay in her guesthouse," Travis said.

Russell nodded and looked back at Kim as though to say the floor was hers.

"You moved into my guesthouse and talked to me so much about friendship that I was beginning to think you were gay. And you —"

Russell gave a snort of laughter.

"I never meant —" Travis began.

"How's Leslie?" Kim asked, letting every millimeter of her anger show.

Travis looked down at his sandwich.

She picked up the ring and looked at Russell. "When I said I had a boyfriend, he almost had a grand mal seizure of old-fashioned jealousy."

"I did not," Travis said as he started to defend himself. But every word Kim was saying was true. "I was shocked, that's all," he mumbled.

"Shocked that I had a boyfriend?" Kim said. "You are . . ." Her eyes widened in disbelief. "You've watched me — stalked me — enough that you knew when I had a boyfriend or not." It was a statement, not a question.

Travis wouldn't have answered that if someone had set his feet on fire. That his mother had listened to Edilean gossip and told him about Kim on nearly every call was beside the point. It suddenly went through his mind to wonder if it was a coincidence that she called just when Kim was getting serious about some guy. And she called when there was going to be a wedding next door to her where Kim was a bridesmaid. His mother had called Penny — who she'd always disliked — and it was his secretary who got him to go to Edilean ASAP. Had it been up to Travis, he might have postponed going to Edilean, but Penny set everything up. Right now it seemed as though the two women had worked together to get Travis to Edilean at a time when he was sure to see Kim again. But that couldn't be true. Surely, all of it was coincidence.

Kim's hands were in fists and she had to turn away for a moment to catch her breath. "You thought . . ." she said softly. "You thought that since you're a big city lawyer and you were born into great wealth, that you know more about life than I do."

"Kim, I never thought that," Travis said as he put down his sandwich. "It wasn't like that at all."

"You assumed that I was a naive, simple, small town girl who was so desperate to get married that I couldn't see the truth about some guy I was dating regularly."

"Kim, you're not being fair," Travis said as he came off the stool. "Borman was a real bastard. He conned Carla into giving him that ring, saying he was going to give it to you when he asked you to marry him. But then he pawned it. I — we — think that he was going to say he knew nothing about the ring and let Carla take the blame."

Kim didn't allow the shock of that information to show on her face. "How did *you* get it?"

Travis sat back down and looked at his plate.

"He bought Borman Catering," Russell said.

Travis looked at him with murder in his eyes.

"You did what?" Kim asked in disbelief.

"He paid a hundred and seventy-five grand for the company," Russell said. He'd finished his sandwich and was working on the second beer. "He was going to pay more, but I got Borman down to that. It's still too much."

"Much too much," Kim said. "Those vans of his are worn-out and Dave's lost commissions because he doesn't deliver what he promises."

"I thought it was too much too," Russell said, "but we were up against a deadline."

Travis looked at Russell in disgust for ratting on him. "Kim, I think we're losing sight of the main issue here. Borman was going to ask you to marry him and I was afraid you'd say yes."

"And when he proposed, he'd give me my ring back!" Kim said loudly. She threw up her hands. "Men! I've had all of you I can take this week. Today I had to threaten Carla with firing her because of what she'd done."

"You should fire her," Travis said seriously. "What she did was a prosecutable offense."

"She was conned by a *man!* It's a hazard of being female. And for your information, in Edilean we don't discard someone for making a single mistake."

"As I did," Travis said softly as he looked at her with eyes begging for forgiveness.

"*You* have made a thousand mistakes. And stop looking at me like that! You already showed me that face, remember? You used it to get the pretty young wife of the old man to teach you how to cook — along with other things."

Russell laughed. "She's got *you* figured out."

"Kim, I never meant —"

"I know!" she said loudly. "I'm sure that from your view you came swooping in on your white horse and rescued me. But I didn't *need* rescuing. I didn't need someone to make me look like a fool, to make me feel that I'm an idiot who can't run my own life. What I need is —" She couldn't take any more. "Out! Both of you get out of my house and out of my life. I never want to see either of you again."

Both of the men got up and started for the door. When Travis passed her she said, "Did you ever think that it's not the Maxwell name that brings out the bad in people? That it's *you?*"

Travis had no answer for her.

Kim slammed the door behind them, locked it, then leaned back against it. "For your information, John Travis Maxwell, *I* want love too."

Two minutes later she was calling the person she wanted to talk to about all this. He answered on the first ring and said he'd meet her right away. Twenty minutes later she was pulling into Joe Layton's parking lot.

Twelve

Joe Layton's solution to every problem was the same: food and work. After he'd spent thirty minutes listening to Kim's nearly incoherent words that she uttered in between copious tears, and feeding her, he put her to work. As he had her help him put the supplies Travis had unpacked on the shelves that he'd installed, Joe couldn't help musing on the fact that their turbulent love life was giving him a lot of free labor.

"I don't get it," she said as she picked up boxes of electric drills and put them on the shelves. "Why would he make so much effort to get a man away from me if all he plans to do is leave me and go back to . . . to wherever he lives?"

"New York," Joe said. "Lives on the top floor of some big building."

"He told you that?"

"No, but I found out."

"That means you've known Travis's last

name and you looked him up on the Internet," Kim said with a sigh. "Reede said I'd find out everything there, but he couldn't wait to send me info. But who wants to find out about someone on the Web? But then, why does everything Travis tells me have to be a lie? Or an evasion? What's happened in his life that makes him think even the most ordinary things have to be kept secret?"

"I don't know," Joe said. They were questions that were bothering him too. He'd given Lucy every opportunity to tell him about her son, but she hadn't. Three times she'd almost said "my son" but each time she'd caught herself. Joe was trying hard not to get angry about it, but it wasn't easy. "Are you in love with young Travis?" he blurted out.

Kim paused for a moment in putting a box on the shelf. "How can I be? I thought I knew the boy Travis, but the adult . . . I don't know who he is. He seems to think he has a right to oversee my life. He takes away from me but gives nothing in return." She knew that wasn't true, but her anger wasn't allowing her to reason.

The red light on Joe's cell phone came on again. He had it on silent so Kim couldn't hear it, but Joe knew that Travis had called him eight times since she'd arrived. He also knew he was going to have to deal with the young man or he'd show up at the door. And with the mood Kim was in now, she might throw an anvil at him.

"Didn't I hear that you were supposed to do something special this weekend?" Joe asked.

Kim groaned. As angry as she was, it didn't dampen her artist's eye as she arranged the small machines on the shelves. She put them up with all the finesse that she used to display her jewelry. "Jocelyn — she's married to my cousin — wants me to go to some little town in Maryland to see if I can find out about some great-great-grandaunt of mine. Joce is doing genealogy charts, and this woman in Maryland had a kid but there's no father listed. This is back in 1890-something. I don't know how I'm supposed to do this. But anyway, Dave wanted to go with me and we were going to make it a minivacation. He was going to . . ." She waved her hand. If she continued talking, she'd start crying again. "I think I'd better cancel my reservation."

She couldn't help thinking about what might have been. What *would* she have done if Dave had asked her to marry him? She'd told Travis she'd known all about the man, but she hadn't. Hearing that he'd pawned the ring he'd slick-talked Carla into "giving" him had made Kim feel sick. She'd not seen anything in Dave that made her think he was capable of such thievery. He'd always been so very nice — boring, but pleasant and likeable. His talks about her going national with her jewelry had always been presented in the most respectful way, saying that it was her decision, and he was only tossing out ideas. And she really had thought the name he'd suggested was just a crude joke.

She'd only heard about Dave's company's failure the day before Jecca's wedding, the day before Travis reappeared in her life. She'd seen that two of his vans were on their last legs, but he'd laughed and said he had too much work to do to order new ones. She'd had no reason to disbelieve him.

But the day before the wedding, when everything was chaos and there were so many people around, Kim had overheard a woman saying she was glad Jecca hadn't used that "dreadful" Borman Catering. Kim had tried to get him for the wedding, but he'd been booked solid. Kim had asked the woman why she didn't like Borman Catering and she'd been told the story of the switched ingredients. And she'd heard that people were canceling their future orders with him. At the time, Kim had been so busy helping Jecca that she hadn't thought about what that meant. When Kim looked back on it, she realized that she hadn't wanted to see that Dave's business was going under. And she didn't want to think about that in connection to how often he asked for the combination to her safe.

Was Dave yet another man in her life who couldn't see past her success?

Kim arranged a hand drill in its case as artistically as she could manage, then started putting up the boxes of bits.

When Joe excused himself to make a call, Kim continued to work — and to think.

Okay, so maybe it was true that she didn't know as much about Dave as she'd told Travis she did, but did that give him the right to . . . to . . . take over?

She thought of Travis buying Borman Catering. Why? But she knew the answer. He paid all that money just to send Dave away. On the drive to Joe's she'd called a client who lived in Dave's building and was told that he'd left with six suitcases and had told the landlord he wasn't coming back.

"The landlord was furious," the woman said. "Dave left so much junk behind and the landlord has to take care of it. But then some man called and said he'd come get everything. The whole building is talking about it. What do you know?"

"Nothing," Kim said and politely hung up.

She'd told Travis she hated the way he'd swooped in and taken over, but there was a part of her that was grateful that he'd saved her from Dave. Kim now wondered if she would have agreed to marry him. Had Jecca's wedding, her happiness, made Kim so envious that she would have said yes just to . . . ? She didn't want to think about what could have happened.

Earlier, as Kim had pulled into Joe's parking lot, her cell buzzed. It was an e-mail from her brother and there was an attachment. Kim hesitated before opening it because she knew what it was going to be. But she also knew she needed to see the truth. She pushed the button and the first thing she saw was a photo of some drop-dead gorgeous woman named Leslie. The caption read WEDDING BELLS FOR A MAXWELL? The article told how the beautiful model had been going steady with the megarich son of Randall Maxwell for months now. *"Travis — über rich, über beautiful — never dates anyone for longer than six weeks. But he and the luscious Leslie have been together for nearly a year now. Can we look forward to a wedding like the world has never before seen?"*

Kim couldn't stand to read the rest of the documents her brother had sent. That one was quite enough.

When she got out of the car, Joe was standing in the doorway, and he opened his arms to her. If her dad had been home she would have gone to him, but Jecca's father was nearly as good.

She'd cried hard for a while, then Joe had ordered in pizza and huge colas and enough cinnamon sticks to fatten half of Edilean. Kim had cried and eaten, then cried some more.

"I don't understand why he lied to me," she said.

"Borman or young Travis?" Joe asked.

"Travis," Kim said. "Dave is . . . He's a real person, so of course he lies."

Joe raised his eyebrows but he didn't comment on that statement. In dealing with his children of opposite sexes he'd learned a hard fact. If Joey came to him with a problem, he was asking for help to find a solution. But if Jecca had a problem, she just wanted Joe to listen. No advice. Whereas Joe had been free in telling Travis what he thought, Joe didn't dare offer Kim so much as a suggestion.

"He lied to me about everything. From day one, I was completely honest with him, but he told me nothing but lies."

Joe had to refrain from rolling his eyes. That's pretty much exactly what Travis had said about Kim. He'd said she'd concealed the fact that she had a boyfriend and had glossed over a story about a missing ring. But Joe made no comment. His cell light went on again and the ID said it was Travis. At the ninth unanswered call, Joe excused himself and went outside.

Minutes later, he was back — and Kim was still ranting.

Joe wanted to help her but he didn't know how. He'd talked to Travis and he was miserable. He said he just wanted to make sure Kim was all right. "She was so angry I was afraid for her to drive."

"I guess that means you followed her," Joe said. Travis's silence was answer enough. "What have you done about this weekend?"

"Weekend?" Travis asked, sounding as though he hadn't thought about it. "You mean Janes Creek?"

"Don't dance around me, boy! What have you *done?*"

Cautiously, Travis told him of renting every room in the two inns in the little town.

Joe gave a low whistle. "Did your dad

teach you to take over everybody's life?"

"I think it's more that I was born with it in me than that I learned it," Travis said gloomily.

Joe almost laughed but didn't. "I'll get Kim to go to that town, but you have to take it from there. Think you can manage that?"

"But Kim said she never wants to see me again," Travis said, his voice full of his despair.

Joe snorted in exasperation. "And that's going to stop you? Haven't you ever had a woman tell you to get lost?" To him it was a rhetorical question requiring no answer. Of course women had said that to Travis, to all men.

"No. Not actually," Travis said. "Never."

"What a world you live in!" Joe muttered, then said louder, "That's because Kim sees *you* and not the Maxwell name. Try being yourself with her."

"But . . ." Travis said, then trailed off. "Will you see that she gets home all right?"

"Of course," Joe said and hung up. He took a deep breath, spent a few minutes looking at the stars and wishing he was snuggled up with Lucy, then went back into the shop. He was going to have to say the sentences that women so loved to hear.

Every male chromosome in him fought against it, but he *had* to say them.

"Kimberly," he said when he got inside, "I think you need to do something good for yourself. Take care of *you.* You should treat yourself to a weekend away. Get your nails done, buy yourself some new shoes."

Joe stood there looking at Kim and wondering if she'd fall for it. Jecca would know he was up to something, but would Kim?

Instantly, some of the misery began to drain from Kim's face. "I think you're right," she said. "I'm not going to cancel my reservation. I'm going to Janes Creek and spend the whole weekend thinking about my jewelry and my ancestors. No men anywhere."

She went to Joe and kissed his cheek. "I understand why Jecca loves you so much." She was smiling even though her eyes were still red. "Thanks for everything."

She left by the front door and Joe sat down heavily in his big chair. When did he become the man who solved other people's love problems? He couldn't even solve his own.

In the next moment he picked up his phone and punched the button to reach Lucy.

"Where are you?" she asked. "I just got

out of the tub and I have on my —"

"Lucy," he said firmly before he lost his nerve, "I think it's time you and I talked about your son. And your husband."

She hesitated. "All right," she said softly. "I'll be waiting for you."

Joe let out his breath, and the tension left his big body. "What were you saying about what you have on?"

Kim did her best to sleep that night, but too much was going around in her head. Her dreams were of Travis and in each one, he left. Just walked away as he'd done so many years before.

She got up at two, started to get some milk, but then poured herself a shot of single malt. She tried to watch a movie but couldn't keep her mind on it. She told herself it was absurd to compare something a twelve-year-old boy did while hiding with his mother from an abusive father to the man he was now. And when it came down to it, Travis had the right to not tell anyone his last name. She'd never been around anyone who had to deal with paparazzi, so who was she to judge?

But no matter what her thoughts, or how rational she was, she still felt betrayed.

When she'd come back from Mr. Layton's

she'd seen that Travis had moved out of the guesthouse. He'd locked the door and left the key on her kitchen countertop.

She looked at the key but didn't touch it. To touch it would make his leaving seem real.

She took a shower, washed her hair, and told herself that everything was for the better. Travis had found out what a snake Dave was; Kim had found out that Travis . . . She wasn't sure what she'd discovered about him. Finding out that he was the son of some rich, powerful man hadn't surprised her in the least.

At 4:00 A.M. she went back to bed and slept until eight. She felt better when she woke up and knew that the last thing she wanted to do was go to work. For one thing, she couldn't bear to see Carla. It was going to take a while before she could trust the woman again. Yesterday morning, Carla had confessed to what she'd done. In defending herself, she'd said that Dave had been so very persuasive as he talked about how much he loved Kim. And Carla had fallen for it. She'd taken the ring out of the display case and given it to him because he'd said he was going to present it to Kim on their weekend together. He'd elaborated on how there would be candlelight and he would be on one knee. Carla's sense of romance had overwhelmed her.

It was Carla's date with Russell Pendergast Wednesday night that had made her rethink what she'd done. He'd leaned across the table and looked at her with his beautiful dark eyes and coaxed the truth out of her. Afterward, he'd been clear that he didn't think what she'd done was in the least romantic. In fact, he'd said that if she didn't want to go to prison, she *had* to tell Kim the truth.

It had taken all her courage but Carla had told Kim the next morning.

At the time, Kim had been angry but it's what she'd thought had happened — and why she hadn't pursued the matter. At no time did Kim think Dave was scheming to steal the ring. Like Carla, she believed the man's hints of marriage and a future together. Her problem had been how she was going to answer Dave's proposal. Travis had shown strong signs of jealousy about Dave, so maybe Travis had plans for the two of them.

Kim hadn't allowed herself to think of that. She'd reminded herself that Travis was as elusive as a nightingale, that he didn't stay anywhere too long.

All that day she'd been nervous, and she'd

kept wondering where Travis was and what he was doing. When there was no call from him at lunchtime, she wanted to go home early. Maybe Travis was doing laps in the pool. But customers kept her late, and as soon as she pulled into her driveway, Reede parked beside her. When she saw his face, she knew what was coming. He'd at last remembered where he'd seen Travis — on a racecourse when Travis had nearly hit Reede and his donkey.

As she walked to her front door, Kim thought about how she was going to defend Travis. She would point out that Reede had been in the way, that he shouldn't have been standing in the roadway. Kim was totally on Travis's side.

What she hadn't expected was that Reede couldn't care less about what had happened in Morocco. In fact, he admitted that the whole thing had been his fault. "That doesn't matter," Reede said, then proceeded to tell her the truth about Travis.

It didn't matter to Kim whether Travis was rich or poor, but it did concern her that he'd not told her such fundamental information about himself.

Why? Did he think she couldn't handle it? Did he think she was so provincial that she'd be overcome to find out he'd spent his life in a different circle than she had? Did he think the truth about himself would change what was between them?

She had no answers to her questions.

The scene with Reede had been bad enough, but then to walk into her kitchen and see Travis and Carla's date standing there was almost more than she could bear. She could tell by Travis's face, white with shock — and she had to admit some pain from what he'd heard — that if she didn't get angry she would have died of embarrassment. She would just plain curl up into a ball and disappear.

Somehow she'd managed to keep cool enough to tell Travis what she thought of him. But when she began to remember how she'd told her brother that she wanted to spend days in bed with Travis, her anger was taken over by the embarrassment. She knew that if those two men stayed, she'd dissolve into tears in front of them, so she told them to leave. But she couldn't bear to be alone, so she went to see Mr. Layton.

Now the morning light was coming through her kitchen window and she was doing her best to be cheerful about her coming weekend. Alone. She tried to think of those old axioms about bowls of cherries and lemonade, but she couldn't seem to remember them. She'd already called Carla and told her she was to take care of the shop Friday and Saturday. There was another girl who could help, but Kim wouldn't be there. Carla hadn't argued or asked for overtime.

Kim packed quickly and was on the road by 10:00 A.M. It was a four-hour drive to Janes Creek, and she used the time to try to think about her next series of jewelry designs. She needed something different, something a person didn't see every day.

She also needed to think about the task Joce had given her to do. Everything she was to research was based on a few sentences that Colin's wife, Gemma, had found in a letter written around the turn of the century.

"Please tell me you're not trying to find more relatives," Kim said to Joce and Gemma the day they'd asked her to take on the project. They looked at her as though to say yes, that is exactly what they wanted, and why didn't she understand?

Kim had to remind herself that neither of the women had grown up in Edilean surrounded by what seemed to be thousands of relatives. Joce and Gemma had come from small families where they didn't know their aunts and uncles, much less their fourth and fifth cousins. Between this lack and their shared love of history, the two women were fiendish at finding out everything about everyone — and as far back as they could go.

"Why me?" Kim had asked when she'd been invited to Joce's house for lunch. She lived in the big old Edilean Manor, the place Kim had so hated as a child. Joce had done a lot with it, and it was beautiful now, but Kim wouldn't have taken the house if it were given to her. She much preferred her one-story newer house with its big windows, and floors that didn't creak with age.

In answer to her question, Gemma had put her hand on her growing belly and Joce had glanced at all the toys around them. She had toddler twins.

Kim grimaced. "If I get pregnant in the next two weeks can I get out of this?"

"No!" Joce and Gemma said in unison.

Joce had done everything. She'd made the reservation at the B&B in Janes Creek and she'd prepared a portfolio with papers that told all that they knew about Clarissa Aldredge, the ancestor she was to search for information about.

Gemma had written a veritable treatise of where Kim should look for the information they sought. Kim glanced at it, saw "cemeteries" at the top, and closed the folder.

She didn't understand why those two women liked doing this.

Kim had been almost grateful when Dave invited himself along. He didn't seem interested in looking for dead ancestors, but at least he'd be someone to share meals with.

When Carla started giggling and talking about the weekend and saying that she had put a ring in the safe before closing time, it didn't take much for Kim to figure out what was going on. Just the weekend before, Dave had admired the ring and made a joke about it exactly fitting Kim. His eyes had said the rest of it.

But that had all changed. Just a few days ago Travis . . . Maxwell — she wasn't used to the name — had shown up and turned Kim's life upside down.

"But that's over now," she said as she pulled into the Sweet River B&B. It was 2:00 P.M. and the parking lot was full of cars bearing plates from the Northeast. She hadn't seen the town but had assumed it was about the size of Edilean. Maybe they were having some local event and that's why they were so full.

She got her bag out of the back, put the portfolio under her arm, and went inside. It was an old house that had been converted into some semblance of a hotel. She could hear voices in the back but saw no one. She thought she should get her camera out and photograph the interior for Joce and Gemma, as she figured they'd like the place. There were carvings everywhere, where the ceiling joined the walls, on the stair posts, and on an enormous cabinet against the wall. She was sure there were people who would love the house, but to her it was dark and gloomy.

"Just like me," she said aloud, then turned at a sound.

"You must be Miss Aldredge," a young woman said. She was blonde and thin and pretty, and was looking at Kim as though she'd been waiting for her.

"Yes, I'm Kim. I'm early, but is my room ready?"

"Of course," she said. "I mean it is now, but . . ."

"But what?"

"Nothing."

Kim got out her credit card but the girl wouldn't take it.

"Everything has been taken care of," she said. "Meals, extras, it's all been paid for in advance."

Luke, Kim thought. Her rich writer-cousin, Joce's husband, was footing the bill.

"All right," Kim said and did her best to smile but she couldn't quite make it.

"You're on the top floor," the girl said, then picked up Kim's bag and went up the stairs.

The room was lovely. Large and airy and done in peach and green florals, with striped curtains at the tall windows. Had Kim been in a better mood, she would have been more appreciative.

Kim started to tip the girl but she refused and minutes later Kim was alone.

She flopped down in a chair. Now what? she wondered. Unpack then go look at cemeteries?

"What a fun life I lead," she muttered.

She knew she was indulging in self-pity. Every self-help book said she needed to look at the positive, not the negative. But at the moment all she could think was that she had lost *two* men in *one* day.

Jewelry! she thought. Think about jewelry. But then she remembered the necklace she'd made for Travis so long ago. He'd said he still had it.

That thought made her realize that she'd never see him again. Why was it that when you asked a man to do something like stop driving so fast that he paid no attention to you? You could tell him a hundred times and he'd still "forget." But tell him one time to go away and never come back and he obeyed absolutely. No second chances. No reminders needed.

Kim told herself to get a grip. The two men she'd lost weren't worth all this angst. Dave was . . . She didn't know how to describe him. In fact, she could hardly remember him. In less than a week, Travis had taken over her mind.

"But not my body," she said as she heaved herself up out of the chair. What she needed to do was to "bury herself in work," that phrase she read so often in books.

That was easy to do when you worked in an office. The other people, the noise, would distract a person. But Kim's job was creating. She did it alone, just her and a piece of clay or wax, or paper and pen. There were no other people to help put her mind on something other than what she'd lost. No boss telling her he wanted the report done *now* so she was forced to think of something else.

Kim looked at the wall in front of her and saw three big white doors. She assumed one was a closet and one led to a bathroom, but what was the other one?

"Lady or the tiger?" she murmured as she

reached for the middle door and turned the knob.

It was a door into an adjoining room that was just as big and beautiful as her room. Standing there, at the end of a four-poster bed, was Travis. He had on a pair of sweatpants that hung down low on his hips, his beautiful upper body nude. Muscles played under his golden skin, richly tanned and glowing with warmth.

Kim stood there, frozen in place, staring at him. In some deep recess inside her she still had a mind, could still think rationally. If Travis was here it meant he had again manipulated her and her life to suit himself.

But those thoughts were at the bottom of a very deep well. Right now all Kim could do was *feel*. Every molecule in her body was alive, vibrating, pulsating with her want, her *need* of this man.

Travis didn't say a word, just turned toward her and opened his arms.

Kim ran to him, her arms going around his neck, her mouth on his. His kiss was hungry, as ravenous as she was for him. His lips were on hers, hard, searching, first on her mouth, then her cheeks, her neck.

Kim put her head back and let his hands and lips take what they wanted.

Her clothes came off. She didn't know

how. She didn't feel buttons being undone, heard no fabric tearing. One minute she was dressed and the next she wasn't.

She laughed as Travis picked her up and flung her on the end of the bed. Covers and pillows billowed out around her and she laughed again. This wasn't polite, respectful sex but pure, raw passion.

Travis stood over her, looking down at her nude form for a moment, then he gave a grin that was so devilish, so wicked, that Kim fell back on the bed and opened her arms to him.

He picked her up with one arm around her shoulders, the other entwined in her hair, and pulled her head back to give him access to her face.

When he put his mouth on hers it was with all the passion he felt.

His sweatpants fell to the floor and she wasn't surprised to feel that he had nothing on under them. Her hands went down his back over the hills and valleys of his muscles. She curved out over the firm set of his buttocks, then down his thighs. His mouth was on hers, his kiss deepening, becoming more urgent with every second.

Kim's hands went to his thighs, then up to put them on the male center of him. He was rampant with desire for her, his maleness strong, hard, big. She felt her body melting with wanting him to take her. She felt like she'd been waiting for him for most of her life.

When Travis began kissing her neck, she leaned back, meaning to lie on the bed, to open herself to him.

But Travis didn't let her lie back. As though she weighed nothing at all, he picked her up with one arm, his other one pulling her legs around his waist.

With perfect aim he set her down on his manhood. He slid in easily.

"A perfect fit," she murmured.

"Did you ever doubt that we would be?" he said into her neck.

He held her to him and she loved that her full weight was on him, that she was touching only him. His hands, his big, strong hands, were clasped onto her bottom and raised and lowered her.

Kim let her head go back, let him move her slowly, deeply, the long strokes filling her as no man ever had before.

When she thought she was about to explode, he fell with her onto the bed. He pulled her up toward the headboard, never breaking the contact between them, as his strokes became more urgent, faster.

Kim wanted to scream. She'd never before

felt this intensity, this sensation that her mind, her body, her very soul was being touched by this man.

When she came, she wrapped her legs around his waist so tight she thought she might cut him in half. But Travis was feeling his own climax and his shudders went through both of them.

He collapsed onto the bed beside her and pulled her close into his arms. Kim put her thigh over his, feeling the dampness of him. His body felt so strange but at the same time so familiar. He was the boy she knew so well, and the man she didn't know at all.

"What do you want to know about me?" he asked softly, his fingers in her hair, his palm against her cheek.

"What did you — ?" she began, but cut herself off. Did she really want to lie in his arms and talk about his father? Did she want to hear more about his isolated childhood? Or should she be one of those girls who demanded that a man tell her about his past sexual exploits? In other words, did she want to lie beside him and ask about the beautiful Leslie?

"Kim," he said, "I'll tell you anything you want to know. I'll confess how I rented out this whole place because I couldn't bear to think of you here with another man. How I got Borman to tell me what he was up to. How I —"

Kim leaned over and kissed him, her breasts touching his chest. "Do you know anything about research?"

"I know everything about it," he said solemnly. "When I want to know about something I call Penny and tell her to do it. She can research anything."

"Oh!" Kim said, rolling off him and putting the back of her hand to her forehead. "How do I deal with someone so spoiled?"

Travis turned on his side toward her and ran his hands over her breasts. "Penny is a necessity. She frees me so I can spend all my time masterminding my dad's evil operations." Bending, he put his mouth on the pink tip of her breast. "You are as pretty as wild roses in the morning. Pink and white against the mahogany of your hair. I've never seen anyone more beautiful than you."

What he said, the way he said it, took her breath away. But at the same time there were images of another woman in her head. "That's not what my brother says about you and . . . and the others." Her tone was light but she was serious.

"Your brother? You mean the guy who stands in the middle of a racecourse holding a terrified donkey?"

The image made her laugh — and it made her brother sound too dumb to know anything.

Travis began to nuzzle her neck. She could feel his whiskers on her skin; she could smell the maleness of him. Closing her eyes, she let her senses take over.

"I love to hear you laugh," he whispered as his lips traveled down her shoulder. "When we were children I knew I'd never seen anyone as happy as you." His mouth went across her collarbone as his hand came up to her breasts. He lifted his head to look at her. "Your love of life, what I learned from you, has sustained me through the years."

She started to ask him why he hadn't contacted her when she was in college, but Travis's mouth descended on hers and she forgot her question.

His hands explored her body, running over her legs, between them. When he touched the soft center of her, she gasped. Gently, he caressed her and she closed her eyes, giving herself over to the sensation of him, to the pleasure of his touch.

Slowly, he moved on top of her. The weight of him felt wonderful, reminding her of his maleness.

He entered her slowly, filling her, and his

strokes were long and deep. He took his time as he watched her, smiling as he saw the pleasure on her face.

It was minutes before Kim's eyes opened and she looked at him in surprise. She could feel the waves in her beginning to rise higher and higher. She'd never felt this way before, never . . . "Travis," she whispered.

"I'm here, baby," he said, then held her as he flipped onto his back, with her straddling him. His hands were on her hips.

Kim grabbed his shoulders, her fingertips biting into him as she rose and lowered on him, their bodies coming together with the force of a tidal wave.

When she felt herself building until she couldn't take any more, he pushed her down to the bed, her thighs around his hips, and came into her with a force to match hers.

He fell against her, weak, sated — and loving. His arms held her to him as though he was afraid she'd disappear.

For a moment she thought he'd fallen asleep but when she moved her foot, he loosened his arm.

"Am I hurting you?"

"Far from it," she said.

Travis moved his upper body half off her, put his head on his hand, and looked at her.

"So what do you want to do?"

"Ask you questions about your past girlfriends," she said with a straight face.

She was rewarded with a split second's look of terror before he smiled.

"You're going to punish me, aren't you?"

"Yes," she said as she reached up to touch his hair. Since the first night he'd appeared in the moonlight at Jecca's wedding, she'd wanted to touch him. "I'm going to make you regret lying to me."

"I didn't really lie."

"Isn't there a law about evading being as bad as flat-out lying?"

"What would I know about the law?" he said, his eyes twinkling. Turning, he put his hands behind his head and looked up at the canopy. When Kim started to move away he pulled her back. Her head exactly fit in the curve of his shoulder. Her hand ran over the light hair on his chest.

"Did you look around this place?" he asked.

She was so distracted by his skin that she didn't at first know what he meant. She lifted on one arm and looked at his chest. "What are all these scars from?" There were three on his ribs, one across the side of his stomach.

"Stunt work," he said and didn't seem to

be interested in saying any more. "This town."

"What about it?"

He rolled over to look down at her. "Have you seen this little town?"

She lifted a bit for him to kiss her and he did. "No," she said at last.

He lay back down beside her.

When he said nothing else, she looked at him. "Was that a hint about something?"

"Didn't you come here for a reason? Other than to marry some lowlife loser, that is."

"I wouldn't have —" She wasn't going to let him bait her into an argument. "Good thing you bought him out for me, isn't it? Are you going to learn to cook so you can run your new catering company?"

"I'm going to make Russell a gift of the whole business."

"For having only recently met, you two are certainly chummy," Kim said.

"Seeing me miserable seems to delight him."

"Why were you unhappy?" she asked before she remembered.

Travis looked at her.

She narrowed her eyes at him. "If you try to make me feel sorry for you I'll start asking you why you came to my art shows but didn't make yourself known."

For a moment Travis looked affronted, but then he gave a one-sided grin. "Sounds like we're even. You think there's any food in this room?"

"If not, you can buy the hotel and use your own catering company. Set up a Maxwell Industries right here in Janes Creek."

Travis shook his head. "You and my father are going to get along well. In fact, he might be a little afraid of you."

"Funny!" Kim said, but she was pleased by his words because he was saying that he was going to introduce her to his father. Maybe even his mother. Again.

When Travis rolled off the bed and stood up, Kim put her hands behind her head and watched him. She had pulled the bedspread over her and it was nice — erotic even — to be covered but to see him in the nude.

All those sports he did had given him a truly beautiful body, with muscles rippling under his skin. There were scars here and there, but they only added to the very male beauty of him.

"Do I pass?" Travis asked, his voice husky as he looked down at her.

"Yes," she said as she smiled up at him.

Smiling back, he pulled on his discarded sweatpants. He walked around, looking at things, then went into her room. He returned with the big portfolio Gemma had made for her.

"What's this?"

"The real reason I'm here."

"Mind if I . . . ?"

"Sure, look all you want. I haven't read any of it."

As Kim watched Travis stretch out beside her and begin to read the paper, she thought how little she knew about him. On the other hand, maybe she knew everything about him. The man who had scars from doing dangerous stunts was the same boy who learned to ride a bike and an hour later was doing wheelies. The boy who sat in a tree and read about Alice and the Mad Hatter was this man who was giving his full attention to some historical documents.

"Did you really not read these?" Travis asked as he put the papers on his stomach and drew her to him.

"I saw the word *cemeteries* and closed the file. What did I miss?"

"Let's see . . . You want the facts presented as a fairy tale or as in a courtroom?"

She was tempted by the courtroom idea. She'd like to see him talking to a jury. But then, he'd probably use his good looks to charm the jurors — and she wouldn't like to see that. "Fairy tale," she said.

"All right." He was smiling. "Once upon a time, way back in 1893, a young woman from Edilean, Virginia, by the name of Clarissa Aldredge, wanted to spend the summer in Janes Creek, Maryland."

"Why?" Kim asked. "Why did she leave Edilean?" She knew her tone told something deeper than her words.

Travis kissed her forehead. "I can't imagine why she'd leave a town where everyone knows everything about everyone else."

"Except people's mothers," Kim muttered.

"Are you going to listen or throw barbs at me?"

"Let me think on that," she said. At Travis's look she told him to continue.

"Where was I? Miss Clarissa Aldredge went to Janes Creek, Maryland, in the summer of 1893. No one knows why she went there but it's my guess that she had friends in the little town and she wanted to spend the summer with them. Okay?"

Kim nodded.

"Whatever the reason she left, all that's known for sure is that when she returned to Edilean in September of that year, she was pregnant. She wouldn't tell anyone about the father, so the townspeople — who are given to a bit of gossip now and then — assumed that he was married. Clarissa never corrected anyone no matter what they said. The big problem was that after Clarissa returned, she was different. Melancholic. Depressed."

"I would think so," Kim said. "Unmarried and pregnant in 1893? It's a wonder she wasn't stoned."

"I think that happened in a much earlier time period. Anyway, it seems that poor Clarissa died a few hours after her son was born."

"Oh!" Kim said. "Joce and Gemma didn't tell me that part."

"Probably didn't want to upset you. On her deathbed Clarissa said to her brother Patrick, 'Name him Tristan and pray that he'll be a doctor like his father.' " Travis put the papers down and looked at Kim. "Aren't the Aldredge doctors today still named Tristan?"

"That name is saved for the ones who inherit Aldredge House." Her voice showed that her mind wasn't completely on what he was telling her.

"Not your branch?"

"No, which is why my brother is named Reede."

"So I remember," Travis said as he slid

down in the bed beside her. "What's wrong?"

She couldn't tell him what was in her mind, that she and Clarissa had a lot in common. Everything was temporary between her and Travis. He'd come to Edilean to help his mother and soon he'd be involved in a big divorce case. He'd go back to being a lawyer, back to his glamorous life in New York. Kim and boring little Edilean would be just a memory. Years from now, would he smile when he thought of her? She tried to put those images out of her mind. They were together *now* and that's what mattered. She gave her attention back to him. "I'm fine," she said. "Go on with the story."

"It seems to me that if Clarissa admitted the father was a doctor and his name was Tristan, wouldn't that make it easy for your friends to find him through an online site?"

"Actually, they did," Kim said. "They told me that they found a Dr. Tristan Janes —"

"Like the town name."

"Yes." She gave a sigh. "He died in 1893."

"I see," Travis said as he began to piece the story together. "Clarissa comes to Janes Creek to visit, falls for the local doctor, they tumble in the hay, but before they can get married she's pregnant and he dies. She

returns to Edilean, has the baby, then . . ."
"Joins him," Kim said.
"Let's hope that's the way it works." He paused. "If your friends know all this, why did they send you here?"
"Joce and Gemma are newcomers."
Travis waited for her to explain that odd statement.
"They weren't born in Edilean. They want me to see if this Dr. Tristan was married and if so, did he have any other children."
"Cousins," Travis said. "Is this about finding more relatives?"
" 'Fraid so," Kim said. "If I do find any young descendants, Joce will probably adopt them and Gemma will want to research the whole family."
"And will you decorate them?"
Kim groaned. "If I come up with some new ideas, yes. Since I met you, I haven't had even one new design for jewelry come to me. In fact I can hardly remember what I do for a living."
Travis's eyes were serious. "Kim, if you wanted to —"
She wasn't certain what he was about to say, but she thought maybe he was going to speak of his ability to pay for things. She didn't want to hear it. She changed the subject. "So when do we talk to the natives

and ask who's old enough to remember 1893?"

"If Dr. Tristan died here, we should look for a grave marker and photograph it. Maybe there's something on it, and maybe someone is buried near him. If he had a wife, she'd be there."

"Maybe we'll be lucky and her name was Leslie." Kim hadn't meant to say that — or anything like it. She wanted to be cool and sophisticated. Instead, she was sounding like someone from . . . well, from a small Southern town. "I'd better get dressed," she said and started to get off the bed.

But Travis caught her arm. "I think I should tell you the truth."

She kept her back to him, the sheet covering her front. She felt as though her words had bared a lot more to him than just her body. "Your life is your own. I'm just in it for the . . ." She wanted to say "sex" but couldn't do it. With her other boyfriends she'd always managed to keep it light between them. One of them had said she made jokes about everything. But this was Travis. The day after he'd returned to town she'd sent an e-mail to her friend Jecca saying the man she'd been in love with since she was eight years old had come back to town. Lover or not, she couldn't make a joke about him and his beautiful girlfriend.

When she didn't turn to look at him, Travis dropped his hold on her. "It took me so long to get back to you because I had to find out about myself," he said softly. "I was a rich man's son and I needed to know if I could support myself. I didn't want to be one of those trust fund guys who lives off his father. What kind of a man would I be if that's all I had to offer you?" When Kim didn't move, he took a breath. "After I passed the New York bar, Dad offered me a high-powered, highly paid job, but I turned him down. He was furious! He shut off my trust fund, so I was on my own. He said I'd not make it and the truth was that I was afraid he was right."

Kim turned to look at him.

"I wanted to get as far away from him as possible, so I bummed a ride with someone" — Travis gave a half grin — "on a private jet to L.A. I stayed with a college buddy while I looked for work. I was so angry that when I heard of an opening for stunt work, it appealed to me. I got the job because I'm the same size as Ben Affleck. I was shot twice for that man."

He smiled at her. "I succeeded and I proved that I was able to support myself. But I'd made it in the physical world by performing stunts. I was good at it, but I could see that my body wouldn't last, so I quit. And besides, it was no life for . . . for you."

"Me?" She blinked at him.

"Of course for you. I told you that my life has always been about you."

"But . . ." She'd thought he was saying one of those things that all men do. She hadn't taken it literally. "So what did you do?"

"My plan was to join a law firm. I was hired by a nice, conservative place in northern California. I thought I would work there for a year or so, then I'd return to Edilean to see you again. I wanted to know if there could be anything . . . adult between us. And if I had a year or two of legal work under my belt, maybe I could get work in or around Edilean."

Kim caught her breath, but said nothing.

"Everything was right on schedule until my mother stole millions out of one of my dad's accounts. He came to me in a rage and said he was going to kill her."

Kim gasped.

"He didn't mean it literally, but I knew he'd make her so unhappy she'd wish she were dead. I knew exactly where she'd gone:

the town where she and I had been the happiest."

"Edilean."

"Right. And knowing that, I knew my hope of seeing you again anytime soon was gone. I knew my dad. He'd have me followed and when he did, he'd find my mother."

"So you went to work for him."

"Yes."

"You didn't plan to stay with him forever, did you?"

"I didn't think that far ahead. It seemed that one moment I was on my way to obtaining my lifelong dream — since I was twelve, anyway — and the next I was working eighty hour weeks for my father. I didn't have time to sleep, much less *think.*"

"But you had time to see shows of my jewelry," Kim couldn't help saying, and there was anger in her voice. "If I meant so much to you, why didn't you say something to me? 'Hi, Kim. Remember me?' It could have been anything. I didn't know your last name and I searched for you for years. I —"

Reaching out, Travis pulled her into his arms and stroked her hair. "How could I come to you? You were doing so well. You were a rising star in the jewelry world. I had an Internet alert on you and it seemed that every day you achieved something new. While I . . . I was still my father's puppet. I needed to prove myself as a man."

"And in bed?" she said and more venom than she meant came out.

"Yes," he said. "I had to prove myself there too. It's one thing to have a girl teach you how to ride a bicycle but quite another for her to teach you what to do in bed. 'Now *where* do I put this big thing?' " he said in a falsetto voice.

Kim couldn't help laughing, then she pulled back and looked at him. "Did you break me up with any men besides Dave?"

"No, but I kept a close eye on them."

"What does that mean?"

Travis shrugged.

"What did you do?" she demanded.

"A few background checks, that's all. Nothing invasive. When I saw that they were much less successful than you, I relaxed. You would scare the hell out of them."

"Thanks a lot," she said. "You make me sound like I wield a sword and ride bareback."

"I like the image." His eyes were laughing.

"You!" she began. "You've put me through hell for years. I missed you and I couldn't find you and —" She broke off when he kissed her.

"I want to make it up to you." He kissed her nose. "I want to spend years and years making it right between us."

For all that she liked what he was doing, she drew back to look at him. "What does that mean? Exactly."

"I love you and I want to marry you. If you'll have me, that is."

Kim suddenly lost the power of speech. "But . . ."

"But what?"

"We hardly know each other. You've been back for a week and before that —"

He kissed her again. "How about this? You take as long as you want to get to know me, and every day I'll ask you to marry me. When you feel that you know me well enough, say yes and we'll go find a preacher. How's that?" Turning, he put his feet on the floor. "I'm starving. What about you? Penny has an uncle who eats so much she said I wouldn't be able to afford his bill. I'd like to see that, what about you?"

"I, uh . . ." Kim's head was still reeling from what he'd just said to her. "Where will you live?" she managed to get out. Travis was on his way to the bathroom.

"With you if you'll have me. I like your house, but I think you should move your workroom to Joe's place. You want to take a shower with me? That way your garage will be free. I believe in taking care of automobiles. Are there any good mechanics in town?"

As he disappeared behind the bathroom door, Kim sat there, staring. The sheet fell away but she didn't notice.

Travis looked around the door. "If you keep sitting there like that, I'll have to come back and make love to you again and I really am hungry. Have mercy on me, will you?"

He moved out of view but Kim still sat there. She wasn't at all sure of what she'd heard or what she was feeling. This weekend she'd expected a man she'd known for months to ask her to marry him. Instead, she'd just received a proposal from . . . From Travis, she thought and smiled. She envisioned him on the bicycle as he flew down the hill of dirt. His face and clothes were filthy, his teeth were coated in grime — but she'd never seen anyone happier. That boy had just asked her to marry him!

She heard the shower water. She took a few more seconds to blink, then she went running. "I like where my workroom is," she said. "I don't have to get in a car to get there, so I can work late at night. You can't —" She didn't say any more because Travis's long arm swept out and encircled her waist.

The shower curtain was trapped between them.

"I'll drive you," he said before he kissed her again. "I'm good at driving."

"Yeah, if you like roller coasters without brakes."

"And you do," he said as he kissed her again.

THIRTEEN

Kim was sitting outside the B&B waiting for Travis. Just as they were at last dressed — the shower had taken a very long time — his cell phone rang. "On this number it's either Penny or my mother or you," he said as he dug the phonc out of his trouser's pocket. "Penny," he said as he answered the call.

Minutes later he told Kim that "an incompetent moron named Forester" was having a meltdown and needed some help. "Sorry," Travis said, "but this will take some time. He'll destroy the entire deal if I don't walk him through it. Do you mind?"

"Of course not," Kim said. "I'll wait for you outside." As she left the room, she picked up her sketchbook. Maybe she'd have an idea or two for her designs. She doubted that she would, since all she could think about was what Travis had said to her. Had he really planned his entire life around her? Was that possible? But then, a part of Kim wondered if she'd done the same thing. Not consciously, as Travis seemed to have done, but unconsciously. Since she was a child and began sneaking into her brother's room where there was an Internet connection that wasn't ruled by her mother's iron parental controls, Kim had been searching for him. Her quest to find Travis had fluctuated with how her personal life was going. After a breakup with a boyfriend she had cried, eaten ice cream, and spent whole days on the Internet.

Now she realized that she'd probably seen photos of the rich Travis Maxwell, but she hadn't given them a second glance. She'd long ago figured out that Travis and his mother had been running from an abusive father. No one ever thought of super rich young men as having been anything but pampered and spoiled. She'd kept her searches off the society pages.

As for what Travis said about their getting married, more than anything in the world, Kim wanted to throw her arms around his neck and say yes. But she couldn't do that. There were too many problems yet to solve. Travis was still too connected to his other life, to his bastard of a father. How could they be happy until all that was settled? And his mother was going to need a great deal of help. As much as they all loved Joe, he was a small town man; he'd never be a match for Travis's notorious father. Randall Maxwell was known all over the world as a man who held his own against anyone — on a global scale. How could Joe, the owner of a small hardware store, cope with that? Travis would have to step in and take care of it all. How long did it take to divorce a superwealthy man who didn't want to part with a dime? Years? How could she and Travis have a life when he was constantly wrapped up in that mess?

It seemed that the obstacles around them were insurmountable. Not that she'd give him up. Not ever. But it was a question of time before they'd have their own lives, their own home, their own . . . children.

When she stepped outside into the cool evening air, she took a breath. She reminded herself that no matter what the obstructions, they'd have each other and there was light at the end of the tunnel. The thought that she did have a future where she wasn't alone — as she'd started to fear — made her smile, and as she did, her mind began to clear. And as she had since she was a child, she began to think about jewelry. In the fading light the leaves on a nearby maple tree looked like moonstones. Or maybe cut quartz. Of course the ones in the shadows were pure garnets. She hadn't used garnets in a long time so maybe now was the time to start again.

There was a little seating area set back under the trees, and she sat down on a pretty wooden bench and began to draw what she saw in her mind. The stones, even the curve of the leaves reminded her of a woman's neck. She could make the gold flow along the skin, then angle up over a collarbone. If she did it right, the necklace could be really sensual. Of course each one would have to be fitted to the wearer, but that would be nice to do. She hated those necklaces that were a stiff, round circle. No one had a perfectly round neck and she thought the jewelry stood out awkwardly.

She was so busy with her thoughts and her drawing that she didn't see or hear anyone until a man almost tripped over her feet.

"I'm sorry," he said. "I didn't mean to disturb you."

Kim looked up to see a short, stout, sixty-ish man standing to her right and holding a broom. He had on an old pair of jeans and a plaid shirt that looked as though it had been washed hundreds of times. He was smiling at her in a way that reminded her of people at home.

"Please go back to what you were doing." He nodded toward her sketch pad in a way that made her think he was curious.

"I like the way the light plays on those maple leaves," she said.

"They are beautiful, aren't they?" He put his hands on the top of the broom handle and stared at the leaves. "Are you one of the people staying here?"

"I am."

"I don't mean to be nosy, but is it a family reunion? We don't usually have this many guests here."

Kim suppressed a laugh as she thought of the truth of why so many people were there. Travis had planned to oversee her and Dave. Only Dave had been sent away. "No," she said. "It's just my . . ." She wasn't sure what to call Travis. Her fiancé? But then he hadn't officially asked her to marry him, not with a ring (what Kim told the young men who wandered into her store was necessary for a proposal), and she certainly hadn't accepted.

"Your young man?" he asked.

It was an old-fashioned term that seemed to fit the situation. "Yes, my young man invited some people."

They were silent for a moment, then the man glanced at her sketchbook. "I'll let you get back to what you were doing, but if you need any help with anything, let me know. Just ask for Red. That's what my hair used to be." He started to walk away.

"We have that in common. Actually," Kim said, "maybe you can help us find someone."

Halting, he looked back at her. There was something about him that she liked. He had a sweet smile. "I have trouble keeping all the newcomers straight, but if the person is over forty I can probably help."

She smiled at his use of "newcomers." It was the same term they used in Edilean. "How about if the person died in 1893?"

"Then I probably went to school with him."

Kim laughed. "Dr. Tristan Janes. I assume the town was named after his family?"

"Yes it was," the man said as he motioned toward one of the empty chairs across from her. He was asking her permission to sit there.

"Please," she said.

As he took a seat, he said, "Will your young man mind that you're having a tête-à-tête with another man?"

"I'm sure he'll be wild with jealousy, but

I'll be able to calm his beastly spirit."

Red chuckled. "Spoken like a woman in love."

Kim couldn't help blushing. "What about Dr. Janes?"

"There used to be a library here, but when the mill closed the town pretty much died with it. They moved all the books and papers to the state capital. If they hadn't done that you could go to the library and read it all. I'm a poor second best. Anyway," he said, "a Mr. Gustav Janes started the town back in 1857 when he opened a mill that ground the flour for everyone in a fifty-mile radius. His only child, Tristan, became a doctor. I read that ol' Gustav, who couldn't read or write, was deeply proud of his son."

"As he should be," Kim said. "Tristan died young, didn't he?"

"He did. He was rescuing some miners and the walls collapsed on him. It took them a week to find his body. He was well loved and hundreds of people attended his funeral."

"And I'm sure that number included an ancestor of mine," Kim said. "It seems that she was carrying his child, who was my — let me get this straight — my great-granduncle."

"I think that makes you an honorary native of Janes Creek."

"Not a newcomer?"

"Far from it." In the distance they heard voices coming toward them, and Red stood up. "I think your young man is returning and I should go."

"The question everyone in my hometown wants to know is whether or not Dr. Janes was married."

"Oh no. I read that he was the town catch, a beautiful young man, but he never married. I'm sure that if he'd lived he would have married your ancestor. Especially if she was half as pretty as you are."

"Thank you," Kim said as Red started to walk away. "Oh!" she called out. "Do you know where he's buried?"

"All the Janes family are at the Old Mill. If you go out there, be careful. The place is falling down. Take companions with you. Big, strong ones."

"All right, I will," she said as he disappeared around a corner and out of sight.

To the left, on the other side of the dense hedge, came Travis, frowning as he spoke on his cell phone. But when he saw Kim he smiled and said, "Forester, just *do* it!" and hung up.

He held out his arm to Kim. "Ready for

dinner?"

"Yes," she said as they walked toward the main building.

Concealed in the bushes and watching them was the older man, Red. He was smiling.

"Sir?" said a man in a suit.

"What is it?" Red snapped.

"You have a call from Hong Kong and Mr. Forester needs —"

Red frowned. "My son took care of Forester. I need you to send someone to the state capital. I want to know everything about the Dr. Tristan Janes who died in 1893."

"In the morning I'll —"

Red gave the man a sharp look.

"I'll call the governor."

"You do that," Red said as he walked away from the hotel.

The man picked up the broom and followed Randall Maxwell to the waiting car.

The sound of the shower running woke Kim, and as memories came to her, she stretched luxuriously. Last night had been wonderful. At dinner a table had been set up for them on a little glassed-in porch, and Travis had chosen the meal ahead of time. They'd had three different wines with their six-course dinner. Outside, the stars sparkled and the moonlight flowed over the soft glow from the candles. By the dessert course they were feeding each other — and it was all Kim could do not to jump on Travis and rip his clothes off.

"Shall we retire to our rooms?" he asked before dessert was finished.

"If you're ready," Kim said in her most demure voice.

"I have been . . . ready for the last hour." He sounded like a man in pain.

Kim gave a very unadult giggle.

They managed to bid their server — the same young woman who'd checked Kim in — good night and didn't so much as touch each other on the long trip up the stairs. Travis opened the door and let Kim go in ahead of him. He closed the chain lock, and turned to look at her.

There were no words needed. She made a leap and was in his arms. Clothes flew across the room and puddled on the floor. By the time they'd covered the few steps to the bed they were naked. They came together with all the passion they felt. And five minutes after their mutual climax, they began again, this time exploring each other's bodies and finding what the other liked.

"What about this?" Travis whispered, his

hand between her legs.

"Yes, very much." Part of her still wished that they'd been together from the start of their adulthood. It would have been nice to learn about one another together. On the other hand, Travis knew some truly lovely things about a woman's body. He knew just what to do to take her to new heights of ecstasy, and keep her there.

As for Kim, she'd learned a thing or two also, and when she lowered her mouth onto the center of him, she was pleased by his gasp. Twenty minutes later she moved back up to his neck.

"Where did you learn to do that?" he asked, his eyes full of wonder.

"Late night TV," she said without cracking a smile.

Travis let her know he wasn't sure whether to believe her or not, but he liked thinking she'd learned from TV and not from another man.

"You make me crazy, you know that?" he said as he rolled her to her back and began kissing her.

They hadn't gone to sleep until 3:00 A.M. They'd fallen across each other, naked, sweaty, and as limp as rag dolls. At some point Travis had awakened. He moved Kim from lying crosswise on the bed, positioned her head on his shoulder, pulled the covers over them, and immediately went back to sleep.

It was morning now, and as Kim listened to the shower running, she kept smiling as she remembered last night.

Travis entered the room wearing a towel and drying his hair with another one. "You continue looking at me like that and I'll need another shower." He gave her a hot little look. "In an hour or so, that is."

Smiling, Kim stretched. "I had a good time last night."

"Yeah?" he said as he sat down on the bed beside her and stroked her hair back from her face. "I did too. How about if today we —"

"Oh!" she said and sat up straighter. "I forgot to tell you that I know where Tristan Janes is buried."

"That isn't what I was going to suggest we do, but we did come here for that purpose."

"Right. To find more of my relatives." Bending, he kissed her earlobe. "Maybe we could just call people named Janes and ask what they know."

Travis got up and headed for the bathroom. "I already checked the local phone book and I asked Penny. There are no Janeses left."

"When did you talk to her?" Kim asked.

"This morning while you were asleep," he called from across the room.

Kim glanced at the clock. It was a little after nine and she didn't think she'd ever slept so late in her life. When they were kids she and Travis had been outside before six. "Are you still a morning person?"

He put his head around the doorway, his cheeks covered in shaving foam. "I'm usually at the office by seven. What about you?"

"In my garage workshop at six."

"Of course I'm having breakfast by five," he said.

"Four-thirty for me."

"I'm in the gym at four."

"I don't bother to sleep at all," she said and they laughed together at their one-upmanship.

He came out of the bathroom, freshly shaved and nude. At Kim's look he paused in starting to dress, but then he turned away. "I don't know about you, but I'm starving."

As she started to get out of bed, she realized she too was naked and hesitated. Travis had his back to her but he was watching her in the mirror. It's not as though he hasn't seen me nude before, she thought as she threw back the cover and walked across the room with all the bravado she could muster. She paused at the bathroom door and looked back at him. He was buttoning his shirt — and he was smiling broadly.

She showered and washed her hair, copiously applying conditioner to make it as silky as she could. When she got out, she dried off, put on the hotel robe hanging from a hook on the door, and began to blow-dry her hair. Travis came in, fully dressed, and took the dryer from her. She was glad to see that he was a bit awkward with the big hand dryer — which meant he hadn't done such a domestic task before. As Kim bent her head forward and felt his hands on the back of her neck and in her hair, she didn't think she'd ever felt anything so sensual. There was something so very intimate, so private, about what he was doing that she thought it might possibly be sexier than sex. What a funny thought! Sexier than sex.

"What's that laugh for?" he asked as he turned the dryer off.

"Nothing, just silliness." Turning, she put her arms around his neck and kissed him. "Thanks," she said. "I enjoyed that."

"Me too." He ran his hands down the back of her body, and gave a pat to her rear end. "Get dressed so I can get some food! You wore me out last night." He left the bathroom.

"You?" she asked as she began putting on her makeup. "You spent most of the time on your back. I was the one doing all the work."

Travis looked around the doorjamb. "So what channels of TV do you watch when you stay up all night? I think we should watch them together."

"Go away," she said, laughing, "and let me get ready."

He went back into the bedroom and put on his watch. "So tell me how you found out where Janes is buried."

With a curler clasped to her lashes, she told him about meeting the caretaker, Red, and the highlights of what he'd told her. Minutes later, she was finished and went to the bedroom to get dressed. Travis sat down in a chair to watch the show.

"So who's here that we can take with us?" she concluded as she started to fasten her bracelet, but then held out her arm to Travis.

"The man said we should take someone big and strong with us? Is that in case a rock falls on one of us and the other can't pull it off?"

"I don't know why he said that. You think Russell is here?"

"Probably. And since I'm footing the bill, I'm sure he's eating truffles and Beluga."

"Sounds good to me," Kim said. "After we go see this Old Mill, maybe we can walk through town."

"And see if there are any jewelry stores to check out?"

"Exactly," Kim said, pleased that he knew that about her.

He smiled as he opened the door into the hallway, and they started down the stairs. "I think I'd enjoy that. Maybe we could find a ring that you'd like."

"I don't copy other people's work," she said stiffly. They were outside the main dining room, which Kim hadn't seen.

"I was thinking more of something you'd like to wear for the rest of your life."

"I —" She wanted to say more but was cut off by a chorus of good mornings. The dining room had eight tables, and all of them were occupied by people she'd never seen before. But they all seemed to know them, as they said hello to Travis and "Miss Aldredge." "You'll have to introduce me."

Travis nodded to a table for four. "That's Penny and you know her kid. I've never seen the rest of them."

"Your room fillers," she said, amused. When Travis went after something he didn't hold back; he covered all the bases. *Am I what he wants next?* she couldn't help wondering.

Penny — Mrs. Pendergast — looked at Kim and nodded toward the two empty chairs at their table. She was a handsome woman, younger-looking than Kim had expected. Her face was unlined, and she'd kept her slim figure, which she showed off in black linen trousers and a white shirt. Peeping out from under her hair, which fell softly to her collar, were the pearl earrings that Russell had bought in Kim's shop.

"Your choice," Travis said.

Kim didn't hesitate as she walked to the table and took a seat. Her eyes were on Mrs. Pendergast. "I've heard nothing but good about you," she said. "Travis doesn't seem able to conduct his life without you."

"He gets in trouble; Mom gets him out," Russell said.

Penny gave her son a look to stop it, but he just smiled.

"And I have heard about you for years," Penny said.

"Really?" Kim asked, surprised. "I had no idea that Travis had ever spoken of me to anyone."

"Did you show her the plaque?"

"Not yet," Travis said as he gave his order to the server. There was an antique sideboard against the wall that was covered with silver chafing dishes, but it looked like he wanted the meal served to him.

Penny leaned toward Kim. "If you want something from the buffet, you'd better get it now before my uncle Bernie eats it all." She nodded toward a corner table where a tall, skinny man was digging into three piled-high plates.

Kim excused herself and went to get scrambled eggs, sausages, and whole wheat toast. When she turned back toward the table, she paused to look at the three of them. Travis and Mrs. Pendergast had their heads together, talking quietly. Actually, she was talking while Travis nodded solemnly, a slight frown on his brow.

The familiarity between them didn't surprise her, but what did was seeing Travis and Russell next to each other. When Kim had last seen Russell she'd been too upset to comprehend much of anything, but now she saw the similarities between the two men. They were the same height, had the same dark hair and eyes, and when they reached for their coffee cups, their hands moved in exactly the same way. Having lived in Edilean all her life, if there was one thing Kim knew about it was relatives. It was easy to see that Travis and Russell were closely related.

With her eyes wide, Kim looked up to see Penny staring at her. Kim raised her brows, as though to ask if Travis knew. Penny gave one sideways movement of her head to say no, and her eyes were pleading. They said, Please don't tell him. Not yet.

Kim didn't like to keep secrets from Travis, but there was more here than she knew about. She gave a curt nod to Penny, then sat down.

Travis and Penny went on talking about what the "moron" in New York was doing about some deal. While it was interesting to see another side of him, Kim was more fascinated by the similarities between him and Russell. She watched Travis's hand gestures, the way he held a fork. When Russell spoke to his mother, she listened to his voice. It was very like Travis's deep resonance.

After a few moments of unabashedly staring, Kim felt Russ's eyes on her, and she looked at him. He was smiling at her as though they shared a secret — and it looked as though they did. A very *big* secret.

When Kim looked at Russell, he raised

his glass of OJ slightly, as though in salute to her. She couldn't help giving a little laugh. Unless she missed her guess, Travis had a half brother.

"Sorry," Travis said as he leaned away from Penny and looked at Kim. "We're ignoring you."

"No one is ignoring me," she said. "In fact I'm being well entertained." She turned to Penny. "Didn't you use to work for Travis's father?"

"For many years." Penny's eyes were alight, as though she was wondering what Kim was going to say next. Announce what she'd just figured out?

But Kim wasn't even tempted to tell. Hearing that he had a brother was going to change Travis's world, and *she* was not the one to tell him. That news needed to come from Russell and Penny — and a lot of explaining was going to have to be done.

"Maybe Russell could go with us today," Kim said.

"Go where?" He was looking at Kim as though he expected her to tell what she'd just discovered.

"To some derelict old building," Travis said. "Last night while I was working, the love of my life was flirting with another man, and he told her where to go today. He said that she'd need the help of someone big and strong. Kim seems to think that's *you.*" His tone was light and teasing.

His words "the love of my life" made Penny and Russell look hard at Kim. Penny glanced at Kim's left hand, obviously noting that there was no ring.

Kim knew there was more going on in the silence than in the words being spoken. "In case all of you forgot, I'm here to find my ancestor."

"And his possible descendants," Travis said.

"It seems that there's a grave site near an old mill, so Travis and I are going to go see it." She looked directly at Russell. "I think you should go with us. If this place is a ruin it'll be quiet there. A person can think. Or talk."

Russell gave a little smile. "I'm about talked out," he said and looked at his mother. "What about you? Finished with your New York business?"

"Completely," she said.

"Penny is going to retire," Travis said to Kim, "and she's thinking of moving to Edilean. Any good houses there for sale?"

"Old or new?" Kim asked.

"Old, small, on at least an acre. I like to garden. But I don't want it to be too far out of town."

"I know a place. It used to be an overseer's house. It would need some renovation." Kim turned to Russell. "And what about you? Where do *you* live?"

"Not in Edilean," he said as he put his napkin on the table and stood up. "When do you want to go to this falling down old building? Anyone bring a camera? Notebook and pen?"

Travis stood up to stand beside Russell. They were exactly the same build and wore the same expressions of challenge on their handsome faces.

Kim glanced at Penny. Why didn't Travis see the resemblance? Again Penny looked at Kim with that expression of pleading. Please don't tell, she seemed to be saying.

Kim hadn't made herself a success by being intimidated by anyone, no matter who she worked for. "Tomorrow," she said softly, and Penny nodded. She had twenty-four hours to tell Travis the truth and if she didn't, Kim would tell him.

Travis was waiting for her by the door. "Russ rented a Jeep and he went to get directions." He lowered his voice. "Kim, if you'd rather that you and I spend time alone together, I can turn this whole thing over to Penny. She'll find out about Dr. Janes."

"No," Kim said. "I think you should —" She'd almost said "get to know your brother" but she didn't. She wondered how he was going to react when he found out that his beloved assistant had had an affair with his father. Travis already had enough issues with his father and he didn't need any more.

"Think I should what?"

"Nothing. Here's Russ. Shall we go?"

Travis wanted to drive, but Russell wouldn't let him. "My car, my hands on the wheel," he said.

Kim rode in front with Russ. Travis was in back with the handwritten directions.

"Looks like you failed penmanship," Travis said. "I can't read this."

"Maybe you should have gone to better schools to improve your comprehension," Russ shot back. "Oh wait. I went to the same ones you did."

"Did you pass any of the classes?" Travis mumbled.

Kim looked out the window to hide her smile. They sounded like her and Reede.

The Old Mill was beautiful. It was wide and low, U-shaped, with the middle part one story, flanked by two-story sections. The building had a low stone wall along the front, which made a courtyard in the center of the U.

For a few moments the three of them stood, looking at the wonderful old building. Part of it had no roof and doves flew out when they walked up. But the two-story section on the left had new tiles on the roof. The little stone wall looked to be falling down, but in places the rocks had been replaced.

"Someone's been working on it," Travis said.

"*That* is perfect," Kim said. She was pointing inside the courtyard to the right. There, behind another low stone wall was a perfect little garden — except that it looked like something out of an eighteenth-century book about gardening. It had gravel paths laid out in the shape of a double circle with an X through it. Inside the eight quarters were wild, weedy-looking plants of different colors, heights, and textures. They had all been carefully, meticulously tended.

"Unless I miss my guess, those are medicinal herbs," Kim said, grinning, "and that means there's still a Tristan here."

Travis and Russ looked at each other, then back at Kim.

"What does that mean?" Russ asked.

"The Tristans are doctors so . . ." Kim said.

"Medicinal herbs," Travis finished for her. "All the Tristans have the greenest thumbs imaginable. When we were kids we made Tris plant things for us. If he planted them they grew for sure. When the rest of us put anything in the ground, half the time it didn't grow."

"So maybe a descendant owns this place," Russ said.

A tile came rattling down from the roof, hit the ground, and broke.

"One who can't afford to restore it," Travis said, looking at Kim. "I think you are going to find some relatives here."

She looked at Russ. "Finding new relatives — ones you didn't know you had — can be very rewarding, don't you think?"

"It can also be terrifying," he said softly. "Traumatic."

"Possibly. But then I always find truth to be better than deep secrets."

"Depends on the truth," Russ said. His eyes were laughing, as though he were greatly enjoying the exchange.

Travis had walked away to the center of the building and pushed open a door. "Are you two going to spend the day in some cryptic, philosophical exchange or are we going to look around?"

"I vote that you scale this wall and walk along the ridgepole. Show us what you learned in Hollywood," Russ said.

"Only if you show us that you know how to do anything at all," Travis shot back as he went through the doorway.

Russ went to the door, and turned back to Kim. "Are you coming?"

"I . . ." There was something about the herb garden that she liked. Maybe it was the shape of it, or the light on the yellow-green leaves of one of the plants, but she was glad she had her sketch pad with her.

Travis came back to the door, and went to Kim. "Why don't you stay here and draw? The kid and I will find the cemetery and record everything." He kissed the top of her head.

She was grateful to him for understanding. When a spurt of creativity hit, it needed all her attention. To put it off might allow it to disappear. And too, unlike her history-loving cousins, Kim couldn't abide cemeteries. "Thank you," she said.

"Don't leave here, don't talk to strangers, and —"

"And don't eat any of those plants," Russ said.

"I'll try to behave myself," Kim said as

she shooed them away. She really did want to put those shapes down on paper.

Travis kissed her again, this time on the cheek, then went to the door.

"I thought you were a ladies' man," Kim heard Russell say, "but you don't even know where to kiss the girl."

"I could show you a lot about . . ." She heard Travis say as their voices faded into the distance.

Kim sat down on a flat stone near the plants she most admired. They were tall, with seed-filled heads that looked as delicate as rays of sunshine. She pulled out her phone, snapped a photo of one of them, and sent it to her cousin Tristan. WHAT IS THIS? she wrote.

Kim started sketching, translating the shapes into jewelry. The chain would be made of long, thin tendrils, like the leaves of the plant. She drew a curved shape with tiny spirals inside it that would clasp one edge of the chain. She'd put a pearl at the center of each one. The earrings had a thin leaf that would curve up a woman's ear.

Her phone buzzed; it was Tristan. ANGELICA, he wrote. WHERE DID YOU SEE THAT?

Standing, she stepped back to get a full view of the garden. When she couldn't get a good photo that showed the design of it, she climbed on the surrounding wall, snapped, and sent it to Tris.

When she started to get down, the loose rocks slid under her feet, which flew out from under her. She would have fallen but a strong arm caught her.

It was Red from the B&B.

"Are you all right?" he asked as he helped her down.

"Fine, but thanks."

"I told you this place was dangerous," he said, his tone sounding severe. "Last year a woman nearly broke her leg here."

Kim sat down in the shade on an old doorsill.

"Don't lean back," he said. "That door doesn't look to be securely on its hinges."

She wiped dirt off her trousers and flicked sand out of her hair. "Are you the town watchdog?"

"More or less," he said. "I was on the way to the garage but made a detour by here. Looks like my worry paid off. You didn't come here alone, did you?"

"No. I have two big strong men with me."

He laughed. "Your young man and . . . ?"

"His —" She hesitated. "His friend."

"But not yours?" Bending, Red picked up her sketchbook. "May I?"

She gestured that it was all right for him

to look at what she'd drawn.

"These are pretty," he said as he brushed off some dirt. "Do you make these into jewelry?"

"Yes. I have a shop in Edilean. That's in —"

"Virginia!" he said. "I used to go fishing there. Nice little town. I like the old houses. I don't remember a jewelry store, but I do remember a place that sold baby clothes." Red sat down on the low wall. "Why would I remember that?"

"Because they are extraordinary," Kim said. "The shop is called Yesterday and it's owned by a lovely woman, Mrs. Olivia Wingate."

"Does she make the clothes?"

"No. Lucy makes most of them."

"Lucy Wingate?"

"No. She's . . ." Kim trailed off. Everything about Lucy was too much of a secret to talk about. "Do you know who owns this place?" She gestured at the Old Mill.

"I'm not sure," he said. "I've seen a young woman here, but I don't know who she is."

"She's under forty?"

He smiled at her good memory. "Yes, she is. I'm sure you could find the property records in the county courthouse."

"Today? Saturday?"

"Oh. Right," he said. "But then, you don't want to waste your time with your young man in a dusty old courthouse, do you?"

"No," Kim said, "I don't, especially since we don't have much time together before he —" She waved her hand.

Red looked concerned. "You sound like he's ill. Oh, my dear, please say that isn't so."

"No, no," Kim said. "He just . . ."

"He's in the military? Facing combat?"

"No," Kim said. "He has some personal business he has to take care of, so he has to leave."

Red sighed in relief. "That doesn't sound so bad."

Kim snorted. "It has to do with his father and from what I've heard . . ." Again, she waved her hand. "That's . . ."

"I understand. It's private, but there's a reason that I'm known around town as everyone's grandfather. I'm a good listener."

Kim smiled. "That's what Travis says he is."

"And is he?"

"Yes, very good."

"Does he have other good qualities?"

"Of course. Lots of them."

"Then perhaps . . ." He trailed off.

"Perhaps what?"

"Sometimes children can't see their parents clearly. They remember that their mother wouldn't let them eat what they liked. What they don't remember is that they wanted to eat paint flaking off an old wall."

From what she'd heard, Travis's father hadn't been around enough to know what his son was eating. Was he having an affair with Mrs. Pendergast all those years? But she couldn't say any of that to anyone, especially not to a stranger.

Red stood up. "I believe I hear your young men returning, so I better go."

Kim got up. "Stay and meet them."

"Maybe this evening," he said as he began to walk quickly. "I just remembered that I have a hundred pounds of ice in the back of the truck."

"It's probably melted by now," she called after him as she watched him hurry out of sight.

"Were you talking to someone?" Travis asked as he came back into the courtyard, Russ behind him.

"The caretaker from the B&B stopped by. He —" She broke off as her phone buzzed. It was from Tristan.

GORGEOUS GARDEN. I WANT TO MEET WHOEVER MADE IT. I SEE COMFREY. IS IT

POSSIBLY BOCKING 14? I NEED SOME TO MAKE COMPOST TEA.

She gave the phone to Travis, he read it, and handed it to Russ. All three of them looked at the herb garden. To a person who knew nothing about herbs, the plants looked very much alike. How could he pick out one from a cell phone photo?

"Told you," Kim said. "There's a Tristan here. So what did you guys find out?"

Travis spoke first. "Dr. Tristan Janes, born 1861, died 1893, aged thirty-two years." He turned to Russell. "What did it say on the stone about him?"

" 'A Well-Loved Man,' " Russ answered. "Not a bad thing to have people say about you. Sorry, but there was no evidence of a wife or kids."

"His father was named —"

"Gustav," Kim supplied.

"Right," Travis said. "No doubt that was told to you by the mysterious man named Red."

"What's mysterious about him?"

"Just that he disappears whenever we show up," Travis said.

"He's probably heard you're a Maxwell and he runs away," Russ said. "Smart man."

Kim squinted her eyes at Russell. He was as much a Maxwell as Travis was.

Russ gave a one-sided grin. He understood Kim's meaning perfectly. "So what do we do now?"

"*We* don't do anything," Travis said. "*You* are going to walk around town and ask questions until you find the owner of this old place. Kim and I are going to look at jewelry."

"Oh?" Russ asked, an eyebrow raised.

"For designs," Kim said quickly.

Travis pulled her arm through his. "Keys," he said to Russell, his hand extended.

"I need to —"

"Keys!" Travis said in a voice meant to be obeyed.

Russ laughed. "Big — Maxwell commands." He tossed Travis the car keys.

Kim was sure Russ had been about to say that "big brother commands."

With a grin, Russ winked at Kim.

He's enjoying this, she thought. And he's going to delight in dropping this brotherly bombshell on Travis.

When they were in the car, Kim asked Travis what he and Russ had talked about when they were alone.

"Nothing much, why?"

"Did you two keep arguing the whole time you were there?"

"Naw," he said, smiling. "That's all done

for your benefit. He was actually good help. There are only six headstones in the little cemetery, and I took photos while Russ wrote down names and dates. I guess your friends will want all the data."

"I'm sure they will," Kim said.

"So what did you do, other than meet a man in secret?"

She ignored his comment as she opened her sketchbook. They had reached the center of the little town and Travis expertly parallel parked the car, turned off the engine, and took the book to look at Kim's designs.

"So this slides around a woman's neck?" he asked.

"Yes, and the earrings go up."

"Not down? Not grazing her shoulders?"

"I'm not much on chandelier earrings."

"Me neither. They get in a man's way." He leaned across the seat and kissed her earlobe. She had on small gold earrings with stones of citrine just off center.

She smiled at him, glad he'd really looked at her drawings. Most people just glanced at them and said how pretty they were, but they couldn't actually visualize her designs.

"Want to wander through every store or go directly to the one and only jewelry shop in town?"

She looked at him in disbelief. "Don't tell me you're a man who likes going shopping with women? Going in and out of stores and looking at every little thing in the shop?"

"Well, I . . ." He looked out the windshield.

"Oh, I see. You're just being polite. You added the jewelry bit on the end to entice me there."

"I'm glad you're not a judge in a courtroom or I'd never be able to put anything over on you. I tell you what, today is yours. I'll go in and out of every one of these insufferably cute little stores, but in the future . . ."

"I'm on my own? You'll get a beer while I wander?"

"Pretty much," he said, and they smiled at each other. That they were speaking as though their future together was set in place, a given, a done deal, was pleasing to both of them.

They got out of the car and stood on the sidewalk, holding hands. So normal, Kim thought. So . . . so satisfyingly, deeply *normal.*

"Where to first?" Travis asked.

"There." Kim pointed to a used bookstore across the street. Its windows were covered in years of dirt and the few books she could see had curled, faded covers.

"Local history, right?" Travis asked. When Kim nodded, he raised her hand and kissed it. "Jewelry store last? To be savored?"

"Exactly," she said.

In the bookstore Kim was glad to see that Travis didn't mind going through boxes that had twenty years of dust coating them and digging for out-of-print books and local pamphlets. He found a cookbook put together in the twenties by the women of a local church.

They looked through it, saw there was no contributor named Janes, so Kim said it was no use to them. But Travis said a person never knew when relatives were going to turn up. Kim started to ask what he meant by that but he'd walked away.

He talked with the shop owner while Kim went through the shelves of books on the history of jewelry. She chose a big one on Peter Carl Fabergé.

They left the store with a box full of books, and Travis put them in the Jeep he'd commandeered from Russell.

"Do you think he walked?"

"Who?" Travis asked.

"Russell. You left him there at the Old Mill without transportation. Do you think he walked to . . . to wherever he went?"

"Probably called Penny and she picked him up," Travis said.

"So how long has she worked for you?" They were crossing the street again.

"Since I started at my dad's."

"And your father let her go so she could work for *you?*"

"Why all these questions?"

"I'm just trying to find out about your life, that's all."

He paused in front of a little shop that had some very pretty clothes in the window. "When my dad rooked me into working for him, Penny said she was going to help me. Dad didn't want to let her go, but she threatened to quit if he didn't, and since she knows more about the business than he does, he couldn't allow that."

"Why was she so adamant about working for you?"

"Felt sorry for me, I guess. I'd just come from Hollywood and my way of handling things was physical. I had trouble even remembering my law training."

"But Mrs. Pendergast took you under her wing and mothered you?"

Travis snorted. "She kicked me fifty times a day. Made me think. Made me put my anger at my father aside enough so that I could do the job. That first year was hell. Do you like that?"

"That your first year was bad?"

"No. I mean that shirt. Those pants. I think you'd look good in them."

"And trying them on would stop me from interrogating you, wouldn't it?"

"I never want to go against you in a courtroom." His hand was on her back as he urged her toward the doorway.

They spent two hours going from one store to another. For all that Travis had said he didn't like such things, he was a dream to shop with. He sat down and waited while Kim tried on clothes, and he gave his opinion on each one.

But for all that he seemed to give his full attention to her, twice he was on his phone, and each time he erased a frown when he saw her. She asked what was going on.

"Closing up business. You ready for lunch?"

As Kim turned away, she was reminded of all that was still facing them, especially the court case for the divorce. "Sure," she said as Travis opened the door for her.

But as soon as they were outside, his phone rang again. "Damn!" he muttered as he looked at it. "It's Penny. I . . ." He looked at Kim in question.

"Take it," she said. "I'll meet you at the diner." But she saw a flash of movement in the window of an antiques shop across the road. It was Mrs. Pendergast's arm, and she was waving at Kim, a phone to her ear.

Kim looked at Travis's back, then at Mrs. Pendergast. She was motioning for Kim to come to the store. They *did* need to talk.

"Thirty minutes, the diner," Kim said to Travis, and he nodded as he frowned at the call, and Kim hurried across the road.

Joe Layton took a couple of deep breaths as he picked up the phone receiver in his office. He was a believer in land lines. Their connections were better, less likely to fade out, and since the call he was about to make would change his — and Lucy's — life, he wanted to hear every word.

It had been simple to get the number of the headquarters of Maxwell Industries, but getting the man himself on the phone wasn't going to be easy. Joe thought maybe he'd tell whoever answered the phone that it was a matter of life and death. That way he'd keep the truth between him and Maxwell. But the snooty woman who was at the end of the line of a long succession of secretaries brought out the truth in Joe.

"You can't just call and expect to speak

directly to Mr. Maxwell." Her tone was patronizing, but at the same time amused. It was obvious that she saw herself as Big City while Joe was Country Bumpkin.

Joe was fed up with all of them. "Tell him I'm the man who wants to marry his wife."

The secretary was silent for a moment, then her tone changed to brisk efficiency. "I'll see if he's available."

It was only moments before Randall Maxwell was on the line. "So you're Joe Layton."

"Looks like nobody's kept a secret from you," Joe said.

"Not if I want to know what's going on, they can't. So what's Lucy up to now?"

"I want to settle this thing between you and me."

"By 'thing' do you mean a divorce?" Randall asked.

"Yes, that's exactly what I mean."

"Layton, you weren't born yesterday," Randall snapped in a voice that often intimidated people. "There's more involved in this than just a few grand."

Joe wasn't intimidated in the least. "Keep your money," Joe growled. "Keep every goddamn cent of it."

"That's an interesting concept. What about the money she stole from me?"

"You mean the money you so conveniently left for her to find?"

Randall chuckled. "Lucy always did like clever men."

Joe didn't answer. When Lucy told him about "accidently" seeing her husband's laptop with his online banking account left wide open, Joe knew Maxwell had meant for her to see it. Lucy said there was five million in the account and she took three and a half. Joe admired her restraint. She spoke of how unusual it had been for Randall to leave his laptop where she could see it. "He must have been under a lot of stress." There was guilt in her voice, showing that she felt bad for what she'd done. The idea that half of what Randall Maxwell owned was hers didn't seem to have entered her mind.

If Maxwell had purposefully left the account open, he'd done it for a reason. If Lucy were a different kind of woman Joe would have thought that Maxwell suspected her of seeing other men and that he wanted to know where she went when she had money. But as Joe heard more of Lucy's story, he thought it was possible that Maxwell was giving his wife freedom.

Maybe Maxwell thought he'd failed with his son, so he no longer needed to use Lucy to hold Travis to him. If Joe knew anything in life it was the pleasure/pain you got from your family. He loved his son with all his heart, but there were times when the boy's wife made Joe want to disown him.

"So how's Travis?" Randall asked into the silence.

There was a soft undertone in his voice that told Joe a lot. Maxwell loved his son very much. "He's a good kid," Joe said. "You raised him right."

It was Randall's turn for a moment of silence. "Lucy can keep the money and I'll give her a divorce — and I'll be fair with her."

Joe drew in his breath. "If by that you mean you'll give her more millions, *don't!* Save it for Travis — and your other kid that I've been seeing around town. Seems his mother is your former secretary. Must have been convenient for you."

Randall laughed. "Layton, you ever want a job with me, you got it."

"No thanks," Joe said, but he was grinning as he hung up.

Fourteen

"So what questions do you have for me?" Penny asked Kim.

They were sitting at a rusty old table outside the back of the antiques store. There was a tall wooden fence on three sides, and leaning against it were dozens of old metal advertising signs. The Mobil Pegasus was directly behind Penny's perfectly coiffed head.

The first thing Kim was aware of was that Mrs. Pendergast had put herself in the position of power. Her chair's back was facing the fence, a solid barrier, while Kim's back was to the door and windows of the store, a more vulnerable position. But more important than that, Penny's words had cast Kim as the one who was to ask the questions and maybe she'd receive answers.

Kim wasn't falling for it. First, she moved her chair so that she was no longer backed against the openness of the store, then she looked at Penny. "I want you to tell me everything."

Penny gave a bit of a smile in acknowledgment of what Kim had done, and shrugged. "Late night, champagne to celebrate a deal, handsome boss, fight with my boyfriend. It all went together to make it happen."

"And afterward?" Kim asked.

Penny took her time in replying, and Kim doubted that she'd ever told the story before. Mrs. Pendergast didn't seem to be the type to share intimate details of her life with anyone.

"That wasn't so easy. I didn't realize I was pregnant until I was four months along. By that time the boyfriend was gone and besides, Randall was . . ."

"Married."

"Yes. Married to a woman who couldn't care less about him or his business, his dreams, or about anything else to do with him." There was a hint of bitterness in her voice.

"So that makes it all right to jump into bed with him?" Kim asked. She was on Lucy's side.

"When you get older you're going to learn that there are always two sides to everything. Lucy married Randall Maxwell because her family pressured her into it. They were an old family, great lineage, but not a cent to their names. Randall supported her parents until their deaths, and he still pays the bills of Lucy's two lazy brothers."

Kim looked down at the table for a moment. "Why did he keep Travis so isolated?"

"Randall had a hard childhood. He was very poor and he's a bit dyslexic. He was bullied in school."

"So he gave his son tutors and privacy?"

"That's it," Penny said.

Kim was silent as she waited for Penny to continue. It was obvious that the older woman didn't want to go on — or maybe she did. Penny had been the one who set up the meeting, so maybe she was hoping Kim would help smooth the way between Travis and Russell.

"Randall thought he was doing well by his son when he had him homeschooled," Penny began. She looked down at her hands. "I know you're friends with Lucy, but . . ."

"I can take the truth, whatever it is."

"I think that at the beginning Randall believed he was in love with Lucy, but the truth was, he was in love with the idea of a family. He had visions of the two of them conquering the world together. He'd make the money, buy her a magnificent house, and she'd be the hostess who was renowned for her dinner parties. It would be like something out of a magazine."

"From what I've seen of Lucy's life now, that wouldn't be for her. She likes to sew and stay with a few close friends."

"Exactly," Penny said. "And Randall likes to *work.* And besides, he hates dinner parties. He loved the thought of them, but couldn't bear the boredom when he was there."

Kim was beginning to see the whole picture. Two extremely mismatched people married to each other. Lucy bullied by her relatives, almost sold by them, to a man who had a chip on his shoulder and something to prove to the world.

It looked like Travis had been caught in the middle.

"What about you? Where do you come in?" Kim asked.

"I . . ." Penny hesitated. "I'm more like Randall than Lucy. I also grew up poor and was desperate to get out of it. I met Randall at a party. I liked him because he was talking business instead of hitting on the girls. I stood to one side and unabashedly eavesdropped. He was so intent on the deal he was trying to make that I didn't think he even saw me. But when the other young men got bored and left, Randall turned to me and said, 'Did you get all that?' I said, 'Most of it,' and told him the numbers. He looked at me for a moment, then asked for my phone number and I gave it to him."

"I guess he called you."

"Yes," Penny said, smiling, "and it was all business. It's always been business between us."

"Except once."

Penny smiled broadly. "And that gave me Russell."

"Was Mr. Maxwell married when you met him?"

"No," Penny said. "He hadn't even met Lucy back then, but he knew what he wanted and he went after it."

"If you two were so alike, why didn't he . . . ?"

"Look at me as a prospective mate?" Penny laughed. "You'd have to know Randall back then. Ambition ate at him. Consumed him. He *had* to get ahead of everyone else or he'd die."

"And Lucy was part of that," Kim said.

"She was indeed."

"But there came a night . . ." Kim said.

Penny shrugged. "When I look back on it, I see that it was inevitable. Randall and I were always together. Travis was just a year old, and I have to say that I was quite jealous of Lucy. I never had time for an outside life and never did find a man who'd put up with my constant working. Anyway, Randall and I stayed late at the office, we had sex, and I was pregnant."

"What did Mr. Maxwell say when you told him?"

Penny shook her head in memory. "He was thrilled. Lucy's pregnancy had been complicated and she couldn't have more children, so Randall was happy to have another child. He wanted to put the two kids together."

"You are kidding, aren't you?"

"Not at all. Randall doesn't live by other people's rules. But in the end I persuaded him to keep his mouth shut, but still Lucy always knew there was something going on between us. She always sneered at me and I never retaliated because I deserved it."

"And you and Mr. Maxwell?"

"We never slept together again, if that's what you mean. And he rarely slept with Lucy. He did what he was so good at and provided lavishly for all of us. I lived modestly but gave my son the best education there was."

"And Russell knows who his father is,"

Kim said.

"Always has. I never hid it from him."

"Did they spend time together?"

"Randall spent as much time with my son as he did with Lucy's. He's not a TV father who tucks the kids in at night."

"And you continued to work for Mr. Maxwell. Does he have any more children anywhere?"

"No. None. Randall's always had affairs, but he's never been serious about any of the women, and he was discreet."

Kim thought for a moment. "He had Lucy at home and you at work and two beautiful sons. I can see why he didn't want to mess that up."

Penny smiled. "I think you're beginning to understand Randall Maxwell."

"Why did he blackmail Travis into working for him?"

Penny's face became serious. "Now that is the clog in Randall's overall life plan. He assumed that when they grew up, both his sons would come to work for him, but neither one wanted anything to do with him. Travis was very angry at his father and Randall couldn't understand why. In his mind, he'd protected Travis all his life."

"And Travis saw himself as being held captive in a beautiful prison."

"That's right. Randall's much better at business than he is at life. I told him not to do it, but he threatened Travis to make him work with him. Randall thought that if Travis was in the office with him every day, he'd catch his ambition bug and that eventually his son would understand."

"But he didn't," Kim said.

"No. Travis had been sidetracked by a little girl who showed him how to have fun."

Kim smiled. "That was a turning point in both our lives." Her head came up. "So what happens now? How do we tell Travis that Russell is his brother?"

"I'm not sure he doesn't know."

"I've not seen any sign that he does."

"Both of them are half Maxwell and they don't let people see what they're thinking."

"Not even me," Kim said softly.

"You didn't exactly blurt out the facts when you realized the truth, did you? From what I've seen, you and Travis are well matched."

Kim thought about that for a moment. "So what now? Will it take Travis years of fighting his father to help Lucy get a divorce?"

"I don't know what Randall is up to right now. He's been very secretive lately. In fact, for the first time in nearly thirty years I don't even know where he is."

There was something about the way she said that last statement that made Kim's hair stand on end. "You wouldn't have a photo of Mr. Maxwell, would you?"

"I can bring one up on my phone," she said as she removed her cell from her bag. "Randall likes to stay out of the spotlight."

"Unlike Travis," Kim said, remembering the photos Reede had sent her. "So how's Leslie?"

"Paid off," Penny said as she handed the phone to Kim.

She wasn't surprised to see a picture of the man she knew as Red, but she wasn't about to say that Mr. Maxwell was here in Janes Creek. "He doesn't look much like Travis or Russell," she said as she returned the phone.

"The boys look like Randall's grandfather, and he was a handsome devil. Have you — ?"

Kim stood up so abruptly Penny didn't finish her question. "Travis is going to think I've left him. I was supposed to meet him at the diner fifteen minutes ago. This has been . . . informative, and thanks for helping me understand Travis better." She gathered up her things and hurried into the antiques store. She hadn't wanted to answer

Mrs. Pendergast's questions about whether she'd met Randall Maxwell or not. Yes, she had. Twice.

Outside the shop, she paused for a moment, trying to remember everything "Red" had said to her. Fishing in Edilean came to mind first. It looked like he'd known all along where Lucy was. And if he knew where she was, then he knew about Joe Layton. And if he did, and if he hadn't raised a stink, maybe that meant Travis wouldn't have to spend years helping his mother get a divorce.

"Maybe we can have a *life,*" she whispered. Now. Not years in the future, but now. She went across the street to the diner, but she didn't walk fast. She had a lot of information running through her mind and the truth was that she didn't know what to do with it all. How much should she tell Travis? How much to keep to herself?

And what would be his reaction to what she did tell him? Anger? He was from a rich and powerful family, so would he jump on a private jet and go . . . Go do whatever fabulously rich people did when faced with stress?

The picture of Travis in a tuxedo with a blonde model haunted her. Was that his *real* life? Had Travis adapted to the glamorous

New York life better than his father thought he had?

Kim knew that whatever happened she needed to keep her cool. She couldn't go running to the two sons of Randall Maxwell and gush about what she'd just been told. Would they smile at her in an indulgent way and say they knew all that? That they'd figured it out long ago? Kim didn't think she could bear that humiliation.

She stopped outside the door to the diner and took a deep breath. She needed to keep a straight face and do what the Maxwell boys did and keep secrets to herself.

There were few people in the diner, and Travis and Russell stood out. They were at a little round wooden table close to a wall, with their backs to her. There was a big bowl of popcorn between them and they were eating and drinking beer as they looked up at a TV screen. A soccer match was playing and both men seemed totally absorbed in it.

Yet again, Kim marveled at how alike the two men were. If they changed clothes, and she saw them from the back, she wondered if she could tell them apart.

Travis turned and saw her. For a moment he looked at her so hard she thought he knew where she'd been. But then his face relaxed, he smiled, and moved a chair out for her.

"You didn't buy anything?" he asked.

"Buy . . . ?" She had to remember that she did go to a store. "I didn't see anything I liked."

Russell was staring at her. "You look like something happened."

"Just looking forward to the company of two gorgeous men," Kim said quickly. So much for keeping secrets, she thought. "So what's good to eat here?" she asked.

"We waited for you," Travis said. He was still looking at her as though he was trying to read her mind. "Ol' Russell here has something to show us, but he wanted to wait until you were here."

Kim refused to meet Travis's eyes. She didn't want him seeing more than she wanted him to know. "That sounds interesting. What is it?"

Russell got up from the table and went to the side wall where there was a package, about two feet by three feet, wrapped in brown paper. As he picked it up and began to open it, he put his back to them so they couldn't see what he had. When he turned around, he was holding what was obviously a picture and from the look of the back of the canvas, it was quite old. He held it facing him, concealing it from them.

"Ever the showman," Travis said.

"You should talk, Maxwell," Russell said as he looked at Kim. "I was curious about these Dr. Tristans so I did a search and some photos came up. Distinctive-looking man is your cousin."

Kim couldn't help smiling. That was one way of putting it about her cousin's extraordinary beauty.

Still looking at Kim, Russell turned the picture around, and she gasped. The man in the portrait looked very much like her cousin Dr. Tristan Aldredge. "Is that him? The doctor who was killed in the mine?" she asked.

Russell leaned the portrait against the wall and took his seat at the table. They were all three facing it. "That's James Hanleigh, born 1880, died 1982."

"But . . ." Kim began. "He really does look like my cousin Tristan."

Travis looked back at the two of them. "Wrong side of the blanket?"

"That's my guess," Russell said. He started to say more but the waitress came to take their orders. Kim ordered a club sandwich and Travis got crab cakes with a triple order of coleslaw and a beer. She wasn't the least surprised when Russell said he'd have the same. She tried not to glance at him but she couldn't help herself. As she knew he would be, Russell's eyes were dancing with merriment. She wanted to kick him under the table.

Their lunch conversation was about how the portrait had been found. It seemed that Russell's uncle Bernie had discovered it.

"I needed to give him something to do to work off all that food," Russell said. "He told me that last night he'd run off some photos of the present Dr. Tristan Aldredge that he'd found online, passed them around to his mother's relatives, and told them to see if anyone in town recognized him. Sometimes blood relatives look like each other," Russell said — and again he looked at Kim with a smile.

"And he found this portrait in one of the stores?" Travis asked.

"No. That would be too easy. He found some old man who said he thought maybe he'd seen a picture of Dr. Aldredge but he couldn't remember where. Uncle Bernie sent relatives out looking and asking and —"

"This all happened while we were at the Old Mill?" Travis asked.

"Every bit of it. I think my relatives were like a locust invasion on little Janes Creek."

"And where did they find it?" Kim asked.

"In the home of a little old lady who bought it at a yard sale thirty years ago for fifty bucks."

"How much?" Travis asked.

"Fifty —"

"No, how much did I have to pay for it?"

"Twelve grand."

"What?!" Kim said.

"She drove a hard bargain," Russell said, obviously enjoying himself, "and besides, she needed a new roof."

"I'll reimburse —" Kim began but stopped at the look Travis gave her.

"So how is he related and how does he fit in the family tree?" Travis asked.

"I haven't found that out yet. Give me the afternoon and at dinner I'll tell you everything."

"So you don't know if there are any Hanleighs still in town?" Travis's tone was that of a challenge.

"Not yet." Russell was calm, amused even.

Kim kept her attention on her food. Her mind was so full of all that Mrs. Pendergast had told her that she couldn't think about finding the descendant of some young man who may or may not be her relative.

When they finished eating, Travis asked if she was ready to go to the jewelry store.

For a moment she had no idea what he was talking about and stared at him blankly.

He smiled at her, his eyes alight. "I agree," he said in a voice that could only be described as seductive. Travis looked at Russell. "Kim and I are going to . . ."

"Take a nap," Russell said.

"Well put," Travis said as he backed his chair out, and held out his arm to Kim. "Thanks for lunch and we'll see you at dinner."

Travis led her out of the diner and to the car. The ride back to the B&B was silent.

Kim knew that Travis was hinting at sex. And why shouldn't he? It was a romantic little town, a charming B&B. They were young and by all accounts in love, so they *should* be spending every waking moment together in bed. Isn't that what she'd told her brother that she wanted? What had she said? *"I'll take all the passionate sex I can get. Days of it. Weeks if I can get it. Months would be divine."*

So now she had it and what she *really* wanted was to call her friend Jecca and spend about four hours on the telephone. Right now what Kim needed more than anything else was the release that discussion would bring.

So maybe I should find Red and ask him

for advice, she thought. Ask the man who caused all the problems how to fix them? She gave a snort of laughter.

"What was that about?" Travis asked as he parked the car.

"Nothing," she said as she got out.

He held her hand as they went up the stairs to their connecting rooms. Once they were inside, he bent to kiss her, but Kim pushed back.

"Sorry," she said. "I have a . . . a headache and I think I should lie down for a while."

Travis stepped away from her. "Can I get you anything?"

"No, nothing," Kim said. "I just need some time . . . alone."

"Sure, of course," he said. He walked to the door to his room, opened it, went through and shut it behind him.

Kim looked at the bed. Maybe if she took a nap she'd feel better, but she knew she couldn't sleep. Mrs. Pendergast's words ran through her head. How much to tell? How much to hide? How much to — ?

"No!" Travis said from the open door. "This isn't all right. None of it is. Something happened to you today and I want to know what it is."

"I can't —"

"So help me, if you say you can't tell me, I'll —"

"You'll *what?*" she shot at him, her voice rising with every word. "Leave? Walk away when things get too much for you? Disappear like you did before? Leave me alone, without a word? Let me search for you for *years* and all the time you were sneaking around at my art shows? Is *that* what you'll do?"

"No," he said softly. "I won't do that ever again. But right now, what I am going to do is stay in this room with you until you tell me what's tearing you up inside."

"I . . ." Her anger left her and she sat down on the side of the bed, her hands over her face.

Travis sat down beside her and put his arm around her, drawing her head to his shoulder. "Does this have to do with Russell being my half brother?"

Kim hesitated for only a second. "How did . . . ?"

"I've not had a lot of experience with relatives, but I'm a good observer. Who else can look at you with the hatred Russ had for me that first day? It was like looking in a mirror, except that one reflection wanted to murder the other one."

Kim let out a deep sigh of relief that he

knew. When her body relaxed, Travis turned her around on the bed so they stretched out together.

"So what happened while I was on the phone to Penny? You were fine while we were shopping, but when you came into the diner you were so white you looked like a vampire had drained you of blood."

"That's a more appropriate description than you know," Kim said with a grimace.

Travis kissed her forehead. "I want to hear every word of it. Don't leave anything out."

"But —"

He leaned over her and looked into her eyes. "No buts. No excuses. And most of all, no *fear.* Especially not of me. Did you murder anyone I love?"

She knew he was trying to lighten the mood, but to Kim all this was very serious. "No," she said, "but I'm considering running your father down with a lawn mower."

Travis's face lost its look of amusement and she saw the man who appeared in courtrooms. He fell back on the bed and pulled her to him so close she could hardly breathe. If she'd had her way, she would have moved even closer.

Where to begin? "Remember last night before dinner when I waited for you while you talked on the phone?"

"To that idiot Forester? Sure. What happened?"

"I met your father." Travis's hand tightened on Kim's shoulder, but otherwise he said nothing.

Once Kim started her story, Travis said little, and listened hard. She told him of her two encounters with the man who called himself Red, and she went over every word she could remember of their conversations. She told Travis of Red's little homily about children eating lead paint but only remembering being forbidden from doing what they wanted to do.

"That sounds like Dad. He thinks he can explain away every rotten thing he does."

She could tell that he wasn't shocked that his father had shown up in Janes Creek. But Travis drew in his breath when she told of Mr. Maxwell fishing in Edilean.

"I never asked Mom where she heard of Edilean in the first place. I never even thought about it, but Dad could have told her. It makes sense. Go on, please."

She told him of when she realized Russell was his brother. "They were giving me looks of pleading not to tell you."

"Penny was. Russ was enjoying every second of it."

"You knew?!"

"One of the things I've learned in being a lawyer is to watch as well as listen. None of you were subtle."

"Do you think Russ knows you know?"

"Of course. The kid is loving every minute of this."

"He's not even two years younger than you are, so he's not really a kid."

"Does your brother see you as an adult?"

"Not at all," Kim said.

"So what happened today while I was in the diner?"

"I met with your Mrs. Pendergast."

Travis was silent for a moment. "Now you're shocking me. What did Penny have to say?"

"She doesn't know your father is here. She —"

"No, wait. Tell me from the beginning. How she contacted you, what she said, you did, every word of it and don't leave anything out."

Slowly, Kim began to go over what happened. She started with the chairs and how she moved hers.

Chuckling, Travis hugged her and gave her a hard kiss on the mouth. "Good girl! I'm proud of you."

Kim liked his kiss so much that she returned it, but both of them wanted —

needed — to talk about what she'd been told.

She started on the easier things, what she thought was least likely to upset Travis. She told him of how Russell was conceived. When Travis didn't reply, she said, "You don't seem surprised."

"I am, actually, but in an opposite way from what you mean. The scuttlebutt around the office is that Dad and Penny were lovers for years. The surprise is that it was just once."

"A one time that produced a child."

"Big, ugly kid at that," Travis said, and Kim heard affection in his voice. "What else? And what are you holding back?"

"Will you let me tell the story in my own time?"

"I think I have, haven't I?" he said softly.

Turning, she looked at him, her eyes asking what he meant.

"I didn't take over."

"You mean like you did with Dave?" she asked.

"I . . ." He hesitated, as what he had to say was difficult for him. "I'm afraid I have more of my father in me than I want. When I took over Borman Catering, I was high-handed, and as you told me, I didn't believe that you could handle something like that on your own. I apologize. I'm not going to do that again. I'm not going to step in and take over your life, but I do think that if we're going to make this work that we need to do things *together*. As a pair, a team. I'm here and I can listen. Maybe if you tell me what is bothering you, together the two of us, can find a solution." He grinned. "That said . . . I admit that I have *never* been told off by anyone as *you* did. I had to check my eyebrows to make sure you hadn't singed them off."

"I wasn't that bad."

"Yes you were and I deserved it."

She snuggled back into his arms. "So this time . . ."

"This time I sat back and let you handle it on your own, and that wasn't easy for me. I can't tell you how much I wanted to let Russell know what I thought of the way he was smirking at you."

"Your brother."

"Yeah," Travis said with a little catch in his voice. "Odd thought, that one. Okay, so tell me more."

Kim took a breath. "You're not going to like this part."

"That means it's about Dad."

"Yes, it is," Kim said and began telling him Randall Maxwell's point of view of

Travis's childhood. He didn't speak during the whole time and when she finished, Kim looked at him.

"I'd guessed some of it," he said. "Not that Dad would ever admit to me that he was bullied by anyone. My guess is that his mouth got him in trouble. He tends to order everyone around, and he was probably the same as a kid."

"You're not upset by this?"

"I . . ." Travis began, and smiled. "No, I'm not. This is hard to admit, but maybe I went to work for him because I wanted to know if I could cut it with my old man. It's not easy being the son of Randall Maxwell. Sometimes when I was doing stunt work the guys would ask me why I was risking my neck every day. They liked to tell me that if they were me, they'd be on a private jet sipping champagne."

"But not you," Kim said. "At least not then. I think you did come to like those things."

"I did. I had lots of champagne. Lots of — well, other things."

"Must have been nice," Kim said quietly.

"Not really. You know something? I received more actual *caring* from Joe Layton than I did from . . . well, from most anyone I ever met. Can I tell you a secret?"

"Please do," she said. She was smiling at his words about Joe, the man who was going to be his stepfather. Joe lived in Edilean, so maybe Travis would too.

"I want to open a camp."

"What kind of camp?"

"A free one," Travis said. "It's been in my mind for years and I thought I'd try it in California, but ever since I saw the preserve around Edilean, it's stayed with me. Joe could build it, Penny could manage it, and —"

"She wants to retire."

"After years with my father this would be a retirement."

"Your mom could decorate the place."

He pulled her up to face him. "How do you think you'd be at teaching kids how to make macaroni necklaces?"

"I taught you how to make a house for a doll, so I can teach anyone anything."

"Taught me? Ha! You ordered me around." He was unbuttoning her shirt.

"Please tell me you aren't going to ask me to shut down my business and work for you."

"I'd never dream of it," he said as his lips touched her neck. "But I can tell you that my secret plan is to take over managing your finances."

"Would you please?" she whispered as his mouth took her breast.

"Think I can get you to give me a recommendation to your local law firm?"

She drew back from her mouth on his ear. "Our very own McDowell, Aldredge, and Welsch? You have to be *born* into that law firm."

"Marriage not good enough?" he asked, but then his mouth was on hers.

An hour before, the last thing Kim wanted was sex, but now all she wanted was release.

"I think we have a future," she whispered.

Travis drew back from her. "What?"

"I think we have a future," she repeated.

"You . . ." He began, but stopped. "You really did think I was going to leave you?"

"Yes. I mean no. I just couldn't figure out where we were going to *live*."

"Your house, if I can get you to move your stuff out of the garage. Joe said —"

She kissed him to silence. "What about the divorce?"

"Joe can handle that. In fact I'm a bit afraid for my father when he goes up against Joe. Do you want to talk *more?*" His voice was full of exasperation.

"Yes!" she said. "Yes and yes and yes! I want to talk endlessly about us, about our future, about — Oh!" Travis's mouth was on her stomach.

"Go on, keep talking," he said as he moved his lips lower on her body.

"Maybe later," she said as she closed her eyes and forgot all about whatever she'd been worried about.

FIFTEEN

When Kim woke up, she could see that it was dark outside. The first thing she noticed was that Travis wasn't in bed with her. They'd made love all afternoon and she knew she'd never enjoyed anything so much in her life. She hadn't realized it, but from the beginning she'd had so many questions that she'd never fully relaxed. All the years of searching for him, of not knowing what had happened to him, were between them.

It wasn't that she'd completely forgiven him, nor did she fully understand his male reasoning, but for the first time since she'd seen him, a stranger standing in the moonlight, she saw the possibility that she *would* get over it.

There was a knock on the door into the hallway, and Kim looked about for her clothes. They were folded neatly on a chair, certainly not where she'd tossed them a few hours ago.

"Just a minute," she called, but then Travis came out of the connecting room. He was showered, shaved, and wearing jeans and a T-shirt. She thought about not getting out of bed.

"Hungry?" he asked as he opened the door and spoke to someone. He closed the door and turned to Kim. "They're going to set up dinner in my room. Or would you rather go downstairs and hear what the Pendergasts have found out about your relatives?"

He made the second choice sound so awful that she laughed. "Russell will miss you."

"He'll miss *you*," Travis said. "Do you think that kid has a girlfriend somewhere?"

"I'm beginning to wonder that too. I guess if he were a New York lawyer that you'd know it."

"Probably." Travis sat down on the bed beside her, and his face was serious. "I didn't realize that I hadn't made myself clear about my hopes for the future."

She knew he was referring to her outburst of fear that he would leave her again. "It's all right," Kim said. "We have . . ." She hesitated. "Some time to think about what we want to do."

The sound of a champagne cork being popped came from the other room.

"I think our name is being called," Travis said as he took her hand to pull her out of bed.

But Kim pulled the sheet close to her and didn't get out. "I'll meet you at the table *after* I've had a shower," she said pointedly.

Smiling, he kissed her hand and left the room.

Kim took a full thirty minutes showering and getting dressed. She put on a blue silk dress that she'd tossed in her bag as an afterthought. When she'd packed she'd thought it was over between her and Travis, that she'd never see him again. Smiling, she remembered that she'd thought he had given up. She had told him off and he'd run away. But Kim was learning that the three Maxwell men *never* gave up.

When she'd finished dressing, she took a breath, smoothed her skirt, and opened the door into Travis's room. It had been set up so beautifully that she stood still just to look at it. Cream-colored linens, blue-green dishes with little seashells on them, silver that glistened in the candlelight. But to her eyes, the most beautiful thing in the room was Travis. He'd changed into a tuxedo, and Kim was very glad of her silk dress.

"May I?" Travis asked, holding out his arm to her. He led her to a pretty chair done in blue-and-white-striped satin. "This is lovely," she said, looking across the table. But when she turned to him, he was on one knee beside her.

Kim's heart leaped into her throat and began pounding.

"Will you marry me?" he asked softly. "Would you be my wife and live with me forever?"

There wasn't any hesitation on Kim's part. "Yes," she answered.

Smiling, Travis bent forward to kiss her, and took her hands and kissed the back of them, then her palms.

Still on one knee and holding her left hand, he reached under the tablecloth and pulled out a long, wide box covered in blue velvet. Kim knew what it was, as she'd seen the same box in her work.

Travis flipped up the lid, and inside were a dozen rings, each one different. Kim didn't need her jeweler's loupe to know that she was looking at world-class stones. Sapphire, diamond, emerald, ruby, they were all there. Each setting was unique, and she knew that each one was the work of an independent jeweler. She would never see the same ring on another person.

With her eyes wide, she looked at Travis in question.

"Mind if I . . . ?" He glanced down at his knee.

"Of course," she said and took the box from him to look at the rings. "I don't know what to say. They're beautiful. How did you . . . ? Oh. Mrs. Pendergast."

"No," Travis said as he filled their champagne flutes. "While Russ drove me here, I called places and had the rings sent. Each one was made by a different artist."

"That's what I thought." It wasn't easy to choose from among the rings.

"They're nonreturnable," he said.

At that she frowned. "You're not going to lavish me with gifts, are you?"

"Since you're supplying the house we live in, and the furniture, I think I have a right to add a few things."

Kim pulled a ring with a large square-cut emerald from the box. Her jeweler's eye could tell that it was excellent quality. She held it near the light of the candle to admire the occlusions, the tiny imperfections that showed it to have been taken from the earth and was not man-made.

She held out the ring to him and extended her left hand. He slipped the ring onto her finger, kissed the back of her hand, and held it as he looked into her eyes.

"Kim, I love you," he whispered. "I have

loved you since I was a boy and I don't want us to be apart again. I want to live where you do, with you."

Kim, ever practical, smiled at him. "I'd like to talk about where, when, how. You seem to have made a lot of plans and I want to know what they are."

"Good!" he said as he removed the lid from a silver platter, exposing two filet mignons. "I like women who know their own minds."

They talked and ate and discussed. Travis told Kim his ideas for the future, that he wanted to live in Edilean and open his camp for the summer. In the winter he'd do law work. "I like it better than I thought I would, so maybe what Dad told Penny is true, that there is some Maxwell in me."

"Do you think little Edilean could be enough for you?"

"Yes," he said, "and I promise that I won't do anything that we don't agree on." He leaned across the table to her. "But I think maybe you have some of your brother in you and your ambition is a bit more than your little town."

"I'm found out!" she said, and they began to talk about her future as she saw it. Dave's ideas of expanding her company hadn't been just his idea alone.

They talked of the coming divorce, and Travis told how he'd decided that Joe and his parents could fight it out themselves. "I'll get Mom a good lawyer."

"Forester?" Kim asked, and they laughed together.

It was while they were sharing a thick slice of chocolate cake that an invitation was slipped under the door. After they finished dessert, Travis and Kim had eyes only for each other and didn't see the heavy vellum envelope.

It wasn't until morning that Kim picked it up and showed it to Travis. It was addressed to both of them.

"Open it," Kim said to Travis. "I bet it's from Mrs. Pendergast and she wants to tell you that Russell is your half brother."

"Too late," Travis said. "You already blabbed."

"That's not how I see it. I think you —" She broke off at the expression on Travis's face. He was still in bed, the sheet just covering his bare lower body. "What is it?"

"It's an invitation to a picnic at one P.M. today, and there's a map of how to get there." He handed it to her, and it was Kim's turn to be astonished.

"It's from your father." She sat down on the edge of the bed. "He says he has a gift for us all." She looked up at Travis. "Think it's a box of pirate's loot? I could use some pearls. And some tanzanite. Of course I'm always low on gold."

He took the invitation from her. "You won't get any of that from Dad."

"Any of what?"

"Gold."

"I sure hope it's not more of his bits of advice about your eating lead paint. I think I'll ask him about his office romance policy."

"You do that," Travis said as he flung back the sheet. "I'd like to see that."

She leaned back on her arms to watch Travis stride across the room naked. "So what do you think he wants to give you?"

"Us. Give to *us*." Travis pulled up his faded jeans. "My hope is that it's freedom. To agree to give Mom an easy divorce."

"You're worried about her and Joe in a courtroom, aren't you? Will your father have half a dozen lawyers at his table?"

"More like twenty, and each one will have a different ethnic origin and race. It will be a global rainbow."

Kim laughed. "My money is on Mr. Layton. I think he can handle anything, and from the way he and your mom were dancing at Jecca's wedding —" She broke off at Travis's look. "All right. No stories of parents and the *S* word."

"Let's go to breakfast and see who else has been invited to this shindig."

Downstairs in the dining room, people had seemed to settle on which tables they were to sit at, so there were two empty seats by Russell and Mrs. Pendergast.

"Oh, how lovely!" Mrs. Pendergast said as she stared at Kim's ring.

Russell was smiling because his mother was looking at Travis in shock.

"You didn't think he could do something like that all by himself, did you? But he did," Russell said. "He even punched the buttons on the phone without any help from anyone. I was amazed."

"I think little brothers should mind their manners," Travis said, a sentence that silenced the table.

Kim looked at Penny and shrugged. "He figured it out."

Penny's eyes were on Travis and they were asking how he felt about all this. Travis put his hand over hers. "Dad should have divorced Mom and given us our freedom and married you," he said softly. "That he didn't shows that he has no common sense."

For a moment there were tears of gratitude in Penny's eyes, then she moved her hand away. "That's enough of that nonsense.

What do you think Randall is up to now with this surprise gift of his?"

"I'm hoping he shows up with a sister," Russell said, and everyone laughed.

All through the meal, Kim noticed Russell and Travis sneaking looks at each other. There were so many new relationships being established! There were the usual — she was going to have to get to know his parents, and he hers. But Travis was getting the worst of it. He had a half brother who'd shown great hostility toward him, and a future brother-in-law who didn't want Travis to marry his sister.

Travis seemed to know what Kim was thinking. He looked across the table and winked at her, as though to say that he could handle anything that was thrown at him.

She smiled, letting him know that whatever happened, she would be there with him.

"You two cut it out!" Russell said. "You're fogging the glassware."

Kim looked away in embarrassment, but Travis just laughed as he clapped Russell hard on the back. "Someday it may happen to you," Travis said.

When Russ didn't reply, Kim said, "For all we know, Russell may have a wife and three children."

When Russell looked at her but made no reply, Kim turned to Mrs. Pendergast.

Penny put her hands up in surrender. "I have been sworn to secrecy."

"More like privacy," Russell said, and for the first time since Kim had met him he wasn't wearing his usual look of amusement. That his merriment had always been at Travis's expense didn't keep Kim from laughing.

Abruptly, Russell said, "If you'll excuse me," and left the table.

"But he didn't eat," Kim said as she started to go after him, but Mrs. Pendergast caught her arm.

"My son has his own demons to fight," she said, "and it's best to leave him alone."

Kim sat back down, but she looked at Travis. His eyes said he agreed with Kim. Without so much as a look at Penny, he followed Russell out of the room, but he was back in minutes. "Russ took the Jeep. I don't know where he's gone. Should we worry?" he asked Penny.

"I should, but not you," she answered. "Who wants to try the peach pancakes?"

SIXTEEN

Russell knew he was being childish at leaving the table without eating, but he'd reached his breaking point. Besides, his invitation to the picnic had included a note asking him to meet his father at the Old Mill right after breakfast. No specific time given, just go there and wait. Between feeling like an intruder among friends and his curiosity about what his father wanted, Russ left.

As he drove, he couldn't help but think about the fact that Travis now knew Russell was his brother. But then Russ had always known about Travis Maxwell. He'd known that living in a big house, seeing his mother every day, being given anything he wanted, was a boy who was his part brother. When he was little and his mother told him he had a "half brother" Russ had started crying. His mother couldn't understand why until Russell had tearfully asked which half of the boy was missing.

After his mother explained that they had the same father but different mothers, Russell had become interested in his brother and often asked questions about him. It was something he and his mother shared.

Not that there was much. They rarely saw each other when he was growing up. She'd be gone for weeks at a time, traveling all over the world, never far from Randall Maxwell's side.

Russell was left at home with nannies, who changed rather frequently, and later tutors came to him. It hadn't been a shock to find out that they were the same men who'd taught his brother.

When Russell reached high school age he'd had enough of living in Travis Maxwell's shadow, and he showed his mother a brochure for a boarding school. She wasn't allowed to say no.

Russell wasn't sure when his curiosity changed to anger. And he didn't know why his animosity was aimed at his half brother and not at his father.

He only saw Randall Maxwell about a dozen times when he was growing up. When he was five, one rainy Sunday morning he was sitting in the room beside his mother's office drawing pictures when a man walked in. He wasn't especially tall and he didn't seem frightening in any way.

The man stopped at the doorway, didn't say anything, but then he turned back. "Are you Russell?"

He nodded.

The man came to stand by him and looked at what Russell was drawing — a picture of the big buildings outside the windows. "You like art?"

Again Russell nodded.

"Good to know." The man left and Russell wouldn't have remembered it except that later his mother said the man was his father. And the next Sunday that Russell went to the office with his mother there was a big box full of art supplies there for him.

His mother said, "Your father is a very generous man."

For years afterward Russell had kind thoughts about his father. It wasn't until he was about nine that he began to be aware of what other people's parents were like and what they did for their children.

Russell couldn't afford to be angry at his mother, as she was all he had. And his mother said they owed his father "everything," so he didn't dare aim his animosity at him. Instead, Russell took his anger out on his brother, the boy he'd never seen, the boy who had everything, including a mother who stayed at home *all* the time. And Russell never forgot that their father lived with *him.*

Russell went to the same college his brother went to, but by then his mind-set was different. He didn't study law. After school he traveled some, returned to the U.S., and studied some more. But he'd never been able to settle anywhere for long. Maybe it was the demons that raged inside him that made settling impossible.

When his mother had called recently and asked him to help Travis, Russell had said no. He'd even laughed. Help a brother who had never contacted him? In Russell's mind it was up to the older brother to make the first move.

That's when his mother told him that Travis didn't know he had a brother. That had been such a shock to Russell that he'd agreed to sweet-talk some girl enough to find out information from her.

But when Russell was finally able to meet Travis, every bit of the anger he'd felt as a child came forward. He'd expected a spoiled, know-it-all jerk, but what he'd found was a man who made an omelet for him.

Since that first day the two of them had

been nearly inseparable. But in spite of their ease together, Russell still felt the anger inside him. He'd liked besting Travis in negotiating the contract with Kim's greedy boyfriend. He'd even liked riding around with his brother. And later, when Kim told Travis off, Russell didn't think he'd ever enjoyed anything so much in his life.

But still . . . What had been difficult for him was seeing the way Kim and Travis loved each other. While it was true that they fought, it was easy to see that underneath it all they belonged together.

On the drive from Virginia to Maryland, Travis, nervous and upset, had told him how he and Kim had met as kids, and how she'd changed his life. For the first time Russell heard the full story of how Travis's life hadn't been the glorious adventure that Russell had always assumed it was.

This morning at the breakfast table had been all that Russell could bear. "Domestic bliss" was written all over the faces of Kim and Travis. And this afternoon Randall Maxwell was throwing a picnic, no doubt in honor of his eldest, number one son.

Russell was thinking so hard that when the car in front of him suddenly stopped he had to slam on the brakes. When he did, the blue velvet box Travis had handed him yesterday slid forward.

"Kim doesn't want them," Travis had said yesterday when he'd called Russ to his room. "Get rid of them."

Russell refrained from pointing out how much the rings cost. Nor did he snap that he wasn't Travis's servant. Russell knew this was brotherly bossiness and not business, so he shoved the box of rings under the seat of the Jeep, intending to give them to his mother to deal with.

Russell turned down the road to the Old Mill. He'd found out — or his mother's relatives had — that a descendant of James Hanleigh, Dr. Tristan Janes's first illegitimate child, still lived in Janes Creek. "She's a widow," he was told, and he envisioned a gray-haired woman with a bun at the back of her neck. No wonder she couldn't afford to renovate the old stone mill.

Russell needed a place and time to sit and think. He knew that it was time to point his life in the right direction, and to do that, he had some difficult decisions to make.

He parked the Jeep in front, wandered past the herb patch — a Tristan garden, he thought — and went toward the back. He hadn't taken but a few steps when he heard a rumble that sounded like falling tile, then a half scream, as though someone had been injured.

He ran toward the sound, through a doorway, and into a room that was missing part of the roof. But he saw nothing and no one, just a stream of sunlight showing dust motes.

"Help?" came a small sound from above his head.

He looked up to see a young woman hanging by her fingertips from a rotting piece of wood that ran along the top of the wall.

"By all that's holy," Russell said under his breath as he ran forward to stand below her. "Do you have a ladder?"

"On the other side," she whispered.

Russell ran toward the doorway into the next room, but then he heard the crack of the old wood and he knew she was going to fall. There was time to do only one thing: put himself directly beneath her. His body would cushion her fall.

He leaped the few steps forward, his arms extended, and got to her just as the wood broke away. She hadn't looked very big as she hung from the top of the wall, but when her body hit his, he staggered backward. His feet tripped over some loose boards, and he went down. The weight and the momentum of the two of them made him skid backward. He felt skin come off his back as he slid across the rubble. Pain ran through him and he grunted — but he didn't let go of the woman he held. His arms were around her so tight it's a wonder she didn't break in half.

When he stopped moving, dust billowed around them. Russell was on his back, the woman on top of him. To protect them from the dust and falling debris, he put his hands over her head, hiding her face in his chest, and he buried his face in her blonde curls. As the dust engulfed them, he inhaled the fragrance of her hair. And when it settled, he still lay there, holding her tightly.

"I think it's okay now," she said, her voice muffled against his chest.

"Yes, fine," he said, his nose still in her hair.

"Uh . . ." she said. "I think I can get up now."

Russell's senses began to return to him enough that he managed to lift his head to look around, but he didn't release his hold on her. She was a small thing and her body felt good on his.

When she pushed against him, he reluctantly released her, and she rolled off to sit up beside him. Russell lay where he was and looked at her. Even with a streak of dirt on her face, she was extraordinarily pretty. Her dark blonde hair was short and rampant with soft curls, one of them hanging down over her left eye. Cornflower blue eyes, a little nose, and a mouth that turned up on the corners completed the picture.

She made a swipe at the dirt on her face but only succeeded in smearing it.

Russell pointed to the side of her right cheek. She pulled her shirtsleeve over her hand and wiped at it.

"Did I get it?"

"Not quite," he said as he reached his hand out. He was still lying where he'd landed, but he raised a hand toward her face. "May I?"

"Might as well. It's not like we haven't met."

Smiling at her joke, he cupped her chin — more than was necessary — and used his thumb to wipe away the smudge. When she was clean, he didn't let go and for a moment their eyes locked.

They might have stayed that way if a timber hadn't fallen to the ground behind them. Instantly, Russell rolled to one side and put his body between hers and the falling wood. Her arms went around him and stayed there even after the dirt settled.

"I think we better get out of here," she

said and again had to push him away.

Russell pulled himself to a sitting position, his eyes on hers, and he was smiling. "Are you — ?" He cut off at a gasp from her. She was holding out her hands and they had blood on them.

In an instant she went from sweetly smiling to all-business. She put her hand on his shoulder and twisted her body to look behind him. "Your entire back is bloody."

When Russell just kept smiling at her, she grimaced. "Okay, hero, get up. We need to get you cleaned up."

She stood and Russell saw that even in her loose jeans and big shirt that covered a tee with MYRTLE BEACH written over the pocket, she was very nicely built. Nothing flashy, but trim and firm.

She put out her hand to help him up, but when Russell moved, the pain in his back brought him back to reality. But with her big blue eyes on him he couldn't let out the groan he was feeling.

When she saw him wince, she slid her arm around his waist and helped him pick his way through the rubble on the floor, out the doorway, and into the courtyard and the sunlight. She guided him to sit down on the low stone wall. "Sit here and don't move, got it?"

"But —" he began.

"I'll be right back. I have to get my medical bag."

Russell's face lit up. "You're a Hanleigh."

Pausing, she smiled. "I am. At least that's my maiden name."

Russell's face fell, but then the light came back to it. "You're the widow."

This time she laughed. "I am Clarissa Hanleigh Wells, I own this pile of rocks, and yes I'm a widow. Anything else you need to know before I get my supplies?"

"You're a Tristan," he said.

She shook her head. "I have no idea what that means. Just sit there, don't move, and I'll be right back." She disappeared around a wall.

Russell took his cell phone out of his pocket. He saw that he had six e-mails and three voice mails, but he ignored them. He was going to text Travis that he'd found Clarissa Hanleigh, but on second thought, he turned his phone off and put it back in his pocket. He'd see the lot of them at the picnic, so the news could wait until then.

He looked up as Clarissa was hurrying back to him. She lithely leaped over fallen stones and rotten timbers, a heavy-looking red leather bag in her hand, as she returned to him.

He just sat there smiling at her in what he knew was an idiotic way.

She stood before him, looked at him for a long moment, and said, "Take it off."

"I beg your pardon?"

"Oh my!" she said. "Where did you go to school?"

"Stanford."

"I could have guessed. Take your shirt off so I can see the damage."

As he began unbuttoning his shirt, Clarissa moved around him, to see his back, and he heard her deep intake of breath. "Never mind. I have to cut this off, and if it's too bad I'm taking you to the hospital."

"No," he said. "I'd rather you fixed it." He heard her pull on sterile gloves, then felt her hand on his shoulder. He had to hold himself rigid as she began to pull the fabric from out of the scrapes on his skin.

"I think you should —"

"No," he said firmly. "You're a doctor, aren't you?"

She hesitated in the cutting. "I had planned to be."

"Wanted to be one all your life? You seemed to have been born to be a doctor? That sort of thing?"

"Yes, exactly," she said. "Is that what you call a Tristan? Named after my ancestor?"

"It's what they call them in Edilean."

"Never heard of the place."

"It's in Virginia, and you have relatives there."

She stopped, with her hands on his skin. "Jamie and I have no relatives."

"Jamie?"

"My son," she said.

Russell drew in his breath as she used tweezers to pull a strip of cloth out of a cut. "Oh. A son. How old?"

"Five."

"I guess he's the reason you didn't . . ." He was concentrating on his breathing because what she was doing hurt a lot.

"He's my reason for living, if that's what you mean. But yes" — she paused to pour water on a gauze to blot the blood away — "Jamie is why I didn't go to medical school. Well, actually, that's not fair. A good-looking football player, a few tequila shots, and the backseat of a Chevy are the real reasons."

"So you married the player?"

"Yes," she said softly, "but he got drunk and ran off a bridge before his son was born. Jamie and I have always been alone."

"Not any longer." He turned to look at her just as she was cleaning a cut, and he gasped at the pain.

"I won't think less of you if you scream.

Or cry."

"And lose my hero status?" he said.

She stopped working, put her hands on his shoulders, and moved her face near his. "You will *never* lose your hero status with me. You saved my life," she said softly as she kissed him on the cheek.

Russell bent his head and kissed the back of her hand.

She removed her hands. "Lifesaving doesn't get you anything else. Who are you, why are you here, and what's this about having relatives?"

As Russell began to talk, he knew that what he was saying was slightly incoherent, but it was difficult for him to think clearly. Between the pain and the presence of this young woman, he wasn't quite himself. He started by telling her the purpose of his journey, how he'd come with his half brother, Travis, to help his fiancée, Kim, trace an ancestor in the hope of finding descendants.

"All of Edilean is related to one another," he said, "so I don't know why they need more."

"You sound envious."

"I . . ." he began. He was going to say that he had relatives, but those people his mother had booked in the B&B only called when they came up with some scheme that her rich boss could finance. Other than that, he and his mother were on their own.

"Go on," Clarissa urged him. "How did I suddenly acquire a family?"

"Shenanigans between Dr. Tristan Janes and Miss Clarissa Aldredge of Edilean, Virginia, back in the 1890s. They produced a child she named Tristan, and the name has been given to succeeding eldest sons."

"And they're all doctors?"

"I think so. You'd have to ask Kim for the facts."

"And she is going to marry your half brother?"

"Yes," he said, then couldn't resist telling her what he'd thought that meant when he was little.

Clarissa laughed and he liked the sound. "That sounds like my Jamie." She was bandaging his back.

"What were you doing here when I rescued you?"

She gave a groan of frustration. "Trying to repair this place, but I'm no good at it."

"I have to agree on that." Her hands were on his skin, smoothing the bandages, and for a moment he closed his eyes.

"There, I think you're done." She walked around him. He still wore the front part of his shirt, which she hadn't cut away, and she smiled at his comic appearance.

He started to pull the remainder of the shirt off, but at a sound from Clarissa he looked up. There were tears gathering in her eyes. It was a natural thing to pull her into his arms, his hands entangled in her hair, her head buried in his shoulder.

"I was so scared," she whispered as the tears began to flow. "All I could think of was that my son would lose his mommy. He'd never recover from it. I'd ruin his whole life because of my stupidity. And it *was* stupid of me to be up there by myself every Sunday morning."

"Yes it was," Russell said as he held her close — and he suddenly remembered that his father had sent him to the Old Mill on a Sunday morning. "You have to swear not to do it again."

"But this is all I have," she said as she pulled away from him. "This old, rotten, falling down pile of rocks is everything in the world that I own. My job barely pays expenses and —"

"I'll help you."

"What?" She drew away to wipe her eyes and look at him.

"I'll stay in Janes Creek and help you."

"You can't do that. I don't know you. I

don't even know your name."

"Oh. Sorry. It's Russell Pendergast. I'm twenty-eight years old and my father is Randall Maxwell."

"Isn't he . . . ?"

"Right. A mega big shot in the world. But I think he may have —" Russell thought that the story of whether or not his father had sent him there to meet Clarissa was for another time. "My mother works for him. Or for my brother at the moment, but he's about to move to Edilean, and my mother wants to live there too. Where's your son?"

"In Sunday school. One of the women I work with takes him so I can spend a couple of hours here." She glanced at the old place. "I think I need more than a couple of hours a week, don't you?"

"This place needs months, lots of machinery and materials, and at least a dozen workmen."

"Or women," she said, and he smiled.

"Right. Where do you work?"

"Guess."

"For a doctor? In a hospital? Something to do with medicine."

"It looks like you're not just a pretty face," she said, then turned red. "I didn't mean . . ."

Russell was smiling at her. "Is there

someplace I can get a shirt? I don't want to go back to the hotel. And breakfast. I'm afraid I left without eating and I'm famished."

"I . . ." She hesitated. "In my attic I have a box of my father's clothes. He was about as big as you. I could throw one in the washer while I make you a pile of bacon and eggs."

"When does your son get home?"

"About eleven."

"I'd like to meet him," Russell said softly.

"And I'd like for him to meet you."

For a moment they looked at each other and there seemed to be an understanding that this could be the beginning of something real, something permanent.

Russell was the first to break the silence. "Would you and Jamie like to go to a picnic with me today at one? I'm sure there'll be lots of food, and I think I can arrange to have some entertainment for Jamie there." His eyes told how much he wanted her to go with him.

"I think we'd both love that."

"Great!" Russell said as he stood up. But that crinkled his back and he winced in pain.

Again, Clarissa put her arm around his waist to help him.

"I may stay injured forever," he said as he

put his arm around her shoulders. "So what does Jamie like? Balloons? Animals? Acrobats?"

"Fire engines," she said. "The bigger, the redder, the better."

"Fire engines it is," Russell said.

"I'm going to go get my car and bring it around," Clarissa said. "Stand here and don't move your back."

"Yes, ma'am," Russell said and watched her hurry away.

As soon as she was out of sight, he typed out a text message to his mother.

I'M BRINGING A FIVE-YEAR-OLD BOY TO THE PICNIC. HE LOVES FIRE ENGINES. I'M GOING TO MARRY HIS MOTHER. R.

Seventeen

When Travis drove into the pretty, wooded area that had been set up for the picnic, he was hoping to see Russell's Jeep, but it wasn't there. Instead, he saw a brilliant red fire engine and what looked to be an entire fire department of men and women in full uniform. They were standing around talking, laughing, and helping themselves to what looked to be a lavish spread of food and drink.

"What's this about?" Kim asked.

"I have no idea, but then for all I know, Dad's planning a bonfire."

She looked at the idyllic setting and let out her breath. It wasn't what she now realized she'd been dreading. She thought maybe there would be white-gloved waiters serving champagne in crystal glasses, and there'd be a hundred people there.

Instead there was just a red-and-white-checked cloth spread on the ground under a huge black walnut tree, with half a dozen red coolers to the side. There wasn't even a sign of a waiter.

The only oddity was the local fire department to the side.

"It's not what I expected," Kim said.

"Me neither," Travis answered. As he spoke, Penny drove up, quickly got out of her rental car, and ran to them. "Is Russell here?" she asked through Travis's open window.

"I haven't seen him. What's the —" He cut himself off as Penny hurried away toward the fire engines.

"Do you think something's wrong?" Kim asked.

Travis was looking in his side-view mirror at Penny as she quickly moved from one person to another. "I've never seen her lose her cool before," he said in wonder. "One time we had two sworn enemies in the office at the same time. Dad and I were worried there'd be gunplay, but Penny deftly moved the men in and around and they never saw each other. She saved a multimillion-dollar deal."

Kim was looking out the back windshield. "Whatever is going on has upset her. She looks frantic."

"Interesting," Travis said as he turned

back and smiled at Kim. "Are you ready to go to this thing? I'm sure Dad — Holy crap!"

Kim looked up to see another car pulling off the road and into the little parking area. "It's . . ."

"Right. That is Joe Layton and my mother," Travis said and his voice lowered. "Speaking of sworn enemies . . ."

"Your mother and Mrs. Pendergast," Kim said as she collapsed back against the seat. "I have a suggestion. Just a little one, but I think you should consider it. How about if we leave here right now and go straight back to Edilean? Mrs. Pendergast can send our clothes to us. Or we can shop for new ones. What do you think?"

"I like the way you deal with a situation," Travis said as he started the engine.

But Joe Layton put his big body in front of the car.

"How about some race driving techniques?" Kim asked. "You could go around him."

"He's too big; he'd hurt the car. Let's get out on your side and make a run through the forest. Maybe we can escape."

Joe was too fast for them. He was standing by Travis's door, and his hand snaked inside to remove the keys from the ignition.

"Come on, you two cowards. Get out and join the party." He opened Travis's door.

Travis squeezed Kim's hand and rolled his eyes skyward. "Give me strength."

Kim got out of her side of the car and stood back to look at Lucy, the pretty little woman who came to stand behind Joe. He was so big that she could disappear behind him.

Kim was curious to see this woman who'd so successfully hidden from her for four years. As Lucy came forward to stand on tiptoe to hug her son, Kim knew she would have done just that. Every minute of those weeks she'd spent with Travis when they were children was so burned in her mind that Lucy's face was there also. If Kim had seen her in Edilean, she would have done what Lucy feared and told everyone she knew. Lucy was the connection to Travis, the way to find him, and Kim would have thought only of that, not of any consequences.

Lucy's eyes met Kim's and there was apology there — from both women.

"Kim," Lucy began as she stood before her. "I never meant —"

"It's okay," Kim said. "I'm sure Mom told you I'd blab, and I would have. I so much wanted to find Travis that I would have sold my own mother into white slavery."

"From what I've heard she could have handled it," Lucy said, and the two women laughed together.

"It's all right between you and Travis now?" Lucy asked softly. Travis and Joe were a few feet away.

"Very, very all right. And what about you and Mr. Layton?"

Lucy gave a sigh that came from her heart. "It's nice to be loved, isn't it?"

"Yes, wonderful," Kim said. "Would it be impolite of me to ask what's happening with the divorce?"

Lucy gave a quick look at Joe and Travis, and leaned forward, her voice a whisper as she took Kim's hand in her own. "Randall has agreed to a peaceful divorce. No fighting. A fair deal. I told him I don't want Travis to have to so much as appear in court. I want you two to have all the time together that you deserve."

Kim couldn't help the tears of joy that came to her eyes. "Thank you," she whispered.

Lucy smiled, and the two women's hands just seemed to cling to one another.

"Hey, you two!" Travis called. "I'm hungry. Let's see what Dad sent us to eat."

Penny was still with the firefighters, and

in spite of his professed hunger, Travis went to her.

Travis greeted the firefighters, told them that if they needed anything to let him know. They all wanted to shake the hand of the son of the man who'd just bought them a new engine.

It took Travis a while before he could make his way to Penny. "What's Dad up to now?" he asked. "It's nice he's contributing to the Janes Creek Fire Department but what's in it for him?"

"I did it," Penny said. Her eyes were on the road, not on Travis.

"You bought a fire engine?"

"I ordered it. Your dad paid for it," she said and stopped, as though that was all the information she was going to give.

"Penny?" he asked.

When they could hear a car coming down the road, she seemed to stop breathing. The car drove past and Penny let out her breath.

"What is going on?!" Travis demanded.

Penny, her eyes never leaving the road, handed him her cell phone. "Look at my text from Russell."

"Oh," Travis said as he read it. "He asked his girlfriend to marry him? Must be catching. I hope he used one of those rings I offered Kim. He —"

"Russell doesn't have a steady girlfriend."

"But he said he's going to marry the mother of a kid who likes fire engines. Who is she?"

Penny turned to look at Travis in silence.

It took him a few moments to get what she wasn't saying. "He just *met* this woman?"

"I think so," Penny said as she rubbed her hands together in nervous agitation. "Oh, Russell," she said under her breath, "what have you done?"

For the first time ever, Travis put his arm around Penny's shoulders. She had always been the one who remained calm through everything. When Travis and his father were at each other's throats, it was Penny's sensible comments, her refusal to let any crisis perturb her, that quieted everyone.

But now she was the one who needed a calm presence.

"Your mother will hate me even more," Penny said, her old self showing, but she leaned her head against Travis's chest for a moment.

He glanced over her head to see Joe and Kim and his mother sitting on the checkered cloth. They'd opened the cooler and taken out lemonade and glasses, and lots of cheese and crackers. Maybe the waiters were missing, but the food looked to be topnotch.

"My mother has eyes only for Joe, and when she sees Russell I think she'll like him."

Penny stepped out of Travis's embrace. "I hope so, but then he does look a lot like you. If there's one thing your mother loves, it's you."

Travis smiled. "Joe said Dad was going to give the divorce without a big court battle. Do you think he will?"

"I know he was quite taken with young Kim."

Travis couldn't help a grimace. "Bastard! Sneaking around like that! He knew where Mom was all these years. When I think of the trouble I went to in hiding from him I could —" He looked at Penny. "How do you know he liked Kim?"

"I talked to him. I showed her a photo of your father and she turned white. I knew she'd seen him somewhere."

Travis nodded. "She came into the diner looking like she'd seen a ghost."

"But she told you the story of how he pretended to be a caretaker?"

"Only after some persuasion."

"Good," Penny said. "Don't keep secrets from each other. Your father and I never — I mean . . ."

"I know what you mean. His life has always been more with you than with my mother."

Penny turned to look at Lucy and Joe sitting so close together on the cloth. "I've always disliked your mother. Not from something based on fact, but from what I assumed I knew about her. The old Travis family name made me think she lived in a world of garden parties and teacups. And I thought she'd like gentlemen who carried lace hankies."

Joe Layton was as far from being a stereotypical "gentleman" as was possible.

"I'm sure Russ will be here soon, so maybe now's a good time to brave it out with a face-to-face with my mother."

"Did she bring any weapons?" Penny asked.

"Only a couple of machetes," Travis joked, but when Penny took a step back, he laughed. "Come on, Kim and I will protect you."

Travis stayed close to Penny as they walked toward the picnic area and his eyes begged his mother not to attack. But then, he realized that wasn't fair. After all, Penny had had a child by Lucy's husband. On the other hand, it wasn't as though a happy marriage had been broken up. The truth was that Travis was so glad to have a brother that he didn't really care about anything else.

As Travis sat down between his mother and Kim, he looked at Joe for moral support. Joe took Lucy's hand and his eyes seemed to say that it would be all right.

"Is there any beer in there?" Travis asked as he watched his mother. She was refusing to look at Penny. "Mom," he said as Kim handed him a beer. "Kim told me you have a couple of brothers. Is that true?"

"Howard and Arthur," she said. "I haven't seen them, well, since I got married. There were harsh words spoken."

Everyone was still, wondering if Lucy was going to say more, but she didn't.

"So what are they like?" Travis asked. He would say anything to break the awkward silence. "I'd like to meet —"

"They're here!" Penny said in a voice of relief and joy. She got up and started running.

"Who's here?" Kim asked.

"It seems that since my little brother" — he looked directly at his mother, but she didn't meet his eyes — "left us at breakfast, he has met a woman, fallen in love, and asked her to marry him."

The others paused with food to their lips.

"Who is she?" Kim asked.

"I have no idea. Everything about my brother is a mystery. Shall we go meet her? It seems that she has a five-year-old son who loves fire engines."

All of them got up and started walking toward the fire truck when they heard a squeal of delight, and a beautiful little boy was running toward them.

"Tristan!" Kim said, then she too started running. "He looks like my cousin Tristan!" she called over her shoulder. "Russell found my cousins!"

Her enthusiasm was contagious, and Travis, Joe, and Lucy hurried after her.

The little boy was already halfway up the side of the truck, all the firefighters helping him up. The happiness on the child's face made everyone smile.

Behind the little boy, wearing a look of pure bliss, came Russell, and he was holding hands with a pretty young woman.

"I like the ring," Kim said to Travis.

He looked at her in question.

She nodded toward the woman's left hand. "It's the four-carat pink diamond from the tray you showed me. It was my second choice. She has taste."

Smiling, Travis nodded. As he'd hoped, Russell had used one of the rings he'd offered Kim for their engagement.

Russell stopped in front of his brother. "Dad said he wanted to meet me at the Old Mill this morning. Seems that Clarissa goes there to work every Sunday morning."

"If Russell hadn't shown up I'd be dead now or at least broken into bits," Clarissa said and everyone looked at her.

"You two have to tell us everything," Kim said, "and I think we're cousins."

"Second cousins once removed," Travis said.

"I need to see to my son," Clarissa said. "Jamie will —"

"He has a grandmother now," Russell said softly, and they all turned to look. Penny was on the ground, but her arms were extended over her head. As they watched, two big firefighters lifted her to the top of the truck to sit beside Jamie. He smiled at her, and when the engine started, Penny put her arm around the child.

"I think he's going to be fine," Russell said as he smiled at Clarissa. "Shall we all sit down?"

"And eat," Clarissa said. "I'm sure you're hungry again."

Like the lovebirds they were, that inside joke seemed to amuse them greatly.

It was three hours later before they were

all sated with food and drink and news. The fire engine had returned and they'd all listened to Jamie's excited description of everything he'd seen and done. He'd been given a hat and a bright yellow coat, both of which he wouldn't take off.

After he'd eaten he wore down and snuggled on his mother's lap. When he fell asleep, Russell took him and stretched him out, his head on Russell's lap, his feet in Penny's.

Everyone had listened in silence as Russell and Clarissa tripped over each other as they told of their meeting. Travis looked at Penny, and communication based on years of working together passed between them. Randall Maxwell had found the Aldredge descendant they were looking for and he'd set his son up to meet her.

When Clarissa told of her brush with death from trying to renovate the Old Mill, Travis again looked at Penny, and she nodded. Randall Maxwell was going to give his son a wedding gift of a renovated building.

But what everyone was most interested in was the first encounter between Russell and Clarissa. They were both shy and reticent when telling that part of the story, but the looks on their faces told it all.

Several times Travis looked at his mother,

and her expression showed that she was as fascinated as they all were by the story. Twice Travis caught her looking at Russell in wonder. He really did look like her son.

At about four they were all winding down from the excitement of the day. Travis and Kim were looking at each other as though they wanted to be alone, as were Lucy and Joe, and Russell and Clarissa.

The odd man out, the only one unattached, was Penny.

"Maybe we should go back to the hotel," Kim said. "We could all meet later for —" She broke off because a long black limo had pulled into the area beside their cars. The back door opened but no one got out and the engine wasn't turned off. Inside they could vaguely see the shadow of a person, but he or she didn't get out.

"That's Randall," Lucy said and she sounded like the party was over, but then her face lightened and she looked at Penny directly. Not with the sideways looks she'd been giving her all afternoon, but full into her eyes. "He's here for *you.*"

Penny shrugged. "He probably wants me to pick up his dry cleaning."

Everyone continued to look at her.

"Mother," Russell said, "you have been in love with that man for nearly thirty years.

Don't you think it's time you showed it?"

Penny looked at Lucy, and her eyes were asking permission. In answer, Lucy snuggled up to Joe. "I have what I want right here."

Penny took only seconds to make her decision. Looking as though she was finally going to get to do what she wanted to in her life, she got up, smoothed the front of her skirt, kissed Russell, then Jamie, then Clarissa on the forehead. She turned her back to them and started a slow, sedate walk toward the open limo. But when she got closer, she broke into a run. They saw her smile when she got to the door. She didn't hesitate as she stepped inside and pulled the door closed behind her. The limo drove away.

The stunned silence of everyone made Jamie stir. He looked up and saw Russell, and smiled that he was still there.

"You gave me a fire engine," he said and slipped his arms around Russell's neck.

"I think we should go," Russ said to Clarissa, and they stood up.

The others stayed seated on the cloth, looking up at them. Russell with the little boy clinging tightly about his neck, holding him in one arm while helping Clarissa with her bags with the other. It was impossible to believe that these people had just met that morning. If ever there were three people who were a family, it was them.

"So what are your plans?" Travis asked.

Clarissa looked up at Russell. As she folded a blanket, the big ring sparkled on her finger. "It's a little early to say yet."

Russell said, "I guess it depends on where I get a job."

"All right, little brother," Travis said, "we're all waiting. What *is* your vocation?"

Russell smiled in a way that said he wasn't telling.

Clarissa looked confused that these brothers didn't know such an elemental thing about each other. "Russell is a Baptist minister."

That silenced everyone.

Russell shrugged. "I trained to be, but I haven't had much practice at it. I was told that I have some, uh, anger issues, and it was strongly suggested that I deal with them."

Travis looked like he was about to laugh, but Kim gave him a look that warned him not to.

Kim spoke up. "You know, half of Edilean hasn't forgiven our current pastor for stealing my brother's girlfriend. Besides, he's been there for years now and . . ." She let the rest of that hang in the air.

"What my dear wife-to-be is saying is that there may be an opening in Edilean for a minister." Travis was looking at his brother with wide eyes, but he managed to recover himself. "I think we should talk about a camp I want to set up. There's a place for you."

"Gladly," Russell said, "but first Clarissa is going to med school. She wants to be a doctor."

"She's a real Tristan," Kim said, and they all laughed. She looked at everyone smiling, then up at Travis. At last she had what she'd wanted since she was eight years old.

"Ready to go?" Travis asked softly.

"Yes," she said. "Always yes."

Epilogue

It was late when Kim's cell phone buzzed. She and Travis were in Paris on their honeymoon and she thought about not looking at the e-mail. But Travis heard it.

"Go on, see who it is. I'm hoping to hear from Mom and Joe."

Kim clicked the phone and read in disbelief. "It's from Sophie."

"Who?"

"My other college roommate, besides Jecca."

"Oh yeah, the blonde bombshell."

As Kim kept reading, she collapsed on the bed.

"Is it bad news?"

"Yes and no," she whispered. "Sophie says she needs a place to hide and a job."

"To hide? From what?"

"She doesn't say," Kim said.

Travis sat down on the bed beside her and put his arm around her shoulders. "If you want to go home, we can."

"No," Kim said. "Sophie said I wasn't to do that. I —" Her head came up. "I'm going to call Betsy."

"Who's that?"

"My brother's office manager. Reede doesn't know it, but he's getting a new employee." She held the phone to her ear.

Travis stood up. "Sounds to me like you're matchmaking."

"Heavens no! Reede and Sophie? It could never work. She's too smart, too *nice* for my brother. However, I think I'll send my cousin Roan an e-mail and ask him to look in on Sophie."

Travis shook his head as he sat down in a comfortable chair and opened a newspaper. It looked like his wife was going to be a while in organizing her friend's life.

Behind the paper he smiled. He was sure he was the happiest man on the planet. "Take your time," he said. "We have a lifetime ahead of us."

ABOUT THE AUTHOR

Jude Deveraux is the author of forty-one *New York Times* bestsellers; her most recent novels include *Heartwishes, Moonlight in the Morning, The Scent of Jasmine, Scarlet Nights, Days of Gold,* and *Lavender Morning.* There are more than sixty million copies of her books in print worldwide. She lives in North Carolina. Visit her interactive website at www.judedeveraux.com or check out the Jude Deveraux Fan Page on Facebook, where she posts daily updates about her writing.

The employees of Thorndike Press hope you have enjoyed this Large Print book. All our Thorndike, Wheeler, and Kennebec Large Print titles are designed for easy reading, and all our books are made to last. Other Thorndike Press Large Print books are available at your library, through selected bookstores, or directly from us.

For information about titles, please call:
(800) 223-1244

or visit our Web site at:
http://gale.cengage.com/thorndike

To share your comments, please write:
Publisher
Thorndike Press
10 Water St., Suite 310
Waterville, ME 04901

BY CATHERYNNE M. VALENTE

Space Opera

The Refrigerator Monologues

The Glass Town Game

Radiance

Deathless

Palimpsest

THE FAIRYLAND SERIES

The Girl Who Ruled Fairyland—For a Little While

The Girl Who Circumnavigated Fairyland in a Ship of Her Own Making

The Girl Who Fell Beneath Fairyland and Led the Revels There

The Girl Who Soared Over Fairyland and Cut the Moon in Two

The Boy Who Lost Fairyland

The Girl Who Raced Fairyland All the Way Home

THE ORPHAN'S TALES

The Orphan's Tales: In the Night Garden

The Orphan's Tales: In the Cities of Coin and Spice

MOJANG

MINECRAFT™

THE END

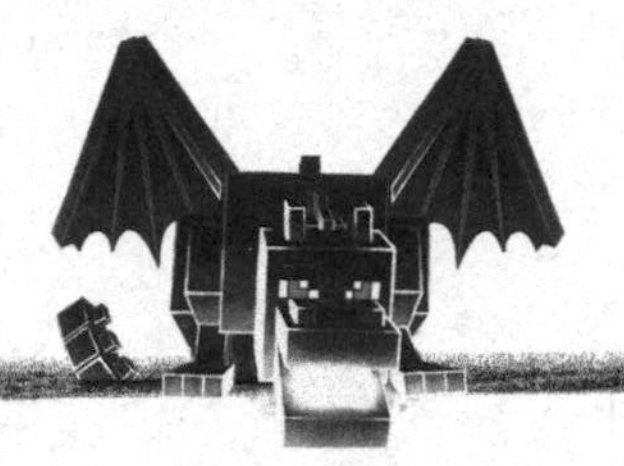

MOJANG

MINECRAFT™
THE END

CATHERYNNE M.
VALENTE

DEL REY
NEW YORK

Minecraft: The End is a work of fiction. Names, places, and incidents either are products of the author's imagination or are used fictitiously. Any resemblance to actual events, locales, or persons, living or dead, is entirely coincidental.

Published in the United States by Del Rey, an imprint of Random House, a division of Penguin Random House LLC, New York.

DEL REY and the HOUSE colophon are registered trademarks of Penguin Random House LLC.

Published in the United Kingdom by Century, an imprint of Random House UK, London.

Hardback ISBN 978-0-399-18072-9
International edition ISBN 978-0-593-15678-0
Ebook ISBN 978-0-399-18073-6

Printed in the United States of America on acid-free paper

randomhousebooks.com

2 4 6 8 9 7 5 3 1

First U.S. Edition

Book design by Elizabeth A. D. Eno

For Aurora and Cole
I am only ever a portal away

MOJANG

MINECRAFT™
THE END

Once upon a time, there was a player.

The player was you.

Sometimes it thought itself human, on the thin crust of a spinning globe of molten rock. The ball of molten rock circled a ball of blazing gas that was three hundred and thirty thousand times more massive than it. They were so far apart that light took eight minutes to cross the gap. The light was information from a star, and it could burn your skin from a hundred and fifty million kilometers away.

Sometimes the player dreamed it was a miner, on the surface of a world that was flat, and infinite. The sun was a square of white. The days were short; there was much to do; and death was a temporary inconvenience.

—Julian Gough, Minecraft "End Poem"

CHAPTER ONE

YOU AND ME AND US AND THEM

It is always night in the End. There is no sunrise. There is no sunset. There are no clocks ticking away.

But that does not mean there is no such thing as time. Or light. Ring after ring of pale yellow islands glow in the darkness, floating in the endless night. Violet trees and violet towers twist up out of the earth and into the blank sky. Trees full of fruit, towers full of rooms. White crystal rods stand like candles at the corners of the tower roofs and balconies, shining through the shadows. Sprawling, ancient, quiet cities full of these towers glitter all along the archipelago, purple and yellow like everything else in this place. Beside them float great ships with tall masts. Below them yawns a black and bottomless void.

It is a beautiful place. And it is not empty.

The islands are full of endermen, their long, slender black

limbs moving over little yellow hills and little yellow valleys. Their narrow purple-and-pink eyes flash. Their thin black arms swing to the rhythm of a soft, whispering music, plotting their plots and scheming their schemes in the tall, twisted buildings older than even the idea of a clock. They watch everything. They say nothing.

Shulkers hide in boxes nestled in ships and towers. Little yellow-green slugs hiding from outsiders. Sometimes they peek out. But they snap their boxes safely shut again, like clams in their shells. The gentle thudding sound of their cubes opening and closing is the heartbeat of the End.

And on the central and largest island, enormous obsidian towers surround a small pillar of grey stone ringed with torches. A brilliant lantern gleams from the top of each tower. A flame in a silver cage, shooting beams of light down from the towers into the grass, across a little grey courtyard, and out into the black sky.

Above it all, something slowly circles. Something huge. Something with wings. Something that never tires. Round and round it goes, and its purple eyes glow like furious fire.

Fin!

The word came zinging through the shade off the shore of one of the outer islands. A huge end city loomed over most of the land: Telos. Telos sprouted out of the island highlands like something alive. Great pagodas and pavilions everywhere. White shimmers fell from the glistening end rods. Shulkers clapped in their little boxes. Leashed to Telos like a dog floated a grand purple ship. A pirate ship without an ocean to sail. Most of the end cities had ships attached to them. No one was certain why, any more than they're certain who built all those big, strange cities in the first place. Not the endermen, though they were happy to name every place after themselves. Not the thing flying in endless circles around a gate to nowhere. Not the shulkers who never came out of hiding long enough to learn anything about anything. The end ships just *were*, as the cities just *were*, as the End just was, like clouds or diamonds or Tuesdays.

Fin! Find anything good?

A skinny young enderman teleported quickly across the island, in and out of the nooks and crannies of Telos. He blinked off in one place and back on in another until he stood on the deck of the end ship, holding something in his arms. His head was handsome, black and square. His eyes were bright and hungry. His limbs were slim but strong. An enderman leaned against the mast, waiting for him. She crossed her dark arms across her thin chest.

Naw, the enderman thought loudly. The words just appeared in the other enderman's mind. Endermen had no need for mouths or ears. No need for sound. Telepathy was so much easier than talking. You just *thought* at somebody and they understood you.

Nothing good, Mo. Just a bunch of pearls. We've got tons of those. Ugh. You take them. They give me the creeps. I was sure the chestplates we found last week would regen by now but I guess somebody else got there first. I got some redstone ore. That's about it. You go next time. You always sniff out the good stuff.

The twin twelve-year-old endermen, brother and sister, Fin and Mo, headed down into the guts of their ship. Fin was technically three minutes older, but he didn't make a big deal out of it. Things like who was older and who wasn't smacked of rankings, of structure, of Order—and Order wasn't welcome in the End.

They'd always lived here. They couldn't remember any other

place. They grew up here. It was their home. No different from any of the hundreds of endermen you'd find on any island in the archipelago. They lived on an end ship crammed with junk they'd snatched up from anywhere they could find it. Some of it was *very* good junk. Diamonds and emeralds, gold ore and lapis lazuli. Enchanted iron leggings, pickaxes of every kind, beetroot seeds and chorus fruits, saddles and horse armor (though they'd never seen a horse). Dozens of sets of marvelous grey wings you could stick right on your back and fly around anywhere you liked. Some of it was just plain old actual junk. Rocks and clay and sand and old books with broken spines. Fin and Mo didn't care. They were scavengers, and scavengers weren't picky. You never knew when you could really use some good old-fashioned clay.

The twin endermen knew there were other worlds out there. It was only logical when you lived in a place called the End. If there was an End, there had to be a Beginning. Somewhere else for this place to be the End *of*. Somewhere the opposite of here. Green and bright, with blue skies and blue water, full of sheep and pigs and bees and squid. Other endermen went there all the time. They'd heard the stories. But this was *their* world. They were safe here, with their own things and their own kind.

Fin and Mo's treasure piled up to the ceiling of the hold. The twins picked their way through their collection carefully. They'd done it a thousand times. There was a well-worn path through the boots and swords and helmets and dragon heads and ingots. Little spaces hollowed out for sitting and eating and living.

And pets.

Hiya, Grumpo, Mo thought cheerfully at the shulker in his box on the far wall. He'd always been there, just like them. They'd never been able to get rid of him, even though they really could have used his spot for more loot. If they whacked on his box until it fell apart, it just came back the next day. Eventually, they'd just given up and accepted him. Gave him a name. Let him guard the junkship some days. You never knew when someone might try to raid your ship. When you had this much loot in one place, you had to stay sharp. Grumpo didn't really *guard* it so much as just *sat there hating everything,* like he always did, but it made them feel safer. He wasn't just a shulker. He was *their* shulker.

If it was a him. They never wanted to pry. They respected the shulker's personal space.

Hiya, Grumpo thought back. He peeked out of his box. They caught a glimpse of his yellow-green head. *I hate you.*

Okay, shrugged Fin. *Good boy.*

I'm not, snapped Grumpo. *I want to bite you.*

Are so! thought Mo. *WHO'S A GOOD BOY?*

The shulker grumbled to himself and shut his box again. His last thought appeared in their heads, the letters very small and angry. *I'm a* bad *boy. I'll bite you tomorrow, you'll see.*

Mo and Fin dug out a basket of chorus fruits from behind a couple of blocks of ore. They divided them equally for lunch. Everything between them was equal. Very carefully, very deliberately, almost militantly equal. The twins worked quietly and happily, side by side, and packed up their meal to take with them.

Guard the ship, Grumpo, thought Fin and Mo. *We're gonna go visit ED. Don't let anyone take our stuff.*

I hate the ship, complained Grumpo, without opening his box. *I hate you. I hate ED. I hate your stuff.*

Good talk, Grumpo! They laughed inside their great black square heads.

Fin and Mo teleported out onto the deck of the end ship. The black sky looked so pretty, with the city sparkling nearby. But they weren't headed to the city. They blinked in and out of sight as they teleported across the island chain. Their ender pearls glowed hot with each jump.

In a moment or two, they'd reached the central island. Crowds of endermen moved between the obsidian towers. Beams of light from the caged lanterns shot out into the dark.

Greetings, Hubunit Paa, Fin thought to a tall elderly enderman they often saw out here. *All hail the Great Chaos!*

May the Great Chaos smile upon you, juvenile male, Paa replied solemnly. It was the traditional answer. All endermen worshipped the Great Chaos. The universe was divided into Chaos and Order. Overworlders believed in Order, but endermen knew it was a lie. Always and forever a lie. The biggest lie ever told. In the Overworld, people believed you could build a fortress strong enough to keep anything out. That you could actually make something perfect. Something that would last. Only endermen, servants of the Great Chaos, seemed to understand that this was folly. It was their holy duty to prove it. Life was so much better when you understood the truth: Anything could happen, anytime, to anyone and anything. The Great Chaos came for everyone sooner or later. It would come for the whole universe someday. The endermen's duty was to help it along any way they could. The holiest pilgrimage an enderman could make was to journey to the Overworld, witness the constructions of the Forces of Order, and sabotage them. Remove one block from a cozy house and the Great Chaos's work could begin. Rain or fire could fall through the roof. Creepers could sneak through a hole in the foundation. Thieves could crawl through and clean you out. Order was so *boring*. Wasn't life so much more interesting once you let the Chaos in?

Greetings, Hubunit Lopp, Mo thought to an enderman who was surrounded by glowing purple sparks, staring out off the edge of the island. *All hail the Great Chaos.*

Greetings, Mo, Lopp replied. *I await the return of my enderfrags. They departed to the Overworld to hunt Order and destroy it. I am tremendously proud of my fragments. They will bring glory to our End.*

I'm sure they'll be back soon, Mo thought comfortingly.

The enderman turned to stare down at them. She was so tall! Something strange flickered in her magenta eyes.

Are you alone? Are you weakened? Do you require endstack with a hubunit of superior strength and power?

Mo took a step back. Mature endermen could get very cagey about a juvenile on her own with no guardians around. It disturbed them somewhere deep in their bones. And Mo didn't like the way the big endermen thought. All stiff and formal and spiky. Long words. And too many of them. Kids didn't think like that. Fin and Mo didn't, and neither did any of the other young endermen they'd met. Some enchantment must fall on you when you came of age that turned you into a snob.

But of course, Lopp thought this way only because there were so many other endermen milling around the ender dragon's island. Alone, an enderman was angry, primitive, little better than a bear who's been hit on the head quite a lot. Only in groups did their thoughts grow all those long and interesting spikes. A group of endermen was called an End. That was why their country was called the End. All the endermen together, the biggest End there could be.

Within an End, there were many different individuals, each in a different cycle of life. Enderfrags were juveniles that fragmented off from a pair of mature hubunits. Nubunits were fully grown endermen who had not yet replicated to start their own Ends. Finally, there were cruxunits, the great, ancient ancestors that had replicated alone and started their Ends out of nothing but themselves. Coming together with other endermen to smarten up and get things done was called endstacking. Of course, it was easiest with the units and fragments of your own End. They'd known you since before you were replicated! But endermen could stack with any other endermen and grow stronger, smarter, safer, sneakier. That was what Lopp was offering: safety. One brick isn't much, though it can hurt if it falls on you. But a hundred all together are a wall.

But Mo didn't want it. She had Fin. That was enough. It had always been enough. When she stacked with endermen who were *not* Fin (and one other she was trying not to think about just now because it was just so *distracting* to think about Kan and Mo had things to do today), it made her itch all over until she wanted to claw her skin off. It made her want to cry. It filled her so full of energy she could barely keep from running and jumping and somersaulting in circles like an idiot. Mo might've been smarter endstacking, but she never *felt* smarter, because she couldn't concentrate for all the itching and crying and somersaulting. Maybe that would all go away in a few years when she became a nubunit. Mo and Fin were still enderfrags, just barely.

Or maybe Mo was just a mess. Definitely a possibility.

No, I'm fine, Mo thought fiercely.

Are you certain? thought the huge enderman with growing concern. *I am available. I am an excellent hubunit. My teleportation and fighting abilities are unequalled.*

I'm fine! Mo shouted in her head, and ran toward Fin. She did not look behind her.

And the ender dragon flew around and around and around, roaring as it went. It dipped and dove between the towers, coming to rest every so often on the small grey courtyard in the middle of the island. There, it roared some more, then took off again.

Fin and Mo teleported up to the top of one of the black pillars. They settled down on the dark stone beside the lantern and watched the ender dragon for a while. It was their favorite thing to do. No matter how long you watched ED, as they called the beast, the dragon never got any smaller or less scary or less interesting. All those nubbly scales along its spine. Those amazing wings. Those huge purple eyes. Every time it passed by they shivered with excitement and fear. But mostly excitement.

Do you ever want to go there? Mo asked, munching on her chorus fruit.

Where? Fin tracked the ender dragon with his eyes. He wasn't really listening to his twin. Who could listen to a sibling when there was a dragon around? It was resting on the little stone courtyard way down on the ground.

The Overworld.

Ugh, why? There's humans *there.*

Humans were the worst thing he knew about. Worse than the void you could so easily fall into. Worse than grown-up endermen. Worse than thieves after your loot. Way worse than Grumpo. Humans hated endermen. They *killed* endermen and stole their *hearts*. The ender pearls that every enderman was born with, the jewels that gave them the power to teleport. Who did that? Who stole *hearts*?

I dunno. Mo stretched her long, dark legs. *Meet new people. Destroy them. Get more loot. Something to eat that's not chorus fruit. Serve the Great Chaos.*

Mo, you know what happened to our hubunits. They went into the Overworld and never came back. If not for the Overworld, we would still have an End.

They got caught in the rain, Mo remembered. A horrible memory. Rain was poison to their people. Standing in a summer storm was like standing beneath a million silver bullets.

It could happen to anyone. That's what the Great Chaos teaches. It gives and it takes. It could happen to you or me or Grumpo. It could happen to Lopp's enderfrags. She stands there waiting for them every day. Have you ever *seen Lopp's fragments?*

No, Mo thought softly.

Fin flicked a chorus fruit over the edge of the pillar. It floated down to the yellow earth. *There you go. It* does *happen to anyone. How many endermen do we lose every week?*

May their noble sacrifice hasten the Reign of the Great Chaos, Mo thought piously.

Yeah, yeah, yeah. But guess who does the Forces of Order's dirty work? Humans. All our problems are because of humans. It's because of humans we can't even remember what our hubunits look like. It's because of humans we can't just pop up to the Overworld for a nice picnic whenever we feel like it. It's not worth it, anyway. I promise. Nothing up there is better than what we have here. The only good reason to visit the Overworld is to serve the Great Chaos. And I wouldn't even do that unless I was sick of being alive. What could be more Chaotic than refusing to serve anybody, after all?

Fin followed the purple spores floating around his skin with his eyes. That was how you could tell an enderman was talking, even if you couldn't hear it. The little glittering violet lights of their telepathy at work flittered all around them.

Is that what our hubunits were doing? Serving? Sacrificing?

I think so. I like to think so. That would mean us being orphans was something more than just a stupid, mean joke the Great Chaos played on us for fun.

Vengeance? Mo thought casually. *We could hunt down humans all night long. It might be fun. Steal* their *hearts for a change.*

Mo, the Overworld is dangerous. It takes people away. Why risk it?

I guess you're right. Besides, we have everything we need right here. She squeezed his dark, thin hand.

The lantern light sparkled everywhere. It was the most beautiful night the twins could imagine. Just like every night. Fin put his long, angular black arm around his twin and rubbed her square head affectionately.

Oh! she thought. *It's coming close this time!*

The ender dragon soared toward them, catching the light from each lantern it passed.

Good afternoon, ED. Mo waved shyly as the creature swooped down toward their pillar. They often tried to talk to it, though it was not tame. It rarely spoke back.

But today, something different happened.

The ender dragon turned its boxy black head toward them. It opened its great mouth. Its insides glowed violet.

Hail to thee and mercy, Mo-Fragment. Its thought blazed and crackled in her head, bigger and louder than any enderman's.

Mo froze, a chorus fruit halfway to her face. *It knows my name! How does it know my name?*

You must be famous, thought Fin. Mo felt his jealousy sizzle in her head.

The ender dragon banked and came round again. It screeched into the void.

Hark, Fragment Fin.

It knows my name too! Wow! The ender dragon turned sharply around a distant pillar. *Hark? What kind of a noise is that? Is it sick? Is it going to throw up? You got all that stuff about mercy. I got "hark."*

It means "hello," Mo giggled in the depths of her mind.

Oh! Hello, ED! Hellllooooo! Hark! Maybe it'll be friends with us! Do you think? Mo?

Mo wasn't so sure. It was coming straight for them now. The purple fire in its eyes didn't exactly look like it meant to make friends. This time, as the creature flew by, it dragged its dark wing over the top of their pillar, knocking them over like they weighed nothing at all.

NOW GO AWAY! ED bellowed in their minds. The crystal lantern next to them guttered in fear. The dragon's tail snapped in the air like a whip and it dove away into the darkness.

That. Was. Fin thought.

So. Awesome! Mo finished for him. Their purple eyes glittered with glee.

Mo grabbed a handful of the silver netting that surrounded the lantern. She could never resist a little more loot.

Race you home! she thought happily, and vanished.

Fin vanished after her.

CHAPTER TWO

THE DOME AND THE DRAGON

Fin sat on a lump of yellow hill on the very edge of Telos. He munched his chorus fruit and stared down at the courtyard below him. It forked off from the main tower of one of the smaller pagodas in the city. Above it, banners hung still in the windless night. Below it, nothing but darkness.

But inside the courtyard? Inside it was the Enderdome.

Mo didn't like to come up here. *If they don't want us, I don't want them,* she always said. Then she buried herself in something or other so she didn't have to keep talking about it. But Fin couldn't stop himself. He loved to watch the enderfrags learning, dueling, playing, sparring, drilling, even their unofficial feuds and brawls. He stayed close enough to stack with them and keep from going totally dangry (dumb and angry, Fin's own word for what endermen alone were like), but far enough away that no one could chase him off. This was where enderfrags trained to survive in the Overworld. To serve the Great Chaos. To fight humans. Fin told his twin he didn't care about the Overworld. She could see his thoughts, so it was true, or she would have called him out. But only partly true. Only mostly. Fin *didn't* care about going up to the big, bright, hot place. But he longed to train with the other fragments in the Enderdome. And the whole point of the Enderdome was to go up to the Overworld someday and punch anything you found there to pieces. He imagined himself in the Dome with the others: top of the class, popular, with ten or even *twenty* people to talk to any time he had a spare thought, instead of just his twin and a cranky shulker at the end of every day.

They were doing teleportation today. Flickering in and out of sight, up to the top of the tower and back down. Out into the hills and back to the courtyard. Here, there, and everywhere. *I could do that,* Fin thought. *I could do it so good. Better than at least half of them. Three quarters, maybe. Yeah. Definitely three quarters.*

Okay, maybe he couldn't do it that well *here*. But back home? On his ship? Fin could disappear and reappear like a deck of cards shuffling. Ace, King, Queen, Jack. Bow, stern, hold, crow's nest. No problem. But that's why he needed to be in the Enderdome with all the other enderfrags! So he could learn to do it everywhere, not just where he felt safe and comfortable. It wasn't *fair*.

Sometimes, when you teleported, it felt like you passed through other places on your way to the place you were going. As though the world got thin when you punched through it like that and you could see through to other Ends almost like this one but . . . but more peaceful, quieter, more full of everything good and useful. Fin wanted to ask about those other places, but he wasn't allowed to train, so he didn't have anyone to ask. The injustice of it burned.

But what stung, what *really* stung, was that Fin and Mo were actually pretty smart, just the two of them. Much smarter than the average enderman alone, if you asked Fin. Or Mo. They never got dangry back home on their ship, far away from anyone else. Imagine how clever they could be if they were allowed to go to the Dome with the other fragments! Endermen were always cleverest in groups, the bigger the group the better. If they were this good as a two-stack, the twins could be gods with two dozen. But they'd never get the chance.

Mo didn't think they needed training in the least. She'd even told him so that morning, as he was heading out. Well, not morning, not really. That was Overworld talk. *Order* talk. But you could make a kind of day and night out of the glow of the end rods. They got brighter and duller on a pretty regular schedule. You could think of them as a clock. If you wanted to. But that was a little bit of blasphemy. Making Order out of Chaos. Time out of timelessness. It was . . . naughty. And therefore thrilling. So, every once in a while, the twins let themselves be bad. They thought of the time when the rods shone brightest as morning, and the time when they dimmed a bit as night. But they never told anyone they'd done it.

There's nothing they can teach us that we haven't learned ourselves, Mo had thought to him that "morning." *We can build, we can hoard, we can travel, we can fight, we can think as straight and as clear as the path between the ender dragon's home and the outer islands. I like our life the way it is. I don't see why it should ever change. Just like you said before. You don't want to go to the Overworld? Well, I don't want to go to the Dome. That's how you know we're twins. We're the same, even when we're different. You don't have to go to the stupid Enderdome to learn how to sit back and have fun.*

The funny thing was, Fin knew she didn't really mean that. She didn't just like their lives the way they were. He caught her staring off into the void lots of times, dreaming of something, someone, somewhere. She would never tell him what. And he didn't pry. He could have found out if he wanted to be a jerk about it. Go peeping into the parts of Mo's mind she didn't broadcast. But that would have been rude, and he would've hated it if she'd done it to him. Fin let her have her secrets so that he could keep his. It was only fair. Fairness was a kind of Order, he knew. But secrets were seeds of Chaos, so he figured it all balanced out in the end. Either way, he knew Mo wasn't quite as happy as she pretended. A brother always knows.

Their one and only friend, an enderman named Kan, didn't understand his fixation with the Enderdome at all. *I hate training,* he always told them. *I am compelled by my hubunits to attend every day and it is boring and violent and it hurts when the other frags hit me. Taskmaster Owari never stops droning on about humans and the Great Chaos, and I spend the whole time wishing I were somewhere else, playing my music with nobody pummeling me. I even wish to be home, and I do not like home much either. When I complain, the Taskmaster only tells me that if I get stronger it will not hurt anymore. Or if I get faster they will not be able to land a blow on me. But I do not want to be strong or fast. I only want the opposite of hurt. You are so lucky you do not have to go to the Dome. Do not tell me any more about how wonderful you believe it is. You do not know. But if it will make you feel better, I can hit you several times very hard.*

But Fin didn't feel very lucky. He felt like a fragment with no hubunits, an orphan with no place in the world. He felt like a freak. Fin just wanted to be normal. He just wanted to be like the rest of them. Why couldn't he be? Why did his hubunits have to go to the Overworld in the first place? Why couldn't life just be *good,* instead of lonely, cast-off garbage? But of course, that wasn't fair. Life *was* good sometimes. And the grown-up endermen had never been cruel about it. They just . . . didn't know what to do with the twins. They were friendly enough when Fin and Mo went into Telos for supplies or to see the lights on Endermas, the great holiday when all the endermen celebrated the birth of the Great Chaos, the beauty of their land, and the strength of their family groups. Their own private Ends. Of course, the twins weren't allowed to celebrate Endermas properly. You couldn't, really, without an End. It was the one day of the year all the endermen made music, singing carols together in vast End clusters. But the twins loved to watch the lights all the same. From afar. From the outside. Like everything else in their world.

Greetings, Fin. Greetings, Mo. The adult endermen would always think when they saw them on the streets. *Are you not afraid to venture alone and weakened after the misfortune which has befallen your life?*

Thanks for bringing it up, Fin always shot back, and it usually shut them up.

It wasn't too long till Endermas now. He would have to think of something special to get Mo and Kan and Grumpo.

Suddenly, an enderfrag flashed into the grass next to him. She was small and stocky, shorter than Fin. Her black skin crackled with purple energy. The enderfrag turned to stare at him.

When you made contact with another person's thoughts for

the first time, you usually saw something welcoming. Whatever it was told you a lot about the person you were sharing minds with. Like a snapshot of their soul. When he looked into Mo's head, the image of their ship greeted him. The door to the hold was always open, and the interior always full of treasure and little beasties from all over the End. Even a tiny ender dragon perched on one of the torches. She loved animals, even though she'd never really seen any other than ED and shulkers and endermites. But she'd heard people talk about the pigs and cows and sheep and foxes and turtles and squid of the Overworld a million times, so she imagined she knew all about them. Mo's mind looked like a home full of happy animals that looked almost but somehow, at the same time, not at all like actual pigs and cows and sheep and foxes and turtles and squid. When Fin looked into Kan's thoughts, he saw musical notes dancing in beautiful spirals. Kan loved music that much. Of course, Fin couldn't see into his own head, because he lived in it. But Mo told him his was a beautiful, friendly room full of open books and pens to write in them, lying on every table and chair and the floor, too.

When he looked at this enderman's mind, Fin saw her End, all those hubunits and fragments and nubs standing close together, arms tangled around one another other until you couldn't tell where one stopped and another began.

Ugh. She was the *worst*.

By the Great Chaos, I believe I have journeyed too far and too swiftly, she gasped in his mind. *I believe you have done likewise, friend! Shall we go back together?*

Good job, Fin mumbled.

His envy burned him up inside. In a minute, she was going to flicker back to the Enderdome and he'd still be by himself with a half-eaten chorus fruit. They looked alike. But they were nothing alike. They weren't friends. They could never be friends. Even the way she thought, all those pretty, formal words. Trying to sound like grown-ups, like the big, tall endermen with their elegant telepathic speeches. Just because she was in the Dome and grown-ups liked her and probably told her she was doing a good job at being a lean, mean, human-stomping machine all the time. Well, those lovely thoughts wouldn't last. They were pretty far from the Dome now. The stack wouldn't hold. Fin had a lot of practice stacking at a distance. You had to, if you lived on the outskirts of everything. But she had no practice at all. If she stayed here more than a few minutes, just the two of them, her thoughts would be more like: *Me strong. You stupid.* And then she'd probably hit him and he'd have to decide whether it served the Great Chaos to hit her back.

Attend a moment, the enderfrag thought. Fin could feel her mind curling away from his. He knew that feeling. All the normal fragments did it when they realized who he was. One of *them.* One of the weird ones. One of the orphans. One of the Endless twins who lived out on that broken old ship like shulkers. The back of Fin's neck prickled all over. Pins and needles, like a foot that had fallen asleep. That was what it felt like when an enderman snickered nastily at you.

I do not know you, the fragment went on. Fin squirmed. *You are not in my training cluster. Why have you escaped the Dome? Where is your hubunit? Where is your End? It is lonely out here on the dunes. These are the hours of instruction. You are not allowed to be alone during those hours. No enderfrag is.*

I am, thought Fin sharply. *I am allowed, and my twin is, too.*

The fragment narrowed her magenta eyes, trying to work it out. *I don't get it.*

There it was. Her thoughts were slipping. Too much time away.

Too much time unstacked. My name is Fin. My twin is Mo. You're Koneka, right?

That is correct. Koneka shook her head. *Yeah. Koneka. But how can you know Koneka, if Koneka does not know you? Why are you out here alone and not in training with us? Alone is dangerous. Come back with Koneka.*

I have no End, Fin snapped. *I have no hubunits! And because I have no hubunits, the Endmoot decided I and my twin must live apart and not go to the Enderdome with you and all your happy little friends. Without an End, we could never be clever enough to deserve training. So they said.*

Oh, thought Koneka.

"Oh" is right, thought Fin. *But I can do anything you can do. You'll see. Someday. When you think about it, I and my twin are* TRUE *spawn of the Great Chaos. Family groups are a kind of Order, not that anyone around here notices. And I'm free of it, unlike you.*

I am gonna go now, Koneka thought sheepishly. *Dunno what do or say. So I go.*

Fine, Fin thought, and kicked the grass.

I am.

Do it then.

I go.

So go.

The enderfrag glared at him. *You stupid,* she thought nastily.

Koneka vanished.

Fin stood up and walked the few short paces to the edge of the grassy island. After a moment, he pitched his fruit over the side. He wasn't hungry anymore. The young enderman watched it tumble end over end into the void. She's *stupid,* he thought. *They're all stupid. It doesn't matter.*

But it did.

Of course it did.

Mo perched on one of the high obsidian pillars on the central island of the End. She rested her back against the silver cage that held the flickering crystal flames that lit the place like little trapped moons.

The ender dragon swooped around and around. Its huge dark wings flapped up and down, up and down. Slowly, effortlessly, as though flying was ever so much easier than sitting on the ground like a lump. Its massive, blocky head moved side to side like a shark's, always seeking something, something it never found. Mo couldn't imagine what a beast like that could want. What could it lack that it could not simply take?

Every once in a while, the dragon crouched on the ground for a moment, but it was never happy there. Always, always it heaved up into the black sky again, resuming its endless circles.

No, the ender dragon's words appeared in her head like someone had written them on a vast bright piece of paper. It answered her question before she even knew she'd asked it. *I am never bored. Not in all the long, hard-boiled, seething history of existence. I ate my boredom when the comets were young. It tasted like death.*

It was happening! ED was talking to her! Her! Mo! Mo the Nobody! Way more than "hark" or "hail to thee"! And Fin wasn't even here! He was off moping at the Enderdome for no good reason. Mo didn't care one bit about the other endermen keeping their distance and making all sorts of rules about them. She cared about her twin, her loot, her friend, and her dragon.

Well, not hers, really. No dragon could ever be anybody's. But nobody was as fascinated by the great beast as Mo was. No one

cared about it the way she did. As far as she could tell, no one else even bothered much with it, or was bothered by it. The ender dragon was like the sun in the Overworld. It was just *there*. It did what it did. You didn't have to try to be nice to it or have a conversation with it or love it. That would be *weird*.

ED occasionally decided the twins were worth speaking to. You never knew if today would be that day or not, though. And it was the first time it had spoken to Mo alone, without Fin. It was a very fickle dragon. And not terribly nice. But terribly *interesting* all the same. The most interesting thing in the world to Mo. She focused her thoughts and sent them across the cool air between the pillars toward the long black serpent.

All hail the Great Chaos! Mo thought joyfully.

If you must, fragment, answered the ender dragon.

Why do you keep going in the same circles on the same island all the time forever? Why don't you ever just . . . fly away? You're so big and strong, you could go anywhere. Do anything. No one could stop you. Why don't you go have adventures? That's what I would do, if I were a dragon.

ED slid one purple eye toward her as it glided lazily through the night.

Who says I am not having an adventure? Right now? Before your miserable mortal eyes?

Uh, I do. Me. You're just flying in circles. That's not an adventure. That's barely an afternoon walk.

You would think that, growled the dragon silently. *You are small. I do not expect anything else from the likes of you.*

Hey, that's not very nice. Mo was hurt, a little. She knew she shouldn't be hurt by what a monster thought of her, but she couldn't help it.

The dragon sailed higher, its thoughts falling down on her like rain. *I am not nice. So that makes a certain amount of sense, does it not? I ate nice, too, when the volcanoes had not yet learned to erupt. It was bothering me.*

Well, prove me wrong then, big guy. Tell me about your adventure.

It has not yet begun.

Then go out and get it!

You understand nothing. You are stupid and small and you understand nothing. I waste my time with you. And my time is precious beyond diamonds.

Tears sprung up in Mo's eyes. *You don't have to be so mean to me.*

I do not have to be kind, either. No law compels me. No creature can force me.

I wish I was a dragon! Then I could say whatever I wanted to anyone and they couldn't do anything back because I'd be so big and black and fearsome and I could breathe fire. And if I was a dragon I wouldn't just flap around in circles like a useless bat. She tried desperately not to cry. *I would burn down anyone who hurt me! Or hurt Fin! I would fly to the Overworld and stop every bad thing from happening! I would destroy everyone who ever hurt an enderman!* And I would bring my hubunits back, she didn't add, but felt, deeply, clutching at her heart. But that was ridiculous. Her hubunits were gone. Even a dragon couldn't get them back. She didn't even remember them, really. If you lined up all the endermen who had perished in the Overworld, Mo wouldn't even know who to save.

ED swung low, its shadow startling several elder endermen, who looked up after it with blank faces. *Child, you are not a dragon. You are a fragment. You are not even that. You are but a fragment of a fragment. And because you are not a dragon, it is beyond the capability of your mind to comprehend that these, right now, here, on this island, among these pillars, are the most enjoyable days of my infinite, endless life.*

I don't understand.

Yes. I said. You are stupid.

I am not!

Go away. I tire of you.

But I want to know about your adventure! Why did you talk to me if you were just going to call me names?

The best time in the world, the ender dragon hummed into her dark skull, *is the time before the adventure starts. Before it starts, it is possible, just possible, that it could end differently than it always ends. It is quiet now. Quiet is a vacation for the mind. Soon the adventure will begin, and at the end of every adventure lies pain. At the end of every adventure, you must ask if it was ever really* your *adventure at all. Perhaps you were only an obstacle in someone else's quest.*

Mo sighed. *I like you better when you're not talking in riddles just to make me feel dumb.*

ED let a ribbon of fire roll out of its mouth into the darkness. *I like you better when you're gone.*

Fine, Mo thought miserably. *Whatever. It's more use talking to Grumpo than you. You're nothing but nasty. I brought you lunch, not that you care. Not that I care either! It's not even for you, I just had it lying around. Whatever.*

The enderman pulled a couple of particularly ripe chorus fruits out of her pack and laid them gently on top of the pillar, where the dragon could easily reach them.

The ender dragon hovered briefly, staring at her offering.

Is it time for that already? it thought softly. *So it must be.*

I don't know what that means, Mo thought.

You are an insect to me. Insects know nothing.

I love you anyway. She always tried to tell the dragon that whenever it talked to her. So it knew, even if it ate love for breakfast and turned it into fire in its mouth.

I have no time for this. Go away. ED's tail vanished into the shadows, flying away from her.

Fine, Mo thought, and kicked the silver cage with the flame burning away within. *It's just a big dumb snake. Doesn't matter.*

But it did.

Of course it did.

Mo left the fruit where it lay and teleported away from the tall black pillar.

After a long moment, the ender dragon returned and snatched them up with its long, fiery tongue. It ate them with great relish.

CHAPTER THREE

KAN

Wake up, I hate you.

Grumpo's thoughts blinked on and off in Fin's and Mo's head like an alarm clock.

Wake up, I hate you.

Fin stretched. Endermen sleep standing up. Beds didn't really work in the End. If you made something to lie down on, it usually exploded. Endermen didn't need much sleep anyway. They were a bit like cats. They just napped wherever they were.

Wake up, I hate you. Someone is approaching the ship. I hate them. Make them leave. It's time for you to make them leave now. I hate them so much. It's happening again. Make it stop happening.

Mo grabbed one of the enchanted iron swords off the sword pile and poked her head up out of the hold. You couldn't be too careful. Humans didn't just live in the Overworld. Every once in a while one would show up here. Or so they'd been told. It hadn't actually happened yet, but sooner or later. It was inevitable. And when they saw ships practically groaning with treasure, humans tended to go a little crazy. And they started out crazy, as far as Mo was concerned.

She scanned the horizon. Telos loomed there, end rods aglow and banners flying. The night beyond was calm and deep. It always was. She didn't see anyone.

Are you sure, Grumpo? Cutie baby Grumpo.

Haaaaaate, hissed the shulker down below. *Want to bite.*

Okay, okay. Mo stuck her head out again.

Anybody there? she thought on a broad frequency that anyone should have been able to hear. *Here, human, human, human!*

I am no human, friend of mine. But I can steal your belongings if you are in the mood for humans today. The thought opened up in her mind. Mo recognized the thinker immediately. Their only friend in the End.

Hello, Kan!

Grumpo growled in his box. *See? He's happening again. I hate him. I hate how he . . . how he* happens. *It's disgusting. He comes around all the time and he does not live here and I hate him. Make him leave. Make him not happen.*

A young enderman appeared on the deck of the greyish-purple ship. He raised one long arm to say hello. In the other, he clutched a brown-checkered note block. Their friend's most prized possession. Kan was longer and thinner than Fin, but because he was always so shy, he seemed smaller than both the twins. He had big, beautiful eyes, but he was always squinting, trying to hide them, trying to make them unnoticeable.

Because Kan's eyes weren't like the wide, clear magenta-violet eyes of other endermen.

Kan's eyes were green.

No one knew why. No one could remember any other enderman who had green eyes, not in all the history of the End. It bothered people. Sometimes it bothered them a lot. Nobody in Telos looked Kan in the eye if they could help it. Fin and Mo had never minded. Some people are just born different, that was all. Some people were orphans. Some people had green eyes. Mo thought they were amazing. Nothing else in the End was exactly that color. Kan's eyes were green like the grass in the Overworld. Green like emeralds. Green like the leaves of a tree in the sun.

Kan raised his dark hands to greet her.

I have run away again, the green-eyed enderman announced triumphantly. *My hubunits attempted to retrieve me, but they could not. I am faster. Taskmaster Owari attempted to drag me back, but she could not. I am stronger. So their training has worked, but not as they hoped. They are all the worst. Every time I think I can bear it, they prove me wrong. May I hide here with you?*

You're always welcome, Mo thought. *Come in, come in!*

That is the opposite of what I said! wailed Grumpo.

And there was the gang. They'd always been like this: Fin and Mo and Kan, morning, noon, and night. Inseparable. The best of friends. Not that Kan's hubunits approved much of that. Not that anyone approved much of that.

Fin and Mo lived on the outskirts of Telos. They lived on the outskirts of everything. They had no End. To everyone else, all these things made them dangerous. To Kan, it made them exciting. Your End was everything. So Fin and Mo should have been nothing. But they weren't nothing. They weren't nothing, at all. What made an enderman an enderman was the End they belonged to, the End that belonged to them. And that was why no one in Telos seemed to know what to do about Fin and Mo, living off on their own in a ramshackle old ship after their hubunits failed to return from the Overworld. Most people thought them frightfully stupid. How could they be anything else when their End consisted of nothing more than two endermen and a shulker? That wasn't an End. That was just . . . a load of junk. So mostly, *mostly*, the other endermen left the twins alone. They had trouble only when they tried to go into the city.

But Kan knew a secret about the twins. They weren't stupid at all. They were much better company than the enderfrags at the Enderdome or the awful Taskmaster or any of the hubs and nubs and fragments Kan had ever met. Maybe it was a twin thing. Kan didn't know any other twins. Maybe they were all like that. Maybe it was like his green eyes. Just some freak of nature. But somehow, just the two of them were enough. Even though a two-stack was usually just barely enough to count to ten between them. Three were the minimum for a decent conversation. Except that Fin and Mo stacked, without any help from anyone. And all three of them were positively *plenty*.

Kan was part of an End, all right. Just like all the other enderfrags. But they never seemed to be much a part of him. He was forever running away from home. This was the third time that week. Kan hated the way he felt when he ran away. He hated the way he felt all the way up until he got to the ship. Mean and dumb and angry and hurt, barely able to remember where he was running to or why. But all he had to do was step on board the ship and the cool cascade of endstacking started up. He could feel himself getting beautifully calm and clever. Because he was home. Not with his End, but with his friends.

Mo had never met any other enderman who'd run away from home even once. But Kan did it every three or four days. Not that

Mo judged her thin, dark friend. She understood, at least she thought she did. Mo would have hated it if she was stuck in some sour, crappy club full of people who scowled at her all the time and told her what to do. Who to be. She would have run away too. And she didn't think anyone should be punished for running away. It was all part of the Great Chaos. Staying somewhere you hated because the rules said you had to was giving in to the Forces of Order.

Mo led her friend down into the hold. Fin was frying chorus fruits in an iron chestplate over the torch flames. You could make a weird kind of sour purple popcorn that way. They'd never found a way to eat it safely, but it was pretty fun to watch the kernels pop. Every once in a while, Grumpo would eat a handful if you sprinkled it into his box like fish food. *Thanks,* he'd say. *I hate it. I want to bite you.* But he always ate it all up anyway. And refused to tell them how he managed to digest the stuff.

Fin waved one long black hand at them, stuck inside the enchanted iron gauntlet that they used as a cooking mitt. The fruits popped cheerfully—Pop! Pop! CRACK!

Kan inhaled the aroma of the chorus corn deeply. It smelled horrific. But it smelled like home.

I like your house so much better than mine, he thought sadly. *I wish I could live here with you.*

No room, Fin thought back jokingly. But the thought that he did not allow to float between their minds was: That would be great, but your hubunits would literally, actually kill us. They'd sweep through this ship like a shadow made of knives and we'd never make gross, inedible popcorn again.

Kan settled into a corner of the ship's guts, between a block of emerald and a pair of old boots. He put his note block between his legs. For a while, he just lay his head on top of it. He didn't think anything. At least not out loud. Endermen could hide their thoughts if they really wanted to. It was just considered incredibly, aggressively rude. Kan didn't cry. Endermen couldn't, not really. But in their minds, Fin and Mo could see an image of the little white sparkles that fell from the end rods on the tips of the towers of Telos, falling all the way to the ground. They understood what that meant the same way any human knows what water falling from another human's eyes means.

Finally, Kan began to tap the brown thatch of his note block. Fin sighed eagerly and sat down with his long legs crossed. Mo leaned forward to hear better. *No one* could play a note block like Kan. Sure, the twins found them every now and again. Mostly when a human failed to kill the ender dragon (as they always did) and dropped one when they got what was coming to them. But when Fin or Mo tried to play it, all they got were short, sharp sounds that they could never fit together into a song.

When Kan played, even the sky stopped to listen.

His hands moved over the top of the block and music poured out. It filled the ship's hold and spilled out onto the deck. The song was sad and bright and angry and hopeful all at the same time. But it was quick and light, too. You couldn't help but tap your feet to it. It made you want to dance and it made you want to hug your friends and it made you want to run out and conquer the world, or at least conquer anyone who tried to tell you what to do.

Grumpo's box top rose up slightly. His yellow-green nub of a head peeked through the crack. Kan stopped playing.

Let me guess, he thought at the shulker, *you hate it.*

After a long pause, the shulker answered: *I don't hate it.*

A gasp rose from all three of the endermen. They couldn't believe it. Of course Kan was good. The best. But Grumpo hated *everything*. Kan often thought the shulker was like his hubunits that way.

I just STRONGLY DISLIKE IT, the shulker snapped back, and slammed his box shut.

Kan turned his friendly rectangular head back to his friends. He had always been the handsomest enderman in the End. Mo thought so. Fin thought so. But whenever the three of them went to Telos and passed others on the long violet streets, they always heard the grown-ups thinking about how ugly and awkward Kan was. How horrible his eyes were. How stupid and weird and even hideous he was. It made Mo so angry. Kan was beautiful! Why couldn't they see it? If only the whole of Telos could hear him play . . . but hearing him play never seemed to help Kan's family like him any better.

I was playing that song this morning. My secondary hubunit heard me. He was so furious. He is right. He has told me time and time again to give up my block. Stop it, *he screamed,* stop that horrible racket! Music is one of the chief servants of Order! How dare you bring it into this house! I cannot stand one more note! Be who you were meant to be! Be one of us! Go to the Overworld! Hunt humans! Serve Chaos like your fellow enderfrags! Eat, fight, and be merry! Why must you mope and sing all the time? You are not a sad parrot! *And then he tried to break my block.*

I'm sorry, thought Fin. *I wonder if our hubunits would have been like that.*

But then, if I try to get away, if I try to save my block, it only gets worse! Without me, my primary and secondary hubunits, their hubunits and nubunits, their other enderfrags and all the rest of them are weaker and dimmer. They roar and chase after me and try to get me back into their End even though I do not want to be in their End at all! I do not want to go to the Overworld! I do not care one bit about the Overworld! It's bright and horrible there! I do not want to be a warrior. I do not care about the Great Chaos!

Mo gasped. That was blasphemy. Real, serious blasphemy. If a grown-up heard them thinking like that . . .

I do not want to be an enderman at all if all it means is hunting humans and fighting battles and breaking things. I just want to play my music. I like this *familial group! Kan and Fin and Mo and Grumpo and the ship! That is my End. They do not understand me. They will* NEVER *understand me.*

We like this End, too, thought Fin.

They were all quiet for a while.

How long before they come to get you? Mo thought delicately. Kan wouldn't want to talk about it, but whenever his hubunits came to pick him up, they tended to do quite a bit of damage to the ship.

I do not know. Kan's thoughts were so quiet they were like whispers. *I wish I did not have hubunits.*

Don't say that, Fin thought fiercely.

No, you don't, thought Mo at the same time.

Now Kan's thoughts were so quiet they could barely see them. They flickered in the twins' heads like candles about to go out. *Then I only wish I had not been born different. I wish I liked to fight and break things like everyone else. I wish I had never heard music in the first place. I just want to be normal. Why did the Great Chaos make me this way?*

I think you're wonderful this way, Mo thought.

Grumpo's box clapped open suddenly. Then shut again. Then

open. Then shut and open and shut and open and shut again, but faster and louder. *SOMEONE IS APPROACHING THE SHIP,* the shulker screeched into their skulls. *SOMEONE IS APPROACHING THE SHIP. SOMEONE BIG. HATE. HATE. HATE. HATE. I WILL BITE THEM. I WILL. LET ME BITE THEM. YOU WILL NOT BE SORRY. EVERYTHING WILL BE BETTER IF I BITE THEM. TRUST GRUMPO. GOOD BOY GRUMPO.*

Fin and Mo turned toward the door into the hold. The terrible thoughts of Kan's secondary hubunit, Karshen, appeared in their minds like flashing lights and sirens.

KAN! WHERE ARE YOU LOCATED IN THE VOID?!

Full of rage. Full of pride. Full of that strange way of talking grown-ups liked so much. There were enough of them here that Karshen could summon the intelligence to speak as he pleased.

KAN! I WILL DISCOVER YOU!

I will go, Kan thought glumly. He tucked his note block under his skinny, dark arm. *I do not want any of your treasure to get ruined like last time. The behavior of my hubunits humiliates me. I am sorry.*

KAN! YOU ARE MORE FOOLISH THAN YOU APPEAR! UNCOVER YOURSELF TO YOUR HUBUNIT! WE DO NOT POSSESS AN EXCESS OF TIME IN WHICH TO PLAY YOUR FRIVOLOUS GAMES. UNCOVER YOURSELF. EVENTS COMMENCE. TERRIBLE EVENTS.

One enderman alone may not be as clever or as strong as many endermen together. But one enderman alone is still plenty strong. They could hear him thrashing around on the upper deck. They heard the slats of the ladder on one side of the mast crack under his fist.

I will go, Kan said again. But he didn't get up.

What's he talking about? Mo thought swiftly. *What terrible events?*

I do not know, nothing was afoot when I left. All was silence. Except for the usual yelling session concerning how much all sensible people hate music.

KAN!

It is the day of my fragmentation, Kan thought glumly. *They do not even remember*.

Endermen were not born the way humans were. The little enderfrags just replicated off the primary hubunit. A tiny black sprite blinking away from a big black block. They looked almost like small black eggs. No pain or drama or cuddles in its mother's arms. A newborn enderman was just part of the primary hubunit one moment, and off on its own the next. But they did celebrate their day of fragmentation, all the same. Usually.

Now they could hear the thoughts of Kan's primary hubunit, Teg. Even louder than Karshen's. Her heavy feet crunched onto the ship.

They're going to wreck the place, Fin worried.

KAN YOU MUST REVEAL YOURSELF TO YOUR CREATORS!

Farewell my friends, waved Kan as he trudged up the steps toward his family. *I will see you again. Someday. I hope*.

It'll be okay, Mo thought after him.

Will it, though?

Ender swear, Fin assured him.

Ender swear, Mo agreed.

Kan nodded. His face looked so pretty in the soft light of the End. *Okay. I believe you*.

KAN, YOU HAVE APPEARED AS IF BY MAGIC. The huge endermen outside blared their thoughts everywhere with very little care for who heard them. They must really have been worried. Usually, endermen were much more careful to keep their thoughts tight and directed, like a flashlight's beam that landed only where you wanted it to.

How did you find me so swiftly? Kan thought dryly.

You always come here, Kan's primary hubunit thought, returning to a normal volume. *Why would we look in an alternative location?*

But his secondary hubunit was still screaming at the top of his mind.

YOU MUST RETURN TO THE HOME NODE IMMEDIATELY, FRAGMENT. THERE IS NO TIME TO EXPEND IN DISCUSSING YOUR FAILURES.

Why? What is at home? More yelling? Kan's thoughts were white-hot with resentment.

The primary hubunit crouched on her black knees. The lights of Telos beyond her enormous head gave her a strange yellowish halo. She looked deep into her fragment's strange, terrible green eyes. She even touched his head. Just a little. Almost as if she cared. And now, even though Fin and Mo and even Grumpo could still hear her thoughts, she sent her words quietly.

Kan, fragment of mine, you must come home and prepare. It is imperative. We must defend ourselves. The humans are coming.

CHAPTER FOUR

THE ENDMOOT

Humans.

Even the word made Mo shudder.

Humans.

Fin had never seen one, and he didn't want to.

Oh, they came to the End. Every once in a while. Like pests. Like Creepers sneaking up behind you on a sunny day. Silverfish leaping out at you from a path you thought was safe. Spiders turning on you just as the sun sets. Or worse, endermites chewing at the foundation of the world until it cracked.

But to Mo and Fin, all that was just stories. Rumors. Memories. Other people's memories. Just as they had been told by the elders what their hubunits were like, they had been told what humans were like. Just in case. In case they needed to know, someday. To protect themselves.

Humans were strange. They were alien. They were hideous. Instead of beautiful, sleek black bodies as tall as trees, they were short and thick and a hundred different colors all mushed together into fat eyes, wet stomachs, horrible reeking feet, and something particularly nasty called "hair." They were violent and angry even when they had everything they could want. If you put a human in a nice patch of swamp or forest or meadow, they'd carve out everything valuable for themselves in half a day, if that. They just sucked it up like squishy flesh tornadoes. And all to build a stupid house or castle or statue, instead of leaving it as it was, unspoiled, which had been far more beautiful than their weird ugly buildings in the first place. Sometimes, they just hit sheep and pigs and even rocks with swords for *fun*. Just to see what would happen. As if they didn't know. And if they saw you, if they so much as *saw* you, they'd get you. You *had* to get them first. That was all there was to it. Survival of the quickest. Once you've seen one human, it's too late. They'll be everywhere before you can blink.

You could get them easier at night. They had to sleep on beds, in houses. Endermen catnapped with their eyes slitted, just slightly open, ready and wary of predators. Obviously, the sensible way to get your rest! One of the elders, a lanky, gruff old one named Sama, had had to explain to the twins that for humans, "sleep" meant lying in one place for hours and hours, totally unable to hear or see anything. This seemed idiotically dangerous, and they told Sama so. The elder had agreed, and they'd gone their separate ways, satisfied to be right all around. That was why humans needed beds and houses, to keep them safe while they did their idiot thing at night. So the best bet was to catch them before they could get into their little fortresses.

And of course, as Fin and Mo knew very well, humans' favorite thing to eat was hubunits.

Not that they'd ever asked anyone what humans' favorite food was. They didn't need to. It was quite literally the story of their lives.

Humans were monsters. Storybook horrors.

And they were coming.

An Endmoot had been called.

Because endermen were most intelligent and careful in their family groups, the wisest an enderman could possibly be was at an Endmoot. From all over the End, endermen came in their family groups to the ender dragon's island to commune and plan. Whenever a decision that affected all of them had to be made, they came to stand in the long shadows of the obsidian pillars and become wise together. It was not every enderman who existed. That was impossible. Endermen ranged far and wide, in every part of the world. It wasn't even every enderman in the End. The End was so vast, each section of it could go eons without communication with another section. But it was enough. Enough to choose the right path.

As long as Fin and Mo had been alive, there had been only one Endmoot: when their hubunits died and no one knew what was to be done with the orphans. There'd never been a need for another. The End had stayed peaceful all that time. A raid here or there from overworlders, sure. But nothing that required a plan of action to handle.

Until now.

They came drifting in like black birds, in groups of four and five, six and eight, sometimes even twelve and fifteen or more. Their lovely broad heads tipped up toward the crystal light falling from the towers, toward the shadows of the eternally circling dragon, who played no part in these affairs and offered no advice. Sparkling violet dust glittered all around the endermen as they gathered. There was Sama, the elder who had explained sleep to them once upon a time. There was Lopp, whose enderfrags had still not returned. There was Paa, who had long ago brought them the news that they could not train at the Enderdome now that there were only two of them. There was Eresha, the Mouth of the Great Chaos, with her many clerics gathered around her. There was Kraj and Karshen and Teg and Wakas and the beautiful nubunit Tapi. Fin even saw Koneka hiding behind her hubunits, awed by so many people in one place. Kan was there too, sulking on a low dune with his note block beside him. His strange green eyes stared off into the distance. Kan kicked at the sand and grass with his feet. The twins saw everyone they knew. Many, many more they did not.

ALL HAIL THE GREAT CHAOS! Eresha thought over the crowd, the power of her mind as commanding as a trumpet.

MAY THE GREAT CHAOS SMILE UPON YOU, answered the masses of endermen.

How do we know humans are coming? Mo thought to her twin. A quick, direct thought between the two of them, not to be shared with anyone else. *Are there . . . I don't know, alarms? Human alarms?*

Can you not feel it? The thoughts of an elder came slicing into their conversation. Rude. But all rules and niceties were off now. The danger was too great for manners. Owari, the Taskmaster of the Enderdome, towered above them. *The twelve seals are nearly in place. And upon those seals the humans will place twelve eyes of ender. When it is done, the great portal shall be complete, and they will swarm into our world. It is the End Times.*

Twelve eyes? Fin recoiled in horror. *EYES? What is wrong with them? Whose eyes did they steal? For what? Party decorations?*

Humans do worse than that, juvenile male, thought Karshen, Kan's secondary hubunit. He was calm and thoughtful now, stacked with so many endermen. Not a trace of his rage left. *They steal our pearls.*

Mo felt sick. Ender pearls were to an enderman as a heart and a soul were to a human. *Why? By the Great Chaos, why?*

Karshen answered: *With it, they can teleport as we do.*

They can't walk? Mo thought in horror. *Run?*

They walk very well indeed, and run better than most. But with an ender pearl, they arrive at their destination somewhat faster.

And that, to a human, was apparently worth ripping the soul from an enderman. They wouldn't even know who it had belonged to. An enderman's entire heart was nothing more than a minecart ride.

It only works once for them, Kan thought from his sullen perch on the edge of the island. Distance mattered little when it came to telepathy. If you wanted to be heard, you could be. His purple spores sparkled brightly. *The pearl burns out into an ember of coal after they use it.*

Oh, that's fine then! Fin cried. *Very efficient! We're just like torches to them! Burn us and throw us away.*

I hate them, Mo thought. *I hate humans so much.*

A howl of rage went up from the minds of hundreds of endermen. White-hot, black-cold, insatiable fury.

The moment I see one I cannot stop myself, hissed Nubunit

Tapi, shaking with anger. *I cannot rest until I kill it. My soul burns until it is dead.*

Good, my friend! Thought an extremely tall enderman standing nearby. *That is right and proper! Let your lust for battle guide you! Strike them all down in the name of the Great Chaos! Break their castles! Take their treasure! Feel no guilt. They would do the same to you.*

It is true that humans are the greatest scourge the world has ever known, as disgusting as endermites, as greedy and ugly as death itself. That thought belonged to the elder Ipari. It floated in the minds of all the gathered endermen, cool and firm. *But we have little time for this. Each and every enderman must feel the portal nearing completion, like locks sliding into place within us.*

The smallest enderfrags looked around themselves suddenly, terrified, expecting a human to appear at any moment.

Ah, the little ones do not understand as their hubunits do, the elder Ipari thought soothingly. *Time in the Overworld does not flow in precisely the same way as it does here. In the time it takes for whatever humans are building their portal to slide another stone, another eye into place, hours or days may pass in the End. We cannot know for certain. Time is the servant of Order. We are not friendly with it.*

I don't feel anything, Fin thought quietly. *Do you?*

No, answered Mo. *Maybe we're getting sick. Grumpo had that cold, remember? He told us to snuggle up close so we would get it, too.*

But we do know the time is short, another enderman, Beigas, picked up Ipari's thought where it left off. His violet eyes flashed. *The portal will open beneath the very earth on which we now stand. And they will pour out like lava. We must fight them. That much is certain. Perhaps we can trust in our dragon to protect us?*

The endernation looked to the skies.

No answer came but a long, low reptilian laugh.

A single word echoed in all their minds: *Fools.*

The End belongs to us, thought Wakas, one of the endermen shepherds. She had a flock of shulkers she tended on the slopes of one of the smaller inner islands. *It is the land of our people. We have lived here since the beginning. They have no right to take our country from us and pillage it.*

Not exactly since the beginning, Vegg interrupted her. Vegg was a strategy master in Telos. She taught the class Fin had watched yesterday from his dunes. Fin watched her now, longingly. She was giving a lecture, a real lecture. And he was here to listen. Finally.

You speak nonsense, Vegg. Be silent, snapped Wakas.

Nonsense? Did we build these cities? Did we raise these towers, block by block? Did we plant the chorus trees? Did we light the crystal torches atop those pillars? No. *We did not. Our ancestors found them as they are. Someone was here before us, and we took their land just as the humans wish to take ours. We took it so thoroughly that now we do not even remember their names or what they looked like. And besides, ownership is Order.*

I would not go that *far,* began Eresha, the Mouth of the Great Chaos. *The human invaders believe everything is theirs for the taking. That is the Order of the universe in their twisted minds. They see a thing they desire; they smash it. They take it. They devour it. They destroy it. They use it in their vile constructions. We must stand against that. We must keep the End safe and whole, and though there is some Orderliness to our possession of this place, it is outweighed by our needs. Endermen must rule the End. The Great Chaos wills it so.*

There is another dilemma, an enderman named Kraj piped up.

A great silence fell in all their minds. Kraj was the oldest enderman any of them had ever heard of. He was a cruxunit. One of the thick, powerful stems from which all other endermen sprang. The violet of his eyes was faded, his spores almost silver. *I am more ancient than many of you. I have seen more things. Suffered more. Experienced more. I have escaped the rain all the days of my life.*

Get on with it, Kraj, Paa complained. *You impress no one.*

Fin and Mo were stunned. They had always been told to respect the cruxunits. But Kraj really didn't impress any of the other elders. As soon as his thoughts fired up, the other endermen started looking bored and restless. They picked at their spores, wandered around, examined the wall of a nearby pillar with sudden intense interest. No one listened to Kraj, and most seemed to intensely wish he'd stop talking at once. The twins took the opportunity to jog over to Kan and settle down on the dry grass with him. The night sky loomed over the edge of the island. It was so beautiful. They'd always thought so.

Kraj kept talking, pointedly ignoring the endermen pointedly ignoring him. The ways of adults were very strange. *I have journeyed to the Overworld many, many times. I have always returned. I have been attacked by humans, cut and beaten. I have barely avoided being caught in the rain. I have served the Great Chaos in the Overworld and the End. And I must warn you that humans have discovered a terrible secret to use against us. For centuries, they could not hide from the ender gaze. Once we saw them, they were ours. But in the Overworld there grows a certain squash, a certain gourd, a pumpkin round and thick. If you had not journeyed as far and as long as I, perhaps you might not have noticed it. Bushes here and there, vines that looked black and welcoming, like endermen, somehow. Friendly. Kind. The humans discovered this. They hollow out these pumpkins and wear them like helmets. When they hoist the gourd-helm over their cursed skulls, we cannot tell the difference between them and an enderman. They can walk among us, spies, secret operatives, double agents! Even now, the humans could already be among us, and we would suspect nothing!*

A terrible shriek of despair echoed around the ender dragon's island. And then, like thunder after lightning, the long, low laughter of the dragon followed.

Is there anything we can do against such a weapon? wailed Lopp.

Is there any way to know which of us are truly endermen? thought Karshen, staring intensely toward the edge of the island. Toward Kan and that blasted note block.

There is not, admitted Kraj. They were listening now, weren't they? Oh, yes. Now they paid attention. Kraj reveled in it. *We must be careful. Never travel alone. Move in groups of four at least, and more if you can gather them. We have never needed one another so much. Fortify yourselves. Have faith in the Great Chaos. It will guide and protect us. It will visit ruin upon our enemies. Place shulkers everywhere you can. They are coming, if they are not already here. We must be ready. We must protect our land from the interlopers.*

Tapi frowned, but kept her thoughts to herself.

But there must be a way to tell, thought Karshen. His eyes narrowed into magenta slits in his black head.

Is he looking at us? Fin thought, terrified.

He's looking at us, Mo thought back. *I wish we hadn't come. He's crazy.*

Karshen glared at them. *Through* them. *It is impossible that the humans have invented something so effective that no enderman can see through their deception. Humans may be strong, but they are wicked and stupid. They use their mouths to talk, like animals. The same mouths they eat with. No one who talks with their eating hole can best the noble enderman. There must be clues that would reveal the spies! If you look closely enough.*

I did not say there were *spies,* thought Kraj hurriedly. *Only that there* may *be. Do not rush to suspicion. The true servant of Chaos accepts all possibilities.*

But Karshen ignored the cruxunit. *A clue,* the hulking hubunit growled in their heads. *If only someone was wise enough to see it. They would not be like us. Oh no. They would be different. Freaks. Outcasts. Monsters. People who simply* cannot *act normal, no matter how you try to accept them. People with no respect, no manners, no love for the End. People who reject the endergroup altogether and run off to be . . . to be . . .* by themselves. *UGH! Humans could never understand the meaning of family. They are the same alone or together: ugly, dumb, unpleasant, annoying, and cruel.* Karshen had worked himself into a fury. His slick, dark shoulders quivered and began to burn red. The berserker rage of the enderman who has a human in his sights. *And LOUD,* he finished.

Stay away! Mo yelled. *You don't know us! You don't know anything about us!*

Please, Karshen! Fin scrambled up. A few blades of grass and grains of sand skittered off the edge of the island, tumbling into the void. *We've eaten with you and drunk with you! You took us in when our hubunits got caught in the rain! You do know us! You've known us since we were little! We don't even know what pumpkins* are!

Karshen bellowed the enderman war cry and bolted toward them, screaming, shrieking. The sound was like a horrible mechanical siren.

KAN! the hubunit roared. He swung his long arms, knocking Mo and Fin aside like black dolls. He kicked the note block off the ender dragon's island into the night with a yelp of joy and triumph. Kan cried out after it, white tears streaming in his mind. It fell silently, slowly, until it disappeared into the dark. Karshen grabbed his fragment's head and smashed it against the earth as though he meant to crack it open. Surely no pumpkin could withstand more than a few blows like that. *I knew it! I knew it all along! Everything makes sense now. You are not my fragment! You have never been my fragment! You are a HUMAN BEING WITH GREEN EYES!*

Kan gave up. He lay on the ground beneath his hubunit and cried.

CHAPTER FIVE

THE SPY

Fin and Mo carried Kan back to their ship. They each put a shoulder up under one of his slender arms and flashed through the island chain with a couple of easy teleports they barely felt. They didn't want to jostle him too much. It was quiet on their ship. The roar of the Endmoot lay far behind them. Only the flicker of end rods and the slow thudding of Grumpo's box like a heartbeat deep within the end ship welcomed them home.

Is your head okay? Mo whispered.

Kan moaned. They heard it only in their minds, but a moan in the mind is much worse than one you hear with your ears. You can't try to moan less loudly so your friends don't worry about you when they can hear the inside of your head. You can't hide anything.

Sit here, Fin thought. *I'll get something to clean you up. I'm pretty sure I've got a potion of healing around here somewhere.*

Why are you helping me? Kan thought bitterly. *You heard him. I am a filthy, disgusting, ugly, loud human. Stop helping. You do not help a spy once you have caught him. You interrogate him. I am ready.*

Grumpo's box thudded several times. They heard muffled laughter.

Listen when Grumpo hates something, the shulker chuckled. *Told you. Told you. No one listens to Grumpo's hates. Grumpo has the best hates. He hates for good reasons. Ha, ha, Kan, I hate your face. I want to bite your face so hard. Do you want to know a secret? If you let Grumpo bite who he pleases, life will be so much better for everyone.*

Shut up, snapped Fin. *Not now, Grumpo.*

You can bite me, Grumpo, Kan thought miserably. *I deserve worse than the bite of a shulker.*

Oh, Kan. Hush. Mo rummaged behind one of the barrels in the hold for a minute. When she emerged, she was holding something in her hand. She gave it to Kan. *Eat this. You'll feel better.*

It was a golden apple. Mo had only two. They were terribly precious. She'd found them in the back alleys of Telos, on top of a pile of dust that she assumed had once been a human. Caught thieving by a righteous enderman, no doubt. They'd probably been trying to heal themselves by eating the apple when the good citizen rushed them. Served whoever it was right. Mo had laughed at the dust. *You died,* she'd thought. *Dummy. Only dummies die.*

Kan ate the apple slowly. His jaw obviously hurt. But slowly, the purple blood dried up and flaked away. The bruise on the side of his head faded and vanished. The enderman sat up straight again.

He didn't look any different. He was as black and beautiful as ever, the angles of his face sharp and clean. His eyes were the same bright, glittering green they were so fond of. There was no sign of pumpkin anywhere. Not one bit of seed or stringy pulp.

Karshen's wrong, thought Mo. *Of course he's wrong. How could you think for a minute you didn't belong here? You're an enderman, just like us. You've always been an enderman. Your hubunit is just . . .*

An idiot, Fin finished his sister's thought. *And a bully.*

But if I was human you would not be able to see *it!* Kan protested. *I would look normal to you! I am human. I am. It explains everything. My music. My . . . my eyes. It is the only thing that makes sense.* The enderman sniffled and wiped his eyes as though he wished he could wipe them away completely. *Humans love music, you know. Oh . . .* he remembered suddenly. *My note block. It is gone . . . gone.*

A memory flashed between them: Kan finding that note block on one of the inner islands years ago. Little Kan with his little shining green eyes, wandering alone on a little scrap of land floating in space with one measly tree on it. Alone because he couldn't stand his house anymore. Because his fellow-fragments had called him *greenboy* again that morning and he hated himself. Hated that he'd cried. Hated that they hated him. Hated his eyes for their greenness. Wishing every day he'd wake up and they'd be pink. And then he saw it, lying on the yellowish earth next to a pair of boots, a broken sword, and a packet of apples and cooked cod, like destiny waiting for its person. He hadn't even known what it was at first. He'd just touched it. Innocent as anything.

But when Kan touched that silly brown block, it sang.

And now it was gone.

Kan, no pumpkin in the world could survive what your hubunit did to you, Mo thought.

You do not know that. Do you even know what a pumpkin is?

Well, not exactly. Almost. Kraj said it was a gourd. I suppose that is some kind of fruit?

See?

Fin shook his friend by the shoulders. *Kan! How could you POSSIBLY be a human? Remember that Endermas when we were all five? Your hubunits let us come to your settlement and share the Enderfeast of Divine Chaos. It was the only year they let us past the home perimeter. Do you remember?*

Yes, Kan mumbled.

Do you remember why they let us?

Because I begged. I promised to put away the note block for a whole month if they let you feast with us. I told them the Great Chaos approved of all lonely people, because they could wander around and make anything happen. That it would be the most Chaotic Endermas ever if you two were there with us. And no one should be alone on Endermas. Rain could happen to anybody. It was not your fault.

Yeah, you did. Because you're a good friend. Almost as good a friend as a musician. And that was seven years ago, Kan. If you've been a human spy for seven years and no one ever even suspected, well, honestly, I think we should just make you king of the End right now, because you'd deserve it. That is a long *game. We were just little babies back then. Babies can't be spies. It's ridiculous.*

I guess you are right, Kan sighed.

He is, Mo agreed. *Your hubunit is just defective. That's all.*

But what about my eyes? No one else has green eyes. *You have to admit, it is terribly hard to explain that away.*

Neither of the twins said anything. It *was* hard to explain.

Just because we can't explain it doesn't mean it's wrong, Mo thought delicately. *It doesn't make you a monster. Some things are just different, that's all. Some fruits aren't quite the same as other fruits, some trees are a little taller or a little shorter than other trees, some cities are bigger and more beautiful, some people are . . .*

But that is just it, Mo, Kan insisted. *Some people* are not. No one *is different in the End. Maybe in the Overworld, what you are saying is true. But here, everyone belongs. The chorus fruits* are not *different colors. Some cities* are not *more beautiful. Everyone looks the same. Everyone* is *the same. Except me.*

And us, Fin added. *I guess we'll just have to be different together. Isn't that what the Great Chaos is all about? Should be all about, anyhow.*

No one thought out loud for a long while. That is to say, they were all thinking, and quite a lot, but they chose not to share it. They made their minds quiet and still as the night sky.

But you are not, Kan thought finally. *Not really. You were just like everyone else until your hubunits were caught in the rain. You are different, but your difference* happened *to you. And maybe when you grow up you could even fix it. You will get big and have an End of your own and you will not be different at all anymore. Everything will be fine for you. You used to be normal endermen. You will grow up into normal endermen. My eyes were never pink. And they never will be.*

I hate pink, grumped the shulker in his box. Thump-thump, thump, thump-thump.

Thanks, Grumpo, Kan thought gratefully. *Very kind of you to say.*

I hate green, too. Thump-thump, thump, thump, thump. The sound of Grumpo's box opening and shutting was uncannily like giggling. *Might bite green later.*

Kan ran his hands over a golden chestplate leaning against the side of the hold. *I just do not think we can rule it out. My being secretly human. Not yet.*

Fin threw up his hands. *Kan, just forget about it! Now, look, you can stay here as long as you want. We'll protect you. We've got plenty of weapons and some explosives so don't worry about that. But I don't want to hear any more about you being human. It's sick. Just a sick joke.*

Mo shook her head. *You can't be, you just can't be. It's not possible.*

Why not?

Because humans are terrible monsters. They're cruel and ugly and greedy. And you're . . . you're wonderful.

The twins saw the white sparkles falling slowly from end rods in their minds again. As they fell, they turned from white to red. They understood their friend was crying in frustration. He rubbed his face with his long, black fingers.

Do you not get it? I want to be human! I hope I am human! Somehow, somehow, I hope my hubunit is right. Because then everything would make sense. Suddenly, I would understand everything that has ever happened to me! My whole life would be like a story, the kind of story where in the end the person reading it thinks: Of course! It is perfect! How could I not have seen it all along? *Everything would fall into place. I would know who I am. I could go somewhere and no one would look at me when I passed them on the road. No one would even care because I would be just like everyone else. I would be normal. And when I played my music, when I played . . . they would* listen.

Kan kept rubbing his face, pulling hard at his cheeks. Scratching. Shoving his fingers miserably into his skin. Mo realized he wasn't rubbing at all. He was *clawing*. Clawing at the invisible pumpkin he desperately hoped was there.

Fin grabbed Kan's hands and stopped him. *Hey,* he thought gently into his friend's mind. *Don't do that. Just breathe.*

Mo jumped up. She'd remembered something. She hadn't thought of it in *ages*. Of course she hadn't, there'd never been a reason to think of it. It'd just been another bit of loot to add to the hoard. She'd found it lying next to a scorch mark that used to be a poor, dead, foolish human who must have tried to go up against ED and failed. The ender dragon had circled overhead, laughing coldly. That particular human had carried quite a lot of treasure and weapons with her into the End, which meant a good day for Mo. Where had she put it? Mo climbed over a pile of enchanted books, loose emeralds, and bows and arrows. One day they really would have to organize all this. But not today. Today, Mo remembered where she'd put things by her own mixed-up system, her own small service to the Great Chaos. Books made her think of paper, which made her think of music, emeralds made her think of Kan's eyes, and whenever she heard her friend play, she felt like an arrow had struck her in the chest. It all made sense, if you were Mo.

And there it was.

Mo pulled something hard and brown out of the mess, dislodging a lot of arrows and emeralds and several old books she fully meant to get around to reading eventually. She knelt next to Kan and put it into his hands.

Here, she thought softly. *See? Everything can be fixed. If you have your End and all its fragments. Anything can come back again.*

It was a note block.

Kan sniffled. He didn't touch it right away. He was almost afraid to. Afraid to believe it was real. Afraid to hope. His glowing spores fell around it like purple fireflies.

The young enderman let his fingers fall onto the note block. He closed his poor, tired eyes. And began to play.

CHAPTER SIX

THE FINAL BATTLE

They were all asleep when Kraj boarded their ship.

He did not come alone. Of course he didn't. Alone, who was Kraj? Nobody. Not even a cruxunit.

SOMEONE IS APPROACHING THE SHIP! Grumpo's voice exploded in Fin's, Mo's, and Kan's heads, ripping them out of a deep sleep. *A LOT OF SOMEONES ARE APPROACHING THE SHIP! WAKE UP! WAKE UP! OH, I HATE SOMEONES! WAKE UP! PROTECT ME FROM THE SOMEONES!*

The ancient cruxunit Kraj approached the stern of Fin and Mo's home surrounded by eight tall, strong endermen. Fin could see them through the portholes, drifting up over the starboard side in powerful silence. He shook his head to clear away the last of his sleep. Mo rubbed her eyes, her heart racing. Kan hung back, glaring uncertainly. None of Kraj's people opened their minds and thoughts. Their hearts were blank and dark as their long, lean bodies.

That's not Kraj's End, Fin thought, a clear, thin, laser-focused thought sent only to his friends. *I know his fragments and his sub-fragments and his sub-sub-fragments. The Great Chaos knows he has enough of them.* There was a reason Kraj was so wise, wise enough to survive so long. With an End as big as his, always around him, always underfoot, Kraj's mind was clever beyond imagining. Never unstacked. Which was why no one liked listening to him. Even endermen got annoyed with know-it-alls.

The eight endermen arranged themselves in formation around Kraj. Two stepped forward to flank the elder. The other six took up positions on the deck.

Proceed, sir, they thought in unison, a loud, hard thought very much meant to be heard over the whole of the ship. *We will protect you and prevent their escape, should they attempt to harm the one or perform the other. All hail the Great Chaos!*

May the Great Chaos smile upon you, proxy-fragments, Kraj acknowledged their obedience, utterly without emotion.

He has a new End, Mo thought, peering out at them. *They're soldiers. They're an army. A little army. Still an army.*

Fin frowned. *But we're . . . we're all on the same side. Why would Kraj bring soldiers to our ship? Why would we want to escape? Why in the world would we want to harm Kraj? If there's an army to fight the humans, we'll be in it. Won't we? Are they here to give us our orders? I don't understand what's happening.*

I do, Grumpo thought dejectedly. *You are going to hate it. I already hate it. But it is your fault because you would not let me bite even one person in the face when I told you to. Now it is going to be terrible and stupid all over you. How boring. And terrible. And stupid.*

Maybe they are here for me, Kan thought unhappily. *Maybe I am to be interrogated. Examined for evidence of pumpkin.*

Kraj and two of his bodyguards floated gracefully toward the heavy wooden door that separated the hold and the underguts of the ship from the deck.

In the name of the Great Chaos and by the command of Kraj the Ancient, open this door, fragments. Obey at once and I will treat you favorably.

If only the grown-up endermen weren't acting so strangely, the twins would have opened up without a second thought. Without a first thought. Why wouldn't they, in these terrible times? Except for Kan, they had nothing to hide.

Except for Kan.

Maybe we shouldn't, thought Mo, her hand paused above the door latch.

If we don't, they'll only break the door down. There're nine of them to three of us, Fin answered. *I don't think we've any choice.*

Well, that's just dumb, Fin. You always have a choice. Sometimes it's a garbage choice. But it's still a choice. Mo rolled her eyes at her brother. She turned to the closed door and thought as loud as she could: *If this is about Kan, you can't have him! He's not a human, we can absolutely promise you that! But if you try to take him, we really do have quite a lot of explosives on this ship. And a lot of other sharp things as well. So you might as well turn around if that's what you're up to.*

Kraj's thoughts were like hard, heavy footprints in their minds. *I am well aware of what this ship possesses. The deformed fragment is the least valuable of its contents, as I am sure you are aware. I am not his hubunit. He is irrelevant to me. As you will be if you do not open this door to your elders.*

Kan was the only thing on board that could get them in any

kind of trouble. The twins shrugged nervously and slid back the latch. They looked up into the pale old eyes of Kraj himself. But those eyes were no longer quite as faded and misty as they had been at the Endmoot. His gaze seemed quite sharp now. Sharp and fierce.

Excellent, Kraj thought as he peered into the shadows of the hold. *Just as Karshen said.* The old enderman looked keenly into Fin's eyes. *Take it all,* he ordered.

His two officers pushed into the hold with satisfaction. They immediately began going through the twins' precious, beloved loot. The soldiers lifted, examined, and commented on each item as they passed them back up out of the hold to their comrades in an orderly chain.

What are you doing? screamed Mo. *You can't! That's ours! That too! STOP! Please stop! No, that's mine, please, not my elytra, those are my oldest pair! They were on the ship when we found it! You have no right!*

One of the endersoldiers picked up a diamond axe in one hand and a crossbow in the other. She brandished both experimentally. *I think I will keep the axe for myself,* she thought approvingly. She was called Tamat. Captain Tamat. She wore her rank and name on the outside of her thoughts like a badge of pride.

Fin tried to grab it back. *No, you won't, because it's mine. I took it off a raider fair and square. I've had it all this time. You're a thief! A robber! Go get your own!* The soldier laughed and shoved him easily to the floor.

But it is my own, she sneered. *Because* I *took it off* you *fair and square. The Great Chaos works in mysterious ways!*

Kan clutched his note block to his chest and backed up slowly.

He kept backing up until his shoulders thunked against Grumpo's box, wherein Grumpo wailed pitifully.

Stealers, stealers, stealers and looters and mobs, moaned the shulker. *Go away! Go away or I will bite you. Go away* AND *I will bite you!* EITHER WAY. BITTEN. *Endermen don't use weapons! Get out!*

Kraj folded his long, shadowy fingers and turned to face them. They could feel his grin in their heads.

Our blessed Eresha, the Most High and Holy Mouth of the Great Chaos, has honored me and my long years of experience and made me commander of the armies of the End. She told me to leave no strategy unconsidered when planning our survival. Why should an enderman not use weapons? Humans use them, and we are better than they in every way. It is foolishness to leave a good sword on the ground when you could just as easily pick it up. It is my solemn duty to prepare our people for war. I was informed by—Commander Kraj glanced at Kan—*certain reliable sources that you unpleasant Endless enderfrags have been stockpiling quite the little armory out here where no one can monitor your behavioral patterns. It should never have been allowed. You are not cruxunits. You cannot just start your own group. When this is over, you will be assigned to an acceptable End and you will mature there like any other fragment. You are not special. Naturally, none of this is yours. You have lived for years on the generosity of the rest of us. Without us, without our love and compassion for your abnormal configuration, you would not have been able to collect all of this. Therefore, really, when you think about it, it was always ours. Good payment for our gentle care.*

Fin fought back tears. *You mean you left us on our own with nothing and ignored us and whispered about us and wouldn't let us stay in the city for Endermas and, and, and . . . wouldn't let us go to the Enderdome, and . . . abandoned us just because our hubunits died and . . . and never came to check on us or see if we were all right.*

I came, Kan thought quietly.

Except Kan, Fin admitted.

Commander Kraj looked puzzled. *Yes, that is just precisely what I mean. We left you alone to grow and learn and have all these riches. If anyone had asked me, I would not have permitted it. Now, I will be asked about everything, and the world will drastically improve. Endless people are dangerous. But we were kind. I do not know what you are whining about. We allowed you to exist! We could have simply exiled you to the Overworld to achieve the lofty life goal of being target practice for some human before he gets around to something more meaningful, like digging a hole in the ground. If you keep up this ungrateful complaining, perhaps I will reconsider our stance on that topic. Careful with those swords, Corporal Murrum. You are no good to the war effort if you stab yourself on the first day. Fin, Mo, your people need you. This is our darkest hour. Everyone must make sacrifices. Everyone must give something up so that the End can go on.*

Corporal Murrum finished up with the swords and bent down to pick up a large round object.

NO! Mo cried out. *Not that! Don't you dare!* She scrambled up and leapt at the other soldier like a cat. She ripped at his hands in a frenzy. *Let go of it! It's not a weapon, you don't need it! It's mine! Please, please let go!* Mo punched at Corporal Murrum's arm. He howled and almost dropped something round and greenish-blue. Mo reached for it but missed. *It's no good for anything,* she protested helplessly, furiously. *It's nothing, it's nothing except mine. Don't touch it!*

Commander Kraj jerked his head to one side sharply. He could afford to be generous. Murrum tossed the object carelessly over his shoulder. Mo leapt up frantically to catch it and held it close to her chest.

We would not leave you with nothing, he thought as the whole work of the twins' lives passed up and out of their ship, out of their home. *You can keep a few things for . . . sentimental purposes. And to defend yourselves, obviously.*

Defend ourselves? But . . . but aren't we endermen? Aren't we part of the End? We'll fight with everyone else. We'll go with you right now! Fin watched as the two soldiers turned over several books, held them upside down, smelled them, and, confused, looked to their commander for guidance.

No, I do not think we will be needing those. You cannot read a human to death. Leave them, Kraj thought. *And do not be absurd. You do not have the necessary training. There is no need for you to fight. We are not monsters! The Great Chaos does not require enderfrags as sacrifices. No, you will not fight, you will simply accompany the ender units to which I assign you in order to add your intelligence to the group and augment their abilities. You are not soldiers, my poor, innocent lambs. You are equipment. Now, what else have you got in here? Do not try to lie to me, Kraj will know. Kraj always knows.*

Mo rocked back and forth, clutching the thing she'd wrested from Corporal Murrum just as tightly as Kan clutched his note block. *If you'd only asked,* she thought through her heart breaking, *we'd have given it to you. This is our home. We want the humans defeated, too.*

Kan looked up. His green eyes went narrow and angry. *You are no better.* His thoughts were a thin, hateful hiss.

Kraj's attention cut away from the twins and refocused itself.

Only a day ago at the Endmoot he'd seemed like such a kind old enderman. Now all that was gone. *Pardon me, fragment? No better than whom?*

Humans! Kan snapped. *You come here and take what you want without asking, without caring, only thinking of yourself and what you can use. You are invading this ship just like they are invading the End. Looting my friends. Ruining their home. Taking, taking, taking. Humans take and take until they cannot even carry everything they stole. They are like big angry horses. They eat and eat because they are too stupid to know their stomachs are about to explode. And that is what you are like too. So I do not see why we should be equipment for anyone if we are going to be eaten no matter which dumb horse is doing the chewing.*

Kraj narrowed his glowing eyes. *How fascinating. You have so much empathy and insight into human beings, young Kan. I wonder where you found all this intimate knowledge of the species? Where this wonderful clarity could possibly have come from? Perhaps I was too hasty in calming your hubunit's fears.*

No, Fin thought quickly. *It's fine. It's just stuff.* He felt sick. He felt like he was going to throw up. *Just junk.* He watched Captain Tamat gather up a dozen different kinds of arrows—Arrows of Regeneration, of Fire Resistance, of Poison, Spectral Arrows, Arrows of Water Breathing, even his precious Arrows of the Turtle Master. She grabbed them like they were all the same, just a bunch of identical sticks, and shoved them out of the hold like firewood, toward the rest of the ender squad.

Take it, Mo joined her twin. *We want to help. We were only saying you could have asked. That's all.*

*That is what I suspected. Poor Endless trashfrags. You will find that in periods of war, niceties are a waste of time as you are a waste *of ender flesh. And almost everything is niceties, in the end. In the End as well! Ah, how marvelous it feels to be in the company of my squad. I feel my brain practically sizzle with intellect. Wordplay! Can you imagine? If only the war had come years ago!*

Thump-thump, thump. Grumpo's box thudded meekly.

Commander Kraj waved his hand dismissively toward the stern of the ship. *Do not bother, shulker. You hate me. I am aware.*

I hope a human eats your eyes, Grumpo whispered. *I really mean that.*

The hold was almost empty. The books remained in a tottering tower in the corner, and a few torches. Two or three swords and a few scattered pieces of armor lay on the floor. Fin watched them congratulate one another on a job well done. *But why do you need our chorus fruits and carrots and cooked mutton? What can you do against a human with that?*

We are hungry, thought the corporal and the captain.

So are we, thought the three enderfrags together.

Why should I care? Captain Tamat thought as she climbed the stairs into the open air. *What are* you *the captain of?*

You had better find some food then, had you not? Corporal Murrum added, somewhat more kindly. But not much more.

Our business is concluded, little fragments, Commander Kraj announced.

Not really that little, Mo sniffed.

Compared to me, you are infinitesimally tiny. Mind your manners or I will cut them out of you. Report to the central island at midnight for your assignments. We have left plenty for you to outfit yourselves, so I expect you to present yourselves in tip-top shape, understood?

They glanced around at the barren hold. Suddenly Grumpo's

box had an echo when it thumped. Kraj stared mercilessly into their unhappy faces.

Enough. You did not deserve such luxuries and you would have no idea what to do with golden swords, which is handily proven by the fact that all you did with them while you had them was serve each other lunch. We have left you items befitting your station in life. Be grateful.

Mo, Fin, and Kan glowered silently.

I said be grateful, soldiers! Or by the Great Chaos, I will make you grateful!

Thank you, Commander Kraj, they thought in a shaky, resentful unison.

That is better. Midnight. If you shirk your duty, I shall personally tell the first human I meet where you are and how good you taste. And if I hear one more word of empathy out of you, young man, I shall happily let the medics dissect you to see if you really are an enderman all the way through to your bones.

And then they were gone. All nine of them, as though a storm had hit the ship and passed on, leaving only wreckage.

Kan stared after the commander. *I remember when Kraj gave me a roasted endermite all to myself to eat at Endermas. He told me I was a handsome lad. He told me a funny story about something from the Overworld called a pig.*

I don't think he means to bounce anyone on his knee anymore, Mo shuddered.

Funny what the word "commander" can do to a person, Fin grumbled.

I hate him, Grumpo huffed without so much as lifting the lid of his box.

For once, I think we all agree with you, Grumps, Mo thought. Kan patted the shulker's box.

Pigs are pink, the green-eyed enderman thought. *Pigs are pink and they eat mud. That is what Kraj said.*

Fin and Mo frowned. That didn't sound right, but they didn't much feel like correcting their friend. It wasn't the time for that.

Well, what have we got left? Kan thought after a long, unhappy session of staring into the nothingness of their future.

Fin sighed. A *damaged wooden sword, a Loyalty trident—I think Tamat stepped on it. A crossbow, a leather tunic for each of us, and it looks like we'll have to fight over who gets the enchanted one. Ooh, a damaged stone sword, how posh!* A lot *of books, your note block, some crappy potions that didn't get completely dumped out, exactly one bowl of chorus fruit, and whatever Mo decided to make such a fuss about.*

The boys kept a respectful distance, but they were dying to see what she'd hit an enderman, a full-grown endersoldier to save.

Mo sat on the floor of the hold. She hadn't moved a muscle the whole time. Just sat there, immobile with rage, holding on to . . . that thing. The thing Corporal Murrum had tried to take. That round, greenish-blue thing that had been so important to her.

It's nothing, she thought, the white lights of her tears glittering in her friends' minds like snow. *It's stupid. I don't know why, I just lost my mind when I saw him tossing it around. He could have broken it.*

Fin leaned in. *What is it, Mo?*

Mo stroked the thing in her arms fondly. *It's mine. It's so mine I didn't even tell you about it. I found it last summer. ED showed me.*

The ender dragon gave *you something?* Kan couldn't believe it. That great huge beast never did anything for anyone.

Not exactly. Not gave. *It showed me. Under the island. Someone must have dropped it. Or maybe it just spawned there. Like magic. Like fate.* She shook her head. *But I told you. It's stupid. I always thought it would . . . do something. But it never did.* Mo pulled her long black arms away to reveal a large, slightly moldy, greenish-bluish-purplish-yellowish egg lying in her lap. *I thought, you know, if I kept it warm in the hold with all the torches and everything, it might hatch.*

Fin sat back on his heels. *What in the name of the Great Chaos is* that?

It's a zombie horse egg, Mo confessed. *And now it's cracked.*

CHAPTER SEVEN

HUMANS

Midnight came.

And went.

The endermen gathered as one nation on the ender dragon's gorgeous barren island. They stood in formation beneath the obsidian pillars topped with crystal flames in silver cages. They stood wearing Fin's and Mo's life's work. All their belongings, stuck awkwardly onto everybody else whether any of it fit or not. The younger endermen ran between units, carrying supplies and orders, lending their intellects to the group, trying to find the right balance of minds for war. Mo was assigned to a flank of archers. Commander Kraj attached Fin far away, to a healing unit. But no matter what they said to his face, no one trusted Kan enough to take him, so he hung back, on the outside looking in, as he'd always been. Only this time, he was clutching a damaged stone sword like it could save his life.

The Great Ender Army turned their violet eyes to the night, ready to lay down their lives for the End. The ender dragon circled above them, roaring fire and hate and vengeance and death to all humans.

They were ready.

It was so quiet they could hear one another breathing in the dark. So quiet they could feel the steady song of the ender pearls inside each and every one of them. Never had so many endermen come together like this. Their intelligence crackled between them like electricity. In that moment, if not for the terrible purpose that had gathered them, the unified nation of endermen could have solved any problem put to them. They could have invented any fantastical machine. If the wisest creature alive in the universe had asked them the most difficult, mystical philosophical riddle, the endermen could have answered it in three or four seconds. That was how clever they were when they were one vast End, which they never had been before, nor would be again.

The air thrummed with anticipation. It was the kind of quiet that happens only before an incredible storm, before an unimaginable catastrophe. Before war.

And nothing happened.

Eventually, everyone went home. People were hungry. They were tired. They were even a little bored. They just didn't know what else they were supposed to do. They had scheduled a war. If the humans had decided not to show up, the endermen supposed that they'd won by default. But had they won? They couldn't be quite sure.

The ship was deathly quiet when Mo and Fin and Kan returned to it. They stood on the deck for a while. A little confused. A little upset. And a little, even though none of the three of them wanted to admit it, *disappointed*. It wasn't that they *wanted* to go to war. Wars were dangerous. You could die in wars. Bits of you could become separated from the rest. Not just arms and legs, either. Souls. Hearts. Memories. But when you've gotten yourself hot and brave enough to do something, and don't get to actually *do* it, there is a very strange hole leftover where you so nicely stacked up all that bravery to begin with.

Unfortunately, constant telepathy means never getting to completely hide how you feel. They knew they were all feeling the same odd disappointment. They knew they all felt they shouldn't be disappointed that they weren't going to get to kill all humans today. And yet the ship never stopped being as quiet as guilt.

The twins faced the prospect of their empty home. They stared down into the shadowy hold. Torches flickered on the walls. At least they hadn't taken those. Grumpo's box sat resentfully silent against the far back wall. Mo had somehow hoped that it would be magically full again. But of course it wasn't. The purple and yellow wood of the ship, wood they hadn't seen in years, practically shone in all the places where blocks and chests and boxes had protected it from dirt and footprints. Except for the mountain of books the army hadn't wanted, it was unsettingly clean.

Like Grumpo, they hated it.

Fin, Mo thought with a panic. *We're* poor. *We don't have anything to eat. We don't have gold. We don't have anything. How are we going to live?*

Fin frowned. *Maybe they'll bring it all back in a day or two. Apologize. Maybe Kraj will tell us some more stories about pigs.*

Pigs are pink, Kan thought distractedly.

Fin nodded. *So they say.*

No, but I'm serious. What are we going to eat? What I mean is, what are we going to eat tonight? Right now? I'm starving.

Can you eat books? Mo rubbed her dark belly. *I suppose we* can, *but would it help? Are books nutritious? Maybe they have . . . good fats. Or something.*

Don't you dare. Fin was shocked. Books were the closest thing he had to training in the Enderdome like the others. Learning. Studying the enemy. *They're all we've got left. Why don't we eat your egg then? At least eggs are food! Zombie horses are way more likely to have good fats! Yum, yum, yum!*

Mo raced to the corner where she'd hidden her egg. She cradled it tenderly in her arms. She examined the crack. It didn't seem to have grown any wider while she'd been gone. *That's so mean. Why are you being mean? If you touch my egg, I'll touch you.*

Fin felt bad immediately. He hadn't meant it. Well, he mostly hadn't meant it. He was *very* hungry and it was a *rather* big egg even if it was also a zombie. It was only that she'd said she was going to eat the books! *Sorry, Mo. I'm sorry. I guess I've got some mean stored up that was supposed to get used on the war and now it just . . . wants to get used any old way it can.*

Mo glared at him and held her egg tighter.

Suddenly, Grumpo's box clapped open and shut. Three times, very quick. They all jumped nearly out of their skins. Three apples flew out of the shulker's lair and thudded onto the floor.

GRUMPO! Fin's and Mo's minds sang out joyfully. They dashed down to snatch up the food.

WHO'S A GOOD BOY? Mo kissed the front of his box all over. The shulker snarled inside.

Not me. I'm not. They're poison. Get away from me.

No, they're not, Fin laughed. *They're good apples and you're a good boy, YES, YOU ARE.*

Very brave of you, to hide something from Commander Kraj, Kan marveled.

I didn't. You can't prove it. I hope you choke, spluttered Grumpo, and then he refused to think anything more at all while the twins called him so many sweet names and said so many nice things about him that the shulker vomited twice in his box. And shulker vomit is not very nice at all.

The three of them stuck the apples onto the ends of their swords and roasted their little feast in the torchlight. Maybe their last feast for a good while. They'd have to start all over again. Start collecting fruits and flowers from the chorus trees like they had when they were little. Like Endless beggars.

They didn't feel very full when they'd finished their apples. In fact, they felt somewhat ill and very sleepy. A shulker is a shulker in the end, and the apples actually were a *little* poisoned. But it was only one apple apiece, for better (still hungry) and worse (slightly poisoned). Mo, Fin, and Kan finally fell asleep sitting up on the hard floor of the ship's hold, back to back to back. Mo curled around her egg, Kan curled around his note block, Fin curled up beside his books. They were exhausted. For the first time any of them could remember, they had no idea what was going to happen next. They dreamed of apples, and pigs, and music, and hubunits, and a rain that could come anytime, even when the sky was clear.

The whispers came hours later. In the absolute dead of night. All hours in the End can be called "the absolute dead of night" but this really was. The end rods were at their dimmest. Total quiet and darkness everywhere you could look or listen—and then.

Whispers.

Outside the door. On the ship's deck. Soft, secret, urgent.

Mo woke up first. Her heart thundered in her head. They'd already taken everything! Why would they come back! She moved protectively in front of her brother and her friend. She hid her egg behind her back. Maybe Kraj had decided she couldn't keep that either.

More whispers. Louder now.

Now Fin woke up. His magenta eyes slitted open in the half-dark.

Someone's out there, Mo told him.

Kan sat up. *Is it my hubunits? Karshen? Teg?*

I don't think so. Mo glanced toward the stern and the shulker's ledge. *I wonder why Grumpo isn't yelling his head off.*

The whispers were right outside the door now. Something knocked hard against the wood. They could almost make out words.

Fin and Mo realized it at the same time. Their eyes got big and wide.

What? Kan looked back and forth between them, not understanding.

Whispers, Mo thought.

Yes, I hear them, too. Is it Kraj? Corporal Murrum? Captain Tamat?

Mo grabbed his hand and squeezed hard. Then she pressed his hand to the side of his head. *Yeah, Kan, you do. You* hear *them. With your* ears.

Someone outside the ship was talking. Not with telepathy. No beautiful thoughts appearing gracefully and instantly in another person's mind. Talking. With their *faces*. A lot of faces. Grumpo wasn't alerting them because Grumpo didn't *know*. The shulker couldn't sense other minds approaching the ship because the people approaching the ship weren't telepathic. Their minds were shut. Their mouths were open.

"Shhhhhh! You klutz."

"Why? Afraid I'll startle the loot?"

"It's another big dumb ship like all the other big dumb ships. Get in there, kill the shulker, open the chests, grab the elytra, get out. Lather, rinse, repeat."

"I don't know. It's creepy here. It's so *quiet*. Just be careful."

"We can go back to the dragon if you want. He wasn't quiet."

"You don't know it's a he."

"Oh my god, are we gonna raid this place or not?"

"Fine."

"Fine."

"You first."

"Whatever. God, you're such a *baby*, Roary."

The endermen stared at the closed door in horror.

Humans.

Here.

Now.

And they had no escape.

The door slammed open. Four *things* poured into the ship. Blocky, hulking, squat, splotchy creatures. Their skin was all different colors when it should have been nice and slick and black. Their clothes were different colors, too—one wore red, one wore turquoise, one wore green, and one wore yellow. *And they were wearing clothes!* Any kind of clothes! An enderman's skin was skin and shirt and coat and trousers and armor all in one. They'd never seen clothes. Ever. Chestplates, sure. But jeans and T-shirts? Fin and Mo didn't even know the words for those things. They didn't seem like they'd be much good as armor. What was the point of them?

The human mob yelled and brandished their weapons. They hurtled into Fin and Mo's private space, their home, laughing and swinging their swords crazily, barely even looking at what they might hit. The one in the turquoise shirt threw herself at Kan. She held a diamond sword high above her head and slashed it down toward him with a yodeling war cry. Sobbing, Mo hit the human hard in the stomach, knocking her back before she could cut off Kan's head.

"Ugh," the human grunted. "I hate these guys. So annoying."

"Ooh!" said the human girl in red. "That one's got green eyes! *Coooool.*"

Stay away from him! Mo lashed back. But the girl couldn't hear a thought any more than she could hear a memory.

I'm fine, Kan thought shakily. *She didn't get me. I've got my sword still.* He groped behind himself for it and found the handle.

Mo fixed the wicked human girls with the terrible gaze of the endermen. Once an enderman has her prey in her line of sight, nothing can stop her. An all-consuming berserker fury takes over and it does not fade until the target is torn to pieces.

But the girls didn't seem to notice that they'd been fixed with the terrible gaze of the endermen. They whispered something to each other and ignored Mo completely.

The boy in the yellow shirt ran up to Grumpo and started whacking his box all over with a trident. A trident! Fin couldn't help admiring it, he'd only ever found one and Kraj had almost made off with it. Tridents were his favorite. He'd always hoped he'd find another one, but he never did. He charged the human in yellow, throwing himself between him and Grumpo. The trident hit him in the shoulder, in the knee, and glanced off his elbow, which somehow hurt worse than the others.

"Get out of the way!" the yellow human snarled at Fin. "I don't have time for you!"

Please leave us alone, wailed Fin. His arm hurt so bad. He kept trying to look the boy in the eye, to fill himself up with that all-powerful, undeniable frenzy that was the legacy of his people. His birthright. But the human didn't seem to care about legacies and he couldn't hear Fin's thoughts. All the human could see was an enderman flashing red with pain and rage, who didn't immediately charge him or bludgeon him to death.

Grumpo was most certainly awake now. He was so angry, his thoughts couldn't even form themselves into words, just one long scream of hate like a knife dragging through their heads.

KIIIIIIIIIILLLLLLLLL IIIIIIIIT! shrieked the shulker.

"What the actual crap," said the human boy in green. "There's frick-all in here. Not even one chest? Worst. Boat. Ever. Koal, dude, are you really having trouble taking out a *shulker*? That's like baby's-first-kill territory. *Weak*. Leave it alone, I think you're just *bothering* it now."

"Let's go, Jax," the girl in red sighed. "This is stupid. And pointless. Somebody else obviously got here first."

"Yeah, sorry, guys," the girl in the blue shirt who'd tried to decapitate Kan apologized. "We didn't know anyone else was raiding this far out. Our bad. I'm Roary, this is Jesster"—she jabbed her thumb back at her red friend—"the big guy is Jax and the skinny one's Koal."

Who are they talking to? Mo thought wildly. She squeezed her egg to her chest. Somehow that made her feel better. *Is this the invasion?*

I don't know! Fin panted heavily, his arm still burning in agony. He turned from one human to the other, his hands curled into claws, ready to fight again.

Jax made a face. "Kind of weird to just be *hanging out* in here with an enderman, but you do you, I guess," he said. "Did you kill the dragon yet? If not, you're welcome to come with us. Once I'm looted up, I'm gonna stab that bad boy in the heart."

"Hey," said Jesster, snapping her fingers. "Hellllloooo? Rude! Aren't you gonna say something? You can still talk with a pumpkin on, you know."

Kan's bright, beautiful green eyes widened. *They are talking to me,* he thought. *I am human. I was human all along. They think I raided this boat. Like them. Like a normal human boy. They think I raided this boat and tricked you into thinking I was a harmless enderman. And I guess . . . I guess they are right.*

Kan took a step toward the humans. The look on his face was so horribly happy and sad all at once. He opened his mouth to talk, really talk, no silky, silent thoughts. Not anymore. Real words. Human words. At last.

"Whoa, Jess!" Koal called out. "Look out! It's coming right for you!"

Koal lunged forward and swung his trident. It caught Kan on the cheek. The wound flared red, but it wasn't deep. The green-eyed enderman stared at the humans, full of hurt and confusion.

"You guys should probably just kill him," the one called Jax said. "Sneaking around is pretty fun, not gonna lie, but it's easier just to clear the zone first thing. Don't worry, they won't even see you coming. They're too stupid to breathe. As long as you've got your pumpkin, you can kill 'em left and right and they still won't figure out what's up."

Fin and Mo just stood there, gawping. Grumpo was still screaming in their heads, like he was trying to drown out the intolerable sound of the humans talking. The place where they'd stacked up their bravery was clean cleared out. They didn't understand. Maybe they didn't want to understand. The twins grabbed each other's hands.

Please just go away and let this not be happening, Fin thought.

Maybe we're still asleep. Maybe the apples really were poisoned. Maybe Grumpo IS a bad boy. Always knew he might be, Mo thought, her mind starting to break under the pressure. She held on to her egg. Her egg was solid. Her egg was real. The egg was love. The egg was life.

Roary cleared her throat. "Awkward."

"Anyway . . ." Jax coughed. "You two want to come kill a dragon? Us humans gotta stick together, you know."

Us humans? the twins thought. *Two?*

Kan crumpled to the floor.

Grumpo's telepathic scream cut off sharply.

Fin clung to his sister.

Mo squeezed her egg as tight as she could, tight enough to make it all go away.

The egg cracked.

CHAPTER EIGHT

THE SIX OF US

You're mistaken, thought Fin angrily. *We're not human.*

Something long and thin and greyish-violet broke the shell of the egg. It had a hard, yellow hoof on one end, like a fist made all out of old thumbnail.

You have got it wrong, thought Kan desperately. *It is me. I am the one. I am human.*

A second spindly skinny thing emerged from Mo's egg. Bloodshot veins snaked all over it in a complicated pattern that looked almost like the design on a pretty vase, only much, much gorier and . . . wetter.

What in the name of the Great Chaos do you mean "kill a dragon with you"? Mo thought accusingly. *I hope you don't mean ED because it will burn you standing.*

Something very big was trying very hard to be born out of her egg. The spindly legs wiggled in the air with effort. The head pushed at the bluish-green shell. A sickly looking head with bits of bright bone showing through the bruised-looking skin. A head with sharp yellow teeth. A head with mold on it before it even took its first breath.

The thing neighed.

The neigh sounded like a coffin opening.

It looked up into Mo's dark, loving face with enormous dark eyes fringed with funguslike eyelashes.

Mumma? the zombie horse croaked in the space between their minds.

"Wow! I heard about those!" Jesster exclaimed. "The eggs are super tough to find! I'll trade you a nether star for it."

Mo wrapped her arms protectively around the undead horse's neck. It was a girl. A mare. Her hair was stringy and moist and smelled like raw beef.

Mumma, the ghoul burped happily. Her breath put out a torch. *Brains. Braaaains?* the zombie foal sniffed around for that special food all zombies love. She fixed her bloodshot eyes meaningfully on Fin's head.

Your baby is disgusting, Grumpo observed from his box. *I hate it. You should put it in the garbage. I can smother it for you if you want.*

Put yourself in the garbage! Mo snapped back. *She's beautiful! Aren't you, baby?*

Mo, don't you think there're more important things going on right now?

Mo glared at her brother stubbornly. *No.* Very gently, she kissed the horse's forehead. *You're all I have left,* she thought softly. *You're my whole old life if my old life was a stinky horse. I don't want whatever is about to happen to us to happen and I don't want to know whatever we're about to know, but you can't stop things happening and you can't unknow something once you know it, so I'm just going to focus on this until it stops happening. I'm never gonna let you go. You have the prettiest sores.*

Mo had no idea what the mind of a zombie horse was like. She'd heard her thoughts, so telepathy was on the table. But could a dead mind even open up enough to fully let someone else's thoughts in? Mo considered it silently. There was no way to know except to try. She smiled at the creature and tried to see inside her brain, her mind, her soul. Mo pushed her mind toward the pony's mind.

She saw a graveyard. It went on forever, over a hundred hills and more. All the dirt was freshly turned. Wiry, crooked trees bent over the tombs. A sickly white moon shone on all of it. Nothing seemed to respond to her thoughts. The gravestones said various things: HELLO. HI. BEAUTIFUL. DISGUSTING. BABY. PUT IT IN THE GARBAGE. WOW. BRAINS. MUMMA. HUNGRY. HUNGRY. HUNGRY. MUMMA. BRAINS. Most of them were blank, though. Not that much had happened to her yet, after all.

A bloated, rotting hand slowly wiggled its way out of one of the graves. The fingernails were fuzzy with purple-black mold. Worms squirmed out of a hole in the palm.

The gravestone above it read: HELLO.

It waved shyly at Mo.

Hi, baby, Mo thought.

"HEY!" yelled Koal. "It's. Very. Rude. To. Give. Nice. People. The. Silent. Treatment." He clapped his hands between each word.

"Mouth go like this," Jax said in an exaggerated slow voice.

He reached out and wiggled Fin's jaw mockingly.

Fin's jaw came off in his hand.

Mo screamed. Not in her head. Not in Fin's head. Not in Kan's head.

She *screamed*. The sound echoed around the ship's hold. The zombie horse screamed, too, in exactly the same pitch, but with a lot more volume. Learning was fun, even for demon ponies.

But it wasn't Fin's jaw.

It was a piece of pumpkin.

In the beautiful black shell of the enderman's face, a shard of warm brown skin showed through.

Jax held it casually in his hand like nothing unusual had happened. "Ew," he said. "Your pumpkin is nasty. It's all old and rotty. I don't know how much longer it's gonna last, buddy."

No, Fin thought, staring at Mo. *It's impossible*.

"What's that, friend?" said Roary encouragingly. "Once more with volume?"

"Impossible," Fin wheezed. His voice was creaky and raw and harsh and husky. Like it hadn't been used in years. Because it hadn't.

Mo raised her hand to her own face. She felt like she was in a trance. The enderman wedged her fingers under her jaw, exactly where Jax had grabbed Fin. She tried to lift up.

A slice of pumpkin shell came away like rotted wood.

Mo dropped it like it was on fire. It fell to the ground. One side still looked black and shiny. The other oozed soft, gooshy, spoiled pumpkin. It even had a couple of seeds sticking out of it. After a moment, the piece of pumpkin shriveled up into dust and disappeared.

Kan raised his hand to his cheek. He slid his fingers under his jaw. He lifted it upward.

Nothing happened.

No, he moaned in his mind. *No, no, no. It's impossible.*

He kept pulling at his face. Kept lifting, kept scrabbling along the line of his jaw to find the edge of the pumpkin mask. The mask that wasn't there. Tears filled his mind. *It does not make any sense. I am the one. It is me. It is not them. Please, please be me.*

"I don't . . . I don't understand what's happening here," Fin said. It was so *hard* to talk! So many muscles! So many different movements! "Can you talk, Mo?"

Mo tried to open her mouth. Her *other* mouth. The mouth underneath the face she'd thought was her real face for all these years. "I . . . I think so," she whispered hoarsely. "It hurts."

Mumma. Paaaain, moaned the undead horse in her arms. Her mouth didn't move, but Fin and Kan heard it, too. Mo stroked the baby's forehead.

See, Grumpo? she thought. *She's not disgusting. She knows when I hurt and she cares, which is more than you've ever done.* The horse began to *gurgle* happily, almost like a purr, if the purr came from hell itself.

Kan lay down on the floor of the ship. He couldn't move. He couldn't think. His brain just wouldn't *brain*.

"Um . . . you're people. Who found a couple of pumpkins and used them to raid the End without getting attacked every five seconds by an enderman with an anger-management problem," Jesster told them impatiently. "Duh."

"But that's not true," insisted Mo. Her throat ached with the effort of talking. And the more she *talked* instead of *thought*, the more she knew that they were right. "We've always lived here. I can't even remember any other place. We grew up here. It's our home. It was our hubunits' home. We're endermen." She said it again, trying to hold on to everything she'd ever known about herself. "We're endermen."

We're endermen.

"I mean . . . except for the part where you're not," Koal said, almost laughing at them.

"What's a hubunit?" Jess asked, confused.

"We *are* endermen! We are so!" Fin tried to shout, but his voice wasn't up to it yet.

"Okay, crazy," Jax rolled his eyes. "Have it your way. We're out."

"Wait," Roary said, holding up her hands. "Wait a minute. This is so interesting. Do you really not know? Do you not remember how you got here?"

"We were born here!" sobbed Mo.

Koal stuck his hands into his yellow pockets. "Fine. Where're your parents?"

"What's a *parent*?" Mo blurted in frustration.

Jess blinked. Roary blinked. Koal opened his mouth to say something, then shut it again and furrowed his brow. Jax laughed—a short, sharp, harsh sound more like a cough than a laugh. "You know, your parents. Like . . . a mom and a dad."

"What's a mom?" Fin asked.

"What's a dad?" asked Mo.

"How can you not know what a mom and dad are?" Jess said incredulously. "The people who look like you only bigger and talk like you only louder, who make the rules and bad jokes and say things like 'Not under my roof,' and 'What time do you call this?' and 'We love you very much but you can't have cake for breakfast.' The people who made you!"

"Hubunits," said Mo.

"Mom and dad," insisted Koal.

"Primary and secondary hubunits," Mo allowed.

Mumma! the zombie horse thought triumphantly.

Roary rolled her eyes. "Okay, okay, what happened to your primary and secondary hubunits?"

"They died," Fin mumbled. "A long time ago."

Kan's green eyes slid open. His brain perked up a little. It might, just maybe, have been willing to brain again. Temporarily.

Did they? He sent the thought toward his friends. *Did they, though?*

Of course they did! Fin snarled, whipping his head around in bitterness.

How dare you? Mo thought. The baby monster in her lap glared at Kan.

All right. Kan's thought was very small and simple. *What is your primary hubunit's name?*

Mo blinked.

How about your secondary hubunit?

Fin opened his mouth to say, but he . . . couldn't. He reached back to all his memories of their End, of their childhood. But . . . it just wasn't there.

"Hey!" Jax snapped his fingers in their faces to get their attention. "What's going on here? Are you having an episode? You guys just keep stopping and staring off into the distance. Do you have a glitch? Do you need help? You need a healing potion or something?"

"Sorry," Fin croaked. "We're talking."

"No, you're not," countered Jesster.

"Yes, we are. We're endermen. Or *whatever* we are. Endermen communicate telepathically. That's what all the little purple sparkles are about." Roary reached out to touch one. It danced out of range. "They let us send our thoughts directly into other endermen's minds. Shulkers, too, if they're willing, which they almost never are. We're talking to our friend there. His name is Kan. I'm Mo. This is my twin, Fin."

"You're *friends* with an *enderman*?" Roary said in total disbelief. "You can't be friends with an enderman."

"We're friends with *lots* of endermen," Mo said defensively. All the more defensively because they absolutely were *not* friends with lots of endermen. But the humans didn't need to know they were the village losers. "Anyway, I think maybe he's . . . like us? Whatever we are?" All right, they were *something*. Something different. But not *humans*. That was too horrible to entertain. Mo took her hand off the purring colt and stroked poor Kan's miserable head. Her fingers left wet, dark marks on his temples. Her new horse was a messy horse. Kan didn't mind. He didn't mind much of anything anymore. What was the point of minding?

"Nope," Koal shook his head. "That's an enderman. A real one. They're *pretty* easy to pick out of a lineup."

"Maybe," Mo said doubtfully. "But he's different, too."

"The eyes," Roary mused. "I've never seen eyes like that on an enderman. Anywhere. Ever."

"I bet you want to rip them out for your next portal, huh?" Mo said.

Jax thought about it, then shrugged. "Nah, we're already here. We're good. You only need eyes for the . . . er . . . outgoing call. And I don't think you need actual—"

"Okay, but back to the actually interesting thing," Roary interrupted. She seemed terribly fascinated by them. Almost like a doctor. You could tell she was just dying to examine them, figure them out, maybe even dissect them. "How can you be human and not remember being human? How long have you been down here? What happened to you? Jax, do we know any Fins or Mos that have gone missing? What if we take the pumpkins all the way off? Maybe their memories will come back."

No, Kan's thought flashed. *No, do not do it. If you take them off, everyone will know. They will attack you.*

You're not attacking us now.

And he wasn't. Kan didn't know why he wasn't. But he wasn't attacking anyone in a room jam-packed full of humans. He didn't even want to. What was wrong with him? Just how much of a freak *was* he?

"This sucks," announced Jax. "Can he talk?"

"I told you, endermen communicate telepathically," Fin began again.

"Yeah, yeah, yeah, psychic monster people. Got it. But *can* he talk? I can talk, but I can *also* think. Ipso . . . you know."

"Facto," Roary finished for him. "You dolt."

Mo put her head to one side. "I guess I don't know." She turned to her friend.

Kan, can you try to talk?

I am talking.

Talk like the humans talk. Can you just try? It's pretty easy. Once you get used to it. You move the bottom of your face up and down and kind of . . . breathe out loud.

"Come on, buddy," Jax said, like he was talking to a big, mean dog who would bite if he didn't get a treat. "Give us a nice talky-talk."

Kan glowered. "No," he rumbled.

But it was so hard for him. His mouth was so little compared to the humans' mouths. You couldn't even see it unless he opened it as far as it could go. His tongue didn't know how to do much of anything besides eat. Words *hurt* coming out of him. Hurt like knives.

"I bet you're fun at parties." Jax sighed. "Look, you can't chatty-chat-chat with us and then be all woo-woo-spooky-mind-meld with him. Manners, people."

Mo wrinkled her nose. Now that she knew it was there, the pumpkin made her face itch. How had she never noticed?

"You're kind of awful," she said to the big boy in the green shirt. He grinned. It didn't bother him.

"Yeah, but he's our awful." Koal sighed.

"I might be awful but I'm not wrong! It's rude. And it puts us at a disadvantage."

"Again, I would like to stress that this situation is possibly unique in the *history of the world*," Roary said. "They've been lost in Monster Central for maybe years. We've got to figure this out. At the very least, you guys, we can take you out of here. We can take you *home*."

"Once we kill the dragon," Koal reminded her.

"Yes, obviously we can't go anywhere until Jax has his little dragon party, but after that, we can take you all back up with us."

Jess crossed her arms and didn't say anything. Fin realized he was staring at her. He hadn't meant to. He was so used to living in a telepathic world that he hadn't even noticed he was concentrating hard on Jess, waiting for her thoughts to appear in his mind. They didn't. She was a closed book. Whatever was making her frown and stare off into the distance, Fin couldn't just *know* it. It was frustrating and horrible and he realized he must look really odd glaring at her like that and yanked his gaze away. How did humans live like that? Anyone could just keep secrets from you and you'd never know!

Mumma remaaaaaain, howled the undead pony in the graveyard of her mind, and snuggled into Mo's chest defensively. To the animal, this was home. She had been alive for only half an hour. She wasn't ready to move to a new neighborhood yet.

"Are you gonna keep that thing?" Koal said, wrinkling his nose. The smell was overpowering. "Like, as a pet?"

MUMMA, barked the horse silently. Red spittle flew from her teeth.

"She's my baby," Mo said lovingly.

"Gross," Jax said. He covered his mouth and dry heaved. A long, empty, gutteral burp came out.

"She's not *gross*. She's *mine*. I'm going to call her Loathsome. Isn't that a nice name for a nice horse who definitely will not eat my brains the minute I'm not looking? Definitely not, right?"

Naaaaame, Loathsome thought lovingly. In that endless cemetery in her head, one of the gravestones suddenly read: LOATHSOME. She snatched up Mo's hand in her rotting yellow fangs. Mo gasped. Her heart stopped. But Loathsome just held her fingers very gently, as if to say: *I could, but I won't. But I* could. The zombie horse made a churning, crunching, bubbling sound in her decomposing throat. A giggle.

"Wow," said Koal, shaking his head. He raised his hands as if to say: It's your funeral. "Just *wow*."

"Shut up!" Mo snarled. "And you better not still be thinking about fighting the ender dragon, because if you have to kill it to get home you might as well start building a nice house here in the End. I won't let you hurt my dragon."

"Your dragon?" said Jax softly.

"Well . . . not mine exactly. Not anyone's exactly. But I love it, and that makes it mine."

"That's not how love works," Jess broke her silence.

"Fine! But I'm not going to let you kill it, because it's beautiful and unique and it breathes fire and knows my name. I'll fight you to the end of the End to keep it safe and I'm pretty sure that *is* how love works."

"We are not going to the Overworld." Fin snapped them all back to attention. "And neither are you. I don't think you're totally aware of everything that's going on here. We knew you were coming. Everyone knew. We were ready for you. We just . . . thought you were coming earlier. And that there would be more of you."

"When they find out you're already here, Commander Kraj will bring the greatest army the End has ever known down on your heads. There're only four of you. You won't survive."

"Six of us," said Jesster gently. "Six humans here, kittens."

"What are you talking about?" Roary said. "Endermen don't have armies. They don't have commanders. What is going *on* down here?"

"We do now." Mo shrugged.

"Ooh, I'm shaking in my enchanted boots," said Jax, waggling his fingers. "I came here to kill a dragon and I don't care how many of your weird freakshow countrymen I have to go through to do it. We're better than them. Endermen are annoyingly strong, but it's not like they're particularly smart. I've always done just fine against them."

Kan strained, moving his jaw unnaturally, trying to speak. Finally, he spat out his words. "Not a freak," he coughed up like sickness. "Not a freak."

"Okay, greenboy, you're not a freak. Happy?"

Kan screamed. His skin flushed red. He bolted at Jax and threw him against the port-side wall. The ship groaned in the sky.

"Get off me! Get off me!"

Koal grabbed Fin by the shoulder. "Call off your friend or I'll stab him in the back," the human boy warned. "I mean it. You care about him, but I don't. I care about Jax."

"Kan, stop!" Fin shouted. "Stop it!"

The enderman stopped. It was so hard to stop. But he did it. He did it because Fin said to. Fin knew the right thing to do almost all of the time. He always had. Since they were small. But had they grown up together? Was it all a lie? What was *happening*?

Roary put her hands on her hips. "I think the first thing to do is get the pumpkins off. It might help. You might remember everything. I don't really know how those things work. We found them growing in patches and started screwing around because it was a boring day and it turned out they were just . . . *massively* useful. Maybe if you wear them too long they mess with your head. It could make sense."

"But the others . . ."

"Don't worry, you can put them back on if anyone turns up," the girl reassured them.

"Grumpo would tell us if anyone was approaching. Any enderman, anyway," Mo said uncertainly. *Would* Grumpo warn them? He was suspiciously silent. Maybe he wouldn't talk to them anymore, now that he knew they were outsiders. She picked a few stray pieces of eggshell off her pony. The pony was already much bigger. She had been the size of a chicken when she hatched. Now she was about the size of a dog.

"I guess it's worth a try." Fin sighed.

Roary knelt down to help Fin take his pumpkin off. Jesster and Koal went over to help Mo. Jax just watched resentfully, rubbing his chest where Kan had hit him. Kan hit hard.

Are you afraid? thought Mo to her brother.

I'm so afraid. Fin trembled. *What if I don't want to remember?*

Too late now, thought Kan.

Roary pushed up and backward. Jess and Koal shoved forward and down. The pumpkins came free with a wet squelch.

Kan looked into his friends' faces for the first time.

He started to scream.

CHAPTER NINE

MONSTERS

Kan screamed into their minds. And apologized. And screamed. And apologized.

But, despite the noise, Fin and Mo couldn't stop staring at *each other*.

"You have brown hair!" Mo said.

"You have black hair!" Fin said.

"You have *hair*," they both said.

"Yeah? Well, *you're* wearing clothes!" Fin accused.

"So are you!" Mo shot back.

AHHHHHH! screamed Kan.

"You have blue eyes, Fin. They're *horrible*!" she giggled with delight. "But they're nice, too. But horrible. But nice."

"You have green ones. They're . . . they're just nice."

Green eyes he'd seen before. All his life. He was used to green eyes. Green and black. It was okay. He could get past it. Even if his twin suddenly had brownish-tan skin and eyebrows and other unsettling things, like a chin.

"Do you remember anything?" Roary asked.

"No," Mo said slowly. "I'm the same Mo I've always been. I'm an enderman."

"You, Fin?"

Fin shook his head. "Same old ender-me."

How could this be happening? How could it be real? How could he not remember being human? Fin was an enderman. He *was*. He had to be. What did anything even *mean* if he wasn't? And another, smaller part of him wondered: Was this why they weren't allowed to go to the Enderdome? Was this why everyone left them to live alone on an old boat? Did everyone, somehow, somewhere deep down, know they were *wrong* all along?

AHHHHHH!

Will you stop that? thought Fin. *If anyone should be screaming, it's us.*

I cannot help it! You are monsters.

No, we're not. We're your friends. Like always. Nothing's different.

Everything is different! To me, you are monsters! Humans! *With hair and skin and big awful* EARS.

But look. Kan, look. She has green eyes. Like you. It's not so bad, is it? She's not so bad. I'm not so bad. Are we?

Mo tried to reach for Kan. Loathsome the zombie pony pawed at her to keep both hands right where they were. *Doesn't the Great Chaos love all surprises?* she thought hopefully.

Not this one, Kan thought. His heart was broken. He couldn't even look at them. *Not this one.*

And then Kan vanished. One minute he was there, the next he was gone.

Kan never did that. Not ever. Just teleported without a word. Without a single thought. Run away from them. Endermen didn't do that. Friends didn't, either.

"This is *so cool*," Roary said. She walked in a little circle around them, checking them out like they were some kind of science experiment. "Maybe it's a spell or a potion. Maybe someone did this to you. Because this isn't how pumpkins work."

"You just said you didn't know how pumpkins worked," Mo pointed out.

"Well, maybe I don't know the exact mechanism, but I know they don't erase who you are when you put them on your head. I've worn one for days at a time and I still know my name is Roary and I like puzzles and exploring diverse biomes and hanging out with my friends and setting things on fire and suspicious stew."

"Yeah, you like it so much you went blind for a week the last time you had your favorite dinner."

"But the time before that I got Fire Resistance for a month! You never know what you're going to get with suspicious stew! I like surprises. *Anyway*, that's not the point; the point is, I might not know the deepest secrets of pumpkin nature, but I know putting one on your head doesn't cause amnesia. So it has to be something else. And I *have* to know what that something else is. Sorry, I'm on your case. And I won't give up till I solve it."

"Could have just hit their heads or something." Koal shrugged. "It doesn't have to be magic."

"Maybe the endermen did it. Maybe they kidnapped you when you were babies!" Roary's voice was breathy with the excitement of a real, honest-to-everything *mystery*.

Fin rubbed his head. All that hair was itchy. He'd never itched like that before. He hated it. "Maybe it's the End itself," he said. "The endermen didn't build all these cities, you know. They don't know who did, either. No one can remember. Maybe if you stay here too long, it does something weird to your memory."

Jesster, Koal, and Roary turned to stare at Fin. He flushed. He'd said something interesting! They were interested in him! And he found that he *wanted* them to think he was clever. Clever and useful. Especially Jess. If these really were his people, if he really was a human, maybe they wouldn't keep him out of whatever they had in place of an Enderdome. If he was good enough, maybe he could belong somewhere. Maybe he could sit next to Jess in the Humandome and train for human battles against various menaces. Maybe he could be so much like a regular human that no one would guess he was brand new at it.

Mo frowned. "But Kan remembers us. He remembers as far back as we do. The Endermas when we were five. All the times he came to the ship when his secondary hubunit chased him out."

"You remember all the way back to when you were five?" said Roary.

"Yes," the twins answered.

"Any further back?"

"Well . . . not much, but isn't that normal? Do you remember a lot of things from before you were five?"

"I guess that's fair," said Jess.

"Okay, but you're just saying 'five,'" Roary pointed out. "Do you mean five years old? Or when you'd been here for five years? Or five months? Or five days?"

"Five years old! Obviously! What kind of a question is that?"

"Do you know that? For *sure?*"

Neither of them could answer. They *wanted* to be sure, but ten minutes ago they'd been sure they were endermen and humans were evil monsters.

Roary started pacing back and forth across the hold of the ship. "See, I don't think you know anything. Maybe it's all connected. The weird endermen making armies and commanders and your friend's green eyes and your memories and all of it. And has anybody else noticed that the end rods have been getting steadily dimmer since we've been standing here? Something really bizarre is going on down here, and we have to rethink *everything*. You two have been living down here with endermen for so long you don't know which way is up. Endermen are monsters, you guys. Do you understand that? They steal and they kill and they hunt. They ruin everything. They're hideous—"

"No, they're not!" Mo cried out.

Loathsome began to chew lightly on her sleeve. The foul foal was almost the size of a bicycle now. Mo wondered when she would stop growing.

"Whatever you say. The point is, endermen are bad. They are capable of anything. They could have done so many terrible things to you to make you believe you were one of them! I can think of like nine or ten without any effort, and I'm a nice person! But what I can't think of is *why*. Why would they convince two humans that they're endermen? What's the point? What's the *plan*?"

"Endermen aren't bad!" Fin protested.

I hate endermen, Grumpo agreed. *They are bad*.

You hate everything, Mo thought. *So what does that prove?*

Just because Grumpo hates everything doesn't mean everything isn't terrible, Grumpo reasoned. *Endermen are terrible. You are terrible. Your twin is terrible. The End is terrible. Burn it all, dragon first.*

Good talk, Grumpo, thought Fin.

Grumpo doesn't talk to humans. The Shulker sniffed. *Humans are terrible.*

"But you met Kan," he said to the humans, who were again looking annoyed with the obvious telepathy going on. "He's not evil."

"Seemed like a pretty normal enderman when he came at me," coughed Jax, rubbing his chest where Kan had hit him.

Koal rolled his eyes. "Oooh, one enderman can cry about how hard his life is. Big deal. Other than Kan, are they even nice to you around here? Are they friendly? Invite you to all the hot ender parties?"

"Not . . . not exactly," said Mo. "We don't have an End, so . . ."

"A what?" interrupted Jax.

"An End. It's like . . . an enderman family. A group of endermen is called an End."

"Super creative," Jax snorted. "And it's called a haunting, by the way. Not an End."

"What? That's horrible." Fin frowned.

"You don't get to say what we call ourselves," Mo snapped.

Koal rolled his eyes. "Well, you're not an enderman, so you don't get to say either."

"Well, we don't have one either way," Fin replied, "so that makes the endermen uncomfortable around us. It's fine, it's not their fault."

Jax looked around. His eyes were calculating. He was working through a big thought. "Hey," he said, squatting down in front of Fin and Mo in a friendly manner. "Where's all your stuff?"

"What stuff?" Fin said defensively.

"You two live here, right? It's a big ship. And if I know anything about endermen I know they love stealing things. So where's all your stuff?"

Mo looked down, her cheeks burning. "They took it," she whispered.

"Who? The nice endermen? The not-bad-at-all endermen? Cleaned you out? You don't even have a scrap to eat or a knife to protect yourself with. Those wonderful, kind, generous endermen didn't even leave you that?"

"Only enough to fight you," Fin mumbled. But he still smarted. He was still angry that Kraj and his goons had robbed them. He was still hungry. Jax was right, but Fin wouldn't give him the satisfaction.

"Well, *clearly* it was worth it. We are soundly defeated, aren't we, guys?"

"Maybe we should take them up to the Overworld," Jess said suddenly. "Sooner rather than later. Maybe they'd recognize something. We could try healing potions. I've got *heaps* of potions at my house. So does Jax. And you never know, maybe someone would recognize them."

"Aw, come on, Jax and me and Roary wanna kill a dragon," Koal said. "That's what we came here for. We can worry about them once we've got the old lizard dead between the eyes. No one's going anywhere until we do, anyway. The exit portal won't appear until that big boy bites it."

"No, you won't touch ED!" screeched Mo. Loathsome screeched with her. "And we're not going to the Overworld either!"

"Our hubunits . . . our . . . our parents *died* there. You can't. It can rain anytime up there. Rain is death . . ." Every enderman knew that. To get caught in the rain was suicide.

"No, they didn't," Roary said, exasperated. "I don't know who your parents were, but they were definitely human! Humans are fine with rain! Promise!"

"I don't want to go to the Overworld!" Mo clung to her baby horse. Fluid oozed down Loathsome's neck. "Fin, don't let them take us. We don't belong there."

"For god's sake, do you even really know that you're twins?" Jesster threw up her hands.

"Of COURSE we're twins," they yelled together.

"You don't look anything alike. What evidence do you have that you're even related at all? Aren't you curious? Isn't any chance of getting your memory back worth it? It's really nice out there, you know. It is. You'll love sunshine. Everyone loves sunshine."

"Well, I *don't*!" Fin snarled. Once, he'd dreamed about going to the Overworld. Avenging his hubunits. Serving the Great Chaos. But it was too much, too fast. All he wanted in this moment was to stay on his ship with his twin and his shulker where it was safe and familiar and solid beneath his feet. He couldn't think like this. He needed to talk to Mo and work it all out in his own good head. He didn't need a bunch of monsters yelling at him. (But were they monsters? If they were, what was he?)

The endermen should have let him go to the Enderdome. Maybe he would have learned something that would have provided a clue to all this.

Mo backed up against the hull of their end ship. "It's *not* nice up there. It's the Land of Order, a miserable wasteland where the wicked rule! It's poison and death! I won't go, I won't. And if you think you're going to sail out of here and murder ED, you've got another think coming. You won't leave this ship. This is *our* territory. *You're* trespassing. And pretty soon the others are going to realize you're here after all and they'll come. You'll find out where our stuff went and you won't like it." *But we won't like it either,* Mo thought to herself. *We're human. We're* them. *The End won't know us. They'll cut us down without a single tear.* "I don't care how many others have come with you. I don't care how big your army is. You're invaders and the End is plenty strong enough to destroy you."

"What others? It's just us," Koal said, confused. "What are we meant to be invading again?"

I hate you all, Grumpo thought passionately. *Grumpo will not be ruled. Grumpo is unruleable!*

Jax stood up straight and clapped his hands together. "Welp," he announced, "I'm bored. This is stupid and I'm bored."

Jax leapt forward, faster than Mo would have thought possible. He grabbed her by the arm, dug into his pocket, and teleported himself, the former enderman, and the zombie horse out of the ship and into the darkness.

Fin blinked after her. His sister was gone and he had no way to follow her.

He was alone for the first time in his life.

Sometimes the player dreamed it was lost in a story.

Sometimes the player dreamed it was other things, in other places. Sometimes these dreams were disturbing. Sometimes very beautiful indeed. Sometimes the player woke from one dream into another, then woke from that into a third.

—Julian Gough, Minecraft "End Poem"

CHAPTER TEN

MAY THE GREAT CHAOS SMILE UPON YOU

Commander Kraj paced back and forth on a pale yellow courtyard above a craggy, forbidding island shore. Captain Tamat and Corporal Murrum paced with him, a respectful distance behind. His bodyguard, their ranks swelled from eight to twelve now, stood gathered round the doorway from the courtyard into a massive tower that soared into the night. Almost a church, you might say, if you didn't know that it was one.

They waited for their audience with Eresha, the Mouth of the Great Chaos.

She was late.

Endermen thought of this place only in hushed, awestruck tones. Terminus, the holy island, where the Grand High and Glorious Cathedral of Entropy lay hidden from all outsiders. Hidden from most endermen, too, in fact. The Mouths of the Great

Chaos had long ago decided that things seemed holiest when most people couldn't have them. They had chosen this place. There was no good beach to come ashore easily. There were many sharp rockfaces and steep cliffs where you could fall to your death before you even realized you had made the fatal slip. And there was no end ship attached to the huge and gnarly city on the north edge of the island. Everything about Terminus whispered death and secrets. Death, and secrets, and Chaos.

Now, endermen swarmed over every inch of crag, cliff, or stone.

They all came to hear from Eresha. What was going to happen now? Where were the humans? Was it safe to go home? The stress and strain of being so vastly intelligent was beginning to wear on the endernation. They much preferred the relaxation of their own Ends, clever enough to decide what to have for dinner, not quite clever enough for higher math.

Eresha, the Mouth of the Great Chaos, had not yet emerged from her residence.

Commander Kraj could see her in her window. Her dark shape behind the banners. The old witch kept him waiting on purpose, he just *knew* it. But Kraj was not just a dotty old enderman no one wanted to listen to. Not anymore. He was somebody now. He was a commander. Commander meant people *had* to listen.

He sniffed the night air. Kraj hadn't slept since the Endmoot. He couldn't afford it. Sleep was weakness. Sleep was laziness. The commander peered into the crowds below. So far below they seemed like one huge black mass to him up here. And to them, Kraj and Murrum and Tamat and the rest of his bodyguard were as invisible as memory.

Commander Kraj shook his huge, square-jawed head. He could feel his wits dulling. He needed more.

Kraj sent out his thoughts into the throng. Just two or three would be enough. *Come to the seventh courtyard of the Cathedral of Entropy, my follower,* he called, the touch of his mind caring, calm. *The Great Chaos has important work for you.*

In a quarter of an hour, three young endermen walked uncertainly through the door. They looked around for their important work. The work given to them specially by the divine source of the universe.

Commander Kraj smiled. His mouth was little more than a tear in his face, but in the endless space of his mind, Kraj's grin was as vast as a mountain range. He could feel strength flow through him as their intelligence stacked with the others' and his own. *Ahhhh,* he thought. *Yes. That is better. That is correct.*

Kraj, my fragment. Another mind cut through his own like a ship through water.

Eresha.

How dare she? Kraj was no one's fragment. He was a cruxunit. Long before Eresha replicated from the hubunit stem, Kraj was whole and undivided, walking the primeval world like a giant. Perhaps having fragments at all had been a mistake. Eresha should have been grateful to him, and to the other cruxunits who survived the eons, wherever they were. If not for them, where would the End be now?

The Mouth took in all of them. Kraj, his subordinates, the platoon that served as his own private brain bank. But not so private as all that. Eresha stood taller and thought more clearly in the presence of so many strong endermen, too. Kraj would have liked to hoard their power for himself. But it didn't work that way.

He couldn't keep his mind sharp and Eresha's dull just to get his way. Ender intellect only multiplied in groups. It could not divide.

Thank you for your gracious patience, the Mouth thought.

Kraj considered that never again would the endermen be this wise and calm. Never again would they come together like this. So many of them. So many. Why had they never done this before? Why did they not *always* stay together like this, and conquer all the worlds above and below?

Eresha was not really an old witch. She was younger by far than Kraj. No cracks spoiled her beautiful dark face. No limp slowed her down. Kraj remembered the day Eresha became the Mouth of Chaos. An Endermas long gone by, when he was young enough to imagine the seat might be his instead of some young enderman's.

We await your orders, Your Excellency, Mouth of Chaos, bowed Kraj.

He didn't mean that obedient bow or those obedient words. Eresha knew it. Kraj knew it. They each knew what the other knew. Telepathy made diplomacy so difficult, hardly any enderman bothered with it.

I have no orders for you, spawn of misrule, the Mouth thought, dipping her head to accept his submission.

What do you mean?

Eresha began her own pacing.

The war is over. More precisely, there is no war. There are no humans here. It is over. It was a mistake.

Kraj stared at her.

Are you not relieved? she thought. *No death, no bloodshed, no horror of loss. Go home to your End. All of us will go home to our*

Ends. We will live in peace again. Return the weapons and armor and supplies to the fragments on the end ship. We will not need them. We need only one another once more. I have communed with the Great Chaos. This is the path of the endermen.

You are a fool, Commander Kraj thought harshly.

You may not speak to me that way, fragment, Eresha barked in his mind.

I am not a fragment. I am older than you. And it seems I am far more intelligent. Only a fool would believe that since we cannot see the enemy today, there is no enemy at all. I tell you, the humans would not just give up. The End is rich and beautiful and vast. What general leading the human horde would simply walk away from such spoils? What knights would prepare themselves for battle and then wander off before the plunder? They are coming, Eresha. They are already here. Just because the mutant greenboy is not a double agent and saboteur does not mean there are none. How can you be so dense?

The Mouth stood very still, controlling her anger in a way no enderman could unless the whole teeming nation of them stood shoulder to shoulder. Perhaps she was stronger than Kraj thought. The crowds below were too far away to have an effect. They were on equal footing. Yet she could keep her temper easily. Kraj could barely stop himself from boiling over.

I have communed with the Great Chaos. This is the path of the endermen. I have spoken, she thought icily.

You have spoken wrongly, snapped Kraj.

Captain Tamat and Corporal Murrum stepped away from their commander in horror. The Mouth could not be wrong. It was impossible. She alone had the ear of the Great Chaos. She could not even be questioned. They stepped away to avoid the lightning bolt or fireball that would surely obliterate Kraj where he stood.

Nothing happened to him.

And what is this enemy you speak of, Kraj? Eresha thought. Her magenta eyes filled with impatience and contempt. She thought he was so far beneath her. Kraj fumed. *Humans? We see humans every day in the Overworld. It is very little trouble to kill one if they irritate you. If you want to find your enemy, it is as simple as finding a house and waiting for them to return to it. Why wash our country in ender blood when, and I cannot stress this enough, nothing is happening and no one is here?*

Yes, humans! The commander exploded. *Of COURSE they are our enemies! Anyone who is not of the End is our enemy. Anyone who is not like us! Anyone outside our great End! They kill us for sport. They steal our hearts to travel just a little faster. They gouge out our eyes to decorate their doorways to our country, where they do nothing but pillage and murder. The End is for endermen!* he thundered.

But it is not, Eresha continued calmly. *You forget yourself. You forget your Enderdome training. It is also for shulkers, for endermites, for chorus trees and the ender dragon itself. Every country is shared among many. And once, the End was for whoever built these great towers and palaces and pillars and roads. For we certainly did not. Some ancestor of ours took it from them, whoever they were. This is the path of the Great Chaos, my fragment. It is not always kind.*

I do not want to be like them. Do you, Eresha? How many times have humans come to the End and cut a path of dead endermen and stolen treasure throughout our world?

Many, Eresha admitted. *I cannot count them all.*

Do you remember your first invasion?

The Mouth of the Great Chaos nodded. *I was a fragment. First of my End. Little cleverer than a bright wolf, even with all my family gathered, for then there were only three of us. Three of us, and two of them. Two were enough. I had never seen anything like it. One seemed to command the very elements. When she killed us, we were powerless to stop her. Frozen in time or burning to death when no fire was nearby. She was like water itself. Like rain. She fell on us and we died. Endermen feared her, but marched on. That is who we are. And wherever he walked, fire followed him. They took everything. It was years before my End recovered. Sometimes, I think it never did.*

Kraj threw up his arms. *Then you know I am right! They must be stopped! You were right before. Why wash our country in blood? We should take theirs! Together, we could march on the Overworld and destroy all their works. Wipe out the Forces of Order once and for all. Together, endermen are unstoppable. It is only because we insist on staying apart like stunted donkeys that we do not rule this universe. Perhaps we should change. Evolve. Perhaps there should be a new law: No enderman shall henceforward ever be alone.*

Eresha rolled her eyes at his little speech. *I also remember rising up to the Overworld and slaughtering a village of humans because I and my fellow-fragments simply wished to do it. This is the balance of the Great Chaos and the Forces of Order. I accept it. I suggest you do, too. There is no threat. Go home. You are no longer a commander, but simply Kraj again. Go home to your fragments and sub-fragments and sub-sub-fragments. I have spoken.*

No. No. Kraj's blood thickened and ran cold. She took his title. He felt it as painfully as a blow from a sword. She couldn't do that. She couldn't rob him like that. She couldn't make him go back to no one listening to him. To everyone laughing at batty old Kraj and paying him no attention. He wouldn't let her.

Telepathy made diplomacy very difficult, it was true. Betrayal was even harder. You couldn't think about it for even an instant before you did it. You had to act faster than the speed of thought. Faster than your brain telling your arms to move.

Just that fast, Kraj lifted Eresha, the Mouth of the Great Chaos, off her feet and flung her off the edge of the seventh courtyard of the Grand High and Glorious Cathedral of Entropy. She plummeted silently into nothingness. Black into black. Enderman into the End.

Kraj, commander once more, stood and watched her fall. He was filled with the most extraordinary calm. And why stop at commander, now that he thought of it? Why stop at all?

All hail the Great Chaos, he thought after her.

CHAPTER ELEVEN

THE HEART OF AN ENDERMAN

Jax materialized on a sandy yellow outcropping of rock. The void yawned away beneath. His toes skittered on the edge, sending pebbles tumbling over and down into nothing. Mo and Loathsome popped into space next to him, fury in her eyes, excitement and interest in the horse's.

"What did you do?" Mo hissed.

"Cut through the crap and made a command decision," Jax said, rolling his eyes. He pointed behind them.

A thunderous roar echoed somewhere far above them. ED was flying in its long, slow circles in the distance. Jax had brought them close to the dragon's island. But why?

And Jax teleported! That could only mean he had an ender pearl. He was packing the absolute soul of some poor dead enderman somewhere. Where? And who was it? Mo didn't suppose she'd ever know the answer to the second question.

"Shall we? After you, my lady," Jax said with a mock bow.

"Shall we what?"

Jax glanced up. "Well, you can stay here while I go up and make quick work of that dragon so we can get out of here and figure out what's up with your whole—" He gestured at Mo, Loathsome, either or both. "—situation. Or, since you and your pet lizard are so cuddly and close, you could come up with me and distract him so I can try to one-shot the old monster and then we can head up to the Overworld as friends who had a fun adventure together killing interesting things. I'd rather the second. I'm not awful like you said. I'm really not. I'm just . . . ambitious and highly motivated by insurmountable challenges. That's what my hubunit used to say, anyway." He winked at her.

"Why do you even care about me or my twin or what happened to us?"

"Oh, I don't," Jax assured her. "I just want to figure it out before Roary does. Can you win at solving mysteries? Because I want to win at solving mysteries. I just want to win full stop. It's kind of my thing."

Mo glared at Jax. "I'm not helping you kill my friend. And I'm not going anywhere with you. I hate you. You had no right to teleport me without my permission. You had no right to *touch* me without my permission—"

"Is he your friend though?" Jax interrupted.

"It's not a him!"

"Whatever!"

"You know I can just teleport away, right?" Mo yelled. "I don't have to stay here with you at all."

Jax crossed his arms. "Go ahead. See, I don't think you can. I think you're not in your enderman suit anymore. I think you can't do anything I can't do, and I don't think you have the ender pearls to do it."

Mo froze. Was it true? Was she stuck moving from place to place on her slow, heavy legs like any other human girl? She hesitated. She knew she should just do it, do it right now, blink out here and blink on somewhere else. But what if it didn't work? What if Jax was right? Mo didn't think she could bear it if he was.

Loathsome gave a low, nervous whinny. Something moved in the distance. Something out on one of the other crags on the underside of the ender dragon's island. Something almost the same color as the great sky beyond.

An enderman was standing out there on the rocks. Probing the air with her long, black fingers.

Mo was so excited she forgot nearly everything that had happened to her over the past two hours. She forgot that no endermen were roaming around on ED's island as they usually would, keeping one another calm and clever. She forgot that nearly everyone had answered Kraj and Eresha's call to arms. She called out to the enderman with her mind, waving her arms in the air.

Hello! All hail the Great Chaos! Help! Help me! I've been kidnapped by this human! He's going to attack ED! Help us! Where is your End? I am Mo, twin of Fin. Do you know me?

The enderman turned toward Mo. It was wearing one of the golden chestplates Fin and Mo had collected and Kraj had commandeered. The metal glinted in the dim End light. The enderman's purple eyes narrowed. Its skin flushed red with rage. It screamed a scream of total hate and eternal fury into the sky. Its thoughts were not elegant. They were not organized into tidy sentences. There was only one enderman, after all. One enderman alone is nothing but the shape anger takes when it wants to walk the world.

DIEDIEDIEDIEDIEDIE

It charged her.

As it crossed the distance between them, Mo recognized the enderman.

No, she thought. *Lopp, no, it's me!*

The enderman did not stop.

Lopp, stop! Remember when you offered to be my hubunit? A unit of superior strength and power? Now would be a great time! Lopp, come on! It's me! It's still just me!

But it wasn't Lopp, not really. Not out here, by herself, with no one else around. There was nothing in her mind for Mo to latch on to. There was no *her* there.

Lopp's fist collided with Mo's face. Loathsome reared up to protect her mother, spraying black and yellow fluid from her churning muscles.

"Idiot!" Jax yelled, stomping toward them. "You don't *call* to them, for frick's sake."

Lopp landed a blow between Mo's shoulder blades. She went flying and sprawled on the yellow rock. The enderman hurled herself at Jax and got a hit in against his ribs. He grunted, but that was all.

"It's just one mob, geez," Jax huffed. "You can't handle one mob by yourself?"

"I don't want to handle her!" Mo shoved back at Lopp's rampaging form. She tried to be gentle. It wasn't easy to shove someone around a cliff that dropped off into infinite space without hurting them. Much harder than just punching them until they fell off the edge. Lopp's dark body flushed where Mo hit her. It seemed to only make her angrier.

Lopp, it's me! It's Mo! I know I look different, but I'm not different! Same old Mo! I'm just a fragment, I'm no danger to you. Take me away from him, we can go find Kraj's army together.

Lopp swung her arms wildly, thoughtlessly. One fist caught Loathsome under the chin and slammed her into the rock wall. The other smashed Jax's nose.

Yes! Get him! Try not to get my horse though. She's going to come with us.

Lopp screeched and lifted Mo up off her feet by her throat.

Wait, no! Mo thought frantically. *That's not what I meant. Please, Lopp. You must remember me. I need a hubunit of superior strength!*

But all the enderman saw was a human girl. An enemy. A monster.

Jax pulled an iron sword out of his pocket. (How did he fit so much in there?) Without thinking about it much at all, he stabbed Lopp through the chest.

No! Mo thought.

"No!" she screamed.

Loathsome gurgled furiously and sank her sharp teeth into the enderman's arm. Jax put one foot up against the sagging, dying enderman to push her off the blade of his sword. Lopp's magenta eyes blazed hate and pain. Her fist tightened on Mo's throat.

DIE, the thing that used to be Lopp thought.

And then, faster than a breath, there was no one at all standing on the outcropping of yellow rock. No girl, no boy, no battle.

The ender dragon howled somewhere far above.

CHAPTER TWELVE

THE OVERWORLD

Space flipped upside down. The black sky and yellow rock suddenly floated above them. Then they flipped inside out. Then a brilliant light obliterated the world around them. It consumed the End and the island and the crag of rock and the rumbling of ED in one huge white flash.

When the flash faded, Mo was standing on green grass. Jax pulled his sword out of Lopp and stumbled backward a little, catching his balance. Loathsome bit down harder. She growled with her mouth full of enderman. But it didn't matter. Lopp was already dying. She'd tried to teleport away, but all it had done was drag them all with her into the Overworld. The enderman crumpled to the ground. Her eyes faded as she fell. Mo reached out after her, but Lopp was gone. Mo's green, human eyes filled with tears.

"What were you doing out there all alone, you dummy?" she whispered. "You died! You didn't have to. Only dummies die."

"Did we just teleport out of the End completely, like, for real? Neat!" said Jax. He looked down at the loot on the ground. "Cool chestplate." He put his hands on his hips and sighed heavily. "I'm gonna have to find another portal. *So* annoying. Doing things twice is stupid."

Mo blinked. She hadn't even noticed that they'd teleported. They'd teleported, and she was somewhere else. Somewhere *very* else.

The sky above Mo shone deep, royal blue. A jungle of trees surrounded her, stretching on as far as she could see. Little red flowers bobbed here and there. Brown mountains rose up in the distance. A few yards away, a bright blue lake sparkled in the golden sunshine. As she watched, dumbfounded, a huge black squid splashed its tentacles out of the water, then slammed them back down, sending up a spray of white foam. It was as though the squid had waved at her, welcoming her to the world.

A single, fat, round-cheeked pig stared at them, its mouth hanging open in shock.

"Oh," Mo said softly. "They're pink after all. Kan always said. I never believed it. But they are. So pink." She reached out her hand to pet the pig.

The pig did not want to be petted. The pig was much more concerned about Loathsome at the moment. Its black eyes slid over the horse, trying to make sense of it. The two animals gazed at each other for a moment. A glob of lung fluid swelled up on Loathsome's chest and, with a massive PLOP, dripped onto the ground.

The pig bolted away.

After a few moments, Loathsome began to nibble lightly on the dead enderman's head. *Brains?* she said hopefully. Like most babies, once the pony had a new idea in her head, she wouldn't be letting it go anytime soon.

But before Mo could teach her horse about eating friends' brains, Lopp disappeared in a curl of smoke. Ender bodies didn't last long. The Great Chaos hates waste. When she'd disappeared, her pearl remained. And the chestplate.

Jax nudged the armor with his toe. "I've never seen an enderman wearing human gear before. Ever." He glanced shrewdly at Mo. "Is this yours?"

"Yeah," Mo said, part of her still so angry that her people had robbed her. And here was Lopp, not fighting in an apocalyptic war of all against all but wearing her stuff like she'd just borrowed a shirt.

He handed it back to her. The metal was warm in the sunshine. Mo gathered it to her like a long-lost teddy bear. She held it tight. It smelled like home. Just a little bit like the End. Like her ship and her brother and her good old life.

"Thank you," she whispered.

"You don't have to thank me," Jax said quietly. For the first time, his voice sounded very serious and gentle. "It's your loot. No one should have taken it from you in the first place."

How Orderly of him, Mo thought. But she was so grateful. To have one piece of her collection back. One piece of *herself* back. Mo fastened it on. It felt good and solid and *real*.

Jax bent down, picked up the ender pearl lying on the ground, turned around, and started walking again.

"Whoa! Wait! Don't you dare," yelled Mo. "You give that to me!"

"No way, I made the kill, I get the drop. That's your loot, this is mine. I'm being *really* fair here."

"But it's *her* pearl! That would be like me taking your brain for a souvenir."

Brains? piped up Loathsome.

No, Mo snapped back.

"She had a name, Jax. Do you know her name? Because I do. You have no right to it. Give it here. I'll take it home. I'll take care of it. It's mine."

"I mean, it's *not* yours. You aren't an enderman. You're not one of them. You seem to be having a lot of trouble with that. I have a lot more right to it than you. And no, I don't want to know her name, that's fricking creepy. All ender pearls look the same and are the same and I like it like that. Look at it this way, if you kill something, doesn't it honor that thing to use all its parts and not let anything go to waste? I honor the strength and power of your weird monster friend. So I will make sure to honor what is left of her by using it in strength and power." But Jax saw the look on Mo's face and knew she wouldn't let it go. "Fine, whatever, take it. I have tons of them. I don't care."

Jax tossed the pearl behind him. Mo scrambled in the grass for it. It was still warm. Poor Lopp. She couldn't stop wondering why Lopp had been so far from Telos. Wasn't everyone still preparing for war? No one knew the "war" was just four kids raiding for loot. It had to be something simple. Something she just wasn't seeing. One enderman alone couldn't hold on to a complicated thought.

Mo squinted. Her eyes burned. She'd never seen sunlight. She didn't know *how* to see it without hurting. It was just so *bright*. How could anyone stand it? That big burning ball of flame hanging over them *all the time*? And all those colors! (Blue for Fin's eyes; green for hers.) They throbbed. So vivid and loud! Nothing like the soothing violet and soft yellow and comforting black of the End. Nothing like anything Mo had ever known.

"Anything look familiar?" Jax asked. His voice was almost . . . nice.

Mo tried. She really tried. "No," she gave up. "I've never seen anything like this place. What is *that*?"

Jax glanced around. "Pretty standard forest biome," he said.

"No, I mean that." Mo pointed up. She couldn't imagine what to call it. It was so big and heavy-looking. So alien.

"That?" Jax followed her eyes. Then he looked back at Mo. Then up again. "That is a cloud," he finished, shaking his head. "Koal was right. Wow. Just *wow*."

Loathsome stood up on wobbily, half-rotted legs. She nibbled experimentally at the grass. She swallowed. The grass slid down her throat and fell out of a hole in her stomach where her ribs showed through.

"This way," said Jax, walking off to the north. He walked with easy purpose and familiarity. This was his place.

"Where are we going?" Mo asked, paralyzed with fear. "Do you think it'll rain?"

But it didn't matter, did it? It didn't matter if it rained. Because Mo was not an enderman. The rain couldn't hurt her. She tried to think. She tried to remember. Tried to remember a time before the End. Tried to remember *anything* other than the End. Tried to remember a time when her life was green and blue and brown. When her life was this world, and not the other. But there was nothing there. Nothing. All she could remember was Fin and Kan and ED and the long night of her home. This was all so *impossible*.

Mo looked at her horse. Loathsome seemed to have stopped growing, for the moment. She was big enough to ride, if you didn't mind the mess. *You still like me, don't you?* she said to the undead pony. *You don't mind whether I'm human or enderman.*

The pony turned and nuzzled her shoulder. It was a very wet, cold nuzzle. Then it was a sharp nuzzle.

Hey! No biting.

Loathsome looked confused. As she was growing older, she was beginning to understand some things about life as a zombie horse. *Mumma. Mumma. B . . . B . . . Braaains?* she asked, uncertain.

No, Mo scolded. *Bad horsey. No brains. At least not mine.*

Loathsome pawed the ground glumly. *Braaaains,* she complained.

"You coming?" called Jax behind him.

Mo didn't want to, actually. She did not remotely appreciate being kidnapped out into the Overworld, a place she'd never *really* even wanted to visit, by a jerk who didn't seem to care about much of anything but looting and killing ED. Well, the looting she could understand. But the ED-killing? Mo had to draw a line somewhere. The until-very-recently enderman followed anyway, though. If she lost sight of Jax, she'd never get back. She'd be stuck in this bright, loud, overwhelming place with no one. Mo scrambled up a little hillside after him. Loathsome did not understand why her mother did not simply ride her, preferably toward any fresh local brains. But she was still very new, and accepted such unexplainable choices.

Reluctantly, Mo kept walking. It was the only option.

On the other side of the hill sat Jax's house. It was a very nice house. Honestly, it was an *amazing* house. Almost a castle. It had four towers, twenty windows, and three gargoyles. The walls were all strong grey stone. Mo, Jax, and Loathsome passed under a huge portcullis on the other side of a drawbridge over the little blue moat flowing all the way around the fortress. Torches burned on either side of every door and window. Pretty little patches of wheat and flowers grew around the banks of the moat. Loathsome stuck her oozing nose into the wheat and sniffed.

Mumma! Graaaaains? she neighed, though it was really more of a phelgmy gurgle.

Mo laughed a little. *Sure, baby. All yours.*

The zombie pony kicked up her hind legs in joy. Bone showed through the grey, rotting skin. Her thick, ridged, toenaily hooves glinted dully in the sun. She mowed through a patch of wheat so fast Jax couldn't shoo her off his landscaping in time.

"Ugh," he said helplessly as the pony started on his flowers. "Can you not . . . *leak* on my garden?"

But Mo didn't seem to care about the murky spinal fluid beading up and dribbling off of Loathsome's body onto his lawn.

"Come on," Jax sighed, resigned to losing his front yard entirely. "The sun's going down. You don't want to be caught outside at night. Trust me."

They left the horse to her first feast and started over the bridge.

Mo jogged a little to keep up. "You're so lucky you found this place! If I were you I'd never leave it! You never know who might try to take it while you're gone."

"Well, first of all, I didn't find it, I built it."

"All by yourself?"

Jax straightened up a bit, quite proud. "All by myself. Took ages. Even designed the gargoyles. But really, it's not that good. There're way bigger castles and stuff farther inland. Some of them are even mine! I was just figuring things out when I built this. I've done way better ones since. But this one's my favorite, because it was my first."

"I didn't realize you built things. I thought you just killed them." Maybe Jax wasn't really so bad. Anyone who could build something so magnificent couldn't be *that* bad.

Jax waved his hand dismissively. "Oh, I don't really do much building anymore. This is all old stuff, from when I was a kid. I got bored. I was spending all my time fighting off creepers and zombies and chasing them away from my houses. Then I realized *I* could just chase *them*, whenever I wanted, and I didn't need any houses for that at all! Way more exciting. I never get bored anymore. Hey! What are you doing! Stop that!"

Mo snatched her hand back guiltily. Where a moment ago there had been a smooth, unbroken stone wall, there was now a square hole.

"All hail the Great Chaos," whispered Mo.

She'd hardly even known what she was doing before it was done. It had been automatic, like a reflex.

"Sorry!"

"What did you do? What's wrong with you? I just told you how long it took me to build this place."

"I couldn't help it! It's just so beautiful and perfect."

"Yeah, it is! So what the crap?"

"You designed it all so . . . so precisely. It's so complete. So correct. So . . . so *Orderly*."

"SO WHAT? YOU WRECK IT?" Jax looked down at her with disgust. "Of course you do. Because you're an enderman. That's what you do. You see something good and you punch a hole in it."

"I served the Great Chaos," Mo argued, steeling her spine. "You do what humans do—you see something and you kill it!"

"What are you talking about?"

"The universe! Lopp!"

"YOU'RE A CRAZY PERSON!" Jax screamed, and stomped off into the house. The portcullis opened into a long hallway with a lot of heads of various exotic creatures on the walls and, naturally, more torches.

"I made it better!" Mo yelled after him. "Now it's perfect, because it's imperfect!"

"Shut up, mob!" Jax yelled back. "I don't have to listen to crazy people!"

Mo ran down the long hallway to catch up with him. Loathsome ran after her. By the time they got to the boy, both were out of breath. Loathsome because her lungs had been born rotting. Mo because she'd never had to breathe the air of the Overworld before. It was so rich and full her body didn't know what to do with it.

"Jax," she panted. "Listen. I'm not crazy. Well, maybe I am, but not because of this. The universe was created in a battle between the Great Chaos and the Forces of Order. They struggled against each other for eons. Sometimes Chaos prevailed, and made the endermen, and the shulkers, and the creepers, and fire itself. Sometimes Order prevailed, and made humans and sheep and pigs and medicine and stones and trees. Finally, their conflict ended as it always must: in a draw. They looked around and all their creations surrounded them: They had made the universe. So everything serves either the Great Chaos or the Forces of Order, and they will always fight. It's in their nature. I served the Great Chaos. I made your house better. More beautiful. More perfect."

"You made it weaker! Anyone could crawl in through that hole!"

"Yes, yes, exactly! And if someone did, what amazing things might happen? What kind of exciting story might start for you? A dangerous one, even. They're more exciting when they're dangerous. You should never be able to predict what will happen next in life. That's boring. That's the Forces of Order. When Chaos reigns, *everything* is exciting, because *anything* could happen. Every second is a surprise. So you can't get mad at endermen for perfecting your houses and all that, because we're *helping* you, really. When you think about it."

"Okay," said Jax with a little smile, the kind of smile that said he thought he'd won the argument already. "Then you can't be mad at me for killing that enderman back there."

"Oh yes, I can."

"Oh no, you can't. I was just serving the Great Chaos. She definitely couldn't have predicted what happened to her. It was one hundred percent a surprise, I guarantee it. It was a very exciting story."

Mo didn't know what to say to that. It sounded right and wrong at the same time. She didn't want to let Jax be right about anything. But it certainly *had* been chaotic. She decided to change the subject.

"What were you going to do with her pearl?" Mo asked hesitantly.

Jax motioned for her to follow him down another stone hall. This one was much more narrow and less grand. "Teleport," he said. "Maybe grind it up to make another ender chest. Dunno."

"I heard that humans can use pearls to teleport." A thought suddenly occurred to Mo. "Wait a minute," she said, stopping in the middle of the grey cobblestone hallway. "Fin and I have always been able to teleport. And if we aren't endermen, we don't have ender pearls. So how could we do that? We teleported just fine. All day long."

Jax looked her up and down. He squinted one eye.

"I bet I know," he said. "Hold still."

Jax got up close to Mo. She didn't like that at all. She didn't like Jax. She didn't like how he looked or how he talked or how he acted. She didn't like that he'd grabbed her off her ship. The only thing she liked even a little bit about the big human kid was that he'd given her the chestplate back, and been quite nice about it. He seemed to be everything she'd been taught humans were: loud, aggressive, greedy, rude, and eager to take anything he wanted.

You're a human, though, Mo thought to herself. *If humans are those things, so are you. And how else did you get an entire ship full of treasure than by taking what you wanted when you wanted it?*

Jax stuck his hand into Mo's pocket. Pocket! She had pockets! She'd never thought about pockets before. Ever. Endermen don't need them. He scrabbled around in there for a minute, scrunching up his face. His face was so close to hers. She'd never been so close to a human. Except Fin. But she hadn't known Fin was human, had she?

He'd been in there a while. How big could a pocket be? Finally, Jax squared his feet and pulled out, one after the other, a strange pale-gold doll, a black egg, and an ender pearl so old its dust was covered in dust. It looked like a collapsed balloon. As soon as the air hit it, the pearl started falling apart.

Jax and Mo stared at the egg, the doll, and the pearl.

"You have a totem of undying," Jax whispered, stunned. "Where did you get that?"

"How should I know? I didn't know I had pockets till just now. But that stuff is *heavy*. How could I be carrying it and not know?"

The ender pearl bubbled into mush and began to seep down through the floorboards. *There goes teleportation,* Mo thought.

"Pockets," Jax said slowly, his mind clearly working through something else entirely. "It's a human thing. It's not really a pocket, it's a shortcut to an empty block of space-time that can hold whatever you want because it's both infinitely big and infinitely small at the same time. You don't feel the weight or the bulk of your stash. There're limits, but mostly you can carry anything, no problem. You could teleport because you had an ender pearl the whole time. So you're no better than me. That pearl belonged to somebody, too. You probably killed them for it."

"I did not!" cried Mo. "I wouldn't!"

But it was so obvious that Jax didn't really care about the pearl or the totem. He reached out his fingers toward the black egg. He seemed almost afraid to touch it. The loud, obnoxious boy was suddenly *reverent*. Full of awe.

"Are you ok?" Mo asked.

"Sorry," Jax muttered, shaking his head. "Look, I'm sorry, I know you're having a whole identity crisis or whatever, but what the *actual* crap, Mo? Why do you have a dragon egg? *How* do you have a dragon egg?"

"Is that a dragon egg?"

"Is that a dragon egg?" Jax screeched in a high-pitched, mocking tone. "YES, THAT'S A DRAGON EGG, YOU MELON. *Where did you get it?*"

"I DON'T KNOW, YOU . . ." Mo wasn't used to insulting people in human terms. She stumbled. "DOUBLE MELON."

Jax shook his head in disbelief. "You've been lying to me this whole time!"

"No, I haven't!"

"You're so high and mighty! Trying to lecture us on right and wrong, killing and not killing. Making me feel bad about myself. Making me feel like I'm *scum*. And the whole time you were carrying around a dragon egg like it's no big deal. Well, it is a big deal, you *freak*. And it's only a *slightly* bigger deal than having a totem of undying when you're supposed to be this poor little lost orphan with amnesia. There's no way you just *found* those things. No one would ever be so careless as to drop one or leave it lying around. In fact, there's no way that egg should even *exist*. You're not going anywhere until we figure this out. Because there's only one way to get a dragon egg for yourself."

"And what's that?"

Jax frowned. "You have to kill the ender dragon."

CHAPTER THIRTEEN

IT'S COMPLICATED

Jax, Mo, and Loathsome had been gone for no more than a few hours.

Fin couldn't remember ever going so long without seeing his twin. Without knowing she was safe and nearby. Without talking to her. It made him nervous. It made him feel unsteady, like he could just tumble off into the night at any moment. The others seemed to have lost a little interest in him once Jax had taken off with Mo. They had other priorities. The mystery could wait until their friend came back.

In the meantime, they were *very* busy.

The humans were building something.

Roary, Koal, and Jesster all had pairs of soft grey wings attached to their backs. They used them to glide from the ship to a smallish island off the port side where they were working. Fin knew what they were. Elytra. A couple of days ago he'd had dozens of pairs of his own. Now, Roary and Koal had to carry him between them when they flew over to their new base. They didn't need anything from the ship. There wasn't much left there anyway, except the small mountain of enchanted books. But Roary wanted them all to stick together over on the new beachhead. She didn't want to leave Fin alone back there.

Fin watched them make quick work of that little island. It was dizzying. Their hands moved so fast and so cleverly. Fin looked down at his own hands. He didn't think he could ever do anything like that. That confident. That purposeful. That *casual*. They must have had some kind of blueprint for whatever they were building, but they never seemed to need to reference it or argue amongst themselves over where to put the next cornerpiece or anything.

Roary and Jesster attacked the grove of chorus trees at the north end of the island. They hacked them up for the wood before Fin could begin to explain how to make chorus corn from the fruits. Koal got busy carving blocks of end stone, the very stuff of the land in the End, out of a little cliff on the west side. Fin didn't think that would be enough to make anything too impressive. You'd have to mine half the islands in the End to build something as big as Telos. And it looked like that was about the size of their plan. But when they pooled the chorus trees and stone at the building site on a flat meadow in the center of the isle, protected by gentle hills on all sides, it quickly became clear the humans weren't relying on just what they could scavenge here.

Something was wrong with their pockets. They could pull anything out of them. Stones, food, weapons, anything. It was like they were wearing his whole ship, as it had been before Kraj and his goons, and shoveling items out as they needed them. It was magic.

"By the Great Chaos," Fin whispered. No one heard him. They had way too much to do.

Roary had half a wall up before Fin knew what he was looking at. She got up on a rise of rock to work on a doorframe. Jess sat cross-legged on the inner side of the new wall, sawing chorus wood up into furniture. Koal dug down into the island earth for a good foundation and started hauling redstone blocks out of his trousers. It was so ridiculous to look at, yet so terrifying. Could all humans do this? Could Fin do it?

None of them seemed to miss Jax at all.

"Well, of course he's our *friend*," Jess said when Fin asked about it. She didn't bother to look up from the stone wall she was building with breathtaking speed. Her pickaxe was a blur. "But he's got his whole mission and he's very focused on it. I'm not about that life. Neither is Roary."

"I'm a *little* about that life," Koal said.

Roary made a gesture with her thumb and forefinger and a tiny space between them. A *little*. She grinned.

"What life?" Fin asked.

Jess bit the inside of her lip. It made her mouth go all crooked. "You shouldn't worry about your sister or Jax. They'll be back. Any minute."

"That's what you told me when they left," Fin said impatiently. "I know. I'm not worried." He was worried.

"No, I know, it's just that when I tell you about Jax, you're *going* to worry, but you shouldn't. He's not a bad guy."

Fin scratched the back of his head. He couldn't get used to having hair. It wasn't right. It was *unnatural*. "It worries me that you're saying that, because nobody said he was bad, but you're already defending him."

Jesster sighed and put down her tools. "Jax likes killing things."

"That's horrible," Fin said.

Jess shrugged. "Is it, though? What do you eat around here?"

"I dunno," Fin said uncomfortably, even though he did know quite well. "Chorus fruits."

"Right, so you kill things all the time. And that's okay, as far as you see it. As long as it's vegetables. And what about endermites? I bet you stomp them as soon as you see them."

"That's not the same thing. Endermites are nasty little pests. They will bite the black out of you as soon as look at you. They're nothing. They're so stupid they barely know they're alive. They're basically mean, walking meat popsicles. It's not like we eat shulkers. And chorus trees are just plants."

"Plants are alive. It's still killing. And I'd bet, if you could get an endermite to talk, they'd have some words about who is a mean, walking meat popsicle."

"But you can't get an endermite to talk. Believe me, I've tried." *I've been lonelier than you can even think of, in your beautiful blue world up there, where everything you could ever want fits in your pocket,* Fin thought, but didn't say.

Jess laughed. "Sure, but you can't get a pig or a sheep or a creeper to talk, either. Jax just . . . Fin, he wants to be safe. He'd never admit it, but that's all it is, deep down. He wants to be safe. He wants *us* to be safe. And you don't know what it's like up there. What comes for you when the sun goes down. We're all on our own in the Overworld, unless we band together, like the four of us. And nothing up there will hesitate to kill us."

"If it's so normal to kill, then why are you acting like Jax is special?"

Jess picked at the corner of the table she was making. "Look, it's fun to fight, okay?" she said defensively. "If you're good at it. And Jax is good at it. We all are, but he's *really* good. So after a while, nobody wanted to mess with him anymore. Even the endermen avoided him. It just wasn't worth it, I guess. So he started wandering out into whatever distant territory he could find. He'd just keep going and going until something attacked him. He became fascinated with hunting rare creatures . . . unique monsters. He took home souvenirs and hung them in his hall. He's a collector. Everybody's got to have a passion, you know? But he's not a bad guy. He wants to be strong and he wants to be safe. Everyone wants that, don't they?"

Fin remembered why they were here. He didn't like it at all. "How did you meet him?"

"Oh, Jax and me've been friends since forever. But we only met Koal and Roary last summer. Jax likes to hunt and fight. I . . . I like to build. I'm the reason he's got all those houses. I taught him how to make something a little stronger and more interesting than a bed with a roof over it. Before me, he was just making big, dumb, plain wooden cubes with a bed inside. No style at all. No *flair*. I love making something out of nothing. Just a wide green field full of trees and boulders and then—presto! Jess happens to it, and it's a pirate ship or a palace or a racetrack. I look at random stuff and I see civilization. Order out of chaos, you know?"

Fin felt a little sick. "I do know," he said, trying to hide his disgust. Chaos was beautiful and alive. Order was ugly and dead. Every enderman knew that. It was like listening to a demon tell him how wonderful living in fire could be. No, it *wasn't* wonderful. It burned your skin off.

"But even though I like to build stuff," Jess went on, "doesn't mean I don't like a good fight or a good hunt. I met Jax in a beach cave. He was cleaning out the cave spiders so you could spend a minute on that beach without having one jump on your head. Horrible things, cave spiders. Poisonous. I was looking for materials to build a library. A place for all the books I find. You can make glass out of good enough sand, you know. A glass library. I liked the idea of that. Anyway, Jax was about to be spider lunch and I gave him a hand. Almost got our heads handed to us. We were just starting out then. He wasn't that good at . . . well, anything. Neither was I. We're loads better now. We traveled together a lot. It's safer in numbers. And last summer we were out hunting skeletons because wouldn't a whole castle made out of bones be fantastic?"

"I guess?" Fin said. It sounded gruesome.

Jess looked at him like he was crazy. He didn't need telepathy to read that look. It *was* fantastic, her eyes said. How could he not agree?

"Well, we followed a skeleton into this huge, amazing swamp. It just went on forever."

Roary jogged over. She settled down next to the half-built table. "You talking about last summer?"

"Yeah," Jess said. "Fin wants to know how we met."

Roary pulled a cooked apple out of her—apparently cavernous—pocket. She munched on it. "You guys saved us from the witch. It was *awesome*."

Jess shuddered, getting into the spirit of her story. "The swamp was huge and soggy and mucky and full of snakes and birds and the moon and quiet. But there's not much good building material in swamps. Not like orchards or mountains. Not for what I like to make, anyway. We couldn't quite get a good shelter up before dark. And as the sun dipped down out of the sky, she appeared in her little swamp hut all lit up with swamp-gas lights. Have you ever met a witch?"

Fin shook his head. There were so many different kinds of creatures up there. He couldn't imagine it. Everyone down here was the same. He never had to worry about seeing something he didn't understand, like a witch or a skeleton or a cave spider.

"They're like chemists with terrible outlooks on life," Roary piped up. "That's why me and Koal were there. I'm sure Jess told you she's a builder, Jax is a hunter—well, I like crafting. Mixing things up and seeing if they explode or create something totally new and totally useful. It's the best thing in the world. Like solving a mystery, but you don't even know what the mystery *is* while you're solving it. Kind of like you and your sister. So the point is, witches have potions, and potions are great, and I wanted them. You know"—Roary leaned in confidentially—"I think I might chuck it all and become a witch myself someday. I could if I wanted. I'm pretty cranky about most things most of the time, I dig swamps and wearing black and filling up potion bottles with horrible chemicals and horrible magic and horror just generally. If this End thing doesn't work out, it's my backup plan."

By then, Koal had seen them talking and put down his axe to join the group.

"Koal came along because he'd never been to a swamp before," Roary said. Koal nodded.

"I like exploring," he said. "It gets me a little bit of everything—collecting, hunting, crafting, building, or at least looking at buildings. And every once in a while you find gold. Or even diamond ore. A little bit of diamond will keep me happy for a week. But it turns out witches are very selfish and they just want to keep all their magic for themselves. One captured us. She put us in a cell made out of hundreds of poison potions. If we'd tried to escape, we'd have shriveled up and she'd have made people soup out of us. Witches are the worst."

"Well, to be fair, you were going to rob her," Fin said.

"Yeah, but she was gonna *kill* us! That's what I call overreacting. She could always make more potions."

Fin thought about Kraj and his soldiers carting everything he and Mo had ever loved out of their ship and how he'd felt. How angry he'd been. If he'd had hundreds of bottles of poison then, what would he have done?

"Jax and I stormed the place," Jesster picked up the story. "The witch wasn't alone. She had a bunch of creeper friends and a zombie butler. Took us all night to get everyone. Then dissasemble the poison bottle jail and let them out."

"You killed *all* of them?" Fin's face was doing all sorts of things. He'd never had one before, so he didn't know how to just look interested and attentive without showing everything he felt. He frowned, his eyebrows went up and then down again, he grimaced, he squinted, he scratched his head. Their story was ridiculous. All those things he'd never heard of, all those places. They were messing with him. They had to be. Or at least exaggerating. Making themselves sound a lot more dangerous and exciting than any twelve-year-old really could be. Fin and Mo were still just waiting for their lives to start. These humans couldn't really have done all this, could they?

Jess looked uncomfortable. "The zombie butler was already dead . . ." she said with a half-hearted shrug. "Technically."

"She'd have killed all of us if she could. They come out at night. They hunt us. Up there, it's everything in the world against humans. Just surviving is a win. You're so judgmental. Has anyone ever *hunted* you? I didn't think so."

He hadn't ever been hunted, of course he hadn't. But that didn't make it right, did it? A lot of the endermen in the End were tremendously mean, but he didn't kill them. Mo didn't kill them. And yet . . . when the humans talked about the Overworld, the swamp and the witch, the beach cave and the poisonous spiders, the castle made out of bones . . . it all sounded so . . . so *exciting*. So different from the End, where every day was exactly the same, and every night, too. Imagine living in a place where you could never know what might happen next. Imagine living in a place where colors other than yellow, purple, and black existed. In a place where the biggest adventure you could find was something much, *much* more interesting than training in the Enderdome.

"They're just monsters," Koal mumbled. "It's no big deal."

All those visions of the Overworld vanished from Fin's head. "Just monsters? Just *monsters*? Like endermen, you mean?" he shot back, much louder.

Jess rolled her eyes. "Yes, actually, *exactly* like endermen. Endermen are *strange*. They're alien. They're hideous. They're violent and angry even when you're just minding your own business not bothering anyone. But if you commit the high crime of looking at them, as if looking ever hurt anyone, they'll get you. You *have* to get them first. That's all there is to it. Survival of the quickest. Once you've seen an enderman, it's usually too late. They're the worst thing I know about. Do you have any idea how many humans endermen kill up there? Because it is a *lot*. And it's not even like they're doing it to get our loot. When we go down, and regen at our spawn point, we leave everything behind, but they never take it. And let me tell you, respawning is no fun. It hurts like I don't even know what. You're so weak. You can barely move. Everything just *throbs*. Unless you've got medicine on hand and a good friend, or a totem to stop your respawn from happening in the first place, you won't feel like yourself again for a long time."

Fin felt his cheeks burn. "Then what are you doing here? It's nothing but endermen down here! Why couldn't you just leave us alone? You're the monsters, not us. You just show up in our territory and expect to do whatever you want, however you want, with whatever you want, and you don't care if it belongs to you or not. Humans are all the same!"

Koal got red in the face. He was embarrassed. He was angry. He was insulted. "If humans are all the same, you're bad too! You're human, you idiot! And if you had a ship full of loot, I bet a bucket of gold you got it by marching in somewhere, seeing what you wanted, and taking it without asking just like all the other nasty, no-good humans. If your ender-friends knew what you were, they'd treat you the same as they treat us and you wouldn't think they were so great then! Get a grip, Fin, deal with your situation, and face the facts! If humans are monsters, you're a monster, too."

Fin fought desperately not to cry. "According to you, endermen are the monsters. So I'm one either way!" he screamed. "Just get out! Go away! If you hadn't come I'd still be in my ship with all my stuff and my twin and my best friend and I wouldn't have any problems! I'd still be happy! *What are you doing here?* Why can't you just go back where you came from?"

"It's COMPLICATED!" Roary yelled back. "Just calm *down*. We're just regular people, Fin, just like you."

"Not like me. I never invaded anybody. And Kraj is right. That's what you're doing, even if you're only an army of four. Why do you think you have the right to just show up on someone else's land and start doing and taking whatever you want from whoever you want?"

"That's just how it works in the Overworld," Koal said. "Everybody does it."

"Then the Overworld *sucks*. And so does everybody." Fin crossed his arms over his chest and let out his breath.

"Did you ask before taking every piece of your collection from the place you found it? Even the rocks and the ore and the wood?" Koal fired back. Fin had nothing to say to that. He hated that he didn't.

"It's complicated," he mumbled.

Roary tried to explain. "You want to know why we came? It's not just one thing. We aren't endermen. Every human is completely different from every other human. Yeah, yeah, Jax wants to kill the ender dragon. Big whoop. Lots of people do. It's like how lots of people see a mountain and some of them want to paint it and some of them want to live on it and some of them want to mine it, but most people just *gotta* climb it. So Jax wants to climb it. But we planned to come to the End for a lot of reasons. I wanted to find new materials. I guess that makes me the miner. There's stone and food and treasure down here you can't find anywhere else. Koal wanted to see a place that's pretty much nothing but a legend in the Overworld. He's your painter. Although he was more or less on board with Jax's plan, and so was I."

Koal looked embarrassed. "I like to travel. But once you've got where you're going . . . it's nice to have something to do. I need activities. Or I might as well stay home."

Roary nodded. Fin got the feeling none of them was entirely *off*board with Jax's plan when it came right down to it. "And Jess wanted . . ."

Jesster rubbed her hands on her knees. She could speak very well for herself. "Jess wants to live on the mountain."

"To rule it? With an iron fist? From this castle? Queen of the End?" Fin clenched his fist. *Grumpo will not be ruled. Grumpo is unruleable. And so is Fin.*

Jesster boggled. "No. Just live here. Who wants to rule? What a lot of work. *Jess* got tired of running from all those sweet, nice monsters who definitely didn't want to kill her or knock down everything she ever built. *Jess* thought if she stocked up enough pumpkins, she could build her own little city and live down here and not have to worry about witches or spiders or skeletons or zombie butlers or creepers or anything. She could just build her library of glass and be happy. *Jess* . . . kind of wants to be *you* when she grows up."

Fin looked at Jess with astonishment. *She* wanted to be like *him*? But . . . Jess was strong and confident. She had everything. She was pretty. Soft brown skin and brown hair in a long ponytail and brown eyes. A friendly set to her chin. Not scary. Not flashing with rage. Not a monster. Just a girl who wanted to build a library. He knew another girl like that. His sister. And when his sister came back, if they were going to figure out what had happened to him, it would be this girl and her friends who would help them, not the endermen. Not now. Not once they saw the twins as they really were. Not Kraj or Lopp or Koneka or Eresha the Mouth of the Great Chaos. Maybe Kan. Maybe. But he couldn't count on that and neither could Mo. If he was going to get help, Fin knew he needed to stop calling them monsters. Whether it was true or not.

Fin dried his eyes and took a deep breath. "Building libraries isn't so bad," he sniffed. He smiled shyly. "I even know where you can find some books."

"Really?" Jess said. Her eyes got big and round. "I could have them?"

Fin nodded. "If Mo says it's okay. She will. But it's nice to ask."

"It would only take a couple of trips to ferry them all over here," Roary said. "What's in all those books anyway?"

Fin shrugged. "I don't know. They're enchanted. I've never been able to get one to open."

CHAPTER FOURTEEN

IN THE ARMY NOW

Go on, thought Commander Kraj. *Take it. It will make you stronger.*

The enderfrag Koneka reached out one skinny arm toward the strange, alien thing. She hesitated, uncertain. She looked dark and calm against the glowing Enderdome courtyard. Almost like a grown-up.

All the other enderfrags in the Enderdome watched her carefully. They waited to see what she would do. Everyone liked Koneka. Some endermen were never alone because they were afraid to lose their minds. Koneka was never alone because the other young fragments just felt better about being alive when she was around. Kraj was big and frightening and angry. He had sailed in like a furious black boat with fifteen other endermen who all had funny titles like "Captain" or "Corporal" or "Sergeant" stuck on their names. He had interrupted Left-Hand Human-Punching practice. He had demanded all the frags gather in one place to listen to him. He had commanded Taskmaster Owari not to interfere or interrupt. Commander Kraj made them all want to teleport far away. But Koneka hadn't, so they hadn't. Whatever Koneka did now, they would all do.

What is it? Koneka thought.

You know what it is, fragment, Kraj scoffed. *Use it.*

Koneka did not move. *It is a sword.*

Obviously. An iron sword, with a Bane of Arthropods enchantment. It is a very excellent weapon. Two of your noble young comrades donated it to the cause. You may thank them after the great battles to come.

But it cannot be a sword, Cruxunit Kraj.

Commander Kraj! Speak correctly to your elder! thought Captain Tamat loudly. But Kraj himself remained calm. The young creature seemed to amuse him with her careful thoughts.

Oh? And why not?

Because you want me to use it. I cannot use a sword.

Of course you can. Whoever told you such nonsense?

One of the other enderfrags piped up, *Taskmaster Owari says that the enderman must not stoop to weapons as the human does.*

Yet another fragment dutifully recited last week's lesson: *Weapons are the tools of Order. They must be crafted according to precise and Orderly instructions. Humans use them to shape and control the world.*

Koneka finished the recital. *The enderman is superior. The Great Chaos needs only the power of our fists, which can never be lost, or shattered, or smelted into something else, or stolen from you.*

Commander Kraj glanced over the crowd of young ones. His eyes met those of Taskmaster Owari. The Taskmaster quite clearly did not approve.

I see, Kraj thought finally. *May I present a counter-argument?*

Taskmaster Owari gave her permission.

Who is your sparring partner, Fragment Koneka?

Koneka pointed to a young enderfrag called Nif in the front row.

Hit him.

Koneka hesitated again. She glanced up at Owari.

Do not look at Owari! Look at me! I am your commander. The Mouth of the Great Chaos has given me dominion over all the forces of the endermen and charged me to create the greatest army the End has ever known or will ever know. What has Owari done? Taught juveniles not to break their toes when they kick one another.

I thought you said that the fragments would not be required to fight, Commander Kraj, Owari thought icily.

I have changed my mind. I will leave no tool unused in the great struggle. Look at me, Fragment Koneka. It is Left-Hand Human-Punching day is it not? So pretend he is a human. Hit him. Show me your left-hand punch.

Koneka dashed forward and struck Nif in the arm. Kraj was right, they did this all the time. Sparring was everyone's favorite. Nif flushed red, but the damage was minor. Koneka didn't hit hard unless it was Unlimited Brawling day. Nif rubbed his arm. He smiled at Koneka, so she would know he wasn't mad that she'd punched him in front of the whole Dome. Nif wouldn't ever be mad at Koneka. They'd been friends since they'd first been replicated. They chased endermites together across the islands and pelted each other with chorus fruits and made fun of Taskmaster Owari behind her back. When it was just the two of them, they were just smart enough for uncomplicated fun like that.

Kraj laid his hand gently on Koneka's shoulder. *Now, take the sword.*

Koneka didn't want to. Everyone knew she didn't. Her thoughts shone clear and bright. The sword was unnatural. The sword was Order. The sword was *human*.

And the sword would probably kill Nif.

Koneka picked it up suddenly. Decisively. She didn't know why, really. She just did it. It felt heavy and cold and foreign in her hand. Her thoughts felt heavy and cold and foreign, too. Kraj was beaming at her. Taskmaster Owari seemed disconcerted. Nif was sweating spores. Koneka's arm was moving into an offensive position already, all on its own.

We are just sparring though, right? Nif thought shakily. *Koneka? It is just practice.*

Hit him, Kraj commanded.

It will hurt him.

We are at war, Enderfrag Koneka. The human threat will not stand here asking questions. Humans will act. They will fight. They will stab. Everyone is going to hurt, sooner or later.

Koneka looked back and forth between Nif and Kraj helplessly. Then her mind filled with the desire to cut Nif down. She didn't know where the idea came from. It just suddenly arrived in her brain, in full color. She raised the iron sword high in the air.

This is unnecessary, Commander Kraj! The angry, brittle thoughts of Taskmaster Owari sliced through the image in Koneka's mind. It dissolved as though she had never thought such a thing. She shook her head as though it were buzzy with bees.

Kraj's mindscape became a wordless snarl.

Surely we need every enderman for the fight ahead, thought Owari soothingly. *Just as you said.* She chose her ideas slowly and carefully. *We cannot afford to waste young, strong warriors on such a simple demonstration.*

The snarl vanished as quickly as it arose. Commander Kraj

laughed loudly into the minds of the Enderdome. *Of course, Taskmaster! You did not think I would allow my enderfrags to actually delete each other? How foolish of you. We forgive you, naturally, you could not know the powerful mind of a cruxunit and a commander. You must take things as they seem, rather than as they are. My demonstration is already complete! Enderfrag Koneka showed no reluctance at all in punching her sparring partner. But she froze when asked to use a weapon on him! Because she knows the weapon is better in every way than a fist. She knows her blows will leave the enemy standing, but a sword will destroy him. Why then, fragments, would we shun weapons when faced with the human horde? Why would we volunteer to be weaker and slower and more defenseless? Ridiculous! Now, we have a number of items to choose from here. Everyone select something and we will begin the real Enderdome. I award you all the rank of private—except you, Koneka. You have already done well. You will be my lieutenant.*

A scuttling sound echoed behind Kraj. In one fluid movement, he snatched the sword out of Koneka's hand, spun, and flung it hard toward an endermite crawling across the courtyard. It died the instant the blade touched its skin.

Bane of Arthropods, Kraj thought with tremendous satisfaction. *How marvelous.*

The other enderfrags ran across the courtyard to Kraj's officers and began to sort through the inventory of Fin and Mo's lovingly collected weapons and armor. Koneka just stared at her sword wobbling a little where it stuck in the stone as the endermite went up in smoke around it.

Why did I imagine killing Nif? she thought. *Why would I ever imagine that?*

But no one was paying attention to her anymore. The commander and the Taskmaster faced each other in the sparring courtyard.

I do not approve of this, Commander.

I do not care what you approve of. I am commander. I speak for all of us.

That is not our way. When enough of us are gathered, we speak together. There is no need for a commander.

But there is. There is, Taskmaster Owari! There has always been, it is just that none of us was clever enough to see it. When we gathered on the dragon's island, so many minds all unified at last, I finally knew the truth. The path we should have taken all along. We have always suffered at the hands of the human world. But why? Why should we suffer at all? Why should they rule the Overworld, where such riches lie, while we skulk and guard our few camps here in the End, where so little grows? If they can take our lands, our resources, we can take theirs, too. We have not, because we hold ourselves back with silly rules like not using weapons or following commanders. I will make us better. You must see that. Under my reign, we will fly, *Owari. We will fly to the Overworld and stop every bad thing from happening. I will defeat even the rain.*

The Taskmaster's eyes flashed dangerously. *What you are talking about is blasphemy, Kraj.*

I disagree.

Reality does not care whether you agree with it. You have elevated yourself. You have created an army, with ranks and duties. You intend to emulate humans. There is no Chaos in this. No divine fire of unpredictability. You have become a servant of Order.

Silence your foul mind or I will silence it for you, Kraj hissed.

Taskmaster Owari folded her long hands behind her back. *You have done more than that, I suspect. Little Koneka was seconds away from killing Nif. She would never do that in the Enderdome. They are practically a paired unit already. There are never fewer than fifty fragments stacked here at any time. Our minds are always calm and civilized in the Dome, so that they can learn. Yet she would have done it. Murdered her friend. And look at your officers! They should be as clever as you, traveling all together. A gang of Krajs! But they obey you no matter what you say, meekly, without argument. Why should they? They are not your End, your family.*

Kraj smiled in his mind. A huge and ghostly smile. *I am a cruxunit. In the Beginning of the End I divided myself voluntarily, to create a family. Perhaps they simply respect their elder.*

I am a cruxunit, too, Kraj. We are equals. Or have you forgotten everything about the Beginning of the End? You must have, to call it the Beginning. The End existed before us and will exist long after. Will you next claim to have built these cities? Your pride is ugly, Commander. *I have taught generations of enderfrags and none of them obeys me meekly because I am an ancient cruxunit. What have you done, Kraj? What have the Forces of Order promised you?*

Do not be angry with me, Taskmaster. We are on the same side. We both want only to survive. The humans are coming. Let us have no conflict amongst ourselves. Kraj reached out a slender, dark hand and gripped Owari's shoulder in a gesture of friendship.

The commander's hand was wet and cold. It tingled, then it began to burn.

That end ship tethered out in the darkness was really something extraordinary, Taskmaster, Kraj mused. *I could never have imagined those twins capable of such . . . industry. I think perhaps it was a mistake to keep them out of the Dome. They will serve us well in the fight. Better still if you had trained them. But how could you have known? How could I have known?*

Commander Kraj pulled his hand away. His fingers were covered in a scrap of leather, to protect his skin. A scrap of leather stained dark cobalt blue. Owari swayed unsteadily.

Yes, truly extraordinary, Kraj thought. *I found this among the other potions. So many potions. This one is a Potion of Weakness. It slows you down, makes you stupid, makes you miss your attacks. And, if a strong, powerful mind is nearby? Well. A weak mind is easy to control. Suggestible. What a wonderfully useful thing. You may call it blasphemy, but you cannot say Order is not* effective. *Like the sword and the fist. The fist is holier. But I choose the sword. There will be plenty of time to let Chaos reign when I own the human world from top to bottom. It is only logical. How else can we be safe, unless they are gone? If a little Order can get the endermen where we should be, why not embrace it, for a little while?*

Owari stared woozily into Kraj's sharp purple eyes.

Yes, the Taskmaster thought, as though it had been her own idea all along. *Why not?*

The ancient cruxunit walked slowly across the courtyard to join the other officers.

CHAPTER FIFTEEN

A LITTLE RAIN

Mo.

The thought wafted in through the window of Jax's grand house like steam off a warm cake. Familiar and comforting and sweet.

Mo.

Mo was asleep. In a *bed*. A bed that didn't *explode*. She'd always slept curled up on the floor of the ship with her brother like stray cats. But Jax insisted she sleep in a proper bed. It was safer, he promised. In the morning, they'd try a few witch's potions on her and see if anything sparked her memory. She didn't really like the sound of "witch's potions." Who was this witch? Did she run a clean kitchen? Could Mo trust her potions? Could Mo trust Jax? What was a witch, anyway? But Jax was determined to know where she'd gotten the egg and the totem. Mo certainly wanted to know, too. Maybe. Maybe she didn't. If she'd done something terrible to get them . . . maybe it was better not to know. He hadn't taken them away from her. She appreciated that, at least. Jax was very strict about that sort of thing, clearly. Her loot was her loot, and he wouldn't take it. If Jax was everything else Kraj and the Mouth had ever said of humans, he still had some morals. More than Kraj did.

On the end of the bed, right next to her feet, Loathsome the zombie horse snored phlegmily. Her big moldy nostrils flared with every gurgling breath.

Muuuumma, Loathsome snored contentedly. *Braaaains.*

Mo.

Mo was dreaming. The thought tried to find her in the dream. Mo was dreaming of the ender dragon's island. Only it wasn't the ender dragon's island. Not quite. The same yellow sandy rock. The same obsidian pillars. The same crystal flames in silver cages. The same tall, black endermen floating in their mist of hazy purple telepathic particles. The same gorgeously horrible, horribly gorgeous massive lizard soaring through the sky. Only the sky wasn't black. It was bright blue, like the sky in the Overworld. The sun shone down like a lamp. Mo stood on top of one of the pillars. An enderman was standing next to her. But it wasn't Fin. Or Kan. Or Karshen. Or Lopp.

It was Kraj.

Without saying a word, Kraj reached out and grabbed her arm. It came off in his strong hand.

Poor Endless trashfrags, Kraj thought. He put his hand on her other arm. It came off as easily and painlessly as pulling up a blade of grass. *You will find that in periods of war, niceties are a waste of time*. He reached down and pulled off her leg at the knee.

And almost everything is niceties, in the end. Still there was no pain. But Mo stumbled, trying to keep her balance. She tried to tell him not to take her leg. She needed it. The army didn't need *both* legs, did it? But no words came out of her mouth. Commander Kraj stretched out his fingers to take the other leg. *Everyone must give something up so that the End can go on.* Mo hopped away. Kraj floated toward her. He was so tall.

Mo dreamed she heard voices coming from far below. Different people, all talking at once.

Go, go, go! Go without me! I'll be fine!

Greenboy. My greenboy.

I can feel it coming. Like a tsunami. First the water retreats, and for a minute you think everything is going to be okay. Then it rises up and washes everything away. I love you.

I love you.

Then, suddenly, the enderman towering over her wasn't Kraj anymore. He had strange blue eyes in his giant ender head. Blue eyes and a necklace of ender pearls. Mo knew those eyes. It was Jax, trapped in an enderman's body. Just the same way Mo had been trapped. Ender-Jax handed her arms back, then her leg. You did it, he whispered to her. *You killed him. I'm so proud of you.*

Mo.

Mo woke up with a little scream. "I didn't do anything," she moaned.

Loathsome looked up at her out of one droopy, goopy eye. The demon pony went tense, ready to protect her mother from anything.

But there was nothing there. Just the quiet little thought in her head.

Mo.

The human girl looked all around the dark bedroom. Not even a torch to see by. She stood up on the narrow wooden bed on her tiptoes and peered out of the window. Mo stared down and out into the moonlit valley where Jax lived. Soft green grass. Hard grey hills. Lilacs and poppies waved back and forth in the night breeze. They shone black and grey in the shadows instead of violet and red.

Mo, it is me.

Two bright green eyes opened up in the dark. Kan was down there in the grass, two stories below, looking up at her. He was sitting on his note block.

Hi, Kan thought.

Hi, thought Mo.

Brains, thought Loathsome decisively.

"Shhh!" Mo hissed.

Brains, the pony whispered.

Kan, what are you doing here? If Jax catches you, he'll kill you. Actually kill you.

I will catch him first.

He killed Lopp.

Kan blinked. *Really? She is . . . just dead?*

Mo nodded. *He took her pearl.*

What a perfect . . . human, Kan spat.

No, you don't understand. She was going to kill me. *She was all by herself. Her mind was nothing but murder and I tried to talk to her but she was just . . . dangry. Like Fin always says. You know what we're like alone.*

Oh? What are we *like?*

Mo went pale. She couldn't be included in "we" anymore. She wasn't "we." She wasn't "us." She was just a human like all the other humans, and Kan was supposed to be her enemy.

Kan relaxed. *Never mind,* he thought. *Sorry. Do not listen to me. It does not matter.*

Mo looked out beyond the shadowy patch where Kan stood. *Wait.* You're *all by yourself,* she thought hesitantly, not wanting to offend him. *Are you . . . ok? Are you Kan?*

I know, it is weird. Turns out I have been by myself a while now. But I am just me. He held up his long black hands in the dark. He was completely calm. His thoughts felt as cool and collected as a glass of water. *See? No raaar. Just Kan.*

What do you mean "for a while now"?

Mo. You are not an enderman. Neither is Fin. Grumpo sure as dark and the Great Chaos is not. So if you think about it, I have been all by myself every time the three of us have been together. And I have played my note block better than anyone alive and not killed anyone or eaten my own toes or walked off an island into nothing.

Mo felt a chill in her guts. She was human. That explained a lot. So what was Kan? What could explain this? *Huh. That's . . . uh . . . that's something we should talk about, don't you think?*

Probably. But there are more important things going on right now. At the moment, I am choosing to believe I have enderman superpowers and leave it at that. I came to rescue you. Kan winced. That sounded stupid. It felt stupid. But he had. He'd come all the way up to the badlands for her.

Rescue me? But I'm fine. We're fine. Jax is gonna experiment on me tomorrow.

Kan blinked again. *Sounds great. Torture after lunch, then? Maybe a little slice and dice before bedtime? Mo, even for a human, Jax is bad news.*

He says it's to get my memory back. He's said a lot of things, Kan. I don't know what to believe. He's pretty mad at me right now, to tell you the truth.

Well, believe that I am your friend. That I have always been your friend. I will always be your friend. I have always told you the truth. I have never experimented on you. And I will never leave you behind. Also believe that it is probably a bad idea to let someone who is pretty mad at you experiment on you. Mo blinked. That had never occurred to her. That Jax might hurt her on purpose. No one in the history of Mo's life had ever meant her harm. The worst thing they'd ever done was simply to leave her alone with nothing. *Let us go. I know where a portal is. If you are quiet, we can just slip back through before he knows what happened. We will be careful so he cannot follow us back to the End. He will not be able to kill ED. Or anyone else. And it will not matter what he is mad at.*

But the others . . .

I do not think they are quite the same. They have all just been hanging out with Fin on this weird little island by the ship. They are not hurting anybody. None of them killed *Lopp. They have not killed anyone. It is strange, honestly. I keep expecting them to start killing and they continue to kill nothing. I do not know what to make of it.*

Are you spying *on them?*

An image opened up in Mo's mind. A beautiful banner unfurling on one of the tallest violet towers of Telos. Kan's smile.

I am a spy after all, he thought, proud of himself. *Grumpo let me hide in his box.*

Mo practically jumped over the windowsill in excitement. WHAT? *Grumpo* NEVER *lets anyone in that box! He hates Fin least of anyone and all he's ever let* him *do is stand a foot away and put one finger on the lid. And he* still *bit him.*

You two ran off without a word to Grumpo and I think he is feeling very frightened. If a shulker can feel frightened. Where did you find Grumpo anyway? I have never met a shulker like that. You know they do not usually talk, right? They do not usually anything. *I guess I never thought about it till now. Till everything.*

I never met an enderman like you either. And I bet until about a day and a half ago, you'd never met a human like me. What was it like in that box?

Crowded. Dark. A weird odor. He refused to let me light a torch. And he said something strange. He said, Stay in here with Grumpo forever. We can hate everything together. *Is that not the oddest idea? I left the box quickly after that.* Mo, Kan thought, sliding his eyes off toward the other windows. Jax's window. *I do not want to keep talking like this. Come out. Come with me. Come home. It is okay. I am not mad. It is not your fault. I understand that now. I was just upset. I just . . . I wanted my life to make sense. And it still does not. But it is not about me right now. We need to make your life make sense. And you can only do that with us. Your twin and your ship and your shulker and me. Your End. Jax is not your End. He is just a hunter who wants to catch something unique. All hunters do. And you are very unique.*

Mo looked over her shoulder toward the bedroom door. *I don't know,* she thought. *Maybe he has answers. You don't know what's happened. I had something in my pocket. I didn't even know about it. A couple of things.* The totem she didn't really understand. It didn't matter to her at all. The pearl she understood completely. But she couldn't tell Kan about it. There were some things too wrong to forgive. And what if he saw Lopp's pearl and knew who it came from? He'd never speak to her again. *One of them is a dragon's egg and Jax said there's only one way I could have gotten one . . . and if I got it that way I should never, ever go back to the End no matter what forever.*

I do not care what you have in your pockets. There is nothing you could have done that would change my mind about you. Mo, you turned out to be a human being *and I am still your friend. I am still here for you, in the awful old Overworld where I do not want to be at all.* Kan held up his long, black arms to her. *I do not want you to be experimented on. Come home. Remembering is so overrated.*

Mo looked over at Loathsome. She patted the horse's greasy hair. She could see Loathsome's huge heart not beating between two gleaming ribs.

Mumma, saaaaaame, the zombie beast thought.

You're right, love. We are *the same. Kan and me and Fin. And you. And Grumpo. And the ship. And home. I don't know how you can be so smart. You were only just born. Or died. However it works. Either way. Both ways.*

Loathsome winked one milky, dead eye. *Brains,* she thought.

I'll climb down, Mo thought.

Kan shook his dark head. He held out his slender fingers toward the stone wall.

A block disappeared.

He lifted his fingers a little higher.

Another block vanished.

All hail the Great Chaos, Mo thought. And in Kan's mind, the image of a golden chestplate glinting in the evening light of the End bloomed. It was Mo's smile.

She held out her hand toward the windowsill. Human or not, the little violet particles still danced around her fingers, more faded and paler than they used to be, but still there.

The stone shimmered and hissed away into the air. Mo stretched out her arm again and erased another square of wall.

May the Great Chaos smile upon you, thought Kan, as the castle disappeared around him.

Block by block, the enderman and the human moved toward each other, making a staircase out of the remains of the wall as they went. Mo stepped down. Kan stepped up. The torches over the moat glowed golden. Jax's house opened up all around them. And when you lay open to the world, strange things could happen that would never find you if you stayed locked up behind orderly walls. Strange things like an enderman rescuing a girl and her zombie. This was the whole purpose of the Great Chaos. That was how Mo knew it was the right thing to do. Human or not, she still believed.

In her infinite pocket, the dragon egg glowed coldly.

Kan grabbed Mo's hand.

I didn't need rescuing, you know, she thought. *I could have just left anytime.*

Kan shrugged awkwardly. *Okay. It is the thought that counts? Can we at least tell Fin I rescued you, though? Very bravely?*

Mo laughed in the quiet between their minds. *Sure, Kan.*

Come on, he thought. *I feel pulled toward the nearest portal. I think I can sense the eyes of ender . . . but we have to be fast. It will be daylight soon. We will teleport. That is easiest. Ready?*

Mo pulled back, frozen. Kan still thought of her as she had always been. It hadn't occurred to him yet that humans couldn't teleport. That she must not've been doing it on her own. And Mo couldn't tell him. She just couldn't. He wouldn't understand. He'd just know that the ender pearl she'd used to teleport all over the End, all during their childhood, used to be somebody's heart, and he'd hate her for it. She wouldn't even let herself think about it. Kan would see the shriveled, dying ender pearl in her mind.

What is wrong?

Nothing. Um . . . Loathsome can't teleport. So. That. Is what's wrong.

Oh, right.

Loathsome burbled. A spit bubble swelled up on her lips and popped. But she didn't neigh. Zombies know how to be quiet. Occasionally.

Mumma, the pony wheezed. *Reeeeeins.*

Kan winced. There were sores and moldy streaks all along the horse's back. But she'd be faster than they could manage on foot by a long shot.

Mo hopped up onto Loathsome's back. It wasn't the nicest. It was a little wet and a little cold and a little slimy. But Loathsome was a little hers, so Mo didn't judge her. She pulled Kan up behind her.

I came to rescue you, he thought huffily. *I should ride in front.*

My horse, my seat preference, Mo thought. *Exits to the side and rear of the minecart.*

What? Kan thought, confused.

I . . . I don't know. What a strange thing to think. I don't know where it came from. What's a minecart?

How should I know? You thought it.

Mo shuddered in the dark. The moon came out from behind a cloud. It lit up Loathsome's green and undead mane. The horse took off away from Jax's great house into the hills, leaving nothing but hoofprints behind her. Neither Mo nor Kan looked back.

They rode for half an hour before Kan squeezed his knees against Loathsome's flanks. The zombie stopped obediently, though she narrowed her eyes and growled a little. Kan wasn't her mumma, and he shouldn't tell her what to do. Endermen had brains enough to eat.

It is here, he thought. *In that spot, but far under the ground. I can sense the portal.*

Kan pointed a short ways off, toward an area with a sand dune on one side and an overhanging cliff on the other, surrounded by huge leafy trees. Mo couldn't see any cave or passage underground, but she trusted Kan. If he said it was there, it was there.

The moon dimmed and vanished. Thunder cracked in the distance. Somewhere behind them, Mo and Kan heard the little speckled sounds of rain starting to fall.

Oh no, Kan thought in terror. *No, no, no.*

The cliff! Mo thought quickly. *Get under it! It'll be enough, the grass hangs over the edge and there's a little hollow there, it's almost a cave. You'll be fine.*

Loathsome ran for the cliff. Endermen cannot bear water. For them, water is death. Kan's breath came in great, hitching gasps. He teleported instantly off the horse's reeking back and appeared in the sandy patch beneath the overhang. Loathsome galloped full tilt after him.

The first drops started to fall.

Mo dismounted. She stood there in the grass, outside the safety of the cliff. The rain fell in big, loose drops onto her warm human skin. It fell harder and harder. She was soaked. She was soaked and it didn't hurt at all. It felt amazing. The crackle of ozone in the air, the smell of fresh greenery in the wind, the excitement of the thunder. All the little tiny hairs on her arms stood on end. But it didn't *hurt*.

Of course it didn't hurt. Mo raised her hands up as far as they would go and looked up into the stormy sky. All that fear, all that grief, all that hatred of the rain that had killed her hubunits washed away. It had never happened. Whoever her parents were, dead or alive, it wasn't rain that had taken them from her. Rain was just water. Cool and wet and sweet. She laughed and spun around. Rain wasn't death. It was *wonderful.*

But then she stopped laughing.

Kan stared miserably at her from under the little cliff. Shivering, frightened, trapped. Rain trickled down off the overhang into a growing puddle. One toe in that puddle and Kan would fade away, leaving only a pearl behind, like a thousand other endermen. The human and the enderman stood helplessly, separated forever by who they were. They'd been able to fool themselves until right that second. That nothing had changed. That Mo could teleport and Kan could survive in the Overworld. That they were still the same people they'd always been. Still an End. But Mo and Kan were nothing alike. They could never be alike.

"We'll go as soon as it stops," Mo said awkwardly. "I'll carry you to the stronghold."

Kan said nothing. He watched the sky. After a long while, he took out his note block, set it on the muddy ground, and began to play. His music filled up the field and the night, sad and sweet and strange. The music of the End echoed through the Overworld for the first time.

Mumma, groaned Loathsome as water dribbled through the holes in her body into the mud. *Raaaaain.*

Yeah, baby, answered Mo as the delicious, delightful storm drenched her from head to foot. *Sure is something, isn't it?*

CHAPTER SIXTEEN

UNDER COVER OF NIGHT

"Let me get this straight," said Roary. The night void of the End yawned behind her. The beginnings of the city Jess planned to build stood out brightly against it. "You've got all those books in your ship, hundreds of them, by my count. And you've never read *any* of them."

Fin shrugged. "I told you, they're enchanted. All got some kind of high-level Unbreaking enchantment on them. I don't know how to get it off. Do you?"

"Grindstone," Roary answered instantly.

"Grindstone," Jess said at the same time.

"Grindstone," said Koal.

"Fine," snapped Fin. "You're all so much smarter than me. It's not like Mo and I didn't try, you know. We didn't have a manual. We did our best. It's not my fault, either. The endermen didn't teach us. How am I supposed to find out about stuff like that if I wasn't taught it?"

The humans shifted uncomfortably. None wanted to tell the poor kid that they'd never gone to school. Or had a manual. Maybe things were just harder in the Overworld, so you had to sort yourself out faster. The kid'd had a hard enough day. Night. Whichever.

"If you didn't know what was in them, why'd you keep so many?" Koal asked.

Fin clenched his jaw. He didn't like having to answer for how he spent his time. Not to strangers. It was *his* time. "I like collecting things. I like the feeling of having *enough*. More than enough. Enough for anything that could ever happen. I hope I die with a full inventory, because that would mean nothing was ever bad enough that I had to use it all up. It makes me feel safe. It doesn't matter what's in the books or that I can't disenchant them. Eventually, if I collect enough things, one of them'll be the thing that will fix the books so I can read them. The Great Chaos will provide."

"I wouldn't think the Great Chaos would be big on books," Jesster said wryly. Fin had explained about all that. Jess didn't like it. Chaos made her nervous. Plans were so much better. "Books are pretty much the Orderliest."

Fin opened his mouth to dig into the religious philosophy of his former people, but Roary cut in.

"Where did you even *find* so many? I don't think I've ever seen so many books in one place outside a real library. It must have taken years."

Fin looked out into the night and blinked slowly as he thought about it. It was *very* eerie to think about. His brain kept sliding off it. He tried to think about the books, but he just didn't want to think about the books, even though he *did* want to think about the books and remember where they came from. It gave him a headache. "You know, I don't really know where we found them. It's weird. I can remember the day I found my Frost Walker boots, my Loyalty trident, the chestplate I use to make popcorn. I can even remember the day Kan found his note block. But I can't remember ever finding a single book. Not one. Not once. And we have hundreds, so shouldn't I remember something about *one* of them? But I don't. They were just . . . always there. From the beginning. Before we found our first sword out there in the islands, the ship was already full of those books."

Roary's eyes lit up. "That sounds like a clue," she said eagerly.

"God, Roary, you're such a dork." Koal put his hands on his hips mockingly. "Sergeant Roary, Kid Detective! That sounds like a *clue*!"

"Shut up, Koal," Roary said affectionately. "End ships usually have shulkers and a couple of treasure chests. They do *not* usually have a mountain of unopenable books. That's not a thing! And how many books have you seen anywhere else in the End? This is not exactly Booktown. Endermen aren't what you'd call serious intellectuals. We have no idea who you are or how you got here, Fin, and that's the first thing you've said that sounds like it might be a—stop snickering, Koal—clue. A path to some answers, are you happy? Ugh, take things seriously for once."

"I could make you a magnifying glass and a stupid hat, if you want." Koal laughed.

Roary threw up her hands and gave up on him. "Fin, it's not just that it would be cool to find out how a human managed to become an enderman and forget how they did it in the first place.

I *need* to know. We need to know. Because if it happened to you, it could happen to us, and I'm not going to get stuck wandering around here for years calling shulkers my BFFs. Ew. This is an operational imperative. We have to disenchant those books and see what's in them. And if it's just cookie recipes, well . . . I don't know. We hope Jax and Mo come back with something. We'll cross that bridge when we come to it. Right now, this is our best bet."

"So . . . do you have a grindstone?" Jess asked Fin.

"Well, I *did*, but Commander Kraj and Corporal Murrum and Captain Tamat have it now. In Telos, with the rest of the armory. I assume."

Roary thought about it. "Telos is big. It's the biggest end city I've ever seen. We gave it a wide berth when we came through. Not worth it. But we have a local guide. I think two of us could get in and out pretty quickly."

"No way," said Fin. "You don't understand. You think you're sneaky. That you're just playing games down here. The End was waiting for you. We knew you were coming by the *taste of the air*, Roary. Yesterday every enderman here was assembled to fight you. And they're still fired up and ready for war. The only reason they're not here now is that no one has come to check on Mo and me, so no one knows you're here. But they'll come soon. Someone will. Looking for Kan or looking for us. Karshen or Kraj. Sooner or later they'll wonder where we went. At the very least, they'll want to tell us they're not going to give our stuff back."

"You don't know that," Jesster tried to reassure him.

"I don't *know* it. But it's still true," mumbled Fin.

Koal rolled his eyes in disbelief. "A war? Against *us*? But there're *four* of us."

"Yeah, but they don't know that. All they knew was a portal was opening. They kind of thought it was . . . all of you."

Jess frowned at Fin. "*All* the humans?"

"Yeah. An invasion. They're just . . . waiting for the other side to show up. I tried to tell you that before. Why, is that a problem? I thought you and Jax liked fighting and killing."

"Well, there's fighting and then there's four on ten thousand," Koal muttered.

Fin started to laugh. He didn't want to laugh. He didn't mean to laugh. But it was all just so funny to him all of a sudden. The last few days of stress and misery and fear poured out in a flood of giggles.

"You don't even"—he gasped between bouts of hysterical laughing—"you don't even know how worked up they all are about you. They're so terrified of the big bad human army. They stripped the End for supplies to fight the oogey boogey human menace and you're just . . . you're just *tourists*. You're on vacation! Building sandcastles and hunting the local wildlife and then you're just gonna scamper off back home and tell your friends what a grand adventure you had. Take souvenirs! Write postcards! See the Magnificent End and Its Many Attractions! Ride the Ender Dragon! Play Whack-a-Shulker! Wish you were here!" Fin had to sit down. He could barely breathe. "We thought you were the scariest thing in the world." But then he thought about Jax, and ED, and how quickly his little universe had disintegrated once the humans set foot there. Everything he'd ever known really *was* ruined. It was just that everything the other endermen had ever known was still just fine. He and Mo were the only casualties of the war with the humans.

So far.

"I don't know," he finished softly. "Maybe you are the scariest thing in the world."

"What's wrong with being a tourist?" Koal shouted angrily. "Didn't you ever want to see anything but this stupid place with its stupid trees and its stupid cities and all its incredible stupidness? You should try being a tourist. It's *interesting*. It's *fun*. It's not *boring*. Traveling makes you bigger and wiser and cleverer and when you lie down in bed at night you have something to dream about. It doesn't hurt anyone. You shouldn't drum up an army just because someone takes their holiday in your neighborhood!"

"Jax is going to kill the ender dragon! It'll hurt the ender dragon plenty! And ED is my friend." Fin stopped and scrunched up one side of his face. "Well, not my friend. But it's not actively my enemy and that's pretty much the same thing!"

Koal looked down at his feet. "Yeah, ok, that's fair," he admitted. "But Jax isn't here and your 'not actively an enemy' is fine. For now."

"We can get in and out of Telos without this Kraj knowing about it," Roary said, choosing to ignore Fin's and Koal's outbursts. "You're forgetting that we came prepared. We've got pumpkins. We can move around the End just as well as you did for all those years, and no one will know, any more than they knew about you. In fact, we can all do whatever we came here to do, without getting caught, and go home at the end with no one the wiser. The endermen can go back to doing whatever it is that endermen do. Win-win-win."

"Except ED. I'm not going to let Jax do it," Fin said in as serious a voice as he could manage, having only started talking with his mouth a few hours before.

"We *have* to—" Koal started. But he didn't get to finish.

"You'll have to take that up with him when he gets back," Jess evaded. "Not our gig."

"But Telos!" Roary said, her dark eyes lighting up with the thrill of the mystery. "Telos can be our gig. It's a real honest-to-god spy mission. We'll sneak in, liberate your stash, and sneak out again. Under cover of night! Not that we have a choice. And if your army friends see us, they'll think we're just prepping, like them, right?"

"I guess . . . probably."

"Once we have a grindstone we can disenchant your books really fast," Jess assured him. "It's no problem, I've done it tons of times."

Roary nodded. "Maybe there's something in there that will help you remember who you are. Maybe the spell that took your memory is hiding in one of them. Or the spell to cure it. You could know everything that ever happened to you in just a couple of hours. Isn't that exciting?"

Fin thought about Mo. Where was she? He hated not knowing where she was. If she was okay. What she was doing. If he was making the right decisions without her.

"I suppose," he said, but he didn't feel it. What he did feel was a big ball of dread right in the pit of his stomach.

"Hey, yeah, you never know, maybe you'll find out something even more devastating than being a secret human!" Koal threw in cheerfully.

Fin thought he might be sick. *Come home, Mo! Yell at these guys with me! It's always better yelling as a team than yelling solo. Where* are *you?*

"I'll go with you, Fin," Jesster said kindly. "I'm the biggest and I have the best weapons. If we all go together, they might get suspicious. Four strange endermen they don't know sneaking around. Roary and Koal can stay and work on the palace. We don't want to fall behind."

Fin nodded. He had to *do* something. All this standing around and talking made him itch. He used to spend all day climbing and cruising between islands, without a care in the world. Now he was stuck arguing with strangers about strange things, no Grumpo, no Mo, no Kan, no purple popcorn, no nothing but them. *Do I really want to know?* he asked himself. *Maybe I should just go up to the Overworld with Mo and start living life human-style. Don't ask questions. Don't pry. Don't look a gift human in the mouth.* But no. He couldn't do it. He couldn't let things go back to the way they were. If he and Mo were human beings, then they weren't Endless. They weren't outcasts. They had a family somewhere. They had people. They had a world where they did belong. And that was worth finding. It had to be.

I can't go back. I can only start over.

One way or another, he had to know who he was and what had happened to him. Even if it was something terrible. Especially if it was something terrible.

Fin straightened his shoulders. His blue eyes shone in the dark.

"Okay, Jess. Let's go."

CHAPTER SEVENTEEN

WELCOME TO MY ED TALK

Kan, Mo, and Loathsome tumbled through the portal. Grey stronghold-stone and underground torches turned upside down, then inside out. They landed stomach-first, sprawled across the outcropping of sandy stone on the underside of the ender dragon's island. Mo was still soaking wet. Kan inched away from her, just to be safe. They could hear the vibrating roars of the great black lizard far above. The earth shook every time it bellowed fire into the dark. Even if they couldn't see it, they could feel it.

Mo stared out into the black sky of the End. She felt the rock under her fingers. She'd been gone only—what? Eight or nine hours? Half a day? More? Less? She didn't know. You never needed to tell time in the End. She didn't know what a proper hour was supposed to feel like. But it didn't matter how much time it was, it felt like a hundred years plus eternity. Nothing looked the same. Not after she'd seen the sun. Nothing could ever look the same again. The End seemed so small now. It looked back at her like a stranger.

Kan grimaced as he pictured the portal they'd just used. The twelve dead, hard eyes of ender that were stuck on to each block of the frame gleamed greyish green. Mo felt ill just looking at them. Loathsome thought they were just beautiful. The prettiest jewels she'd ever seen. She rather wanted to eat one. Loathsome looked at Mo for permission. She was so hungry. She was always just so hungry. Mo nodded.

The zombie horse squealed in delight and snapped at the eyes as they stepped through the portal. She chomped as fast as she could, chomping while falling, popping them like bubbles, slurping, crunching, munching, relishing. The eyes crunched like candy between her sharp yellow teeth.

Without those eyes, Mo figured Jax wouldn't be able to come through that portal. He'd have to hunt down yet another stronghold before he could track them down. As the trio regrouped safely back in the End, that thought at least was comforting.

Mmmmmumma, Loathsome hummed with satisfaction as she slurped up a bloodshot mess of eyeball off her blistered lip like spaghetti. *Veeeeiiiins.*

Yummy, Mo said as she fought to keep from throwing up. She couldn't remember ever having a mother, but she felt it was generally important for parents not to shame their children for their tastes. The baby was eating, that was the important thing.

Kan shuddered. He patted the horse. Carefully. Gingerly. Those teeth meant business. Loathsome went stiff. No one but Mo had ever patted her in her whole sixteen hours of life. The undead pony froze mid-snack. But Kan's hand was cold and hard and heavy. To a zombie, that feels very nice indeed. People who were not Mo were obviously bad and wrong, the horse knew. But at least one of them was . . . acceptable. Barely.

He wasn't that *bad,* Mo thought.

Who?

Jax. I think really he's just a kid like us. He likes to hit things and take things and do what he likes without anyone bothering him.

He likes to kill things, Kan corrected her. *He wants to kill the ender dragon.*

I know that's bad. But he gave me back my chestplate. Kraj likes to kill things and he stole it from me. And Kraj hasn't been a kid since the dawn of time.

You like him.

No, I don't. Mo sighed. *Right now, I like anyone who helps me make sense of all this insanity. He's one of only four humans I know. Five, I guess, counting Fin. At least he hasn't hurt me yet. If anyone I used to know down here sees me, they will. You know they will.*

Mo's green eyes filled up with tears. She remembered Lopp's face, twisted up and furious and cruel. Lopp, who once asked her if she needed a hubunit. She didn't want to see anyone else look at her like that. Not ever. Mo needed a hubunit now. But she'd never say so.

Kan put his arms around his friend. The pearl where his heart should have been pulsed fast, the way any human boy's heart would have.

I have an idea, he thought.

Is it to give up and hide forever with me and my horse?

No. *Mo, someone, somewhere knows the truth about us. About what happened to you and Fin. About why I am . . . the way that I am. There is not anything in the universe that* somebody *does not know. Now, let us lay it all out. What do we know? Not much, I admit.*

Me and Fin are human beings.

Therefore, you came from the Overworld.

Sure, that's logical enough. Endermen come from the End, rain comes from the sky, humans come from the Overworld. Ah! Therefore, *we had to come down to the End at some point. With the pumpkins on. Through a portal. Jax says that's the only way for a human to travel between the Overworld and the End.*

Right. And it had to be some time ago, because you and Fin and I have all these memories of growing up together. And your pumpkins were not exactly fresh.

Mo picked at her fingernails. How strange it was to have fingernails in the first place. *We also know that you aren't like other endermen,* she thought. *You have green eyes. You can play music. And when you're by yourself, you don't go halfwit berserker dangry on everything. But you aren't wearing a pumpkin and you're not human.*

Kan sighed. *I think your mystery is easier. I wish it were not. Believe me. I never thought that more than anything in the world, someday I would wish I were a human being with a pumpkin on his head. But here we are. At least we have somewhere to start with yours. I am just . . . a freak.* A *greenboy.*

Kan, don't say that.

It is true.

Mo touched his cheek. His skin felt like wet ink, even though it was dry. *If you're a greenboy, I'm a greengirl,* she thought. *Our eyes are exactly the same. If you're a freak, I'm a freak. Freak Club. Population two.*

They were almost close enough to kiss.

You mean three, Kan thought bashfully. *Fin, too.*

Yeah, thought Mo, a little embarrassed. For the first time, she saw an advantage in *not* having telepathy. *Three. Sure. Fin, too.*

Kan's pearl thundered in his chest. Why had he brought Fin into it? What a fool he was. The moment had passed. The thing about telepathy was that you couldn't hide your feelings from anyone. Especially not from the girl you'd known all your life. He tried to hide how much her words meant to him. But she knew anyway. With telepathy, you couldn't put on a tough face. You could only change the subject. So he did.

So if you came to the End at some point, someone must have seen it. Everyone knew when Jax's portal was about to open. They knew right away. So if you came through a portal, somebody knew then, too.

Mo caught on to where Kan was headed with this. *So who's old enough to remember two humans coming through a portal years ago? Kraj, obviously.*

For once, I doubt he will want to regale us with tales of the past. Right now, he is not even Kraj anymore. He is Commander Kraj. The "commander" makes all the difference. One look at you and he will command you out of existence. And me for helping you. An earsplitting shriek broke through the air far above them.

Mo's thoughts lit up. *ED? The ender dragon?*

There is nothing in the End older than ED.

There is nothing in the End meaner *than ED. It's not going to tell us what color my shoes are. Huh. I have shoes. I'm wearing shoes. Did you see my shoes?*

I saw your shoes, Kan thought. *They are awful. I thought you said ED showed you where to find Loathsome's egg?*

Yeah, because the meanest people are the ones who are occa-

sionally nice. You can never totally hate them, since they really were so kind to you that one time a million years ago. So they can keep on hurting you while you wait for that one nice day to come around again. Also, it probably hoped she would eat me.

Brains, agreed Loathsome. Kan narrowed his eyes.

Let us go talk to it. Maybe today is a nice day.

Kan got up to start the climb up the rockface and over the lip of the island to the grand plain where the ender dragon lived.

Wait, Kan! Mo grabbed at him. *I can't.* The enderman hopped back down. *You know I can't.*

Why can you not?

Mo laughed. She pointed at her face. He still didn't get it. *No pumpkin. I look as human as I am. Have you ever seen the island* not *crawling with endermen? They'll see me. They'll kill me. And they won't even know it was poor little orphan Mo they killed.*

Okay, so we just teleport up to the top of one of the pillars. Easy. No one will see us up there.

Mo went pale. *I . . . I can't do that either.*

What? Sure you can. I have seen you teleport tons of times.

Mo slumped miserably. She couldn't look him in the eye. But she didn't need to. As soon as she thought about it, he knew.

Oh, he thought. *Oh. Um. Huh.* Kan looked away. Kan looking away was the most awful thing that had ever happened to Mo. And Mo was still in the middle of the worst day of her life. *Silly, I guess. I should have thought of that. It is . . . a lot to get used to. And everything.*

But Mo knew that under all that he was just wondering who it was. Whose heart and brain and soul she'd used as a public bus for so long. She hated herself. But should she hate herself? She didn't remember ever killing an enderman, let alone collecting their pearl. So the Mo that did that wasn't this Mo, right here, right now. That was another girl, a girl she'd never even met.

I suppose you are right, Kan answered her thoughts instantly. *This Mo is my friend. This Mo gave me a new note block when my hubunit destroyed mine. This Mo let me in and fed me whenever I ran away from home. This Mo loves a dead horse like her own baby. She could never hurt her people. Whatever that Mo did, I do not know her. All hail the Great Chaos, right? This whole mess is truly Its work. I have served the Great Chaos all my life. Why stop now?* Kan looked up, toward the ender dragon's lair. *Maybe the Great Chaos is just another way of saying life is crazy so you might as well get crazy, too.*

Kan sent his mind toward Loathsome's. He saw the infinite graveyard and the wiry trees and the sickly moon. He saw the gravestones of Loathsome's first memories, and now there were new ones. One said: YUMMY EYEBALLS. One said: DOUBLE MELON. One said: MUMMA'S FRIEND.

Stay here and we will come back for you, Kan thought to the graveyard. *Do not go anywhere till we get back. Do not even move.*

Remaaaain, Loathsome moaned.

Good, Kan thought. *Okay, Mo. Hold on to me? I will do it for both of us.*

Mo hesitated for a second. Jax the human being had just grabbed her. He hadn't cared what she thought or what she wanted. Kan the enderman was asking. Even though part of him was disgusted with her right now. What did that mean? Did it matter? She took a deep breath and stepped into the enderman's arms.

And quicker than she could let that breath out, they were standing on top of a towering obsidian pillar. A crystal flame crackled beside them in a silver cage. And far off on the other side of the island, the ender dragon flapped its enormous black-and-purple wings in the night, soaring toward them.

The dragon turned toward the eastern bank of pillars. It meant to pass right by. Its endless circling wouldn't be interrupted by a couple of brats. Mo and Kan held their breath. The ender dragon glided past on their left side—and turned its head.

ED looked at Mo. Directly at her. At her green eyes. At her black hair. At her human face.

And the ender dragon laughed.

It sounded like rocks banging down a mountainside and landing in a lake of fire. It sounded like a hundred people screaming at once. It sounded like stars dying. The ender dragon's thoughts exploded roughly into their heads.

Is it that time again already?

What? Mo thought, reeling from the force of the great reptile's mind.

It brings me pleasure to see the face of this primate uncovered. I did not expect you so soon. ED's Jurassic laughter banged around their skulls again. *Well done, child of the sun. Very quick. And the other one? He is likewise . . . revealed?*

Fin? I left him back at the ship. He's fine. He's safe.

So you knew? Kan spluttered. *You knew they were human all along?*

The ender dragon chortled. It sounded like thunder broken across the knee of the world. Its massive eyes slid shut. *I am the infinite lightning night-lizard at the end of the universe. I am the master of time and death. The fire of creation is my youngest brother. In my stomach, galaxies churn in cosmic acid and are digested into meaninglessness.* ED opened one vast violet eye. *You can't fool me with a pumpkin, dummy.*

Then you must remember! You must remember when they arrived.

ED flapped lazily around their pillar. *I do.*

Kan's excitement made the purple particles floating around his body glow like fireflies. *You must know what happened to them. You know why they do not remember anything.*

ED rolled onto its back midair and thrashed its mighty tail. *I do.*

Tell us! Tell her! Kan cried out in the space between their minds.

The ender dragon flexed its claws. *Nah,* it thought.

Why not? Mo pleaded. *I need to know. Who am I? Who is Fin? What should we do? Just leave and never come back?*

I would seriously consider it, if I were you, the dragon mused.

But this is our home. Up there . . . the way Jax talks about it . . . it's hard and lonely and everything wants to kill you. You have to know so much. *No one helps you or tells you the right thing to do. There's an Order to everything, but you have to figure out what it is while creatures try to eat you alive. You're just . . . on your own. By yourself. Without an End.* Mo's cheeks burned. Her thoughts went very quiet. *If we just found another couple of pumpkins, everything could go back to the way it was.*

You have come to the infinite lightning night-lizard for advice, ED thought as it dipped down and up again in a graceful loop the loop.

Yes!

I have never been asked for advice before. It is . . . annoying. Will it make you go away?

Yes, Kan thought. *We promise it will.*

Very well. Heed my words, mortal children! Life is very difficult and complex above and below. In the End and in the Beginning.

You must make your own decisions, and not rely on the world to tell you what to do so that you do not have to think. Nevertheless, there is a path, and you are always on it. Your choices created it. Your actions move it beneath your feet. You have crafted it as surely as any iron sword. The future is uncertain—up to a point. Then it is very certain. And inescapable. You are nearing that point now. And ultimately, the easiest, most correct, and wisest choice is to let me eat you.

Mo threw up her hands. *Oh, fine, if that's all the help you're going to be.*

ED shrugged its scaly shoulders. *You wanted my advice. I am selfish. As the universe is selfish. And hungry.* The ender dragon turned and flew straight at them. Then it stopped—and hovered. Not flying, simply existing without gravity. *I have known you a long time, Ultimo. It's really best if you let me eat you.* The dragon pouted. *You* never *let me eat you. You're no fun at all.*

Kan's mouth hung open in his sleek black face. *Ultimo? Who is Ultimo?*

But ED ignored him. *Do you know?* It asked Mo.

Know what?

ED sighed. *What a pity.*

You do not make any sense! Kan thought. Frustration burned in his green eyes.

The universe makes no sense, fragment. So I fit right in. Now get out. You promised. Leave me alone. I have much to prepare.

Wait, Mo thought. She trembled a little. ED was so big, so impossibly big. It could destroy her without even noticing. *I have to ask you something else. One last question.* She winced, then stuck her hand into her pocket and fished around. Jax had done it before, but she hadn't wanted to explore it herself. She had no idea what an empty block of space-time would feel like. She'd thought it would be creepy and unpleasant, and it was. Cold, dry, vast. It felt *grey*, if *grey* could be a feeling. Mo didn't like it. She felt her hand brush by many things she didn't recognize or understand by touch—and then her fingers fell on the thing she wanted.

Mo pulled the dragon's egg out of her pocket. She showed it to the ender dragon.

I have this, she thought nervously. *I have this and the human boy said . . . he said . . .*

Something hotter than the core of a planet ignited deep in ED's eyes. White ultraviolet flame popped in its pupils. Its breath quickened. The big, shiny black-and-purple egg was reflected in the dragon's eyes.

ED, Mo thought. She didn't know how it could be possible. But she had to ask. *Did I . . . did I kill you?*

With a scream of pure rage, the ender dragon reared back and vomited a thick, boiling stream of white-purple lavafire toward their pathetic little pillar.

Just before the flame reached them, Kan and Mo blinked out of existence.

The pillar erupted in a tornado of violet fire. It burned for a long time after they'd gone.

CHAPTER EIGHTEEN

TELOS

It was quiet in the city.

Fin felt like himself again. Tall, dark, and strong. Magenta eyes and a square jaw. Jess looked magnificent as an enderman. But all endermen looked magnificent. Fin had always thought they were clearly the most beautiful species, if you wanted to be objective about it.

"Just walk casual," Fin whispered. "And don't talk. You're supposed to be telepathic."

They stood on the edge of the city center. Black figures moved silently back and forth on the streets. Behind them, Fin and Jess could just see the shape of their ship floating off the island shore. He repeated the plan to himself. *In and out. In and out and back to the ship with the grindstone. Koal and Roary will meet us there. No problem.*

Jesster cocked her head to one side. "I'm not, though."

"Yeah, I got that," Fin said, distracted.

"That's very odd, don't you think?"

"No? You're human."

"So are you, Fin. But you communicate telepathically with Mo and Kan and I presume all the other endermen down here. I'm no different than you were when we met now. A human with a pumpkin on her head, which makes her look like an enderman. But I'm not an enderman. The pumpkin doesn't give me mind-reading powers. But you have them. Why? What's different?"

Fin rubbed his eyes, exasperated. "Knock me dead if I know, Jess. Yesterday I wanted to kill all humans. Today I am one. It's a lot. Let's just get this over with."

"Can you read my thoughts? Even if I can't read yours. Might be useful."

Fin tried. Nothing. He looked hard into Jess's mind. He searched for that image that always greeted a telepath when they tried to read a new person. Mo's ship, his open books, Kan's music, Koneka's family. In Jesster's head, he saw a perfectly-built cathedral. Beautiful, soaring, intricate, each stone in its place, the architecture precise and perfect. And the door was shut. She was human. She didn't know how to let her thoughts out or let others in. It was no use.

"No," he said.

"Too bad," answered Jess.

"Yeah."

"Where's the armory?"

Fin pointed to one of the fattest, tallest pagoda towers. Its purple roof forked up at the ends like the branches of chorus trees. All the buildings in the End looked alike, but not identical. Whoever built them liked things just so. The buildings matched the trees and the land. It all went together. Fin imagined that appealed to Jess the builder quite a bit.

"On the third level. Where the courtyard looks like a big mushroom. There's a door and a couple of shulkers there."

"Like your shulker?"

"No," Fin laughed. "Grumpo talks about biting me a lot. These actually will."

Jesster patted her hip. She wore a long diamond sword with a Fire Aspect enchantment on it. It was easily the most fantastic weapon Fin had ever seen. It would have looked so good hanging over Grumpo's box. Really tie the whole room together. Oh, well. He squeezed the handle of Koal's crossbow. The boy had lent it to him. Kraj had left them with so little to protect themselves.

"Hold on to me and I'll teleport us both right in," Fin said, holding out his hand. The ender pearl in his infinite human pocket was still good. He didn't know about it yet, because he hadn't had a moment to think about why he could teleport when he was just a human boy. But it lay there in his pocket anyway, putting out the last dregs of its energy for him to use.

Jess took his hand and the next thing either of them knew, they were standing inside the Telosian armory.

Fin and Mo's collection surrounded them. Fin gawped. The twins hadn't always kept their treasure organized and tidy, but at least they treated each item with care. Each thing was precious to them, even if it wasn't necessarily sorted into categories and stacked neatly. Nobody seemed to care about their stuff here. The room was huge, and everything Fin and Mo owned was thrown into great sloppy piles for anyone to take whatever they wanted without cleaning up after themselves. Weapons, armor, food, ore, potions. All just tossed together into a teetering, tottering trash heap. It glittered in the torchlight.

Fin had never really realized just how *much* they'd collected. The endersoldiers must have dumped it all back here when the war failed to get with the warring. Ready to be passed out again at a moment's notice. No *wonder* Kraj had commandeered it all. There was hardly anything in the enderman armory that *didn't* belong to them. If not for Mo and Fin, it seemed as though the End would have had to defend itself with a couple of small sticks and a stern expression.

Jesster opened her mouth to say something. Fin held his finger up to his lips. Funny how quickly and easily he made that gesture. Endermen never had to. No quiet like the quiet in the End. You didn't think with your mouth, so you wouldn't *shush* with it anyway. He'd never even seen anyone do it before. That he could remember, anyway, which wasn't saying much. Yet his finger flew up like he'd done it a thousand times. Instinct. *Habit*.

Jess pointed instead. She pointed to something dull and grey sticking out from under a small mountain of boots. The grindstone.

Fin glided across the room. He saw that Jess was impressed. His chest puffed out a little. Yeah, he could move like an enderman. Easy. Can't you? It wasn't really gliding. He just moved his feet in a certain quick way that looked like gliding. Instinct. Habit. Fin landed on the small mountain of boots. He reached down to wiggle the grindstone out of the trash heap as quietly as possible.

All hail the Great Chaos, Commander Kraj.

May the Great Chaos smile upon all your works and deeds, Corporal Murrum.

Fin's head snapped up toward the door. He glanced quickly at

Jess. She was standing out in the open in the middle of the armory, totally unprotected.

Hide! He thought. *They're coming! Kraj and Murrum are right outside!*

Jess blinked. She spread her hands. *What?*

Of course, she couldn't hear him. Ugh! Humans! Telepathy was just so much better than talking.

He tried to communicate with his eyes. Hard stare at Jess, hard stare at the door. Fin waved his hands as if pushing her back. Jess got the message. She ducked down behind a stack of water buckets and shovels just as the two grim, straight-backed soldiers walked into the armory. Fin was shocked to see one of them was Koneka, the juvenile enderman from the Enderdome. She looked . . . terrifyingly blank. Behind them more endermen followed. Kraj's personal brain squad was no longer just fifteen but fifty-nine soldiers. Kraj spoke only to Murrum. The rest were just there to make the commander cleverer. Living, breathing buffs.

You may deliver your report, Corporal Murrum. Kraj clasped his hands behind his back. He looked younger than he ever had. Power made him feel feisty, Fin supposed.

The portal is gone, sir.

Kraj looked benevolently at his underling out of the corner of his purple eye. But beneath that benevolence Fin felt the threat of the old enderman's anger.

Sire, Murrum. Not sir. It is sire, now.

Of course, sire, of course.

The Mouth of the Great Chaos blessed me with a royal title.

Corporal Murrum squinted and squirmed uncomfortably. *I thought* you *decided you should have a title. After you threw Eresha off a cliff because she ordered everyone to disband the army and go back to their homes on account of there being no human invasion after all.*

Commander Kraj's eyes bored into Murrum's. *Where did you hear this utter slander?* His thoughts thundered skull-to-skull.

S . . . s . . . some of the endersoldiers were talking after hours, that is all. Sire.

The Lord of All Endermen towered above the poor soldier. *You are MISTAKEN. Eresha is completely fine and resting comfortably at her house. It was she who chose to honor me. I am the humblest of all endermen. You know that, Murrum.*

I apologize deeply, my lord. The corporal shifted back and forth uncomfortably. *Well. In any event. The portal is gone,* sire.

Closed?

No, sire. Gone. Can you not feel it?

Of course I feel it! Do you think me a weak old enderman without his senses? Kraj exploded.

No, sire! Corporal Murrum cowered.

Fin's knees ached, crouching on the mound of boots. They were so slippery. He tried to hold on with his toes. If he moved, Kraj and his goons would hear.

Thc commander collected himself. *Humans are a clever, sneaky species. They specialize in deception the way spiders exercise the weaving of webs.*

Certainly, Commander, Murrum thought miserably. *Shall we start returning all this to the Endless fragments, then? Since the portal is gone and there is to be no war.*

Kraj looked at his manservant incredulously. *Return it? Whatever for? I need it. All of it. I cannot foresee a time when I will not need it. The human army would not just give up their ambitions, Murrum! No! The answer is simple. They are already here. Thou-*

sands of them. All around us, every moment. Why, they may be here in Telos already. In this very tower. In this very armory. We no longer feel the vibrations of the portal because they have shut it behind them. They do not intend to return home. No mercy, no surrender. What a cruel and heartless strategy from a cruel and heartless people.

The horror of the ruthless, calculating human heart settled down onto Corporal Murrum's shoulders. *How do you know, sire? Have you had word?*

How do I know? Why, I have thought about it long and hard. I have imagined with the powers of my very good and fully stacked brain. And I have come to a logical conclusion. To me it is perfectly obvious that this is what has happened. I am the wisest enderman ever to live, after all. With my End—Kraj gestured at the squad behind him—*no one can outthink me. No, Corporal Murrum, they are hiding their vast army among us. This cannot be denied.*

What will you do, sire?

Fin's legs screamed with the effort of holding still, keeping a grip on the grindstone, and not sliding down the pile of boots head over feet.

I will protect my people, of course. Do not fear. Pumpkins are just fruit, after all. And fruit can be . . . bruised. A dark smile showed itself between the words of Kraj's thoughts. *Everyone must be interrogated. One by one. I shall do this sad but necessary work. It is a sacrifice I am willing to make. We will uncover the saboteurs. We will punish them. But not as we usually do. That is too quick and merciful. We will make an example of them, so that every human ear in the Overworld hears what happens to invaders and plunderers in Kraj's Kingdom. And finally, the End will return to its great peace once more.*

And that's when it happened. Fin couldn't hold still any longer. If he just moved his right leg an inch or so, he'd be on flatter ground. He wouldn't have to hold on so tight. It'd be fine. He could do it without making noise. Sweet relief was just an inch that way. Fin slowly worked his foot over.

A pair of boots, held in place by his heel, slipped and started to slide down the pile. The boots had hard metal soles. Fin watched it happening with horror. He remembered finding that boot. On the outer islands, with Mo, a million years ago. They had a middling-strength Blast Protection enchantment on them. Pretty good boots, all in all. They were gonna make *such* a loud clang when they hit the ground. But he couldn't stop it. It was like it was happening to someone else. In slow motion. Fin was frozen.

Just then, a loud crash sounded from across the room. It totally swallowed up the sound of the old boot clattering onto the armory floor. Kraj, Murrum, and the fifty-eight soldiers behind them snapped to attention. The Lord of All Endermen shrieked like a teakettle devouring an air raid siren and shot across the room toward the water bucket skittering across the floor. The commander punched through the stack of water buckets with one black fist. Fin's heart jumped into his throat. Jess was back there!

But she wasn't.

Kraj kicked the other water buckets aside in a fit of rage.

Perhaps it was a stray endermite, sire. Murrum tried to calm his master.

Kraj shoved him aside. *You fool! THEY. ARE. HERE.*

How strange, Fin thought. Kraj was right. The humans *were* here. But he was so wrong, too. And Jess. She'd covered for him. Why? He wasn't anything to her. Why would she risk Kraj's wrath for him?

Fin suddenly saw a glint in the torchlight. Jess's eyes, between a teetering pyramid of gold and a barrel of cocoa beans. Not using telepathy was garbage, Fin decided firmly. How could humans stand it? If Jess had been like him, she could have just shown him what she wanted him to do in an instant.

Jess mouthed something. Fin squinted in the dim light, trying to make it out.

T-E-L-E-P-O-R-T. Go! Leave me.

No way! Fin mouthed back. *Not a chance!*

Ender-Jess, still slick and tall and black in the pumpkin helmet that disguised her so well, rolled her purple eyes. While Kraj raged at the water buckets, she crept out from behind the gold stash in complete silence. Jess slipped into formation with the fifty-nine-strong squad waiting patiently for their commander to come to his senses. Fin tensed when he saw Jess was standing right behind Koneka, but if the fragment noticed, she didn't give any sign. Fifty-nine was a lot of people. If you didn't count, you'd never know there was one extra. Fin sighed with relief. Jess was awfully good at this.

Sound the alarms, Murrum, Kraj roared. *Intruders! Endermen! With me! We will carve out the human menace!*

The brain squad came to attention. They turned as one to march out of the armory and into the city again, where they could rejoin the assembled forces of the End. 2-3-4-*Hup*! In perfect time, they beat their path through the great door.

WAIT! The Lord of All Endermen's booming thoughts sliced through the minds of everyone in the room. Kraj seemed bigger and taller than ever as he flowed over to the troops. *Fee-fie-fo-fum,* he fumed, *I smell the blood of too many endermen!*

Kraj's dark hand fell upon Jess's shoulder.

I do not know you, soldier, he thought coldly. *What is your name? To what End do you belong?*

Jess stared up miserably into those boiling purple eyes. She couldn't understand him. She wasn't telepathic. To her, there was nothing in the armory but silence and danger.

I SAID GIVE ME YOUR NAME, SOLDIER! bellowed the thoughts of Kraj. *DO NOT DEFY YOUR LORD!*

But poor Jess could no more hear his words than she could hear Jax snoring in the Overworld. And if she spoke, no pumpkin in the world could hide what she was. She tried to inch her hand toward her sword.

Kraj's body flushed a deep, ugly red. His fury built and built until it was flashing and clanging inside him like a fire alarm. Fin couldn't believe it. With so many endermen around, Kraj should have been in total control of himself. The mindless rage of the berserker enderman should have stayed a million miles away. But there it was, plain as the red on the commander's face.

HOLD HER STILL! Kraj commanded. The ender squad obeyed without question. Koneka and another soldier seized her arms in a grip worse than any iron.

Sire! protested Murrum. *It is only a fragment!*

Are you really going to let her get caught right now? Fin asked himself. *Really, Fin? She tried to save you, and you're just going to watch him lose his mind on her? Move your feet, you coward.* But Fin couldn't. He wanted to. He really, really did. But his feet wouldn't do what he told them to.

Commander Kraj raised his fist into the air. In one terrible blow, he threw Jess across the whole of the armory. She crashed through a jumble of pickaxes and smashed into the far wall. Jesster sank to the ground. She moaned. She put her hand up to the back of her head.

It came away covered in shattered pumpkin.

Slowly, horribly, the helmet cracked and fell forward. Kraj and Murrum and fifty-eight endermen itching for war stared in fascination at their first human invader.

The scream of triumph that came out of Kraj in that moment could have shattered every glass bottle in the room, had he screamed out loud and not directly into all their minds until they ached. It sounded like the devil's nails down all the chalkboards in hell.

SEE? DO. YOU. SEE? I WAS RIGHT! AS RIGHT AS RAIN!

He went completely red and bent his head to charge Jess.

Fin's feet still wouldn't obey him. But that sound knocked the fear right out of him. Fine. If his legs wouldn't work, his arms would have to do. In one fluid motion, Fin pulled up his crossbow, yanked back the firing mechanism, and shot the Lord of All Endermen directly between the shoulder blades.

"All hail the Great Chaos," Fin whispered.

It happened so fast.

Kraj crumpled like an old umbrella. The red light of his anger went out. He hit the ground, but it hardly made a sound.

Oh no, Fin thought. *What have I done? Poor old Kraj. All his long, boring stories. I killed him. And his stories. I killed an enderman in the End. In his own land. What a good human I turned out to be.*

Two things happened at once. Corporal Murrum teleported in the direction of the crossbow bolt. And Jess leapt forward, flaming diamond sword in hand.

She mowed her way through the fifty-nine endermen bodyguards. Jess slashed left and right, slicing down and ripping up. It wasn't even a contest. Her blade cut through them like they were nothing.

No, thought Kraj weakly. *No, I need them!* Jess spun around and hacked another soldier in two. *Stop! I was right! Murrum! I was right! There she is! The human menace! Among us! I was right!* The endermen warriors tried to fight back, but they were no match. Some of them broke and ran. They blinked out, teleporting away, abandoning their commander. Koneka looked directly into Fin's eyes. One, two, three more went down.

By the Great Chaos, I believe I have journeyed too far and too swiftly, Koneka thought, just as she had that day they met out on the dunes above the Enderdome. But now her thoughts were the color of heartbreak and horror. She vanished in an instant, just as Jess's sword sliced through the space where she'd stood.

Kraj howled. *STOP! I need those soldiers! I need my End! I don't want to go back! I am the wisest of all endermen! I am . . . I am the wise . . .* The last of the squad sank to his knees and toppled forward. Jess panted in the middle of her carnage. The bodies were already disappearing, leaving their pearls behind.

Kraj's mind dissolved into a mindless scream of blind and thoughtless rage. And then it was silent too, and all that was left was a withered greenish-grey gem with a dull, dark shine deep within it.

Corporal Murrum bore down on Fin. He was alone now. *Nobody here but us humans,* Fin thought in a panic. Murrum's mind was a blank. All it wanted to do was kill. There was no one home behind those familiar purple eyes anymore. Murrum didn't see Fin, he didn't see anything. He just saw a target.

I had to, Fin thought, *I had to do it.* He closed his eyes, clutched the grindstone to his chest, and waited for the worst.

It didn't come. Endermen flooded into the armory in a black wave. They followed the death cry of Kraj into the room. As soon as the mass of them drew near, the stack initiated, and intelligence returned to the corporal's eyes. Intelligence, and cold hate.

Seize them immediately, Murrum ordered. Jess lifted her sword again but they rushed her too fast. She got one, two, and then they had her. *Keep the human for questioning. The fragment known as Fin murdered our beloved commander. We will also ask him a question. That question will be: What method of execution would you prefer?*

"Fin, just teleport away, don't risk yourself!" Jess yelled. What was the point of staying quiet now?

"I'm not leaving you!" he yelled back without thinking.

"Well, that's completely stupid!" Jess hollered.

Murrum staggered back, away from the sound of Fin's human voice. *Oh*, Fin thought. *Oh, I actually am an idiot. Endermen don't talk*.

Faster than Fin could regret his recent life choices, Corporal Murrum grabbed his head and slammed it into the wall. He felt the pumpkin crack and fall off. Fin turned a human face back to Murrum.

Fin? Murrum thought in total confusion. *It is not possible. I have known you since you were a young fragment. It is not true. It cannot be. Kraj . . . Kraj knew. He always knew. He was truly the wisest of us!*

I'm sorry, Murrum. And Fin was sorry. He really was. *Do I still get to pick how I'm executed?*

No, the corporal thought. The enderman turned to the crowd behind him. *Take them both to the Cage!*

Something big and hard and a lot like a fist hit Fin in the back of the head.

Lights out.

CHAPTER NINETEEN

REMEMBER?

Fin woke up.

A cold, black wind hit him in the face.

He was lying on a hard floor. And the floor was moving.

He tried to open his eyes. His head throbbed. Everything was blurry.

"Morning, sunshine," a voice said.

That's Roary, Fin thought. *Couldn't be, though, because she's safe back on the ship with Koal.*

"Welcome back to the program already in progress," another voice said wryly, a voice that unmistakably belonged to Koal.

Am I *on the ship?* Fin wondered. *Seems unlikely.*

Jesster's voice cut through his grogginess. "About time you rejoined the land of the living."

I thought they said they were taking us to the Cage, thought Fin blearily. *Not the ship.*

Look around, dummy. The cool, familiar thoughts of his sister flowed into Fin's head and even though his eyes still burned, they flew open.

Mo sat directly across from him. Kan stood next to her.

Chaaaaains, groaned Loathsome silently, curled up between them. Jellied black fluid oozed between the links of the thick chains holding the zombie horse prisoner. She kicked out her hind legs. The chains clanked.

And next to Loathsome was a very large purple box.

Thump-thump, thump, thump-thump went the box.

I hate you, Grumpo thought from inside it. *This is all your fault. I want to bite you so bad.*

"Grumpo!" Fin yelled. "I missed you so much!"

I didn't miss you at all because I hate you.

"WHO'S A GOOD BOY?" Fin asked in the voice you use to call a cuddly dog.

It is not me. I am a bad boy. Also not a boy.

"I hope you're not too mad," Fin said.

Grumpo thumped his box. *I don't judge. I hate you no matter what. I would hate you just the same even if you turned out to be a human with a pumpkin on your head. Oh. Wait.*

Fin laughed a little. "This is pretty messed up, huh?" he said to all of them.

Everyone was there, and everyone was clearly going to stay there for a while. Mo, Kan, Loathsome, Jess, Roary, and Koal stood against the silver bars of a massive cage hanging in the air a couple of hundred feet above the ground. Each had one arm locked to a bar of the cage and one foot locked to the floor. The cell swayed in the wind. Darkness waited below them.

"What's going on?" Fin said.

"Well, you've been out to lunch for ages," Koal chuckled. "The rest of us have been catching up."

Fin turned to his sister. "You came back!" He wished he'd said something cleverer, but his brain was having a rough go of it. "Where's Jax?"

"That's all you have to say?" Mo laughed. "I don't know, probably stroking his hunting trophies. Kan brought me back." The green-eyed enderman gave her a stern look. She'd promised. Mo rolled her eyes a little. "Kan rescued me. We teleported back to the ship and it was crawling with army boys yelling about Kraj and vengeance. So it sounds like you kept yourself pretty busy while I was gone."

"We've been sentenced to death by ender dragon." Roary sighed. "Good work, everyone."

Fin looked a little more closely. He peered through the bars to what lay outside the Cage. Obsidian pillars. Crystal flames. Silver cages. The ender dragon's island. Wonderful.

"Wait. Where is it? ED doesn't like to wait."

"It's flown by a few times," Mo said.

Flaaaaaaame, croaked Loathsome.

Mo patted her stiff, dirt-caked mane. *Yes, yes, you're very smart*.

"They're gonna hold a big ritual so everyone can see that Kraj was right and the human menace is real," Jesster explained. "Murrum is feeling pretty cut up about the whole thing now that his boss is toast and unavailable to yell at him or smack him around, so he wants to make sure everyone knows what a saint the old guy was. Spoiler," she said to Koal and Roary, who didn't know Kraj from any other enderman, "he was not a saint."

"None of you seem very worried."

ED would not hurt me, Kan thought. *I am an enderman. I have not done anything. You all are in big trouble, though.*

Why don't you just teleport away, Kan? Mo thought miserably. *Leave us. Save yourself.*

If I could take you all with me, I would. But I ran away too many times. I did not learn enough at the Enderdome. I am not strong or fast enough to take you all. So I will not leave. He took Mo's hand, and she smiled. *You are my End. You cannot leave your End.*

Fin was pretty sure Mo didn't think ED would burn her either. He was also pretty sure she was wrong. Fin had never liked the old beast as much as Mo did. It made him uneasy.

"These things tend to work themselves out one way or another." Roary shrugged.

"That's a very Chaotic thing to say," Mo observed. "You should come to church with us sometime."

Fin groaned and rubbed his head. It felt like he'd stuck it in a torch and let it slowly roast there.

"Never mind your head," Mo said eagerly. "We've been waiting for you to wake up."

"Why?"

Roary pointed at Fin's feet with a suggestive bounce of her eyebrows. Fin looked down.

He still had the grindstone.

"Wow! I can't believe they didn't take it off me!" He reached down with his unchained hand to make sure it wasn't damaged. "But it's no good without the books."

Koal smiled the smile of someone with a really good surprise ready and waiting. "We're way ahead of you, kid."

Mo reached out for him across the cage. He reached too. They couldn't touch. "Do you know what today is, Fin? So much has happened I forgot."

Fin shook his head.

"Happy Endermas, Fin," she said sweetly.

Oh. Oh wow. He just . . . hadn't realized. It had been the furthest thing from Fin's mind.

"They got us presents," Mo grinned.

Roary and Koal dug deep in their pockets for a minute. Then, Roary pulled out a book and tossed it onto the floor of the cage. It slid and spun over the wood and landed against Fin's big toe. The human girl reached in again and pulled out another one. And another. Koal already had five or six out. He pushed them toward Mo. Not all the books they'd had on the ship. But a lot of them. A respectable selection.

"Happy Weird Mysterious Murder Monster Day, guys," Koal said.

Fin picked up the book in his hand. He turned it over a couple of times. He and Mo locked eyes. They hadn't had a chance to talk about this. But they didn't need telepathy to sort out what to do next. It was now or never.

"Come on!" Roary coaxed. "I'm dying here!"

Koal crossed his arms. "This is going to be such a huge bummer if that's just a janky Bane of Arthropods spell."

"You first," Mo said.

Jess showed Fin how to use the grindstone. The book didn't seem to respond for a minute. Then it quivered. It swelled up like it meant to heave out a huge belch. It shimmered.

And it popped open.

All five humans, one enderman, one zombie, and one shulker leaned forward.

"Luck of the Sea Enchantment Level One," Fin read slowly. "The Luck of the Sea enchantment increases your chances of catching treasure rather than junk or fish. No *way*," he said in disgust and disbelief.

"I told you!" crowed Koal. Roary kicked him. "Sorry, though, Fin. Sorry."

Ha ha, Grumpo laughed in his box. *It is funny when you fail.*

Fin slumped down against the cage bars. "I can't believe it. I really thought . . . I really thought we would find something in there. Some answers. Anything." He threw the book onto the floor of their cage. "I'm gonna die and the only thing I know now that I didn't know before we went and royally screwed everything up in Telos is that you can add the Luck of the Sea enchantment to any fishing rod."

"Fin," Mo said softly.

"I'm really sorry, Mo. It all happened so fast. I didn't mean to kill Kraj. You don't know what he was planning, though. It's probably not the worst thing for the End that he's gone . . ."

"Fin," Mo said again.

"But I know that doesn't make it any better. I didn't kill him because of what he was planning. I just killed him because he hurt Jess and I hated him for it."

"Fin! Look!"

Mo pointed at the book. The stupid, useless Luck of the Sea Enchantment Level One book.

There was handwriting on the other side of the enchantment instructions.

Fin's handwriting.

As if in a trance, he picked up the book. At long last, Fin was front and center, reading to the class. He followed the words with his fingers.

It is always night in the End. There is no sunrise. There is no sunset. There are no clocks ticking away.

But that does not mean there is no such thing as time. Or light. Ring after ring of pale yellow islands glow in the darkness, floating in the endless night. Violet trees and violet towers twist up out of the earth and into the blank sky. Trees full of fruit, towers full of rooms. White crystal rods stand like candles at the corners of the tower roofs and balconies, shining through the shadows. Sprawling, ancient, quiet cities full of these towers glitter all along the archipelago, purple and yellow like everything else in this place. Beside them float great ships with tall masts. Below them yawns a black and bottomless void.

It is a beautiful place. And it is not empty.

"What is this?" Fin asked his twin.

"I don't know. Keep reading."

We have always lived here. We cannot remember any other place. We grew up here. It is our home. No different from any of the hundreds of endermen you'd find on any island here in the archipelago. We live on an end ship crammed with junk we snatched up from anywhere we could find it.

Fin flipped through the pages.

Kan's eyes aren't like the wide, clear magenta-violet eyes of other endermen.

Kan's eyes are green.

> No one knows why. No one can remember any other enderman who had green eyes, not in all the history of the End.

"What in the name of the Great Chaos?" Fin whispered. He'd gone pale. He flipped faster through the book.

> I'm going to call her Loathsome. Isn't that a nice name for a nice horse who definitely will not eat my brains the minute I'm not looking?

Mo trembled all over. "Skip to the end," she said, clutching her horse so tightly even the dead skin bruised.

Fin turned to the back of the book. He read aloud.

> I am afraid. So much has happened. Kraj is dead by my own hand. Eresha is dead. I have lost my twin. The ender dragon is dead. Poor Loathsome. Poor Grumpo. Poor all of us. The End itself is coming apart. The islands cannot hold. The sky is falling. If I try to forget what I'm looking at, it's beautiful. Really. So beautiful. The towers of Telos are falling like confetti. It is coming. The great tide of memory will wash over me and I will know nothing about all this grief. And do you know? I think I welcome it.
>
> I have retreated to the ship. Lying on the deck, I can watch the night tear itself apart. When I close my eyes, I can hear Kan playing somewhere far away. Good. He is alive. I'm glad. He's coming to find me. To be part of my End.

It's almost here. I can feel it moving through the islands. Completely inevitable. Why fight it?

All hail the Great Chaos. Blessed be the Beginners.

See you on the other side, Ultimo.

Fin flung the book away from him in terror and bewilderment. It skittered across the wood floorboards, through the bars of the Cage, and soared out into the empty night. It looked like a white bird as it plummeted away from them.

"What is that? What *is* it?" he cried, panicked.

"Okay, okay, calm down. Let's try another one," Roary suggested. "Magic is always weird. There's an element of unpredictability in any enchanted object."

Roary disenchanted another book with the grindstone and started to pass it round to Fin, then thought better of it and handed it to Mo.

"The Feather Falling enchantment reduces damage from falling and damage from ender pearl teleportations," Mo read.

Then she turned over the page.

"This is my handwriting," Mo told them quietly.

She began to read from the other side.

It is always night in the End. There is no sunrise. There is no sunset. There are no clocks ticking away.

But that does not mean there is no such thing as time. Or light. Ring after ring of pale yellow islands glow in the darkness, floating in the endless night. Violet trees and violet towers twist up out of the earth and into the blank sky. Trees full of fruit, towers full of rooms. White crystal rods stand like candles at the corners of the tower roofs and balconies, shining through the shadows. Sprawling, ancient, quiet cities full of these towers glitter all along the archipelago, purple and yellow like everything else in this place. Beside them float great ships with tall masts. Below them yawns a black and bottomless void.

It is a beautiful place. And it is not empty.

"I don't understand," Fin said, rubbing his cheeks. Nothing seemed real. What was this, what *could* it be?

Mo skipped to the end.

I am afraid. So much has happened. Kraj is dead by my own hand. Eresha is dead. I have lost my twin. But I believe he is alive. The ender dragon is dead. Poor Loathsome. Poor Grumpo. Poor all of us. The End itself is coming apart. The islands cannot hold. The sky is falling. If I try to forget what I'm looking at, it's beautiful. Really. So beautiful. The towers of Telos are falling like confetti. It is coming. The great tide of memory will wash over me and I will know nothing about all this grief. And do you know? I think I welcome it.

I have retreated to the ship. Lying on the deck, I can watch the night tear itself apart. When I close my eyes, I can hear Kan playing somewhere far away. Good. He is alive. I'm glad. The music is getting closer now. He's coming to find me. To be part of my End.

It's almost here. I can feel it moving through the islands. Completely inevitable. Why fight it?

All hail the Great Chaos. Blessed be the Beginners.

See you on the other side, El Fin.

Roary disenchanted another. And another. And another. Koal had already stepped back. He wanted no part of it. It was all way too serious. An explorer has to expect a bit of getting sentenced to death by dragon. It was all part of the adventure. But this was too out there.

They took turns looking through the books and reading out loud. But it didn't matter. Each one was the same, in either Fin or Mo's steady handwriting.

> It is always night in the End. There is no sunrise. There is no sunset.
>
> It is always night in the End. There is no sunrise. There is no sunset.
>
> It is always night in the End. There is no sunrise. There is no sunset.
>
> See you on the other side, El Fin.
>
> See you on the other side, Ultimo.

They weren't entirely identical. Some names changed. Some events didn't pan out the same way in every book. They didn't have time to really read them all. Soon they were numb to it. They checked the beginning and the end and moved on to the next disenchanted enchantment. It was all there. Their whole lives. Everything they'd ever experienced and a few things they hadn't yet. Over and over and over again in their own handwriting. And how many more of these had they left in the ship in that massive mountain of books?

Mumma, explaaain, thought Loathsome raspily, nuzzling Mo's hand.

I can't. I can't. I don't know.

Kan ran his hands over the books.

I'm in there, he thought. *In all of them. I'm playing my music as the world ends. That's something, I suppose.*

Fin strained for his sister. "Who is Ultimo?" he whispered to her.

"I have no idea," she answered. "Who's El Fin?"

"I don't know!" Fin spluttered.

Mo quirked her mouth to one side. She didn't want to say in front of everyone. But she didn't have a choice. "The ender dragon called me Ultimo," she confessed.

"Uh . . ." interrupted Koal. "Wait a minute. Go back. Ultimo? *The* Ultimo? Supreme Brewmaster Ultimo?"

"El Fin the Archmage?" said Roary, and her eyebrows said she was impressed.

I hate them, Grumpo huffed in his box. *They sound like losers.*

Jesster shook her head. "No way." She laughed. "We all like playing pretend, but no way. Ultimo and El Fin are *legends. Magicians'* magicians. Iconic. And they weren't twins. They're also dead. Presumed dead, anyway. Might as well be talking about King Arthur and Dracula. And like, no offense, but I saw you in action in the armory, Fin. I like you a lot. But you're not exactly iconic."

Fin tried to ignore that. He'd done his best, hadn't he?

"Saved you, didn't I?" he mumbled.

"Yeah, I saved you, too, my friend. Don't get it mixed up. This is not and never will be a damsel situation."

Fin couldn't help himself. In the midst of all that confusion and strangeness, he smiled a little.

Mo raised her hand from Loathsome's boil-covered back and set it back down again thoughtfully.

"What does it mean?" she asked no one and everyone.

But there was no answer to that, at least not one you could find in a cage hanging in the dark.

There was a commotion down below. A lot of grunting voices and soft thuds. Everyone lurched to one side of the cage to see what was going on down there.

A figure was standing on the sandy earth with its hands on its hips, looking up at them with intense irritation from inside a circle of severely wounded endermen.

"Oh my god, you freaking *dorks*," Jax shouted.

CHAPTER TWENTY

UNKNOWN VARIABLES

"Why'd you run off?" Jax called up to Mo from the ground. He sounded genuinely hurt.

"You were so mad at me. And you were gonna experiment on me."

"To help you!"

"I don't need help!" Mo shouted.

Jax laughed. "Cool story, you just hanging out in cages for fun, then?"

"We're going to be executed, *obviously*," Koal rolled his eyes. "Keep up."

"Dingus over here killed their president or whatever so now it's this whole *thing*," Roary jabbed her thumb over her shoulder at Fin.

"How can you be so casual about this?" Mo said. "They're going to kill us. You're acting like it's a joke."

Jess shrugged. "Nah. Jax is here now. We'll just escape. It's cool. We do it all the time."

"The ender dragon is out there somewhere, you know that, right? It won't just let us go."

"It's what I came for!" Jax yelled up. "One in the chest, one in the gut, two between the eyes and we're out of here."

"I'm not going to let that happen," Mo said quietly. Her voice was dead iron.

Koal's head snapped up. He looked out through the bars of the cage nervously. "Do you hear that?"

The ender dragon's island lay mostly empty. Even of the ender dragon. If the old lizard was here, it was hiding very well. Not like it at all, Mo thought. Jax had made quick work of the gang of enderguards below. The group was, for all they could tell, alone.

But then Mo could hear it, too. Then Roary. Then Jess. Then Fin. Then Kan and Loathsome and Grumpo.

Voices. Voices in the void.

Voices singing Endermas carols in unison, so loud that everyone could hear.

O come ye, Great Chaos,
Lawless and triumphant,
Come ye, O come ye to the End.
Come and reward us,
Born your loyal fragments.
O come let us obey you,
O come let us assist you,
O come let us adore you,
Great Chaos above.

"Shoot us down already, would you?" hissed Jess.

Jax gave a very dramatic sigh. The human boy unholstered the crossbow on his back, took aim, and before Fin and Mo could scream that it was too far to fall, shot out the rope that held the Cage to the obsidian pillar.

They tumbled through empty space. Five kids, an enderman, a zombie horse, and a monster in a box.

Jesster, Roary, and Koal seemed completely unconcerned. Koal even waved at Fin in midair. Roary turned over on her back and made swimming motions with her arms. Jess checked her watch as they fell.

They had their elytra and Feather Falling boots. No fall could do much to them other than jazz up their funny bones. Fin and Mo used to have those things, too. But not anymore. They shot down through the sky with nothing to slow them down.

O sing out, Great Chaos,
Sing of pure anarchy.
O come, O come ye to the End.
Come and exalt us,
Bring ruin to our enemies.
O come, thou holy entropy,
O come, thou blessed discord,
O come, unknown variables,
Chaos is born!

Grumpo hit the ground first. The lid of his box shot open, exposing the shulker to the air. He shrieked in rage and humiliation. Loathsome landed next. Her spine broke in half and her skull split open. But she was already dead, so it didn't really bother her.

Mo had always thought dying would happen fast. So fast you wouldn't know what hit you. But now that she was about to die, it all went so slow. A crawl, really. She had so much time while she plummeted toward certain doom. Time enough to see endermen flowing in toward the island from all sides, still singing their carols.

O come let us embrace you,
O come let us nourish you,
O come let us delight you,
Chaos is nigh.

Time enough to reach up toward Fin tumbling after her. Reaching for her hand, not catching it, reaching again. To see his blue eyes accept their fate. Time enough to see Kan, so far from her, teleport to safety without them. What else could he do?

Time enough to look up at the quickly retreating pillar where the Cage hung and see the ender dragon hanging upside-down below it like a vast and horrible bat. Its enormous black wings hugged its body. Its tail tucked up beneath those leathery curtains closed over ED's glowing face and ultraviolet belly. With its wings shut, you could hardly see it in the dark. Jax certainly didn't see it. He was standing right in front of it and he had no idea. If he had, he'd never have turned his back on it like that.

ED had been there all along. Waiting. Listening. An inch away from their feet.

As Mo fell, Jax began shooting out the crystal flames at the tops of the pillars. It was starting. The End. Whatever the End was going to be. This was it. One, two, three, the lights went out.

The last thing Mo saw before she hit the ground was Jax taking aim at the last lantern. Behind him, the ender dragon slowly opened its colossal reptilian wings.

Mo landed on Grumpo's box. Fin landed on top of her. They felt something horrid crack beneath them. Then, it seemed to sag and go soft and they were falling again.

The lid of Grumpo's box slammed shut over them. Thump-thump, thump, thump-thump.

O come, thou holy entropy,
O come, thou blessed discord,
O come, unknown variables,
Chaos is here!

The twins woke in an enormous purple chamber. The ceiling towered above them. The floor stretched out in all directions. Row after row of elegant columns connected the two. Torches lined the walls. Soft, golden light greeted them.

In the middle of the room they saw a raised platform made of the same purple stone as Grumpo's box. But it couldn't be. Grumpo's box was tiny. Stairs led up to a squat, square cube that looked very much indeed like Grumpo's box. And on top of that, angrily, resentfully, perched a naked shulker with nothing to protect it. A nub of pale, glowing, yellowish-green flesh. Not much bigger than a softball. Not much tougher than a gob of spit.

"Are you okay?" Mo asked gingerly.

"Is this your *box*?" Fin marveled.

Grumpo seethed on his podium.

"This isn't a shulker's box," Mo said. "I know shulkers. This isn't right."

"It makes a certain sense, you carrots, since I am not a shulker,"

Grumpo said. “Anyone with half a brain would have figured that out by now.”

Grumpo *said*.

Grumpo talked. Out loud. Like a human.

Up above, outside the box, they could hear a riot of sounds. Furious sounds. The sounds of fighting.

“What are you then?” asked Fin. His throat was dry and thick.

The little softball-sized glob of slime rolled his eyes.

Grumpo bowed humbly. “I am the Great Chaos. Ugh, I hate the two of you so much. I really, *really* want to bite you.”

CHAPTER TWENTY-ONE

ALL HAIL THE GREAT CHAOS

"Sorry, you're the what?" Mo said.

"You heard me, Ultimo. You always hear me. I am so tired of having this conversation. I have had it every way it can be had. It was fun at first, but once a thing becomes predictable, I become allergic to it, and the pair of you are giving me hives."

"You're the Great Chaos. The god of the endermen." Fin shook his head. "No, you're not. You're Grumpo! You hate everything and you yell at me and sometimes I give you an apple or a bit of cod for a treat at the end of the day."

"You can stuff your cod," the shulker growled. "I hate it."

Fin smiled. "There's my boy. WHO'S A GOOD BOY?"

"I am neither good nor bad and I am not your boy!" The shulker thundered. "God is a limiting word. I existed when the universe was new. I will exist when it burns itself out. I knew the Beginners, the builders of the End. I saw them come ashore, and do their work, and embrace their extinction. I am the eternal unpredictable stroke of chance in the cogs of creation."

Mo scratched the back of her hand. "What about the ender dragon? It talks like that. It said it was the infinite lightning night-lizard at the end of the universe."

"The ender dragon is my *dog,*" Grumpo scoffed. "I got lonely a millennium or two ago. I needed someone to snuggle and amuse me with its tricks. Everyone needs someone to snuggle, you know. The development of a self-aware soul was a very good trick. As was fire breath. I am proud of ED."

"If you're so great and powerful, why do you look like a lump of snot?"

"—like a shulker," Mo quickly added at the same time.

"To observe you in this cycle and many others. The sight of my true form would liquefy your livers in an instant. Also everyone leaves me alone and I don't have to listen to those stupid carols. Once you're a god it's bye-bye to privacy. Paparazzi everywhere."

Fin said, "To observe us? Why?"

"Because I hate you," the Great Chaos grinned. "I hate you with such passionate intensity I cannot let you out of my sight. You really cannot imagine how much I hate you."

Mo sat down heavily on the floor. "Why is any of this happening? Why did you call me Ultimo? I don't understand."

"Aw, precious," Grumpo said kindly. "You don't understand because you're thick as a cake. That goes for the both of you. But don't feel bad. That's partly my fault. My dog ate your homework."

"Jax is gonna kill your dog if we don't get back out there," Mo pointed out.

"And why would I want to stop him? Someone always kills the ender dragon. It is the beginning of the cycle."

Mo felt as though she almost had it. She could feel the corner of it in her teeth but she couldn't get it out. The cycle. The enchanted books. The dragon's egg. Ultimo. All the pieces were there. But she couldn't make them fit.

"Chaos abhors a cycle," Fin said. He didn't know where that came from. It just popped into his head.

"*There* he is. There's the Fin I know. Of course, it's not entirely true. Scripture is like that sometimes. It sounds very clever, but the truth is so much more complicated. The cycle has never troubled me. I exist within the cycle. I set the cycle in motion. It's you two that broke it."

"How? What have we done?" Mo asked.

"You're stuck," said Grumpo. His voice sounded thick and wet. "And you cannot get out." The shulker's face, as much as a shulker had a face, grew serious. There was something almost like pity in his grey, milky eyes. "Oh, I have tried to help you. I told you not to let Kan on board. I told you to kill the humans. I told you you would be happier if you let me bite them. I even told Kan he could stay with me forever, because that would have been something *different*. Something chaotic. But you never listen. Not until it is too late. There will come a moment, after it is done but before it all begins again, when you will remember everything. You will know it all. What has come before a thousand times. What will come again. And you will cry your eyes out because you are human and that's what you do. I don't say that to mock you. It's nice that you can still cry. Gods cannot."

"Grumpo, please."

"I am not Grumpo."

"But you are," Fin insisted. "Part of you is. You can't live with us for so long and guard us from intruders and eat our popcorn without being a little bit ours. Our good boy."

The Great Chaos sighed. He squelched resentfully on the purple stone. Then, he spoke.

"I have said all this before and I will say it again. I hate you, Fin. I hate you, Mo. I hate you more than the last time I told you I hated you," Grumpo began. "The ender dragon is the heart of this world. It beats in the center of the End, round and round in circles, steady as a pulse. Nothing works without ED. And since the beginning, humans have come questing after it. To find ED and kill it for no particular good reason other than that it is killable. Every time my poor doggo dies, another one must be born. *That* cycle was perfectly acceptable. A world must have a heart. The ender dragon vanishes, an egg appears in its place, and a new ender dragon rises. But something as powerful and ancient and loyal to the Great Chaos who is its master does not die without leaving . . . a wake. Let's call it that. When a ship passes by at great speed, the sea churns and ripples after it as water is displaced and replaced again. That is what happens when the ender dragon dies. What is going to happen in about . . . oh, I would wager ten to fifteen minutes, give or take. A great wake pulses out from its body. It travels through the End like the tide. It touches everything and everyone. And it makes them forget. The world resets. What came before is gone. There is only the now."

"Why? How can that be good for anyone?" asked Mo.

"Why does your body respawn when you die?" Grumpo shrugged as well as he could without shoulders. "It is how ED decomposes. You shouldn't judge. You always were very judgey, Ultimo. It's a nasty habit."

"I am not Ultimo!" snapped Mo in frustration. "I'm just Mo! Just a girl with a ship and a horse and a twin."

The shulker laughed throatily. "Of course you're Ultimo. Ultimo the Magnificent. Supreme Brewmaster Ultimo. Do you think zombie horses listen to everyone? Sort yourself out, child. And you, you are El Fin the Archmage, the Flame in the Night. You were famous back home. Everyone wanted to learn from you. Ultimo lived in a vast graveyard with every kind of plant and mineral at her beck and call—people always get buried with their best loot. They used to say Ultimo could brew a potion to do anything under the sun or moon. Impossible things. Things no one else would even think of. El Fin lived in the desert, in a palace made entirely of torches. You met by chance, as far as I can tell. The two of you geniuses came down to the End for your turn at killing my dog many cycles ago. And you did it, didn't you? Bang—right between the eyes. But you just had to gloat. You didn't hop through your exit portal with your prize like most people. You stayed for *ages* and got caught in my poor puppy's wave of amnesia because you were just too proud of yourselves to practice basic personal safety. Disgusting. And so you go. Over and over.

"Some cycles are short. Some long. But they all end the same way. When you wake up, your pumpkins keep the Endermen from seeing who you really are, and of course you don't remember. The death of the ender dragon washes your mind so clean you can actually hear the thoughts of the endermen. Human minds are usually too noisy for that. And so you make certain assumptions. Humans are so good at making patterns out of nothing. Order out of . . . well, me. You patch over anything that doesn't fit. You *make* it fit. You look around at a ship and presume it's your home. You meet your neighbors and all of you are far too embarrassed to admit you don't remember one another so you invent reasons why you're feeling so out of sorts that morning. You do not need to stack, like the other endermen, to retain your mind, and you assume you must simply be . . . special. Not that you were never one of them. You see a shulker in a box and assume he's your pet. You have no parents, so there must be a story that explains why they're gone. And what archmage obsessed with fire does not hate the rain? Even when you would not know your own face in the mirror, some part of you remembered that. And then? You meet a strange boy who seems to like you, and imagine that you have been friends all your life. Mortal imaginations are astonishing. It's never more than a day before the End forgets that it's forgotten anything at all."

Mo looked inside herself. Was it true? Was it real? Was she Ultimo the Magnificent? But there was nothing. She couldn't remember any of it.

"What about Kan?" she asked. "He's not like us. He's not human."

Grumpo shut his eyes. "Ah, Kan. My enderman. My best enderman. I am the Great Chaos. The unknown variable is the gift I bring to the world. Kan is simply . . . Kan. He was born different. Those green eyes. A mutation. Mutations are the most valuable things in the universe. Without mutation, nothing ever changes. Because he was different, he did not belong. Because he did not belong, he sought out strangers when they came, hoping they would love him as his own people refused to. Don't get excited—you treated him no better than anyone else. Not during that first cycle. When the ender dragon's wave caught you, he was hiding nearby, trying to work up the nerve to talk to the beautiful brewmaster. And when you woke up . . ."

"He was there, so we thought we were connected," Fin filled it in.

"Yes. But that is the miracle of mutation. By imagining that you were connected, you *became* connected. Where there is Fin and Mo there is always Kan, now. And he has spent so much time with you, his thoughts embedded into the very brains of a pair of powerful humans, that he has developed beyond any other enderman I have ever known. The cycle has been messing with all my endermen. Each one of them bends and breaks and warps a little more with each version of this tiresome story. Or else they would never have thought to make Kraj a commander or organize an army or even make poor Eresha into the Mouth of the Great Chaos. Before all this started, none of them would have even dreamed of such fancy things! And frankly, it's terrible. Have you met Kraj? Ugh. He's *such* a bore. But Kan has changed the most. He's nearly human himself these days. And that music. That music. He is my proof. He is my justification. Kan's song is the illustration of all I am. From chaos comes beauty. You three became an End in yourselves. No one could have predicted it."

"How many cycles have there been?" Mo felt numb.

"This will be the thousandth cycle," answered the god of the endermen.

Fin and Mo gave up. They sprawled out on the floor and just lay there, unhappy and overwhelmed. Gravity was too much to bear just then.

"Why not just *tell* us?"

"What fun would that be? I told you. I tried to help. I tried to tell you. I tried to make each cycle different. But you are so stubborn! Humans love Order. They can't get enough of it. And you insist on being yourselves over and over."

"Wait . . . are we twins? Grumpo, is Mo my twin?"

The shulker chortled. "As I understand things, which is quite deeply, you met two weeks before you passed through your gate into the End. You are near strangers to each other. Isn't that just *fabulous*?"

"We have to break the cycle," Fin said finally. "That's all there is to it. We get out. And then we won't be stuck and everything will be normal forever."

The god of Chaos laughed.

"You always say that, Archmage. I have heard it nine hundred and ninety-nine times."

Mo didn't laugh. Mo frowned. She thought about Loathsome and Kan. She thought about Jess and Jax and Roary and Koal. She thought about Kraj and Eresha and Karshen and the note block echoing in the rainy night of the Overworld. It was all her End. If their shulker wasn't lying, they must have lived down here much longer than they ever lived up there. And until a few days ago, they'd been so happy.

"There," Grumpo crooned. "There's your trouble, Fin. She *likes* it here."

Fin ignored that. "You say this has all happened before. I read the books. I know you are at least telling part of the truth. But what about them? The humans fighting ED up there? Jess? Have they been part of the cycle before?"

Grumpo seemed surprised, almost. Taken aback. "No," he said thoughtfully. "They are new."

"So there's a chance," Fin leapt up. "There's a chance we can change things. We can break the cycle and escape. We'll take Kan with us, Mo, if that's what you're worried about. We'll take him and we'll start a new life. Build a house. Till a field. Together."

Mo looked so uncertain. "If we're together, everything will be okay. That's how the universe works. Weren't you listening?"

Fin grinned at Mo. The old playful grin she'd known all her life. All her life that mattered.

"Ooh, I can't wait to see how this turns out," Grumpo snarked. "What suspense."

Something crashed down on top of the box. Dust trickled down through the stones.

"You'd better hurry," Grumpo said as if it didn't matter at all to him. The pair got up to go. They climbed the platform stairs toward the lid of the box.

"Please, my children," the Great Chaos called to them in a suddenly soft, gentle voice. "Remember, no matter what happens, no matter what you do or say, no matter if you live or die, no matter if you achieve your dreams or drink their ashes, I will always, always hate you. Until the end of time, I will hate you more than anything in the cosmos."

Fin frowned. A strange idea came into his head. "Grumpo, when you say you hate us, do you really mean you love us? Is this a Great Chaos thing? Are words meaning the same thing as the dictionary says they mean too much Order for you? It's a pretty terrible joke, you know."

"You wish," snorted the shulker. He nodded behind him. "Please exit through the gift shop," he joked to himself. Neither Fin nor Mo laughed. They didn't know what a gift shop was.

The sound of the door closing echoed through the Great Chaos's lair.

"See you back on the ship," he said to the shadows.

CHAPTER TWENTY-TWO

THE FINAL BATTLE, AGAIN

Ultimo the Magnificent and El Fin the Archmage exploded out of the shulker's box. They landed on a battlefield already burning.

The enderman holiday choir hid behind pillars or simply fled. The ender dragon roared in injured fury. It dodged and flew between the pillars, bleeding freely from one wing. Jess and Koal were encamped in the center of the island on the stone courtyard, weapons drawn, waiting for ED to drop low enough to end it all. Roary ran between them, doling out healing potions. Jax whooped and hollered. He danced in the scorched earth. He reloaded his crossbow for the killshot.

"No!" cried Mo. She leapt at him and knocked the arrow out of his hand.

"You *melon*," he snarled. "What are you doing?"

"I'll explain later!"

Jax rolled his eyes and shrugged her off. It was time for battle and he had no interest in listening to her innermost thoughts.

The ender dragon saw them. Its white eyes blazed. It folded its wings and dove straight for them.

"Yeah! Let's go! This is it!" Jax laughed with delight. "Final checks, everyone! Got your coats? Got the keys? Anybody need to go to the bathroom? No? Then let's DO THIS!" He notched another arrow and put the dragon in his sights. He fired.

ED opened its monstrous purple jaws. It ate the arrow like it was nothing.

Then it ate Jax.

It happened right in front of Mo. One minute he was there, dancing from foot to foot, trash-talking an ancient deity's favorite pet. The next minute he was gone. A lonely bow fell from the sky.

"Oh my god," gasped Fin. "Oh my *god.*"

"ED, stop!" screamed Mo. "It's me! It's me!"

But ED was the infinite lightning night-lizard at the end of the universe and it didn't care. ED was doing what it was made to do. Protect the End from outsiders. Nothing else mattered. And Mo was an outsider, too. She'd never been anything but.

The ender dragon turned on her. With a shriek it swooped down to devour her as well. Mo took off at a dead run. But it wasn't just ED. Everyone was shrieking. Everyone was screaming. Everything burned around them.

Kan? Mo thought wildly. Where was Kan? Where had he teleported to? Was he safe? Fin shoved her down just as ED pulled up, catching his upper arm with one claw. El Fin the Archmage cried out in pain.

Mo ate sand. *This. This is the Great Chaos. Death and battle. It seems like a game until everything's on fire and your friend is dead.*

Roary tossed her a healing potion from behind a pillar. The dim light of the End caught the glass bottle. It sparkled briefly—and then ED barreled through again. The bottle shattered. A rain of healing misted down, too diffuse to help anyone.

Especially Roary. Lying face down on the rock. Her eyes closed.

Fin screamed wordlessly. *No, no, no!* They knew now! They were supposed to be fixing the cycle! Everything was supposed to be okay!

"Help!" yelled Koal over the din. "Fin, Mo! Help!"

They scrambled over the broken stones through the storm of flame and debris toward Jess and Koal. A pair of endermen had them pinned down, punching at them with bare fists.

"Karshen," breathed Mo.

It was Kan's secondary hubunit. And Koneka, the fragment Fin had met outside the Enderdome. The fragment from Kraj's brainbank squad. Two wasn't quite enough to achieve enlightenment. It was just enough to be *really* good at fighting and know why you wanted someone dead.

Fin searched the ground—a sword. Someone's, anyone's. No. Not anyone's. His. Theirs. Their treasure. Borrowed by an enderman and left where it lay. Mo was already crawling toward a trident.

She was closer than he was. Fin waved to Mo.

Go, go, go! Go without me! I'll be fine!

Karshen hit Koal over and over. Koneka went at Jess with bare teeth. Fin got his hand around the fallen sword. Mo rolled over with the trident clutched in her blistered fingers.

But it didn't matter. Not much does when there's a dragon involved. ED sped through the air toward the little grey courtyard. Fin's legs pumped under him, willing the distance between him and Jess to disappear. Jess, who just wanted to build her library and live here in the End like they had. Jess, who saved him. Jess, who he saved. Jess, with her long brown hair and her constantly rolling eyes. Fin sobbed. He hadn't even gotten a chance to tell her how glad he'd been that she wanted to stay.

Mo almost made it to them. She would have made it. But unknown variables will have their way.

Loathsome rocketed out of nowhere. Her bloodshot eyes streamed tears. The undead demon horse collided with her mother, knocking her out of the courtyard. The mare turned round to look at Mo just as ED opened his mouth and emptied his gullet onto Jess, Koal, Karshen, Koneka, and Loathsome, engulfing them all with white-hot fire. The humans went to ash in an instant. Fin didn't even have time to call Jess's name. Koal's face went slack with total disbelief, then drifted away like dust. Till the last second, he simply knew he was going to escape. He always escaped. Karshen dissolved into smoke. Koneka looked up at the infinite blackness of the End. *It is lonely out here on the dunes,* Fin heard her think, and then she was gone, too.

Loathsome burned. Her undead body was the candle. Her long mane was the wick. She burned and burned. Mo sobbed. She held her arms out to the horse, but she couldn't touch her. The flames were too hot and fierce.

Mumma! Loathsome cried out in her mind. *Slain. Slaaaaain.* The dead horse stumbled to her knees.

Why, Loathsome? Mo's thoughts were soaked in tears. *Why didn't you stay safe like we told you, you beautiful dummy?* She stretched her arms out to the creature she could never touch again. *Don't die. Only dummies die.*

Mo reached out into Loathsome's gentle ghoulish soul for the last time. She saw the infinite graveyard. The wiry trees. The sickly moon. The gravestones, all written over with new things. EATING FLOWERS. RUNNING IN THE RAIN. MUSIC. CAGE IN THE SKY. MUMMA. DRAGON! MUMMA. ULTIMO THE MAGNIFICENT.

And one read: GOODBYE. A rotting, moldering hand scrabbled up out of the grave dirt.

I love you, Mo thought to the graveyard of her baby's mind.

The hand waved sadly. Then it went still.

Fin and Mo stood in the middle of the carnage, slack-jawed. They'd never had a chance. How could anything happen that fast? It wasn't fair. You couldn't fix it. If it wasn't fixable, it shouldn't be allowed to happen that fast.

Through his tears, El Fin the Archmage whispered, "We can still break the cycle. If we find Kan. He can teleport three of us back to the Overworld. That's not too much. ED's still alive. If we leave now, it can't start over again."

But Mo couldn't move. She couldn't leave Loathsome. She couldn't even leave Jax, flying around up there in the belly of the ender dragon. *Three days ago I was happy,* she thought, and lay down on the earth with her hands over her head. What did it matter what happened? She wasn't Ultimo the Magnificent. She didn't even have a brother. She was nothing.

The song didn't have time to start out quiet. It burst into the air at full volume, rich and lovely and sad and sweet and complicated, like everything else. Mo knew that song. She turned her head, looking for the source.

Fin tried to see through the smoke and his own tears. He knew that song, too. *But Kan shouldn't be here. He should stay safe. Stay away. Grumpo told us. Kan never stays away.* Ash settled onto his hand. Fin stared at it and shuddered. He dropped below the smoke layer and crawled to where Jax had dropped his crossbow. He wrapped his arms around it and held it tight. ED wasn't going to get Kan too. It just wasn't.

But ED wasn't going after Kan. It wasn't moving.

It was *listening*.

The ender dragon cocked its head to one side, listening intently to the music. Its muscles held perfectly still. Kan advanced out of the shadows, playing his note block better than any note block had ever been played or ever will. His green eyes glowed in the black fog.

Mo put her hand on Fin's arm. He nearly jumped out of his skin.

You scared the life out of me! he thought wildly.

Mo looked deep into his eyes. Eyes that had been purple until three days ago. She held him tight. And between their minds they understood everything in an instant. They didn't have to plan. They didn't have to argue.

Kan can't die, thought Mo. *No matter what it costs*. And a moment after that: *And none of the rest of them, either. It's not their fault their vacation turned into our nightmare. They don't deserve to lose everything.*

I don't want to remember anyway, Fin thought. *We failed. I don't want to remember we failed.*

The End is what counts. Our End.

They were both holding the crossbow.

Fin let go.

Mo stood up and strode across the island. The End burned behind her. Her hair glowed in the light. ED turned to see her. It heard no more music. It saw no other prey. Only her. The ender dragon spread its black wings into the sky, bellowed to the heavens, bent down, and launched itself toward her. Mo didn't flinch. She aimed and she fired true.

Game over, the ender dragon bellowed into her brain. *Try again?*

The bolt took the ender dragon between the eyes. The lights went out in ED.

But not before the colossal bulk of its body slammed into Ultimo the Magnificent, crushing her mercilessly against the stony earth.

Ash, smoke, embers floated through the air. Kan and Fin ran to her, never once thinking they could make one bit of difference.

They found two things where Mo died.

Her body, and a glistening black-and-violet egg.

CHAPTER TWENTY-THREE

A TIDE OF MEMORY

Fin alone sat on the deck of the ship. The night flowed all around him. There was a certain taste in the air. A tang of ozone and burnt obsidian. Telos crumbled in the distance. The End was coming apart. Getting ready to be reborn. Only this time without her. And no one would know the difference.

He remembered everything. El Fin the Archmage. His life in the Overworld. What pigs looked like. How many times he had discovered how big Grumpo's box really was. Everything. In that magical space between the End and the Beginning, his mind was completely clear.

But he didn't much care.

He held a book in his lap. One of the ones from the hold. The empty hold. At the end of the last cycle it'd been crammed full to bursting. No war that time. No Commander Kraj. This time he'd have to start from scratch. In every way. The book was *Curse of*

Binding Level Two. Fin turned to the first page. *You can add the Curse of Binding enchantment to any piece of armor such as helmets, chestplates, leggings, or boots* . . . it read.

El Fin the Archmage turned the page over and began to write on the back.

> I am not afraid anymore. So much has happened. Kraj is dead by my own hand. Eresha is dead. Karshen and Koneka are dead. Mo is gone. The ender dragon is dead. Poor Loathsome. Poor Grumpo. Poor all of us. The End itself is coming apart. The islands cannot hold. The sky is falling. If I try to forget what I'm looking at, it's beautiful. Really. So beautiful. The towers of Telos are falling like confetti. It is coming. The great tide of memory will wash over me and I will know nothing about all this grief. And do you know? I think I welcome it.
>
> I have retreated to the ship. Lying on the deck, I can watch the night tear itself apart. When I close my eyes, I can hear Kan playing somewhere far away. Good. He is alive. I'm glad. He's coming to find me. To be part of my End.
>
> It's almost here. I can feel it moving through the islands. Completely inevitable. Why fight it?
>
> All hail the Great Chaos. Blessed be the Beginners.
>
> See you on the other side, Ultimo.

A cool hand slipped into his.

"Not if I see you first," Mo said.

Fin went pale. Then he tackled her in one of the greatest and fiercest hugs in recorded human history. "You're alive!"

One of the Telosian pagodas tumbled off the side of the island into the void.

Mo patted her pocket.

"Totem of Undying. Brings you back feeling like roadkill. But it brings you back. I understand how to use it now. So here I am. You can't keep a good brewmaster down."

They lay back on the deck of their home, looking up at the starless night. The starless future. They listened to Kan's music, getting closer and closer as he walked toward them. Not teleporting, but walking, as his friends did. As his End did. He would be here soon. He quite literally couldn't be late.

"I wish we'd fixed it, like you wanted," Ultimo said. "I think I've said that exactly a thousand times."

"I don't know," Fin sighed. "Maybe we're as fixed as we're going to get. It's only . . . them. Jess and Jax and Roary and Koal. They didn't deserve to get mixed up in our little dance down here. They should be up there. Kicking pigs and dancing in the rain."

Mo brushed her long, dark hair out of her face.

"About that," she said. "I don't think Ultimo the Magnificent can really take an L that big. It's just not in her nature. But . . . you know what that means."

Fin nodded.

"Can you make that choice for them?"

El Fin the Archmage squeezed her hand. He stroked her face with his hand. Not his twin. But still his family.

"You saw them. The cycle is getting worse. It's evolving. It's changing the laws of nature. Endermen use weapons and build armies and . . . apparently humans don't respawn. I'm only here because of my totem, and here's hoping I remember to grab another one on the next go-round. They should have woken up in their own beds. But you saw them. They were just lying there on the ground.

Cold and quiet and *gone*. We can't leave them like that. We just can't. And you never know. Grumpo said they were new. Maybe this is what changes everything. Maybe this time it's different."

Mo nodded. She pulled a few things out of her infinitely deep pockets, assembling them on the deck with the practiced ease of an expert. Five potions in a neat row. Regeneration potions, but more powerful than any the Overworld had seen since Ultimo the Magnificent lit out for parts unknown.

"If it's not," she said as she finished, "that's okay, too. I've had a good thousand lives with you, Fin. A thousand more won't hurt."

"But will they remember us? If this works? If they come back like we do? Will we remember them?"

Mo sat back on her heels. "No." She sighed. "I don't think we will."

"I don't want to forget again. I don't want to forget Jess. Or any of them," he added quickly.

"Me neither. But we never remember." She capped off the potions. "At first. Maybe this time there will be some small thing that's different. That sparks us. Like it did this time. Maybe it'll be Grumpo or Loathsome or ED or something Kan says or the glint in Roary's eye. Maybe it'll even be awful old Kraj. Maybe it'll be Jax calling me a melon or Koal laughing or Jess swinging her sword. Maybe all of us together . . . maybe we'll *stack*, even though we're humans. Become something more than we were separately. Something. Something new. Something . . . Chaotic. And maybe we'll begin to remember next time. Before it's too late. When there's still time for remembering to matter. Maybe this time, we do it all right. And everything changes."

Kan's dark head appeared over the side of the ship as he floated toward them. He let his note block fall silent. They didn't have to say anything. They never did.

Fin, Mo, and Kan walked down into the hold together and sat down to rest. Then, Mo decided nothing could really be awkward when the universe was collapsing. She snuggled into Kan's side. Fin leaned against their backs. And they waited. The slumber party at the end of the world.

"Can you feel it? I can feel it coming," she whispered. "Like a tsunami. First the water retreats, and for a minute you think everything is going to be okay. Then it rises up and washes everything away. I love you."

"I love you too, Ultimo," Kan said. He squeezed her tight. "You really were magnificent."

Mo winked. "You too, green. You too."

"See you on the other side," whispered El Fin the Archmage.

The wave of memory passed over the ship an hour later. Fin and Mo and Kan fell asleep long before it came. The world shifted, and tilted, and righted itself, and remembered nothing.

About an hour after that, the shulker box at the back of the ship creaked open. Something emerged. Not a shulker. Not an enderman. Not a creeper or a skeleton or a witch or a human. Something the color of a shulker, and the shape of the unpredictability of all life.

Very gently and tenderly, Grumpo fitted a pumpkin onto Fin's head, and then Mo's. He'd do the same for the others when they turned up. It wouldn't be long now. Grumpo tucked in the vines and made sure they looked nice and neat. He bent down and kissed each of their foreheads.

"I hate you both so terribly much," the Great Chaos whispered.

And vanished.

The atoms of the player were scattered in the grass, in the rivers, in the air, in the ground. A woman gathered the atoms; she drank and ate and inhaled; and the woman assembled the player, in her body.

And the player awoke, from the warm, dark world of its mother's body, into the long dream.

And the player was a new story, never told before, written in letters of DNA. And the player was a new program, never run before, generated by a sourcecode a billion years old. And the player was a new human, never alive before, made from nothing but milk and love.

You are the player. The story. The program. The human. Made from nothing but milk and love . . .

Shush.

Sometimes the player created a small, private world that was soft and warm and simple.

Sometimes.

—Julian Gough, Minecraft "End Poem"

CHAPTER TWENTY-FOUR

THE END

It is always night in the End. There is no sunrise. There is no sunset. There are no clocks ticking away.

But that does not mean there is no such thing as time. Or light. Ring after ring of pale yellow islands glow in the darkness, floating in the endless night. Violet trees and violet towers twist up out of the earth and into the blank sky. Trees full of fruit, towers full of rooms. White crystal rods stand like candles at the corners of the tower roofs and balconies, shining through the shadows. Sprawling, ancient, quiet cities full of these towers glitter all along the archipelago, purple and yellow like everything else in this place. Beside them float great ships with tall masts. Below them yawns a black and bottomless void.

It is a beautiful place. And it is not empty.

The islands are full of endermen, their long, slender black limbs moving over little yellow hills and little yellow valleys.

Their narrow purple-and-pink eyes flash. Their thin black arms swing to the rhythm of a soft, whispering music, plotting their plots and scheming their schemes in the tall, twisted buildings older than even the idea of a clock. They watch everything. They say nothing.

Shulkers hide in boxes nestled in ships and towers. Little yellow-green slugs hiding from outsiders. Sometimes they peek out. But they snap their boxes safely shut again, like clams in their shells. The gentle thudding sound of their cubes opening and closing is the heartbeat of the End.

And on the central and largest island, enormous obsidian towers surround a small pillar of grey stone ringed with torches. A brilliant lantern gleams from the top of each tower. A flame in a silver cage, shooting beams of light down from the towers into the grass, across a little grey courtyard, and out into the black sky.

Above it all, something slowly circles. Something huge. Something with wings. Something that never tires. Round and round it goes, and its purple eyes glow like furious fire.

Fin!

The word came zinging through the shade off the shore of one of the outer islands. A huge end city loomed over most of the land: Telos. Telos sprouted out of the island highlands like something alive. Great pagodas and pavilions everywhere. White shimmers fell from the glistening end rods. Shulkers clapped in their little boxes. Leashed to Telos like a dog floated a grand purple ship. A pirate ship without an ocean to sail. Most of the end cities had ships attached to them. No one was certain why, any more than they're certain who built all those big, strange cities in the first place. Not the endermen, though they were happy to name every place after themselves. Not the thing flying in endless circles around a gate to nowhere. Not the shulkers who never came out of hiding long enough to learn anything about anything. The end ships just *were*, as the cities just *were*, as the End just *was*, like clouds or diamonds or Tuesdays.

Fin! Find anything good?

A skinny young enderman teleported quickly across the island, in and out of the nooks and crannies of Telos. He blinked off in one place and back on in another until he stood on the deck of the end ship, holding something in his arms. His head was handsome, black and square. His eyes were bright and hungry. His limbs were slim but strong. An enderman leaned against the mast, waiting for him. She crossed her dark arms across her thin chest.

Nothing good, Mo. Just a bunch of pearls. We've got tons of those. Ugh. You take them. They give me the creeps. I was sure the chestplates we found last week would regen by now but I guess somebody else got there first. I got some redstone ore. That's about it. You go next time. You always sniff out the good stuff.

The twin twelve-year-old endermen, brother and sister, Fin and Mo, headed down into the guts of their ship. They'd always lived here. Here on the ship with their two brothers and their two sisters. Jax and Koal and Jess and Roary. And every day, their dear friend Kan would visit. Kan was tall and dark and thin like all the enderfrags were. Taller than Roary but shorter than Jax. He had big, beautiful eyes, but he was always squinting, trying to hide them, trying to make them unnoticeable.

Because Kan's eyes weren't like the wide, clear magenta-violet eyes of other endermen.

Kan's eyes were green.

And he played the note block better than you'd ever believe a note block could be played.

Jax liked to tease Mo that she was sweet on Kan. Brothers were like that.

They couldn't remember any other place.

They grew up here. It was their home. No different from any of the hundreds of endermen you'd find on any island here in the archipelago. They lived on an end ship crammed with junk they'd snatched up from anywhere they could find it. Some of it was *very* good junk. Diamonds and emeralds, gold ore and lapis lazuli. Enchanted iron leggings, pickaxes of every kind, beetroot seeds and chorus fruits, saddles and horse armor (though they'd never seen a horse). Dozens of sets of marvelous grey wings you could stick right on your back and fly around anywhere you liked. Some of it was just plain old actual junk. Rocks and clay and sand and old books with broken spines. A moldy greenish-blue egg with weird veins running all over it. Fin and Mo didn't care how ugly it looked. They put the egg by the fire and hoped for something unpredictable to happen. Something new.

The family of endermen knew there were other worlds out there. It was only logical, when you lived in a place called the End. If there was an End, there had to be a Beginning. Somewhere else for this place to be the End *of*. Somewhere the opposite of here. Green and bright, with blue skies and blue water, full of sheep and pigs and bees and squid. They'd heard the stories. But this was *their* world. They were safe here, the seven of them, with their own things and their own kind and their own story.

One big happy End.

ABOUT THE AUTHOR

CATHERYNNE M. VALENTE is the *New York Times* best-selling author of dozens of works of science fiction and fantasy, including *Space Opera, The Refrigerator Monologues,* and the Fairyland series. She has won or been nominated for every award in her field. She lives on an island off the coast of Maine with her partner, her son, and several other mischievous beasts.

JOURNEY INTO THE WORLD OF MINECRAFT™

Learn about the latest Minecraft books when you sign up for our newsletter at **ReadMinecraft.com**

THE OFFICIAL GUIDEBOOKS

Learn about the latest Minecraft guidebooks when you sign up for our newsletter at **ReadMinecraft.com**

READ THE OFFICIAL BOOKS FROM

Learn about the latest Minecraft books when you sign up for our newsletter at **ReadMinecraft.com**